Women in Red

A Novel

Jordan Rosenfeld

LUBBOCK, TEXAS
WWW.BOLDFACEBOOKS.COM

Published by Boldface Books, an imprint of Bookadelphia
www.BoldfaceBooks.com
www.Bookadelphia.com

Originally published 2015 by Booktrope Editions

Cover Design by Greg Simanson

Library of Congress Control Number: 2015910140
ISBN 978-1-935619-40-6 (trade paperback)
ISBN 978-1-935619-41-3 (epub)

10 9 8 7 6 5 4 3 2 1

www.jordanrosenfeld.net
jordanwritelife@gmail.com

This book is dedicated to the magnificent artists whose medium is the body, whose movements are the kind of graceful and effortless that only come through commitment, strength, and hard work. You inspire me in my own craft.

1

STELLA'S WALK OF SHAME was eight blocks, enough time to let the chill air snap her awake, the wind to whip away the musk of sex.

She snuck in the back entrance at the Fuse, and squeezed past Eduardo, jockey small, who bussed tables with such windy grace the dishes appeared to whisk themselves away. She edged sideways past him as he uncrated wine glasses glistening like treasures snug in straw and tossed her a grin that would have made her younger self blush. As she punched in and tied the black apron over her starched white button-down top and black slacks, a needle of envy pierced when her gaze landed on the evening hostess, Geena, encased in a slinky bronze-hued dress. It had been years since Stella had cause to dress up, much less in something form-fitting, leaving limbs unencumbered.

"Hey, Red." The deep male voice was so close to her ear she jumped and whipped around, bonking heads with Jason, who was her same height. Now the space between them was as awkward—in public—as it had been erotic not even an hour earlier.

"Very creative." She rubbed the sore spot on her head. "If I dye it again, you'll have to change my nickname."

"Nah, don't change it." He traced a tendril with one finger, trailing heat down her cheek. He smelled like sweet almond oil. "Not too many girls can pull off fire-engine scalp."

Stella made an exaggerated smile, trying not to show her annoyance at being called a girl. "Well, I *was* shooting for 'zombie blood' red." He held his hands out like a prayer for forgiveness. "Just can't get it right, can I?"

Well, he could get a few things right. She recreated in sensual memory the gentle sloughing of his closely cropped dark hair against her inner thighs, the flex of the strong muscles in his back as he moved into her. They'd been sleeping together for a few weeks, and though they were good together in bed, and she liked his lax cheerfulness—a kind of laid-back, listen-to-Rasta-music-and-smoke-the-occasional-joint kind of chill—he wasn't her intellectual match. There was no cause to introduce him to her daughter as anything more than her boss.

Friday nights meant a steady slam for their surprisingly busy little Northern California town, Luma, less than an hour north of San Francisco. Because the restaurant was only fifty-person capacity, service required a clean choreography between waiters and bussers. The rhythm generally worked except when they hired someone new, or someone was on the rag. Tonight, though, there was a pulsing Latin beat, and Stella's feet carried a salsa step from one patron's table back to the kitchen. Just a couple of steps—nothing that anyone would notice—but her blood thrummed with energy.

She served an elegant salt-and-pepper type at the corner window table some cold gazpacho and a murky glass of Merlot. He was alone, reading the news on his iPhone. A tech geek, probably. She admired those who could eat out alone on a weekend night without self-consciousness. He smiled, and she'd have never made such direct eye contact, but he had one blue eye and one green, a hypnotizing feature. He returned her gaze with such intensity that for a moment she couldn't swallow, as though those eyes of his could see right into her. She quickly fumbled for the parchment of specials tucked into her apron pocket.

He brushed the menu with long, artistic-looking fingers, then spoke to her. "There's something about the way you move that tells me you dance."

One eye was oceanic gray-blue, very pale, and she wondered then if he could see out of it. Despite the white hair, his hands were smooth and unwrinkled, his age indeterminately youthful. A man who'd gone gray before his time. She had the sudden urge to pull him to standing and Charleston with him around the restaurant. "I danced when I was younger—it was my big dream." She looked past him through the window at the leftover holiday lights still entwined around the trees in the center of the street.

He frowned slightly. "Nothing wrong with dreams."

She shook her head. "Childhood is for dreams; adulthood is all about practical realities. Not as much fun, but maybe that's the price of growing up."

The man's eyes snapped to the front door then, as though he was expecting someone after all. All eyes in the restaurant, including Stella's, quickly turned to see a tall brunette in a crimson, body-hugging vintage dress sashay in on red stiletto heels. She clutched a black beaded purse in one hand and a red flower—possibly a hibiscus, though Stella couldn't imagine where one would get such a thing in California in February—in the other. The woman's black hair was draped in a sleek loop at the back of her neck. She held such erect posture that Stella became aware of her own slumped shoulders, her former ballet director's voice shrilling, "Shoulders back! Neck long!"

The crimson-clad woman scanned the restaurant and then zeroed in on a short, bald man and his wife, regular patrons, right behind Stella. The wife's eyes narrowed to slits, and the entire restaurant held its breath as she made a beeline for his table.

"I have something very special for you." The red-clad woman stage-projected, suggesting melodrama to follow. Stella tensed, prepared herself to intervene.

The man looked to his wife, eyebrows peaked in confusion, and shook his head.

As the wife grimaced, perhaps on the verge of throwing down her napkin and storming out, the woman in red tipped up her head, opened her mouth and produced a single, vibrant, operatic note that drowned out the rhythmic background music and sent chills up Stella's arms. The note shimmered, hanging in the air like something with a consciousness all its own.

And suddenly, the woman multiplied into many, or that's how it appeared to Stella. From the back entrance, from the front, and even from the bathroom, more identical scarlet-clad ladies appeared, walking with the precise and careful gait of African women balancing jars of water on their heads. They, too, struck the same haunting note, their voices blending into a sound so rich and smooth that time disappeared into its vortex. The notes expanded, grew bigger than the source, like smoke clouds rising from flame. Stella was no opera buff—it sounded like *La Traviata*—but the effect was overwhelming. It was just music, Stella told herself, so why did she feel as though her heart was dough rising up out of its bowl, lifting her mood with it and creating a giddiness that made her want to jeté around the room? The music swelled and filled the room until the waves of air pulsed through her with a force that left her skin tingling, and when the ensemble hit a crescendo, throwing out their arms and tilting their heads up to the ceiling as though offering their music to the heavens, she felt its vibrations down her spine. She wasn't alone; the restaurant patrons spontaneously wept, as though they were all standing before a miracle. All activity in the Fuse had stopped; even the chefs stood ogling, open-mouthed.

And when it was done, whether moments or minutes later, the first woman bowed and produced a card to the shell-shocked man and his wife. Aloud, she read: "Happy Birthday Chuck, from Harvey. Thanks for being our biggest earner of the year."

The man tapped a hand against his heart and laughed, and relief replaced bewilderment in his wife's eyes.

The red-clad women bowed their heads, clutched their purses, and filed out the front door as though there was nothing unusual at all about what had just happened. Stella imagined them returning to some gash in the sky, an alternate universe. Before Stella could think, she'd grasped the wrist of the last woman leaving. "Who are you?" she said. "Where did you come from?"

The woman's lips were as red as Stella's hair. She smiled and cracked open her beaded purse, extracting a white business card that she handed to Stella, her fingers bracingly cool against Stella's own.

The last woman had strutted out the door before Stella looked at the card.

Frivolity Inc: Spectacles for All Occasions

Stella's gaze drifted back toward the man with the multicolored eyes in the corner who had asked if she danced; he would surely have been awed by the performance. His empty seat was pushed out, his spoon still abandoned in his half-finished soup, as though Stella had imagined him entirely.

2

ELEVEN O'CLOCK, her body heavy in her shoes, Stella clocked out and tried to escape before Jason caught up with her, but he waited at the back exit looking handsomely tired, all the crispness slumped out of his shirt, a slouch in his stance. She could imagine the eager way they'd collapse into each other if she would allow herself—how desire would energize their fatigue.

His eyes were shiny. "What a night, huh? You ever seen anything like that?"

She knew she was supposed to say no, she hadn't—except she had, many times, in a way: every time she'd walked into a rehearsal with the San Francisco Ballet, smelling that signature scent of rosin in the wood floors and sweat; when her sister dancers snapped their bodies into alignment and moved in unison like they all shared a mind. It had just been so long since she'd felt that kind of awe, felt *moved* by anything artistic, that the women were like something she'd dreamt, or a story someone had told her. She shrugged.

"Can I walk you home?"

Her eyes followed the bold lines of his neck as they trailed into the cavern of his shoulders. She could easily rest her head there, inhale the sweet powdery scent of him. Nothing like a little carnal drift to edge her away from thoughts of the violin she could not afford and the guilt of failing her daughter. But the women in red had inspired a more profound urge; even though her bones ached with the effort of hard work, the desire to dance was a nuclear star-burst working up from her soles.

"I'm dead tired," she said. "Another night?"

Jason's dark eyes dropped for a second in disappointment. "Never a dull night, eh?" He walked away so fast Stella felt as though *he'd* dismissed *her*.

She hurried on her way. If her mother knew that several nights a week, she did not, in fact, stay at the Fuse until midnight but walked alone to dance in a dark grove, she would have an aneurysm. And some part of Stella wilted at the thought that now, at twenty-nine years old, she even considered what her mother thought. But that is what came of still living with one's mother, wasn't it?

Despite that she'd been on her feet all night, jogging felt good—energy rippled up her thighs in static bursts of electrical impulse. Out of breath, she dropped her bag at the foot of the mighty, famil-iar redwood, inhaling the sharp and earthy scent of trees and dirt. She toed the redwood mulch at her feet. If she had an audience, it was composed only of night-peeping creatures. She plugged in her headphones and found the latest Beyoncé album.

Years ago she'd have laughed to imagine herself dancing to pop-ular music or hip-hop. Her training in ballet commanded precision, grin-through-groans beauty, and even ten years later her body knew its poses as intimately as she did her own edges. Yet the movement she craved was an alien bursting-out of those rigid forms—it was beat and blood and heat. Since she rarely danced in front of a mirror she didn't even know what she looked like anymore, only how it felt—as though she were breaking free from some tightly enclosed shell, every dance a birth.

*   *   *

She was sweating and panting when a shadow materialized in the dim light between two trees and then disappeared. It was tall and person-shaped, and it cracked an instant whip of terror up her spine. She yanked out her earbuds and dropped to a crouch, ready to run. There were recent reports of gang-related violence in the neighboring town of Hollis, and though she knew it was unlikely in this remote spot, she was instantly alert.

When nothing happened, she called out, "What the fuck do you want?" into the night, half-wondering if she had hallucinated the witness she secretly craved.

"You're so light when you move, like you're flying." The voice was low, vaguely familiar, and definitely male.

"I have pepper spray and a very large knife." She regretted her empty pockets.

In the shard of light cast from a neighboring high school football field, his Roman nose and wide, pale cheekbones emerged first, then his hair, so silver it seemed spray-painted on his head. Even in the dark she could make out the pale glow of his marble eyes, the light blue one almost phosphorescent.

It was Gazpacho Man, from the restaurant.

"I'm sorry if I scared you, I don't mean you any harm." He held out his hands as though passing a plate to her.

"No? You're just spying on me in the dark?" Her pulse hammered out the beat still echoing in her ears. She pulled herself straight, trying to make herself seem taller than five-five.

"That was my spectacle back at the restaurant." Pride made his voice sound like a smile.

She didn't know what he meant for a moment, until the memory returned to her. "The women in red?"

He nodded and bounced lightly on his toes. "What did you think of it?"

Even in the shadows she could see the light of expectation in his eyes, as though her opinion mattered to him.

"It was . . . surprising." What she wanted to say, if he was not a stranger accosting her at night with unknown intentions, was that it made her ache to perform again, to be looked upon with the same admiration as she had regarded the women.

"It delighted you, right?" He spoke with an almost childlike anticipation.

She wished she could see him more clearly. In the light of day, she would be able to tell if he wished her ill or good. "One more time, what do you want?" She leaned forward into a lunge.

"This is not the first time I've watched you dance." He held up his hands warding off her protest. "I'm not a voyeur. Frivolity Inc. is my entertainment company. I think you should consider working for me." In the shadows he was insubstantial, as though a strong beam of light could dissolve him.

Stella took a step back, assessing the quickest exit routes. Backed up against the trees, she'd have to run right past him to get away, and, though lean, he looked swift and strong.

"So why not say so in the restaurant?" She heard her voice split with fear and hoped he didn't hear it too.

He stepped backward, snapping a twig. "I was prolonging the pleasure of watching you dance. I didn't plan to interrupt you tonight."

"You're really inspiring confidence." She flexed her feet. Could she run very far, tired as she was? "The pepper spray is cocked and ready in my pocket."

He sighed and dropped to a squat, as though trying to make himself smaller. "I'm not a threat to you. My name is Julien. I employ talented performers of all kinds. I walk by here often, and the first time I saw you dancing, I was entranced. You have a gift, my dear." His voice took on an admiring depth that Stella was not immune to. "I didn't want to spoil it. But tonight, in the restaurant, I heard it in your voice, how you missed it. Only someone who has a real passion for dance, maybe a forbidden one, would steal away into the dark to do so. I'm guessing that whoever is at home doesn't know you're here. Or what you've given up."

In the rare times Stella's mother, Margaret, had taken time out of her prima ballerina career to actually tend to her, she spouted mnemonic statements of parental advice: "Stranger danger," was among the first and also the most ironic, as Stella was often cared for by whatever young ingenue trailed Margaret that week. The words rose in her mind again now. "You're an incredibly presumptuous person, you know that, Julien?"

Julien smiled and laughed, running his hand through his short hair. "Yes, Stella, I know. I like to think it's also one of my charms."

Stella took a step back. "You know my name?"

"You told me at the restaurant," he said. "Who could forget a name like that?"

Her muscles softened their anxious hold. "I have to go."

"Wait, Stella, listen. Consider working for me. Come in for an interview. You'll be very well-paid and have flexible hours, so you can afford the things your intelligent, talented child needs. And all the while, you'll be back dancing in the light, giving others the same joy, rather than hidden away in a dark wood."

She felt herself stiffen. "I dance for myself," she said. "There's nothing wrong with that."

"But it doesn't have to be that way." Julien took several steps toward her, until they were close enough to shake hands.

Despite all the tense protest in her body at this stranger's presumption—how could he think he knew what would make her happy?!—she flashed back to being on stage amid the veil of gray cast by bright spotlights, the audience a hidden river of silhouettes. And before she could ask him about anything else, like the sudden realization that he knew about her daughter without her having said anything, he turned and walked out of the clearing with a long, confident stride, a composer exiting the stage after a standing ovation. It was all so bewildering, like one of those figures from a dream so palpable and familiar you spend the rest of the day wondering if they were real or not.

3

TEN-YEAR-OLD IZZY waited outside Luma Elementary School, alone. Her braid was unwound and hanging free of the purple band Stella had laced it in that morning. Her cheeks burned the telltale red of a fit of emotion, and her eyes were glazed with held-back tears. But the detail that set Stella's heart to pounding was the sight of her daughter's empty hands wringing together.

Stella parked and jogged to her. "Izzy, where's your violin?"

Izzy's lower lip trembled, but she turned and walked fast ahead of her mother, clearly trying to put distance between herself and the classmates who trickled out and cast curious looks in her direction. Stella dashed after her and touched her daughter on the shoulder.

"Honey?" Up close she could see that Izzy's right cheek was an angrier red than the left. "Please tell me what happened."

"Not here," Izzy muttered.

Stella sighed and led her child to her old brown Toyota Corolla, which looked even more like a jalopy than usual in the dim winter light.

They drove past the rows of pop-up condos that appeared in a matter of nights like rogue mushrooms after a rain. Stella had no idea who was going to buy these homes, since everyone she knew was either losing one or lamenting they couldn't afford one. Izzy sat in stony silence, her face turned away.

"Can you tell me now?" Stella asked as they neared home.

"First Jadon Green said it's stupid that I call my grandmother Gigi. Then he asked why my dad never picks me up from school." Stella's inhale stuck in her lungs. "And what did you tell him?"

"I said he shouldn't ask personal questions."

"Well, that sounds like a good answer to me." Stella took a steadying breath.

But Izzy wouldn't look at her. "So then he asked if you were a . . . a . . . lesbian because why else would I not want to talk about it."

Stella pressed her palm into the hard leather seam of the steering wheel cover. "Did you tell him that being a lesbian is as normal as being a boy or a girl?"

Izzy sniffled. "No. I told him that maybe if he had two moms instead of just one he wouldn't be such a jerk."

"Honey, that's just antagonizing him." Stella shook her head and reached out for Izzy's hand, but her daughter pulled away.

"Then he called me a bastard."

Stella stepped on the brakes harder than she intended at the stop sign, jerking them both against their seat belts. "He did not."

"He did. So I hit him."

They had just pulled onto Stella's street, and she parked the car with a lurch in front of their house.

"Isadora Scarlet Russo . . ."

Izzy turned to look at her mother with no remorse in her eyes. "I didn't even hit him hard, but it was like it didn't have any effect on him at all, like he didn't get it. So then, I couldn't help it, I just did it . . ."

"Did what?" Stella felt the answer before she heard it as a lump at the base of her throat.

"I went to hit him back without thinking, and I was holding my violin . . . but I missed, and it smashed against the wall behind him." Izzy's voice split with grief.

Stella could almost hear the twang of the instrument as it cracked with a ten-year-old's fury.

"Where is it now?" Stella asked, trying to keep her voice soft and not crusted with frustration at what it would take to get another violin. She'd been saving for a "real" violin, five and ten dollars at a time; but often the money had to be yanked, crumpled, from its hiding place at the back of the freezer for groceries or extra pain meds for her mother.

Izzy shot an agonized grimace at her hands, as though replaying the awful moment when she'd sacrificed the one thing that meant the world to her over a silly schoolyard slight.

"In the dumpster at school. It's ruined."

Stella's eyes were drawn to the peeling brown paint of her rented condo, the frizz of autumn flowers crisp in their pots like gnarled old men. She tried to keep the anger from shattering her calm voice. "Izzy, that violin doesn't even belong to us! Now we're going to have to pay for something you can't use, and frankly where are we going to get the money for a new one?" Stella knew she shouldn't be putting these worries on Izzy. But they were lucky—lucky!—to have her mother's disability checks just to be able to pay the rent.

Izzy exhaled loudly and opened her car door, casting a dark-eyed glower. "Well maybe it wouldn't have happened if I just had a stupid father."

Stella leaned over to put a hand on Izzy's shoulder, realizing too late that her urge was not to soothe her daughter but shake her. Izzy shrugged her off and leapt out of the car.

"Izzy, we are not done!"

Izzy whirled around, her braid unraveling like a snake shedding its skin. "What did you do that made my dad go away?"

Stella closed her eyes to ride out the sting of those words. She stepped out of the car. "It wasn't like that, I've told you. We were young; he wasn't ready for fatherhood."

Izzy stared up at Stella and for a quick flash, though it had been eleven years since she had last seen Dylan, Isadora's face was his in feminine form: the broad, high cheekbones, the lush green eyes, the full lips, set with the same look of fierce determination to achieve.

"He didn't want *me*, is what you mean."

Stella shook her head. The truth would be kinder to Izzy, but it meant untangling the lies she'd told for so long that she didn't know where to start.

"*I* wanted you," Stella insisted, "and that is all that matters."

Izzy exhaled loudly. "No it's not. I'm supposed to *solo* at the recital. But you probably can't even come to that anyway even if

WOMEN IN RED   17

I did have a violin because you'll be *working* . . ." She turned and stalked off into the house, her small shoulders hunched forward.

After several deep, hitching breaths that failed to calm her much, Stella went inside. Margaret sat attentively in the living room with furrowed brows. "Izzy's school called," Margaret said, muting Oprah on the TV. Her mother's blonde hair was several days unwashed, and Stella was sure she was wearing the same ratty floral blouse that she had for the last three days. Stella felt a pang of guilt; she should be a better help to her mother.

"We just left school; they called already?"

Margaret nodded, glancing peripherally at the TV screen. "They asked if Izzy knows anything about the broken violin that's assigned to her for band. A child complained to the secretary that she broke it on purpose and put it in the trash. That doesn't sound like our Iz."

Stella shook her head and slumped into the couch. "It was self-defense."

"So she did break it?" Margaret's cheekbones rose to an appalled height.

Stella had the urge to pull her mother's hair back into a tidy bun, button the gap revealing the thin skin above her collarbones. "Some idiot kid called her a bastard because her father never comes to pick her up."

Margaret sighed. "Oh heck. But Stel, she's ten. Maybe it's time to tell her everything."

"What's to tell? I chose her life over dancing. I wasn't going to make *him* do the same thing—he was the far more talented one anyway."

Margaret twisted her hands in her lap. "That's not true. I think Isadora is the sun and the moon, but I was heartbroken when you stopped dancing."

On TV, Oprah tossed back that famous head and laughed silently on the screen at something her guest had said; Stella felt absurdly mocked.

"Mom, *you* told me it was the right thing to do." Stella dug her fingers into the thin corduroy of the couch.

Margaret reared back slightly. "No, I told you that's what I did, when I got pregnant with you."

Stella shook her head. Her mother's memory was getting worse. When she leapt up to get space from her mother she caught sight of Izzy's head disappearing back into her room.

"Ah shit, she heard us." Stella rushed in to see if she could do damage control but Izzy's purple door, bejeweled with stick-on sequins, wouldn't budge.

"Please let me in, Iz!"

"Go away."

"Honey, I don't know what you think you heard but . . ."

"Go AWAY!"

"No, I'm not going away."

"Why not? You didn't want me, he didn't want me. Leave me alone!"

Stella pressed her face against the cool wood of Izzy's door, which smelled faintly like mothballs and paint. "It's not true. Adults are very complicated. We say things . . ."

She felt her mother's hand suddenly at her lower back, and jumped; she hadn't heard Margaret's wheelchair.

"Let her be, Stel. Give her some time."

Stella pulled back from the door and whispered to Margaret, "Time to let a little overheard seed of doubt bloom into something worse? Trust me, I know how that works." One of her mother's weak white calves had emerged from under her blanket, and the sight of it elicited a lick of rage up her neck, a reaction just as quickly smothered by guilt.

"I'm just . . . I'm going to run errands. Take some time to think about how the hell I'm going to afford a new violin for my child who will otherwise hate my guts."

"We'll find a way," Margaret said.

"Oh *we* will? Somewhere between finding a way to keep up the rent, food on the table, and your medications?"

The words were out before she could stop herself. Margaret's eyes drooped just slightly and she bit her lip as she wheeled away from Stella.

"Mom, I'm sorry, I didn't . . ." Stella stared at the ratty hair at the back of her mother's head as she disappeared with a squeak of wheels around the corner to her own room.

Stella was left alone, standing silently in her living room with a familiar feeling of the earth dropping out beneath her feet.

And then she remembered the card tucked into the pocket of her work apron.

4

MARGARET TURNED the tiny silver tack over and over in her fingers, regarding it with the disgust you might give a bloated tick found gorged on your inner thigh. She tested its sharpness against the pad of her index finger, gasped when the sharp point made a bright bead of blood appear there. The same tack had sat lodged right in the meat of an intercostal muscle not far from her sacrum all night and half the morning until her granddaughter had shrieked and asked why her back was bleeding.

The poster over her bed of Faye Harlowe reclined on a velvet couch—an actress no one Stella's age or younger would ever recognize—was folded down at one corner, and there was a fresh spot of blood in her bed as bold and humiliating as if she'd been deflowered there. There was no hiding it. Stella washed the sheets; she'd have to explain it away somehow.

She'd assured Izzy it was nothing. Didn't hurt a bit.

And when her granddaughter was satisfied after putting on the Band-aid, and left her alone, she'd exhaled a shaky breath and tried to steady her hands. It hadn't hurt a bit. And still didn't, even though she could feel a raised, hot lump with her fingers, and the bleeding hadn't stopped right away.

The problem was: it *should* have hurt. There should have been a hot, throbbing ache or an annoyed bruised sensation every time she pressed her back against her wheelchair. But there was nothing, and that nothingness had invaded the skin and muscles around the tack. The doctors had been arrogantly conclusive that she would never, not ever, regain feeling in her legs. They did not traffic in any promises or miracles of a hopeful sort, but relied on "wait-and-see" strategies. They had never said that the paralysis would remain confined to her legs and buttocks. They had never assured her that things couldn't get worse.

She pressed the tack into her thumb this time, the sharp pain almost pleasurable, the welling blood reassuring that life still pumped in these veins. But if the numbness could spread, how far and how fast would it go?

She tossed the tack into the garbage and wheeled to her writing desk. It had become her soothing enterprise, this old-fashioned writing of letters. And what was she if not old-fashioned? She didn't use the computer because it made her eyes feel swimmy—a long-term effect of her decades-old concussion. She hadn't cottoned to the fancy phones that were like mini-computers either, and spent twenty minutes texting a few simple words to find out when or where Stella might be. But pulling out the smooth cream paper that had been her own mother's favorite brand, Crane, and tapping the tip of her fountain pen against it to produce a smooth glide of ink—that was her speed exactly; she danced her pen with the same rhythm she'd once used her own legs. She wrote:

Max,

Sometimes I wish I hadn't waited so long to find you again, so many stupid years lost to old grudges. But that's all I'll say about that. Today I'm wondering, what if I hadn't spent the night on a thumbtack? Would I have noticed anything different this morning? Or would it creep up on me, catch me in my sleep, the paralysis choking me like a night prowler? Right now it's moving up my buttocks — you remember them? Smooth, round, incredibly firm—you used to grip them when I sat astride you (oh how cheeky I've become). It's not enough that this killing numbness took my legs—do you know how badly I miss the feeling of sand and earth against the soles of my feet? And speaking of feet—you used to kiss them once, starting with the little toe, sometimes snaking a tongue between the crevices after we bathed, even though those feet were as rough and battered as a native's. I'm sure I sound melodramatic, but that's what you love about me, right?

I will always prefer this method of communication because then you can hold that image of me as I was in its full glory. In your memory I still stand tall, en pointe, my thighs flexed and strong—pistons powering me past pain. In your mind, I am haughty and glorious and forever at age, well let's just say twenty, even though you didn't know me then. You can picture it, though, can't you?

Tell me it's going to be okay. Tell me again. I believed you once.

5

THE ROOM GLEAMED, light from a high chandelier reflected off polished wood, evoking thousands of hours of pointing toes at the barre, arms held so firm and straight they stung with effort. Stella's eyes followed the intricately laid amber slats all the way up the walls and the ceiling. Other than a wall of mirrors and a wall of windows looking out on the turgid excuse for a river that ran through town, the all-encompassing wood created a feeling of standing in an elaborate ship's cabin. She half expected Julien to show up in a white and brass captain's uniform. An enormous desk sat at the far end of the room, almost as an afterthought. It was a room to perform in, and her breath caught at the near obscene amount of space in which to move, imagined herself making a weightless leap across its expanse.

But when she saw her own image in the mirrors her heart sank. Her red hair stuck out from her head in chicken wings, looking more *cheap hooker* than *zombie blood* after all, after she'd run to fight the cold. Her nose and cheeks were pink, blue circles cratered her eyes, and her clothes—all black—hid her body in a dark blob.

What the hell was I thinking? Stella turned quickly and strode toward the door, to leave, when she heard his voice.

"Glad you found my office okay. Name the music; I'll pull it up on the computer. Sorry it's only an audience of one."

Stella turned back to find Julien standing in the room as though he'd materialized there. No captain's uniform, though. He wore a pale blue silk shirt and dark slacks over shiny leather shoes. Not a scuff on them.

"You want me to dance? I thought this was an interview." Her voice was thick from the cold, unwarmed.

His smile softened the angles of his face. "Well, dancers interview by auditioning, don't they?"

She exhaled sharply. "I didn't prepare anything. You didn't tell me that's what I'd be doing."

His lips parted slowly revealing two perfect rows of white teeth — the kind displayed by motivational speakers and talk show hosts. "I didn't want you to prepare. I want you to bring the same spontaneous energy to this audition that you do to your grove of trees."

A cloud parted outside and a thin band of sunlight shot through and illuminated his long, angular face. He was undeniably handsome, but she felt no spark of attraction, merely admiration, as though he were a sculpture on display.

"I thought you had watched me enough already."

He frowned, a deep crease opening between his brows that marred the symmetry of his face. "Stella, I know it's been a long time since you performed . . ."

"Why is it that you seem to know things about me? What kind of a business do you run here?" She tried to smooth the wild coils of her hair away from her face, but they sprang back.

He walked toward her. She supposed he expected her to take a few steps toward him, but she stayed put, planted her hands on her hips. A part of her wanted to stalk away, to refuse what others would consider generosity. Desperation put her at a disadvantage, and she hated that.

When he was only a few feet away he stopped and smiled. She was again startled by the one blue eye, and the other green; what kind of odds produced such an anomaly?

"Imagine waking up every day and coming to a job where you get to be yourself, do what you love, live your passion." He held out his arms wide, as though this were a showroom for the great life she was about to begin living. "A job where you will receive praise, an incredible salary, and freedom. A job that doesn't always require you to work late nights, a job you can be proud of. A job that will help you invest in your daughter's talents, that is unlike any job you have had before or will again. More than that, we're a team, a family. You'll become part of a larger whole. You work for me and you will live and breathe creativity and passion. I promise you."

Despite her pride, his words made her thirsty for all the things he promised. "To have all that, all I have to do is audition for you today? What if you don't like my audition?"

He smiled. "Gain always involves risk, n'est-ce pas?"

Reflexively she straightened one leg, mortified by the sound of her knee popping loudly, and unwound her scarf from her neck. "I haven't done an official ballet performance since I was eighteen."

He wrinkled his nose. "Not ballet. Not anything formal. Just dance. You tell me the music, and you dance."

"Okay. Do you have . . ."Toxic. Britney Spears?"

His lip turned up as though she'd said something funny. "I have to admit that's not what I expected you to ask for."

Stella sighed. "It's got a good beat. Look, why don't you just tell me what you're expecting." She began to twist the scarf back on.

"No, no." He tugged the scarf from her hand. "I didn't say I was disappointed. I like that you can keep me guessing, Stella."

He made soft eye contact, and though she wanted to keep from smiling, her lips betrayed her.

He fiddled with his computer, and before she was ready the oddly gentle beat trickled out of hidden speakers, Britney's sugary vocals were a sudden shower from all around her, loaded with warning about bad boys.

He raised an eyebrow, leaned back against the desk, and threw an arm toward her. "Whenever you're ready."

Stella unwound her scarf and dropped her jacket. There was so much light in the room reflecting off all the polish, shining into her face, she felt more lab rat than yearning dancer. She was sweating with nerves before she even began to move. But the music was contagious, and she closed her eyes and popped into rhythm. She tried to pretend that she was snug in her grove of trees, shaded by night, but she could feel the light behind her eyes. She tried to remember the feeling of being on stage, not the first nausea-inducing moment when she looked out at the sea of faces, but the moment when her conscious mind slipped down somewhere into the intelligence of her body and there was no "me" or "them," only a pulsing interface between the two.

"Open your eyes," Julien said. Though his voice was soft, he enunciated the words with such force she snapped them open with soldierly obedience.

"There's a sacred bond between audience and performer." He talked as he circled around her, far enough away that there was no chance of running into him, but closer than a normal audience.

"The performer needs the audience's love, adoration, praise. The performer needs the witnessing of the audience, for without their eyes, what is she?"

Stella tripped over her own foot and went down painfully on her right knee. She forced a deep breath that made her lungs burn. His speech was more than distracting, and she wanted to tell him to shut up so she could focus, but he kept his slow circle and she pushed back into motion.

"The audience needs an object of worship, a place to project their hopes and longings, an escape from the sad and tragic realities of their own lives. It's a symbiotic relationship," he said, his voice taking on the smooth monotone of a PBS narrator.

Stella settled into something of a groove. She loved pop and hip-hop, because she could bring all the precise movements she'd learned from ballet together with something powerful, an energy that began in her belly button and spread out, hot, alive. Britney agreed, singing about sipping from a devil's cup.

"So, all those years you've been dancing alone, you've been depriving yourself, but also others. You have a gift, and you've been withholding it."

That was something she'd never considered, her dancing being a gift. When morning sickness had prevented her from even being able to exercise for the first trimester, she'd felt keenly as though something had been taken from her, almost as if a limb had been removed, a sensation that only ever dulled with time but didn't stop its sting. It made no sense, this stranger giving her what she wanted, but she wanted it suddenly with a child's need, the kind that leads to tantrums of rage if the object of desire is denied. But admitting that felt dark and twisty, a vine of shame crawling her spine.

"You could have such a different life, Stella." He pressed on. "Or you can go back to the one where you serve food to people in a restaurant, take care of your sickly mother, and live your little life out of the spotlight forever."

Stella's breath roared inside her chest, her pride a shield. Who the fuck did he think he was? He could save his lectures for someone who needed his pity.

She dropped to a crouch. "Thanks for the opportunity," she said, panting as she reached over for her discarded jacket and scarf. "I'll be just fine on my own."

Julien shook his head slowly. "I don't agree, Stella. You're raising a musical prodigy. That takes time and money you don't have . . ."

Stella wheeled around. "How the hell do you know about my daughter, or my mother? This feels like stalking."

He laughed, then held up his hands. "No, no, please don't get me wrong. I've done a little research the way any scout would when headhunting new talent. I knew the first time I saw you dance that I wanted you to come work for me. I honestly and truly want to help, Stella. I'm sorry if I've come on too strong, too soon."

Stella bundled herself back into her jacket. "I've gotta go." Without waiting to hear more lectures about what she was withholding from the world, she strode past the mirrored walls to the exit, even though it felt a lot like turning her back on a dream.

*　*　*

That night she tripped over the rubber mat at the back entrance to work and scraped her knee. "Fuck!" she said, pulling herself up from the concrete.

Geena, the hostess, glared at Stella as she led a couple to a nearby table. Stella mouthed "sorry" but Geena had already turned away. A sour taste filled her mouth. She had hardly eaten, and an acid churn of three cups of coffee scorched the base of her throat. Stella's hands were trembling, and a strange buzz filled her head as she filled salt shakers. She kept seeing Julien's one blue eye and one green in her mind like glowing cat's eyes in a dark night.

The rhythm of the evening was bump and jostle. Even the drone of soft jazz felt off, too slow, her body moving too fast against its serpentine slide. Jason smiled politely at her but didn't make his usual eye contact, and she got the cold prickle at the base of her neck that it might already be over between them. What should it even matter? She'd been the one to put him off. But now, as he grinned his wide-mouth smile at Geena, whose breasts were sirens barely contained by the low V of her shimmering black dress, Stella battled a black possessiveness, tempted to insert herself between the two of them like a jealous wife.

"Excuse me, Miss, this isn't what I ordered." The annoyed comment came from a young man with a crew cut she'd just served a steaming plate of fettuccine and shrimp. He pushed it away from him as though the very sight offended him.

He held himself rigidly, no smile on his pale face, a network of freckles making him look younger than he probably was. Usually if she got an order wrong she knew instantly what the mixup was, but she continued to stare at him, blankly, racking her mind.

"What did you order?"

"The tri-tip steak, medium rare. Extra horseradish."

She eyed him suspiciously. Holly, a fellow waitress, had just laid that very same dish down at a table opposite the crew-cut man, and Stella had the feeling he'd simply changed his mind once he got sight of the glistening slab of prime meat.

"You're sure?" she said. "Because I have a really good memory of you ordering the fettuccine."

His mouth tightened into a hard line. "Who the fuck cares what you remember," he said softly, so only she would hear. "Now I want the steak."

Anger docked hard inside her like a boat moving too fast into its slip. She felt it as a cinching just below her belly button, took a step away from him. "There's no need to be rude."

"If you can't follow a simple fucking order, then maybe there is." He whipped his cloth napkin into a hard line, and Stella tensed with the fear he was going to snap it against her leg.

She looked around to see if any of her fellow servers or the hostess could possibly have heard him, but all were busy.

"Steak it is . . . *Sir*." She added the last in as sharp a tone as she could muster.

She stomped off to the kitchen and delivered his order with the hopes that a slammed kitchen would mean delay. Unfortunately their chef, Frankie, was on his game tonight, and Crew Cut's steak was up before she cared to return to his table.

She let it sit on the counter longer than necessary, and took the wine orders of two other tables before she finally moved back toward him. As her feet crossed the slick black tiles of the dining room floor, a lucid clarity settled over her. The music was liquid and moody, and before she had time to let her rational mind kick into gear about consequences, she faked a stumble and the nearly two pounds of beef, sitting in a good inch of hot juice, slid with a wet slump into the man's lap.

"Hey!" He was on his feet in a pinch and grabbed her by the lapels of her starched white shirt. He smelled like tobacco and cloying, musky cologne. Her heart beat in her throat. "Bitch, you did that on purpose!" he said.

"Get your fucking hands off me." She wrenched herself away from him so abruptly that the two top buttons of her shirt popped open, revealing her dingy white laundry-day bra.

Jason dashed over to them from across the restaurant. "What happened?"

"He grabbed me." She pointed at Crew Cut, whose eyes were two blazing slits, his jaw a grimace of rage.

"Your server dumped that steak into my lap. First she brings me the wrong order, then she refuses to get me the right one, and now she's being outright hostile."

Jason held out his hands as Stella stared Crew Cut down. Fuses were snapping off inside her, turning everything down to a dark seethe. The patrons of the restaurant were pretending not to watch behind their menus and wine glasses.

"I'm so sorry." Jason began to clean the man's chair, offered him napkins. "We'll get you another steak, on the house, and your clothes—send us the dry cleaning bill, please."

Stella whirled on Jason, hoping that the thread of intimacy that existed between them might turn this in her favor. "He called me a bitch, and he swore at me for no reason." Jason shot her a pleading look to be quiet, which only enraged her more. "Let the idiot go," she said. "You don't need customers like that."

"Don't think I'm past suing your joint for harassment, injury, and slander." Crew Cut pointed a long, thin finger at Stella. "You need some taming, lady." His eyes were cold, hard. "Breaking in, just like a wild stallion." Then he strode out of the restaurant dripping steak juice in a slippery path to the front door.

"I can't believe what an asshole he was." Now that he was gone, Stella expected Jason's offstage support.

But Jason herded her toward the back pantry with a hand on her low back. "Go home." On a different night, she'd have seen that kind of contact as an invitation.

"Go home? I just got here."

"You are not in a good space tonight, I can tell. And that's the kind of guy who *will* sue. So go home. In fact, I want you to take a week off."

"Are you kidding me? He grabbed me, did you see him? He said 'fuck' to me several times."

"So what, Stel? This is the service business. People are assholes. That's what tips are for. If he comes back any time this week, I don't want him to see you here."

"You're just pissed because I didn't go home with you last night, aren't you?" Stella ripped off her apron while trying to hold her shirt closed at the same time.

Jason's mocha cheeks flushed momentarily, though it was hard to tell in the dim light. "I'm not doing this here."

Stella shrugged into her jacket. "I shouldn't have done *anything* with you *anywhere*. It's like a golden rule: don't sleep with the boss. But I'm an idiot." Shame wicked up her body.

Jason sighed and ran his palm over his scalp. "Just go take your vacation now. We'll see you in a week."

All those lost tips added up in her mind in a mounting panic. But then, behind it, she saw the gleaming room of mirrors and polished wood like a sanctuary in her mind, Julien's white grin beaming down at her as she danced for him.

"You know what? Fuck this job. If you can't stand up for me, and you can't be mature about whatever is between us, then I quit." She had already put down her apron and receipt pad so she did not have the satisfaction of throwing anything in a final act of punctuation. Instead, she reached behind Jason and yanked down a pile of aprons that hung on the door; they fell with an anticlimactic sigh of cloth, like a woman slipping out of a coat at the end of a long day. There was no satisfying clatter or crash.

She gave one great groan of frustration.

"Now who's being mature?" Jason crossed his arms against his chest.

Stella narrowed her eyes, resisting the urge to jab a finger into his strong pecs. "I've had a better offer anyway. See you around." She turned on her heel with the first moment of relief she'd had in days, pressed out into the cool evening.

She'd made it halfway home before it occurred to her that she had no guarantee Julien would hire her. Especially after the way she'd behaved.

6

A PATTERING SOUND rattled the peace of Margaret's letter writing. She dropped her pen, signed her first initial, and wheeled out to the kitchen, where she found her granddaughter seated and fidgeting at the kitchen table.

Isadora's long fingers were tapping manic energy on the stack of schoolbooks she was supposed to be using for her homework.

Every couple of minutes, Margaret felt Izzy's eyes on her—and in the weight of their gaze boiled questions that she didn't want to be asked, questions her fight with Stella had awakened. Without the violin to preoccupy her, Margaret suspected, curiosity was sneaking in to the child's thoughts, and she turned up Oprah a notch louder in the hopes that it would ward them off.

Izzy got up and helped herself to cereal—the loud, crunchy kind—each bite sounding like an accusation. *You know. You know. You know.*

One of many insulting commercials about feminine hygiene products with a slim-waisted girl dancing in a white bikini on a beach came on, and Margaret muted the TV, aware she was opening herself to whatever the silence would bring. She turned to find Izzy staring at her, mouth full of cereal, fingers drumming on the table.

"Not even a couple days off the violin and you're going nuts, eh?"

Izzy set down her spoon and licked her lips. "My fingers itch, like when you can't sit still cuz you've had too much sugar."

Margaret nodded. "I felt that way for a long time after my accident." She pointed to her useless legs. *Wet noodles.* Hard to believe the cadaverous limbs had once been strong enough to propel her into a series of thirty-two fouetté turns at the end of a grand pas de deux, that famous sequence that finished almost every classical ballet.

"You did?" Izzy asked, pushing back a glossy hank of copper hair to little avail; its density caused it to fall right back into her face. "When did it go away?"

Margaret sighed. "I don't know. Sometimes I still feel it. Like how a wild animal must feel when caught in a trap. Sometimes I even forget, and I feel the impulse in my legs to just jump up and reach for a book on a tall shelf. But Isadora, that's not going to happen to you. You are simply on a sabbatical until you can get a new instrument."

Izzy bowed her head, and Margaret read guilt in her crimped cheeks.

"I don't know why I did it." Izzy dithered her spoon in her Cheerios. "I was just so mad at that stupid kid, and my violin is like . . . it's like my arm. It was like I was just hitting him with a part of me, and I didn't stop . . ."

Her breath cascaded toward a sob, and Margaret wheeled herself over beside her granddaughter. As she thrust an arm around the child's thin shoulders, she was keenly aware that Izzy's lanky frame did not come from her own solid family line, but that the child uncoiled daily with the genes of the father she did not know.

"Children who are still learning about the world and themselves can be cruel without meaning to," Margaret soothed. "Kids who are scared, or afraid, often try to make other kids hurt so they don't feel so alone. I'm sorry you ruined your violin, but I understand why you did it."

Izzy's bottom lip hovered at a tremble. "Stupid Jadon Green doesn't know what it's like."

Margaret sighed. She didn't want to shut the child down, but to ask the hanging question was to invite the inevitable. "What it's like to . . .?"

"To not even know your own dad. To not even know if your mom wanted you."

"Oh Isadora, your mother wanted you so much. Do you know how much?" She tilted Izzy's chin up and peered into the flinty green eyes. Margaret had only met Dylan a handful of times. Stella, caught in the fury-lust of new love, had squirreled him away as though he were some precious sculpture too rare to be viewed. But Margaret didn't need to remember him, for he emerged almost fully formed in her granddaughter's angular face, with its patently Irish complexion, the red hair, the green eyes.

"How much?"

"She chose *you* over dancing, Isadora. She loved ballet the way that you love the violin, with her whole being. She never wanted to be or do anything else. But when she knew that you were coming, she gave it up in a heartbeat. You have to understand that."

Izzy's bottom lip quivered. "Did you know my dad?"

And there it was. There was surely an answer that could assuage this question without leading her into trouble. Margaret thought for as long as she could without appearing to be avoiding the question. "He was a dancer, too, like your mother. It's no surprise you've got music in your blood. He was very handsome, and you look like him."

"He was a dancer, too?" Izzy's eyes widened. "I thought maybe he was a musician. I hoped. They both danced in the company—the San Fernisco one?"

"San Francisco, yes."

Izzy chewed on her lips. "So why didn't he . . .?"

Margaret's long-dead nerve endings sent spider webs of pain up and down her legs, a phantom in her brain, but so alarmingly real she had to take a deep breath before continuing talking.

"Isadora, sometimes people have secrets for good reasons. If your mother hasn't talked to you about this, then I am sure she has such a reason."

"I bet he never knew," Izzy said after a long moment's contemplation. "That's why he never contacted us. She didn't tell him."

Margaret shook her head. "Honey, it's not a good idea to guess. Maybe you just need to ask her."

Izzy stood up and shook her head wildly. "No. It's okay, Gigi, don't worry. I won't say anything to her about this. I just wanted to know a little bit about him."

Margaret stared at the child and the room tipped in her vision. She clutched the sides of her wheelchair as though to break a fall, but she hadn't moved. Something had been opened, set in motion, even. She didn't know exactly what, or whether she should feel guilty, but the very quality of the air in the room between them crackled, charged.

And when the door opened only three hours later, when Stella burst into the house, danced across the living room as though trailing a cloud of sparks, Margaret had the feeling that everything was about to change.

"What are you doing home so early?" Margaret asked.

Stella's answer was to wave a dark rectangular box in the air. Izzy stood so still and wide-eyed she looked frightened by the spectacle of her mother, whose hair stood in frantic red spikes, eyes dark-lined and overly bright, and trailing a scent like male cologne behind her.

"Oh. My. God," Izzy cried in little-girl delight, rushing at her mother. "A new violin?"

Stella laid the instrument case down between them with a Vanna White–style flourish. "It's no Stradivarius, but it will keep your genius from going to waste."

"I thought you couldn't afford one." Though Margaret's voice was soft it still sounded like an accusation.

Stella glanced up at her mother only briefly, not making eye contact. "I quit my crappy job, and got a new one today," she said. "This is courtesy of my new employer."

Izzy stopped her tactile admiration of the instrument in its blue velvet cushioning long enough to look up at Stella. "You quit the restaurant?"

Stella nodded. "Yup. This jerk insulted me, and my boss didn't back me up. So, as of today you are looking at the newest dancer for Frivolity, Inc. A company that specializes in performances for all occasions."

She sounded like an infomercial. Margaret found swallowing difficult for a moment. "Izzy, can you go fetch me my vitamins, the ones in the pink bottle?"

Izzy reluctantly put down the violin and ambled off at a leisurely stride.

"Please tell me you are not talking about . . . exotic dancing?" Margaret was aware of the tight and prudish tone to her voice, but unable to control it.

Stella's eyes crimped in around the edges and the hinges of her mouth dropped her lips slack. It was a look Margaret remembered

all too well from when Stella was a raging teenager, a creature
tamed only by dance.

Stella's mouth tightened. "Mom. God, I wouldn't, I can't even
believe you'd think . . ."

Margaret held up her hands in a defensive flat-palmed posture.
"Okay, I'm glad."

"You can't be happy for me, can you, that I get to dance again?"

Margaret reared back. "What? That isn't true."

"Sure it is. I get to dance again and you don't—if the tables were
turned, well . . ."

Margaret shook her head. A cold, liquid sensation chilled each
knob of her spine, another of the strange hallucinations of a body
that had lost so much functioning. "If you're happy, I'm happy."

There was no chance to defend herself as Izzy returned with her
Valium, which she shook into her hand, comforted by the clatter of
pills against the sides of the bottle. Izzy picked up her new instrument, plucked its strings, then tucked it beneath her chin where the
flat callus marked her hours spent practicing. She let out several
tremulous notes that transformed the air in the room to light, her
eyes closed in the half-slits of concentrated pleasure. Then, in a rush,
she set it down on the table and thrust herself into her mother's
arms. "Thank you Mama, thank you. I'm so sorry. I won't be bad
ever again."

Stella laughed. "You weren't bad, honey. You were defending
your honor. You're my girl, after all. Just don't use your expensive
instrument next time."

Izzy murmured her agreement into her mother's side.

There should have been nothing but joy in the room, but Margaret
sat back feeling as though the featherweight legs that hung useless
from her waist had suddenly turned to stone.

7

GIGI HAD FALLEN ASLEEP with her head thrown back and her mouth open to the low drone of the TV, one of many sounds that Izzy had to tune out. Sometimes just people's voices were enough to irritate the surface of her skin. She liked real sounds not cluttered up by artificial ones. The buzz of bees when the delicate white flowers on the orange tree bloomed; the faint rattle and horn of the train that passed through town; the clack of shells she collected with her mom at the beach in the little velvet bag by her bedside. And of course, music—the sweet air moving between her bow and the strings. It wasn't even the sound of her violin, exactly, that she liked so much, as the way it made her head go calm when the notes came out just right, like a thousand tiny shapes sliding into slots designed just for them. She even liked the hum of the computer in Gigi's room, where she wasn't supposed to be without permission. But she knew after Gigi took the yellow pill, the blue pill, and the white pill in combination, she would sleep for over an hour.

Her fingers trembled over the keyboard as she pecked out the words: *San Frensisco Ballet.* She spelled it wrong, but the search engine corrected her by asking, "Do you mean San Francisco Ballet?"

She clicked on that link, and it brought up the page of the ballet with lists of staff and ticket sales. She surfed the page for a half an hour without finding what she wanted, so she tried another search, prickling with nervousness that Gigi would wake up soon and stop her.

A fourth search revealed a "forum" for former dancers and something called an archive that sounded like it might hold old articles. She tried typing in her mother's name in the search function, and was shocked to discover a list of articles featuring her. She clicked on **Youngest Performer in a Decade Asked to Join San Francisco Ballet.** Up came a grainy photograph of her mom, looking so young—something about the softness of her cheeks and tilt of her eyes made Izzy feel as though she was seeing something make-believe. There was none of her mother's too-busy energy and constant impatience in the image. No tired lines at her face, and her smile was so big, like Izzy would feel getting to play her violin at Carnegie Hall or meeting Yo-Yo Ma. Her mother wore a leotard and a little crown and stood on her tiptoes in pretty ballet shoes, her arms hooked overhead. She looked like one of those graceful white birds they saw at the beach—her mom had called them herons—like a little wind could lift her right off the ground. It made the inside of Izzy's chest feel bumpy. This version of her mom was happy, no matter what Gigi had said. The person in that picture looked the happiest ever in her life, and Izzy couldn't imagine that having a baby could compare to that. Her mom never smiled like that now.

She scanned other articles until she came to a photograph of the whole company in that same year, 1992. Standing directly to her mom's right was a man who looked barely older than a teenager. He was so much taller than her mom, his leg muscles all bulging and strong, she would have had to look up at him to see his eyes. The longer she looked at the photo, the more her fingers ached to pick up her violin and chase away the itching in her mind. He was so familiar, like she had seen him a thousand times, when she was sure she didn't know him at all. The picture was black and white, but she could swear he had red hair and pale skin. And there was something about the triangle of his chin, with the dent in it, that made shivers tickle her neck. The names of the dancers were all in a list below the photo and the moment Izzy read "Dylan Wheeler" she knew that she had found what—or *whom*—she was looking for.

From there, it wasn't hard to open her Gmail account like Trista had taught her when they were supposed to be doing homework, or to create a simple Facebook page, uploading one of the old dance photos of her mom she'd found. Then she could search. There were three Dylan Wheelers, but only one who matched the image in the photo. Only one whose page proudly proclaimed that he was the youngest director of Santa Maria Dance—a town she knew was not so far away—only one Dylan whose voice she was sure she would know as though it had read her a thousand bedtime stories, whose long fingers matched *her* fingers as they plucked the strings of her violin. She tried to write how Stella talked, heart thumping so wildly against her chest it sounded loud enough to wake her grandmother.

Dear Dylan,

I know that it has been a very long time, and you are probably surprised to hear from me. But if you would like to talk to me, or care to meet me, please let me know.

Sincerely,
Stella.

She logged out of all the pages as quickly as she could, thirst overtaking her. She crept out of Gigi's room, poured herself a glass of lemonade, downed it so fast it made her stomach hurt, and then shut herself into her room, fingering the new instrument that gleamed at her with promises of happiness.

8

STELLA HAD NO IDEA what to expect of her first official day of "work." Upon returning the day before to fall at Julien's mercy and beg him to hire her, she'd met a slender redhead who handed over hiring paperwork as though it had been all ready to go; she'd passed her audition or whatever it had been.

"Take this, too," the redhead said without introduction. "Come to this address tomorrow in these clothes." She handed over a shopping bag from a local dance shop. The fact that Stella had no idea what she would be doing, or how hard she'd have to work, didn't matter in that moment; he'd bought her child a violin!

Now, the giddy realization that she would not have to go back to serving demanding patrons slid over her with the same smooth glide the black leotard and pleather dance skirt did now.

She followed the directions to the address the secretary had given her in a part of town she vaguely knew, but when she pulled up to the old, defunct textile mill—situated between dilapidated tin warehouses overlooking the river—her heart pounded with anxiety. Was this Julien's idea of a joke, his answer to her failed audition, getting her hopes up only to destroy them as punishment for how she'd run out on him? If not for that violin as a proof of faith in her, she'd have turned right back around and begged Jason to give her job back.

Half of the windows in the ancient building were shattered, and the cement of the parking lot was buckled and cracked. And yet a warm yellow light glowed from within, and when she got out of her car, tightening her sweater against the autumn chill, soft music and voices emanated from within.

The front entrance was propped open with a pedestal bowl full of white camellias floating in water, but the entrance was dark. She could see only enough to find her footing and not trip over pebbly debris on the floor. Enormous wooden spools, empty of the twine and yarn that had once been produced here, loomed like water wheels in the first room of the warehouse. A flutter of wings above her alerted her to birds that roosted in its high, open ceiling beams.

Shadows writhed on the walls, and she hurried toward the light and the voices, overcome by a childish fear of the dark and what unknown things lurked within it. She had a sudden suspicion that people weren't even supposed to be there, and the idea aroused a rebellious pleasure in her before settling back into anxiety.

A hundred feet more and she hit a candle-lined walkway sprinkled with more white flower petals, and as though she'd passed through some sort of protective membrane, pop music that had been a distant echo now throbbed in her ears, followed by a murmur of voices talking. Was she late?

The line of candles stopped at a beaded curtain, through which she could make out bodies in motion, then the yeasty smell of sourdough bread and wine hit her nose.

She stripped off her sweater and left it on the floor behind her. When she put her hand through the curtain and pushed her body after it, she was greeted by a rose-colored spotlight and an audience of people dressed in evening gowns and tailored suits all staring at her. Midway between catching her breath she noticed Julien—a tall, dark blue silhouette in the corner of the room, holding a glass of champagne and gazing at her with the intensity of an inventor watching his creation come to life. His gaze unnerved her, so she looked around at the scrolls of black velvet draped over exposed bones of wall that had long ago deteriorated; took in the gurgling fountain of red wine that people dipped glasses into; and watched as, on a dance floor designated solely by an outline of white tea light candles, a smattering of other dancers were all suspended in different positions as if her very entrance had caused them to pause.

Before she could gather herself, Julien pointed a long finger at her, then at a woman standing beside a makeshift DJ stand, and music erupted from the speakers. It was the same Britney Spears song she'd asked him to put on in her audition, and Stella was flush with adrenaline that she was going to have to perform now, with no practice. If there had ever been an audition it was this; he'd thrown her right into the maw of one of his spectacles to see if she would flail or shine.

Even more miraculous than the way her own body picked up the thread of music and performed as she had at her audition, only with more confidence, was the quick and perfect timing of the women who moved around her as though they knew exactly what she would do—who mirrored and shadowed and complemented her with eerie precision.

And when it was over, she thrust her body to a stop, her companion dancers halting in sync. As the assembled audience burst into exuberant applause, endorphins powered through her body, like after great sex. And then Julien was at her side, his arm looping through hers, a glass of champagne slid into her other hand, and his warm, low voice commending her in a whisper in her ear, "You are everything I hoped you would be, and more." A sheen of sweat dotted his brow and the pupils of his eyes were nearly pinned and glossy, as though he was a few glasses of wine deep, and yet his breath didn't smell of alcohol.

Hands were on her arm, her shoulder, even touching her neck, faces pressing in too close, breathing a sour combination of wine and cheese on her, and yet she didn't mind.

Magnificent, wonderful, sublime—words poured onto her body like benedictions, and the first green shoots of her hunger uncoiled, opening Venus flytrap mouths to receive the praise. Julien kept hold of her with one arm, steered her through the guests, his company of dancers trailing behind them. She sipped the champagne in her hand, swallowed a bite of a pastry filled with cheese, and let him lead her out of the party, away to another area of the building.

The walls were almost completely crumbled away, just bare beams exposed, and piles of dust and spare bits of string and wire, the skeleton of something. Julien sat on the ground on a blanket and pulled Stella down beside him. The women gathered in a coil around them, a hedge of bright eyes and high cheekbones, smooth faces peering back at her as though she were a queen and they were waiting her command.

"Well." Julien smoothed a wrinkle at his knee. "How'd our Stella do?" Even though a part of her still bristled at being claimed by this man, with his grand promises and his uncanny ability to fulfill aspects of herself that she had all but given up on, the phrase, or maybe the warmth of its delivery, touched her. How long it had been since she'd been part of something, of someone?

The women exchanged glances with each other, and then, one by one, nodded.

Now that Stella's heart rate was returning to normal she realized that several of the faces were barely out of their teens. A couple could have been her age—it was hard to tell beneath their makeup—and wore identical black wigs.

"Shall we have her take the vow here, or should we wait until we return to Headquarters?"

Headquarters, like they were some sort of crime-fighting agency. Stella stifled a giggle. The champagne was already working on her.

"Give her the vow *here*," said a woman with a cinematic mole to the left of her slight nose and a pale thatch of blonde hair peeking through the top of her wig.

Julien nodded thoughtfully. "Yes, I think so." He turned to Stella. "Finish your champagne, lovely."

Stella tipped the glass back and downed it, head filling with echoes of performances that had ended with bouquets of roses thrust at her feet, with the same palpable energy of hands against her body, of praising faces, Dylan standing back a pace away from the crowd, watching her with the satisfaction that she was his alone later on. She nodded, dizzy.

Julien stood and helped her up. The strange troupe followed behind them as he led her further into the heart of the old building, to a room whose windows were all completely broken out. Moonlight danced around the broken glass and cast a liquid light on the floor. Julien shoved aside debris with his foot and clapped his hands. The women assembled in a semicircle around Stella. It had really been a long time since she'd drunk champagne, for her head felt as though it would detach from her body, or as though her neck was elongating like Alice in Wonderland's under the influence of the "eat me" cookie.

Julien reached into his pocket and withdrew a red silk bandanna. "Eyes closed, lovely."

Panic stabbed through her, but the women around her were all placid and composed, so she took a deep breath. He tied the bandanna around her eyes, fingers lingering at the back of her neck. His hands were warm, and he smelled like Old Spice, faintly sweet. She had the alarming urge to kiss him, though she would never, and before she could do much more thinking, he spun her in circles just like they were playing a game of pin the tail on the donkey.

Then he pushed her slightly, and as she was sure she would fall painfully to her knees, another set of arms took hold of her, turned her and spun her again, and yet another person caught her.

As she whirled dizzily from one body to the next, Julien spoke: "I pledge to Frivolity Inc. my talent, my commitment, and my secrecy."

The physical whirling stopped, though the blackness still danced inside her head, unsettling her stomach. Julien's strong hands pressed warmly on her shoulders. "Repeat it, Stella."

She repeated the words.

Julien continued, "I treat the company of Frivolity like my family. It comes first, but for every sacrifice I make, there is a greater reward."

For a beat Stella hung at the edge of repeating the words. Her daughter came first. But then, Julien was obviously a man of ceremony. She repeated the words.

"I respect the sacred bond between audience and performer, and always, no matter what, will honor it."

She repeated the words, and then Julien took her hand in his, followed by a sharp sting in the pad of her ring finger. She cried out, as Julien whipped the bandanna off, and saw that all the other girls were holding up their fingers. From their wigs they'd each produced some kind of pin.

"A blood vow." Julien's face was leonine in the dim light. "Go." He shoved her lightly toward the girls and she moved on rubbery legs. The faintest hot pain of her old knee injury lit up the left knee as she pressed her finger against that of the first woman, who said simply, "Yvette."

They followed: Aja. Chloe. Lucy.

The last woman to hold up her finger pronounced, "Lina," and raised a pale eyebrow at Stella in a meaningful way, as though there was more to say, and then winked. Stella realized that Lina was the one who'd given her the violin, the hiring forms; not a secretary after all.

Stella tried to look at her finger, at the trail of blood mingled with her own, tried not to consider diseases transmitted, when Julien was at her shoulder again, whispering into her ear.

"Come on," he said. "I want to show you something."

The champagne had now worked its full effects on her and she drifted high, weightless, and giddy. She traveled on the energy of his arm out into the cool night, let him lead her along a reedy stretch of the river to a rusty footbridge, the suede of her ballet slippers scraping softly along its crusted ridges. It shimmied under their weight as they walked, but he held her up, close to his body, until they stood almost directly in its middle.

"Look," he said, pointing at the yolk of moon as it broke apart on the water. Stars winked in and out overhead and down the river, in the little harbor in town, she saw that all the boat masts were strung with lights, like an early Christmas.

"Oh." She inhaled briny air. "It's gorgeous."

"I always feel more alive when I'm near water," he said. "It's life-giving on so many levels."

She nodded. She was afraid to look at him.

His voice blended with the night. "I know that the way I came to you was . . . unorthodox. Maybe even a little unfair," he said gently. "And I never meant to scare you or cause you to mistrust me. But I knew the minute I saw you dance in the woods that I wanted you. In the company. My instincts don't fail me, and tonight I feel validated. You should, too."

Stella took a deep breath and ventured a look at him. "It's exciting." She blew out a white puff of air. "I don't want to admit it. I'm proud. And I'm afraid that if I give in to the thrill of performing again, I'll never want to give it up again."

"Why would you have to?"

She raised her eyebrows at him. "I'm not nineteen anymore, and even then, I've only got so many good years left in me."

Julien shook his head. "If you look that far down the road, Stella, you'll miss it, all of this. And it is, I promise you, just beginning."

The moon spread apart and re-fused in the water at their feet as the river moved.

"If you say so," she said. "I'm not used to the long-term view."

Julien pulled her to him then in a hug that was more fatherly than anything else, something of a relief.

"You're my star, Stella. I've been looking for a long time, and I found you."

Stella shivered. "What was all that vow stuff about?"

Julien didn't answer for a good long minute, leaving Stella to wonder if she'd offended him.

"I take this company very seriously, Stella. It's everything to me."

A breeze swept over them, so bracing it hurt.

"It's time to go back," Julien said, as if some mythical clock had chimed the end of this surreal moment.

*   *   *

Stella woke behind the wheel of her car, not remembering having gotten in. She was still parked in the String Factory parking lot, but the light from inside had gone dark, and she had the strangest feeling of having dreamt the whole thing. But her finger was still marked by a crusty line of blood, and a fetid mixture of sweat and alcohol seeped from her skin. Her cell phone registered that it was two a.m. She shook the sleep out of her brain and drove herself home. There were no cars on the road, and the gray night sky and empty streets had a slightly apocalyptic feel, like a zombie might come dragging a human corpse along.

She tried to be as quiet as possible when letting herself in. As she tumbled through her front door, into the foyer where mail was stacked to the point of tipping and shoes warred with books for space, where the house had the contained smell of having been unopened for too many days, her limbs went numb and leaden, overcome by weariness, like the energy it would take to disrobe and walk to her bed was too much work. She vaguely remembered this sensation at the end of a performance from her dancing days, when all the sets came down and the costumes were retired.

She tiptoed to the kitchen to fix herself some peanut butter toast when the telltale squeak of her mother's wheelchair made the breath catch in her throat, like she was a teen again, caught sneaking out.

"Late, isn't it?" Margaret wheeled around the corner into the kitchen.

"Or early, depending on how you look at it," Stella said, popping bread into the toaster.

"What was it like?"

Her mother's hair stood up in featherlike tufts from her head, putting her in mind of some newly hatched bird.

"Exhilarating."

"Goodness, what happened to your hand?" Margaret asked in that shrill, overly concerned tone that Stella still cringed away from as a grown woman.

Stella looked at her hand in the light. Crusted over with reddish brown blood, from a distance it could look like a serious wound. "I don't know." She wiggled her fingers. "Must have cut it on something."

"And you only just noticed?" Margaret raised an eyebrow.

Stella's bread popped up, and she burned her other fingers slightly in her quick grasp of it. She slathered it in peanut butter and thrust a bite into her mouth. "Yup."

Margaret continued to stare at her, and Stella turned quickly to the sink and washed her hand, rivulets of pink streaming down the drain.

"That was a beautiful instrument you brought home yesterday. Your new boss just gave it to you?"

Stella wheeled around. "What do you want to ask me, Mom?"

Margaret held out her palms. "No, nothing, I'm not trying to sound disapproving. I'm asking questions because I care, because that's what mothers do."

Stella took a deep breath and another bite of toast. "I'm sorry. I'm just tired and stressed. I'm sorry for being rude to you yesterday. I just . . . well, you know it's complicated."

"I know," Margaret said. "I just want to say one thing, and then I will shut my mouth."

Stella braced her back against the sink and finished her toast in two bites.

"You should talk to her about her father. Even if it's only to tell her that she's not going to get the chance to know him. The more

she wonders, the more opportunity she has to come up with fanta-
sies that might be worse for her in the long run."

Stella felt the magic of the evening sink as though to the bottom
of that moonlit river with the weight of all these realities. Her
probing mother; her fatherless daughter, and both of them needing
something from her she didn't have to give.

"Duly noted. I'm going to bed now. Thanks for your concern."

"Stella," Margaret started, but she didn't finish her thought in
time for Stella to hear it as she marched off.

9

HEADQUARTERS. **THE WORD** sounded silly in Stella's mouth and did not match the vision of the cornflower blue two-story Victorian in front of her. She'd pictured something squat and half abandoned, a ramshackle warehouse down by the river, its tin roof rusted, tangled in ivy. She parked down the long driveway as instructed and walked around the back. The front of the house was immaculate, paint still fresh and unchipped, elaborate white molding and shell-shaped tiles like something out of a historical society; the yard, however, was forgotten and untended, littered with broken white angel statuary and the brown remains of plants indistinguishable in their deaths from weeds. Cigarette butts and beer bottles tossed into a corner of the mostly dirt yard gave the impression of a frat party just recently left off.

She climbed the steps of the back porch noticing a not unpleasant soreness in her limbs from the previous night's dancing. A screen door was open, and through it wafted the gentle strains of Bach and conversation and the scent of something spicy and sweet. She slipped inside.

Four women were perched around a table in the bright, folksy kitchen, three times the size of her own. Her boot heels clicked crisply on the red tile floor. Bright ceramic chickens and pigs hung on the walls. The women smiled up at her and waved. Unvarnished and free from costumes, they were unrecognizable to her from the other night.

"Stella!" A tall blonde stood up and held out her hands. The mole on her cheek was at least familiar. "I'm Chloe."

Stella admired the all-American features, blue eyes, blonde hair, poreless complexion of the girl, the kind you'd find in a magazine ad selling soap or shampoo.

Stella frowned. "You all look so different by daylight."

"All the mystery is gone." This from the only woman she did recognize, the redhead who'd given her the violin. "We're all pumpkins again."

"Lina, so dramatic." Chloe waved at Lina like a bad smell. "Did you bring your sleeping bag, Stella?"

Stella looked at her hands dumbly as if it was their fault for being empty. Chloe all but leapt across the kitchen to Stella's side to pat her on the shoulder. "Don't worry, we've got extras."

"I didn't realize this was a sleepover," Stella said. "I . . . need to let my daughter know."

Several of the women exchanged glances.

"Why are we sleeping over?" Stella asked.

Chloe retrieved orange juice from the fridge. "We always do when we're planning a new spectacle," she said, "since we tend to stay up most of the night anyway. Part of the whole 'company first' deal."

"Besides, *she* might be coming," whispered a dark-eyed girl with a bob and a French accent.

"Yvette, you're just hoping. You know he doesn't bring her out so soon into a new initiate's . . ." Chloe stopped abruptly. Stella realized that the French woman sitting behind her had poked or pinched her in censure.

"I hear the spectacle's going to be at that mansion up on Evergreen terrace." Chloe changed tacks.

Lina shook her head and cracked eggs into a chipped white bowl on the table, her brow furrowed. "We don't know anything until Julien tells us."

Yvette stood up abruptly. "I'm off to smoke. Keep your lectures to yourselves." She marched off through the way Stella had come, the screen door banging hard against its jamb.

"Yvette has trouble adjusting to change." Lina beat the eggs hard with a fork.

"You mean me?" Stella touched her collarbone self-consciously.

Lina raised a dark red eyebrow. "*Oui, oui.* Yvette was the star for a long time, and once you see her dance, you'll understand why."

Stella had a vague feeling she knew which one had been Yvette whirling in the dark around her, the one who seemed to anticipate her own movements before she even made them.

"Do you mind if I sit?" Stella pointed to an empty chair, silver back with red plastic seat, just like something out of a retro diner. Lina nodded. The seat let out a squeak of air that was vaguely fartlike and Stella had the urge to shout, "I didn't!" but nobody looked up.

Only then did she realize there was another woman in the kitchen, so quiet and sullen and hunched into a chair near the oven, legs tucked up beneath her, Stella hadn't noticed her. She had the perfect skin and sullen scowl of a teenager, with long black hair to her waist.

The table was littered with bowls and dough, cut apples and flour, and each girl—except the dark-haired one in her own world in the corner—engaged in some part in it.

"I have to be honest," Stella said. She shifted in her chair again, which farted even more loudly this time. "I feel like he's over-touting my talent. I haven't danced in ten years, I mean not formally. I'm rusty, I know that."

"Lucy, bring the flour over here, honey," Lina said to another raven-haired girl, her face heart-shaped, a young Cher.

Lucy shot Lina a glower of adolescent annoyance that only Stella caught, and delivered the bowl of flour with a *thunk* on the table.

"Stella, Julien doesn't select us for our technical perfection, if you hadn't noticed. The dancer you were back in the day—and I've seen the clippings on you—probably wouldn't have caught his attention. He's not interested in perfection, but personality, spark, authenticity."

Stella briefly wondered what she meant by clippings.

"So right now, you're the star because you've got something new, something we don't already have. Aja, make yourself useful; check the oven."

"Not your slave." Aja didn't so much as speak as eject the words like something foul out of her mouth. Her body, praying mantis-like in her fold, now unfurled to a staggering height—maybe six feet as she stood to turn the oven on, her feet encased in heavy black boots hitting the floor with a thud.

"Ignore Aja." Lina pursed her lips. "She was the hip-hop queen before you."

"Still am," Aja said, "And your first fucking pie is gonna burn you don't get it outta here."

Lina pulled the dough ball to her, kneaded it fervently. Stella was a serviceable cook—the bare minimum. Now that Izzy was old enough to boil noodles and make sandwiches, some days it felt as though she barely needed Stella for much of anything.

"Give it ten more minutes." Lina glanced sidelong at Aja then rolled her eyes in Stella's direction. "Go put those pans away so I can have some space to work."

Stella waited for Aja to protest, but she did not. Lina commanded some sort of top-of-the-hierarchy power as far as Stella could tell.

"Dancing ain't the end-all be-all anyway. Some of us got other talents." Aja turned around and laid sharp eyes on Stella.

Stella now spotted a tattoo beneath her right eye, like a tiny curlicue or a snake, and others on her arm, elaborate, twisting designs that seemed full of symbols, but Stella didn't want to stare. Aja's hands-on-hip posture was hard and full of attitude.

"You'll always be his darling songbird, Ayj." Lina began to work the dough into a pie tin.

Stella cleared her throat. "So . . . what are we doing here this morning? Just baking pies?"

Lina looked up and raised an eyebrow. "Just? Honey, there's more to being part of a company than the fun stuff," Lina said. "This here is chop wood, carry water. Or, make pies because Julien loves them, and we want him to be happy."

Stella remembered the work of a dance company for the brief time that she'd been in one—it had been hours of drills and rehearsals, cigarette breaks to ward off hunger, and rubbing each other's sore muscles before the stern clap of the choreographer's hands meant back on the floor, in position. *Shoulders back! Neck long!* Not baking pies.

"Who's gonna tell newbie that she's got less than twenty-four hours to learn the spectacle?" Aja popped a slice of apple into her mouth.

Lina slapped a second slice out of Aja's hand. "I think you just did, and not very nicely, either."

Aja shrugged and grinned. "Yeah, that's the beauty of this gig—it's always new and it's always a little fucking scary. Especially for the new girl."

Lina clucked like an old grandmother, though she couldn't have been more than thirty.

"Stella, if you'd like, you could fill this pie with apples for me. Aja, go make some beds or something."

"Okay, *Mom*." Aja stomped off to the porch, where the faint drift of Yvette's cigarette wafted in.

"Don't mind her." Lina sighed. "She's just rough around the edges."

Stella stared after her, trying to decide how she felt about this whole scenario. "I was never good at . . . fitting in," Stella said. "Me and groups—not symbiotic."

"Well, but you danced in a company when you were younger, right? You know how to follow the rules and do what's expected of you, I presume."

"Yes."

"So the only thing to remember is that you just do what you're supposed to do, do it well, practice, and don't let any of these little bitches throw you off your game." Lina smiled with all her teeth, and Stella laughed despite herself.

"This is a house full of women, after all, most of them too young and raw from their experiences, so you're going to have to duck occasionally, expect a fair amount of on-the-rag bullshit, and otherwise remember that most of them are just little girls underneath it all, looking for a tit to suck or a skirt to hide behind."

"So when do I get the 'but it's all worth it' speech?" Stella asked, as she layered apples atop each other and watched, mesmerized, as Lina shaped a crust without even looking.

Lina smiled, her gently freckled cheeks rising high, and picked dough out from under her long fingernails. "You danced last night. You felt it, right? I know you did, because I felt it, and when I feel it . . ."—she winked at Stella—"the magic is really on."

"You make it sound supernatural or something."

Lina raised an eyebrow. "What else do you call it when you can come into complete sync with a group of people and mesmerize a group of strangers?"

Stella nodded. "It *was* pretty spectacular, the way you all danced with me like we'd choreographed that routine. You're all great at improvisation."

Lina stood up, pressed her palms to her lower back with a wince and arched backwards. "Julien showed us the videos of you dancing in the woods, and in his studio. We knew how you moved."

"Videos?" Stella asked, her mouth suddenly tasting like copper. As in plural?

Lina put a hand to her mouth in mock distress. "Ooops, did I say too much?"

Stella shrugged. "That's a little creepy."

Lina shook her head. "Julien is very committed to his work, that's all. Okay, hand me that bowl of egg yolk."

Stella did as she was told, watched Lina slather the clear goo on the surface of her pristinely latticed crust, wondering all the while which, if any, of all revelations and warnings she'd learned about, she should heed.

10

IZZY WOKE IN A PANIC to the crunch of wood being smashed into bits, a twang of a snapped wire whizzing in the air, and that horror of knowing she couldn't take it back. It took a very long minute, in which she peeled her sweaty body off her bed, to realize it had only been in her dream. Her mother had been standing before her, wearing gauzy red clothes, her hair flying out around her head like that of a crazy fairy, and she'd been laughing at Izzy, holding hands with a faceless man. They were leaving without her and they didn't even care, and Izzy had stomped on her violin in protest, to show that she hated them.

Izzy shook her head to clear it. Her digital clock pulsed 6:45 a.m. No one had woken her to get ready for school, and the house had a sense of empty quiet, as though she were alone. She tiptoed out into the house and was relieved to hear the rhythmic snores of her grandma.

Her mother's bedroom was empty. She had left without saying good-bye. Izzy's dream choked her throat for a moment before she thought things through. Her mom had a new job, one with new hours, early hours. She wouldn't leave them. Izzy stole into Gigi's room and perched at the computer. She pulled up a web page on African tree frogs just in case her grandmother woke and asked what she was doing. Then she logged into the Facebook page she'd created for her mother. There was a message waiting for her. The sweat on her body chilled her and her finger was slick with sweat as it poised on the mouse.

Dear Stella,

Yes, surprised is an understatement. Frankly, I never thought to hear from you again. But I'm glad. Really glad. I hope that you are well now. And if you don't think it will compromise your mental state any, then I'd be thrilled to see you. I'll actually be in town in your neck of the woods in two weeks. I'm director of a modern dance company now, Santa Maria Dance, and we're doing a one-weekend show at the Phoenician Center for Performing Arts. I'll leave two tickets at will-call if you think you can make it, and perhaps we can have coffee after.

All my best,
Dylan.

Izzy wanted to get up and tap dance or run circles around the room. She wanted to pounce on her grandma's bed and shout her excitement. The man whose hair and eyes she could claim as her own, the man who had provided the other half of her DNA, was real, and he was close, and maybe he even still cared about her mother. She wasn't entirely sure what he meant about her mom's mental state, but the truth was, she didn't really care. All she had to do was get her mother to go to the show in two weeks. She was up for the challenge.

11

MARGARET HAD WATCHED Stella that morning, flitting around the house with an ease and lightness in her step that she hadn't seen in years, a lightness that revealed a dancer's life within her. Her daughter's feet didn't plod, flat against the floor with the gloomy effort of obligation. She was lifted, and for every light step she took, Margaret's own legs sank heavier, more like iron anvils, useless. Out of nowhere surged a rage she had not felt in ages. She pounded her dead thighs, the sensation a distant vibration as though someone were banging on a door at the end of a long hallway. She had a vision of tearing the new clothes down out of Stella's closet. Even as the thought horrified her, she couldn't dispel it, took pleasure at the visceral sense of how those silky new tops would feel between her teeth as she ripped them to shreds.

She threw open her robe and scowled at her white, shriveled worms for legs—small and misshapen, twisted from how they'd broken, fused with the metal of that tin can of a car as it crumpled nearly in half, never to work again because of where the accident had severed her spine. Dark red scars worked up through the pale flesh like subterranean parasites, ropy and ugly. These legs were hideous, not the strong, curved calves and chiseled thighs that had once given her near-superhuman power to propel her entire body across a stage in a couple of leaps. There had been nights when she'd peeled away her ballet shoes, soaked, to find a toenail torn off, the slipper's lining crimson, a gluey mixture of sweat and blood cementing the shoe to her flesh. But rather than the horror someone else might feel at such a sight, she'd felt nothing but pride; suffering was equal to how hard you worked. During the dance there was no pain; nothing but energy and power, almost a madness. Beneath the surface it had occurred to her that perhaps it wasn't normal to enjoy such torture; it wasn't healthy to equate pain with success. But it came with the territory of dance.

She hadn't craved that pain in years, probably because the medications had dulled it out of her, softened all the hard edges along with the nerve pains and turned her into this feeble excuse of rotting flesh.

She didn't want to feel this envy now, but it was oozing up like muddy water through her nonetheless, every time Stella moved through the house with this new stride or put on her makeup for work. Margaret suffered a spasm of rage, an echo of her former self, who had revolved between two poles of pleasure and pain, and who only rarely in between had really even considered her daughter.

The more Stella moved toward happiness in dancing again, the more Margaret missed that person she had been, even felt the phantom of her old self moving inside her, a demon gestating, a calculating talent who had taken what she wanted. A person who had been secretly glad when her nineteen-year-old daughter had wound up pregnant, had convinced her to have the baby, because then she didn't have to corrode with jealousy each time it was her younger, more beautiful daughter up on the stage instead of her.

It was that person who had fallen for *him*. He had seen what she was and had eaten her up. Even as she knew that he pandered to her, that he egged her on for something in his own ego, she had let herself fall, for a moment, for a little while, barely long enough to call it a relationship. It had cost her everything. Everything. She looked at the wretched legs, felt her pudding-soft middle, and made a decision.

She wheeled to her room, scooped up all the pill bottles—the Neurontin for her nerve pain, the hydrocodone and Tramadol for pain and muscle spasms—and wheeled herself to the bathroom, twisted open the easy-to-unlock bottles meant for weak and help-less old people, and poured all of them, a little shower of miniscule shapes, into the toilet, where they bobbed gently for a moment before sinking.

She wanted to know what sensations were available to her body without all that dulling—maybe the drugs were numbing her. She would even take pain again, a welcome distraction.

12

STELLA WAS FOLDED FORWARD, stretching her hamstrings, when the front door of the house burst open and Julien strode in. He must have leapt up the rotted gap in the front porch. She snapped upright, aware that her hair was probably flying out in wild red spikes around her face.

In her sweatpants and Bob Marley T-shirt she felt a ragamuffin compared to his sleek gray slacks and silver button-up shirt. He brought that distinctly masculine smell of aftershave into the room, and she noted the way her mood brightened, as if under a warm light, when he smiled at her.

She smiled shyly, and an instant he was giving her a warm hug. "Glad to see you're making yourself at home. Girls not behaving too badly?"

"Only as bad as usual," said Lina from the doorway to the kitchen.

His smile was like something chained had been set free inside him when he set eyes on Lina. "Oh dear girl, are you making apple pies again?"

Stella turned to see Julien fold Lina into his arms in such a tender way she felt almost inappropriate watching, and yet it wasn't sexual, just as though Lina was his most favorite person in the world.

"I wouldn't dream of disappointing." Lina's smile did not match Julien's; hers looked almost forced. "Are you alone?"

Julien craned his head back to the front door with a look that Stella read as concern. "For now," he said. "*She*'ll be joining us this evening. It's her spectacle, after all."

* * *

Several hours later, after nothing but stretching and washing dishes, and the emergence of the rest of the women from upstairs and outside, the entire group, plus Stella, were seated around the living room in various stages of sprawl, eating apple pie—at least those who would consent to eat. Stella noted that Aja and Yvette both had the telltale behaviors of anorexics: chain-smoking and eating only tiny bites of fruit. She'd been one herself, at least the dance-induced kind, when she was a teen.

Julien lounged in a worn leather recliner with a clipboard on his lap and a mug of coffee in one hand. Lina perched just to the left of him, and blonde, perky Chloe to his right.

"Spectacle number sixty-five will take place tomorrow at ten p.m. This is another private spectacle, at the home of one Steven Ernestine . . ."

"Evergreen Mansion, I told you!" Yvette chimed in.

Julien shot her a stern frown, eyebrows pinched together. "What do I say about guessing and rumors?"

Yvette dropped her head and mumbled, "Respect the spectacle; await the revelation."

Julien nodded. "Mystery is important. It's crucial to what we do. We don't ever want word to spread ahead of time, or the purpose of our work is ruined. We'll be doing some sort of mermaid theme, but I'm afraid there won't be any restful lounging on rocks or dainty swimming. You will exert yourselves and it will be, as always, unforgettable. You know how Lady I. is."

"I knew it," Aja mouthed to Lina, in Stella's line of sight.

"And we will be dealing with partial nudity."

The saliva in Stella's mouth suddenly thickened, grew too hard to swallow. Julien had never said anything about nudity. As if he sensed her discomfort, he looked immediately at her. "Don't worry, you'll be wearing body makeup, the lighting will be dim, and you will be able to dress fully after the spectacle before you mingle with the guests. Tasteful, as always. We're not doing porn here."

Stella exhaled slightly. She supposed she could handle that. And for all she knew, she wasn't even going to be featured in this event. "Okay, let's all move to the basement. I've got the trusses and hoists arranged there and Lady I. will join us shortly to begin."

Stella did not want to be the new girl asking too many questions, but it was out of her mouth before she could stop herself. "Trusses and hoists?"

Julien didn't smile. "I usually like to let the Lady do the explaining when it's her creation."

Stella felt strangely chastised and nodded, folding her hands into her lap until, on the cue of all the others, she rose with the rest of the women and followed them down to a surprisingly large and musty-smelling basement that looked something like a torture chamber. A large blow-up swimming pool took up a good portion of the floor, and above it hung, as he had described, a trellis of leather and polyester straps and harnesses. An ancient water heater creaked in the corner, and the room smelled rank and fetid, like years of mice had pooped and bred in its walls.

The girls buzzed and whispered to each other, and Stella's tummy rumbled with both nervous excitement and a childish kind of anxiety—none of them were talking to her; she was the new girl, the outsider.

It wasn't long before the door at the top of the stairs opened again, and all the girls turned with an almost trancelike synchrony toward the steps. Stella half expected the ghost of Princess Diana to descend, from the reverence of their gazes. Even Aja's grim smile had softened in anticipation.

A woman's shapely legs in sheer black hose and shiny black heels appeared first. The rest of her emerged in slivers of shimmering green. Her dress was form-fitting, of a delicate green fabric, as though it had been woven of lily pads, revealing a pale and smooth décolletage, strong shoulders, a long, Hepburn-like neck, and the most startling shade of turquoise hair, cut into a twenties bob around her round face. It was the oddest color of hair, so unnatural it should look wrong, but instead, the effect on the dark-eyed woman was very much as though she were a sea nymph stepping out of the ocean to command a human lover. Stella worried that it was cliché wearing red, wanted to bleach it right off her head.

"Isis," said a voice, maybe several voices all at once. Stella wasn't sure—a giddy sensation overcame her, as though she'd been suddenly drugged. There was something about this woman, right away, that made Stella want to sit at her knee and wait for some kind of revelation.

The heart-shaped face, the perfect almond eyes under the bob reminded Stella of someone—an old actress from the era of movies when men danced and women smoked.

Julien was at the bottom of the stairs, waiting for Isis. He took her hand and kissed her cheek. Stella couldn't have moved unless pushed at that moment, her body an earthbound piece of marble, upon which hundreds of moth wings beat at the idea of being strapped into the strange hoists.

"Girls," Isis crooned, holding open her arms. Several of them rushed in. When they'd pulled away, Isis scanned the room and alighted on Stella at last. Her mouth lifted into a slight, one-sided grin.

"Strap her up." She pointed to a contraption dangling from the ceiling. "Let's make our new star soar."

* * *

By the time the girls were all packed into two cars the next evening, makeup on and costumes in their bags, Stella's ribs and limbs were rubbery and sore, bruised in the places where the straps had held her. Isis had assured her that the hoists at the spectacle's location were much fancier and easier on the body, that she would feel weightless, and look it, too.

As the troupe made their way down the residential streets, the homes became more elaborate, gaining more stories gables, turrets, and scalloped tiles the farther uptown the girls went. Stella felt momentarily disconnected from her body, her life. Her job of only a week before was like something she'd dreamed. She couldn't even remember exactly what Jason had looked like exactly, or remember the sweet privacy of dancing in her grove of trees. And as their vans pulled up to the back of an estate so sprawling it didn't seem possible that it existed in the same town as her dingy condominium, it hit her she had forgotten to call Izzy to tell her she wouldn't be home.

She frantically searched her bag for her cell phone and found it lit up with messages and an all-caps text from her mother: WHEN U HOME?

She swallowed her guilt back like a too-large bite of food and texted, "Late 2nite. Home by time u both up. Xo."

A split-second after she'd hit send, the phone was yanked from her hand, and she looked into the lovely, grim-lipped face of Isis, her blue hair glowing with supernatural beauty under the yellow outdoor lamps.

"No time for that, honey. You're on in ten. And for the future, get that sort of thing straightened out ahead of time. Think of your home life and your work life as a separation of church and state. No mixing."

Her eyes were hard, but she smiled and gripped Stella's shoulders. "This is going to be one of my best. Now come. The ocean awaits."

When Stella thought swimming pool, she imagined the well-used, four-lane pool at her community center where she used to do laps, with low lights and a chemical fog in the air, the mural of waves on the walls half chipped away and the floor of the pool a dingy gray. So when they followed a black-and-white-clad young man in a black tuxedo servant's jacket—and Stella had only a moment to consider the fact that their patron was rich enough to have servants—into the marvel of a pool room, she almost hooted her surprise aloud.

The room was as big as a football field, the pool larger than Olympic size. It was U-shaped, the tiles at the bottom of the pool alternating in glittering cobalt blue and gold. At the two open tops of the U, waterfalls spilled down from rocks, like something out of a Hawaiian idyll, backlit with a glow that turned the water multi-hued. Most of the ceiling was skylight—a series of silver beams and windows to the night sky, and somehow, suspended from these beams, were chandeliers of blue glass. Cranes on either side of the pool, embellished so as to seem part of the scene, provided the framework for the sophisticated version of the hoists that had bruised Stella's body in the basement of Headquarters.

Stella's seaweed-colored wig itched and her bruises still throbbed, but she didn't care; she had not been in a space so palatial or glamorous since the San Francisco Opera House. Surrounding the pool were guest tables laid in cobalt blue cloth and silver candlesticks, everything glittering as though dusted with diamond powder. A buffet and bar, staffed by well-dressed servants, took up two walls.

Even Isis stood in obvious admiration, her eyes wide, her smile a crescent moon. Isis clapped her hands and the girls fell into circle around her, and with quick commands she sent them to various positions in and around the water. Stella watched Chloe, Yvette, and Lucy strip out of their robes—revealing their slender torsos painted so expertly to appear covered in green scales that their nudity was essentially hidden. They eased into clear floating chairs, almost invisible in the water, to take positions. Several male servants did double-takes at the half-naked girls in the water.

At last it was Aja, Lina, and Stella remaining, and Stella looked up at the hoist and harness with a bubble of trepidation inside her. She wondered where Julien had gone. Probably off handling the business with Mr. Ernestine.

Two young men in swimming trunks did elegant crawl strokes to the center of the pool, and Isis put her hands on Stella's shoulders. "This is it, darling. Don't disappoint us."

Stella looked over at Aja and Lina for support. Aja was scowling. Lina poked her in the arm. "You snap out of it, or else."

"Or else what? I *disappea*r?" Aja said, waving her hands as though she had a wand that worked magic.

Lina didn't smile. "You don't take this seriously enough. You can get over your snit that it's not you up there center stage tonight."

Aja shook her head. "Funny how every time you say something like that, I hear a threat."

Lina raised an eyebrow and looked at Stella as though she wanted to say more, but seemed to think better of it.

It took about fifteen minutes, but eventually Stella, Lina, and Aja were strapped into their various places in the harness. Either Isis had been lying about the comfort of this rig, or Stella was more bruised than she realized. Added to that, the plastic strap that belted her waist made her breasts poke out noticeably, and she was sure everyone would stare at her and point, maybe laugh, frozen with fear that when show time arrived she would choke, forgetting all the moves they'd learned the night before and make a mockery of the entire company.

The water was also bracingly cold. Her bare nipples, disguised by makeup, still hardened in shock against the chill. There was no

more time to chat, however, for Isis gave the finger-to-the lips sign
for all-quiet on the set, and people began to file into the room, laughing and talking to one another. When everyone was seated, a young
bride with blonde hair coiffed into a braid around the crown of her
head swept into the room at the arm of a much older man wearing a
silver-gray suit, and the room broke into applause. Stella supposed
the man to be Mr. Ernestine, some sort of microchip genius with
deep ties to Silicon Valley's success. She couldn't help but judge the
much younger woman at his side, barely in her twenties, as being
one of those gold-digging trophy wives.

But none of that mattered. She spotted Julien at one of the tables,
chatting earnestly with a matronly looking woman. Moments before
the music cue hit he looked straight at Stella and raised an eyebrow
and one corner of his mouth in a slight smile. Bolstered, she looked
to Lina, held out her hand, and despite it all—the pain of the straps
and the cold water, and disappointing Izzy—in moments she was
walking on water and the room was cheering.

Afterwards, they each had their own room to change in, which
Stella found refreshing after the noise and glare of an audience. She
was stripped down to just her underwear, trying to wipe off the
greasy green and blue paint from her torso, when she heard the
door to her dressing room open. She covered her breasts with one
hand and shrieked.

"It's only me, come to congratulate you." Julien strode in. His
hair had been cropped since earlier in the day when she'd last seen
him, and his oddly colored eyes pulsed. He held out a tiny cluster
of pink and white roses.

"Um, do you mind if I get decent first?" she asked, shivering.

He waved a dismissing hand. "You're already more than decent!"

As though unaware that she was mostly naked, he came over to
her and pulled her into a hug. Her breasts pressed painfully to his
chest, and his heart thumped against hers. Suddenly it all played out
in her mind, so quickly and vividly it made her feel seasick—him
walking her backwards to the big white vanity style sink, lifting her
up onto the cold porcelain base, wrenching off the flimsy excuse for
panties she wore beneath the sheer mermaid skirt. . . . It wasn't that
she wanted him. More like she was waiting for him to exact a price.
She shook her head to clear the image. She wasn't going to make

the same mistake twice of sleeping with the boss. She wasn't prepared to entangle herself with a man who was already so involved, in whatever way, with so many women.

She took a step out of the hug.

He didn't even seem to care that a green and blue imprint of her torso was smeared onto his gray shirt. When the silence lengthened she smiled and hugged herself. "I'm really grateful you hired me. I really love what you're doing—it's very avant-garde, exciting."

His expression changed only slightly, nothing as dramatic as a frown; in fact she couldn't quite tell what he was feeling. A murky nervousness filled her.

"And we are grateful to have you," he said. "I told Isis after you rose up like Venus on the surface of that water that I might just be a genius."

She smiled and looked behind her for her towel. "I'm just going to get dressed and join the rest of the ladies." She hoped this would cue him to leave.

"You're not like the rest of them," he said so softly she wasn't sure she'd heard him. And despite herself, his words kindled a sudden warmth she couldn't recall ever having—of male approval of the sort a father might bestow. He stared at her another long moment and then bowed his head, and left the room as swiftly as he'd arrived.

13

STELLA TUMBLED INTO BED at three in the morning, jerking in and out of sleep on a rolling tide, her body still remembering its dance in the water. Her home looked even stranger than the last time she'd been in it, as though someone had rearranged small things just enough to throw off the map of familiarity in her head.

She was deep in a dream of dancing at the top of a Christmas tree whose ornaments were all beautiful women hung from hooks, when breath on her face woke her with a scream.

She opened her eyes to see Izzy rear back, her sweet face a mask of surprise, and then amusement.

"What time is it?" Her voice was more croak than anything.

"Nine. You overslept," Izzy wrapped her arms around herself.

"Honey, I only fell asleep around three. I'm exhausted."

"Your face is a mess," Izzy sneered. "You look like a clown."

"That's what you woke me up to tell me?"

Izzy plunked down at the end of Stella's bed. It had only been a week since she'd started her job, but in that time she'd barely laid eyes on the girl, and in that week, her daughter seemed to have lengthened and changed. Could your child become a stranger in such a short time?

"I won free tickets to some ballet next week, and I really, really want to go."

"Ballet? You ask Grandma if she wants to go?"

Izzy's full lips rolled into an instant pout. "No, I want YOU to go."

Stella nodded. "Okay, just give me the date. I'll ask at work if I can . . ." As soon as she said it she had a sinking feeling. *Separation of church and state,* Isis had said. "Since when have you been interested in ballet anyway?"

Izzy shrugged. "I like it. I always did. I just thought you might. Especially now that you're like, dancing again, too."

"You're not still thinking about that stupid thing you overheard awhile back? You know that I *chose* to give up ballet."

"But you just took a job to dance again," Izzy said into her hands.

Stella sat up and moved over to sit beside her daughter. "Honey, there are lots of other kinds of dance besides ballet. A lot of professional dancers don't really have a life because ballet comes first. And it's hard on the body and even how you feel about yourself . . ."

"But Gigi kept dancing for a long time, right?"

Stella sighed. Yes, her mother had kept dancing after having Stella, through an addiction to amphetamines, and would have continued if not for the accident.

"Gigi had help. Lots of friends, other dancers to assist her. And Gigi is just . . ." Stella couldn't find the words, because beneath all the sentences that sounded true were the shadows of lies. She could not fix her memory on a single person who had cared for her more than a handful of times, most of them young dancers in awe of her mother, who spent their time rifling through her mother's costumes, or talking on the phone to their boyfriends.

"Listen, my job now is more like performing, like theater," Stella said. "We do all kinds of things, not just dancing, and it's not so rigid. And it's fun. And I don't have to give up being with you."

"I didn't see you at all yesterday," Izzy pointed out.

"Okay, but that's just because I'm in training mode," Stella said. "It will get more regular."

Izzy frowned.

Stella squeezed her, kissed her head, and then went into the bathroom. Mascara and leftover black and green greasepaint were smeared all over her cheeks and eyebrows. She washed her face as best she could, and when she came out, Izzy was still sitting there.

"Just promise me you'll come to this show with me, Mom. That's the only thing that matters to me. I don't even care if you miss my recitals."

"I won't miss your recitals, and I'll come to the show. How's your new violin?"

Izzy broke out in the first carefree grin of the morning. "It's great. I really love it. I didn't even know how crappy that last one was."

Stella frowned. She'd worked her ass off to rent that crappy violin. "Well, that's something."

14

MARGARET'S FINGERS pressed sweaty indentions into the paper—he always wrote on the same strange lined blue paper, like something from a kid's notebook. This time it had been ripped out roughly, its edges jagged rather than smooth as usual. No care taken.

> *Margie—*
>
> *I will never forget your body as it was, don't fear. I don't want to hold your memory; I want to hold you. I want to see you again. Please. Soon? I promise not to dredge up anything ugly. We've moved past all that. Let's capture the good stuff, what remains, while we are still young enough to do so.*
>
> *—M*

After the delighted flush came a rush of shame that his words could make her so eager, followed by terror. There was no way in hell she would let him see what she'd become, withered, wrinkled, useless. A fifty-four-year-old woman in a body that creaked and throbbed, and acted twice that old.

And yet . . . what if? What if he saw her still as she once was? He'd been one of the few who adored her in such a pure way, without

expecting much in return. He didn't need to be the man at her arm
or in the spotlight so long as he was the man in her bed. It would
all have been fine if she'd never gotten pregnant. Or perhaps if she'd
never waffled the way she had. Her mistake with him was letting
him into her uncertainty. Telling him about New York.

She rescued more of his letters from their envelopes in the box,
smoothing the papers one on top of the other. One floated to the
ground, and when she tried to reach for it, a spasm of pain shot
from the base of her spine right down her left leg. It was bright
and hot, such a surprise that she dropped the box right onto the
floor, all its contents spilling into a tangled mess. She gripped the
sides of her wheelchair. She was so accustomed to numbness in
the legs that the sensation brought an adrenaline rush with it that
was almost pleasurable. Ah, pleasure; between deep breaths she
reminded herself that was the point of all this. Just like dancing:
one had to endure pain to create pleasure. She panted as the leg
twitched; it had the feeling of something near death coming back to
life—a Frankenstein gift that all of these painkillers and nerve tonics
had dulled into stupidity. She breathed through the pain like they
had taught her in Lamaze class, though in the end she'd opted for
the blissful anesthesia, the operating room rather than the sweaty
laboring bed, and for them to cut the baby out of her, none of that
messy pushing, altering her womanhood irreparably. And maybe
it had been the beginning of the end then—her stomach muscles
didn't recover as quickly as she'd hoped, and there was always a
tiny burning fire just below her belly button, a reminder of what a
woman gives up when a child enters the world through her.

She gazed at all the papers that had previously been so organized
in the box. Old papers, most of which she should get rid of, but
which she kept as much for nostalgia as anything else. She could
see the cream-colored official form with its official stamp on it. *Legal
Order of Restraint.* Oh what a time. She'd only kept that because it
had his signature on it. That's how badly confused she'd been. Love
and hate mixed together. But that was the past.

She kneaded her leg with her hands, always horrified by the soft,
fleshy texture of what had once been her pride. As she massaged
the leg, which did in fact relieve the pain, her fingers grew curious.
It had been a week since she'd stopped the medications and while

there was more pain, there was also more sensation. She stroked the inside of her own thigh, imagining it was his muscular hand. She trailed it up, only over the thin cotton fabric of the pajama pants. She had barely been able to feel the urine pass through her body in years; she could feel when her bladder was empty, but that had been the cruel joke of it. Above the belly button, all the sensation. Below, demarcated by the line where Stella had entered and then altered the world, she'd felt only occasional flashes of sensation, mostly unpleasant; she wasn't even sure she would recognize pleasure again. Her fingertips rested atop the hard little nob there. Heat, she felt that! And when she moved her finger against it, no more vigorous than pressing the button on a phone, imagining his hand in control, his fingers sliding beneath the fabric, into the flesh, something small, a flash mostly, like a tiny strike of lightning, pulsed beneath her hand.

15

THE SPECTACLE WOULD be held at a beautiful three-story house with a wraparound porch up E Street where Stella often took Izzy for ostentatious trick-or-treating (gold-foil wrapped Godiva chocolates and full Ghirardelli candy bars) and Christmas light displays worthy of a department store window. She couldn't argue with the gig—they were paid the same whether the spectacle was for a business event or a spoiled child whose parents didn't lie awake at night hoping that if nothing else, they would not squash the talent out of their child.

"Rites of Spring," Isis called this spectacle, designed for a sweet sixteen birthday that elicited a jealousy so potent in Stella she could taste its bitterness on her tongue.

Stella and the girls were all dressed in pastel leotards and gauzy green wraparounds; she supposed they were meant to be flowers, tulips even, and while she'd admired the prior spectacle she couldn't help but feel this one was uninspired, clichéd even. But she kept her mouth shut; perhaps there was only so much you could do when the subject was barely more than a child. Although the "child" herself, and ten of her friends, were all dressed in bikini tops and sarong skirts, and were all of them so surprisingly ample-chested for such young girls that she wondered if they'd all been given the gift of breast augmentations for their fifteenth year.

They'd just begun to dance; it was a modern piece, full of just enough melancholy and angst—clenched fists and limbs drawn back in on the body as though in emotional pain—coupled with optimistic enthusiasm, spinning open, reaching toward one another and undulating around each other like girls playing tag. Stella saw birthday girl Sophia, her hair loose and sultry around her shoulders, yawning and casting snide glances at her friends, who spent more time adjusting their endowments and trying to capture the weak sunlight on their pale skin.

First came the old familiar crush of disappointment that started in one's head—where you weren't supposed to stay, anyway, when dancing—and its slow circular spin down her shoulders, like ice water, chilling her, making her muscles feel jerky and spasmodic. And behind that was a dark rage; how dare these girls, these spoiled, ungrateful little shits who had everything they could ever want, sit there and sneer at the hard work of women who were just trying to get by? It surprised Stella how much she wanted to slap the expressions right off those teenage faces.

What happened then so startled Stella because it seemed as though her anger had taken human form, had conjured the wraith of the woman staggering in through—literally *through*—the big hedges. Her white blouse had torn open in the jagged fingers of branches, carving bloody scrapes into her arms. She had long dark hair, not unlike Aja, but she was rounder, softer—except in the eyes, which were cold and hard and seemed capable of turning to stone anyone who looked into them.

"Ho-ly shit!" Sophia now sat up with rapt attention. "That's awesome." She pointed as though this bloody apparition was part of the show. Stella was pretty sure that was not the case. The woman had now made it all the way into the yard, and the parents and the birthday folks all stood staring at her as though no one was quite sure if she was real. And even Stella, who had, like all the girls, stopped dancing, stood assessing the scene. Despite the bloody arms and the torn-open blouse, hair half-tumbling out of an uneven ponytail, there was an otherworldly beauty to the woman; she possessed a quality as though she came bearing information about the other side of the veil, some truth the rest of them could only know after death. And then the woman opened her mouth as though to begin singing—Stella immediately recalled the first moment she'd encountered the women in red at the restaurant—and issued one howling ravaged cry: "Julien! You liar, you asshole!"

Julien had already begun moving toward the girl, face impassive. This was when the murmur among Frivolity Inc. began, a series of soft and hard consonants coalescing into a name: *Brooke. That's Brooke. God, look at Brooke now.* Just before Julien reached her, Stella took another look—at the purple hollows below the woman's cheeks, red blotches on her skin as though she'd had a late in life case of the chicken pox, and a protruding little drum of a tummy that Stella instantly knew, in a way that made her shudder: pregnant. This mess of a woman was pregnant.

Julien took the woman's arm in his and led her calmly away. He gave a quick nod to Isis, who cued the music back up, but before the girls could resume their dance, Aja made a choked cry and dashed toward Julien and Brooke. Julien, seeing her coming out of his periphery, in a move so graceful it almost looked choreographed, too, grasped Aja's wrist in his other arm, pulled her against him, and hustled the two women off the property.

Isis now shot them a look of such seriousness that they picked up dancing as though nothing had happened, and Stella channeled the adrenaline of the strange experience into a performance that suddenly had the formerly too-good-for-it girls' attention.

When it was over, Isis hurried them out of the place. Julien and Brooke were nowhere to be found, but Aja sulked against the van, smoking and red-eyed. The women rushed her and began a chorus of questions:

Why was Brooke here?

How did she know about the spectacle, and is it true what she said?

Obviously she's been back at the meth again . . .

Aja kept her mouth firmly clamped during the interrogation and then at last, "She's hurting. That motherfucker better do her right," is all she would say.

"She's obviously into the drugs again, Ayj." Lina reached inside the open window of the van and extracted a pack of Marlboros and a lighter, helping herself despite Aja's scowl.

Aja stood up tall at her impressive height and leaned in over Lina like she meant to crush her with her bare hands. "*Don't* talk to me about her. You turned your back on her!"

Lina inhaled slowly but didn't cower. "If that's what you want to call letting someone go who steals, lies, can't show up to work on time, and when she does can't function, so be it."

Stella had the oddest feeling that this dialogue was for her benefit. Her foot gave her a sudden cramp and with the pain came the reminder that she was supposed to be somewhere.

"Fuck! My daughter has tickets for me to see a show. I have to get home," Stella said.

Lina looked at her through a cloud of smoke. "You'll get there when you get there, Stella. You know the deal."

Stella bit her tongue, literally, blood rising up with its copper-penny tang. Twice in one day she'd wanted to hurt someone; this was not like her at all.

*   *   *

Stella was panting by the time she got her mother on the phone—she'd run all the way to her car.

"Izzy went to the theater on her own . . ." Margaret's voice was tight, strained, full of disapproval Stella didn't have time for.

Stella ribs contracted painfully, as though they would split open like a too tight seam. "What do you mean she went on her own? How could you let her go alone? The bus is teeming with perverts and kidnappers."

Margaret sighed. "I didn't *let* her go. She left me a note during my late afternoon nap that she had taken the bus. What can I say; she's your child through and through."

Stella snapped her cell phone shut and dug around her car for her keys, which she'd tossed in a rush on her way to the spectacle. She found them at last beneath the driver's seat and jammed them into the ignition.

Lina was suddenly at her door, peering in through slitted eyes at the window. "I wouldn't run off so quickly. Julien will want to do damage control back at Headquarters."

She sliced an impatient hand through the air in front of Lina's head. "My little girl is on public fucking transportation. So excuse me if I don't bother tracking down His Highness right now."

"If you value your job—" Lina said.

"And if you value your head, you'll get it out of my window," Stella revved the car.

Lina withdrew herself, frowning, and Stella squealed out of the parking lot, nearly running over a passerby.

She made it to the theater in fifteen minutes, praying to every deity she could think of that Izzy was there and unmolested. She parked in a twenty-minute zone and dashed for the theater. The show was almost half over already, and she had no idea if they'd let a minor in without a parent. She didn't relish the idea of picking her way through a dark theater crying for her daughter, but she would do it if she had to.

The box office beneath the marquee held one bored-looking female attendant with bleached-blonde hair and one redheaded child, talking animatedly to her. Stella sprouted tears of relief at the sight of her. Izzy rushed out when she saw her and threw herself at her mother, hugging her as though she had not been so desperate to see this show that she'd undertaken a dangerous mode of transportation on her own.

"Mama, you made it!"

Though Stella wanted to luxuriate in the feeling of her child pressed against her, she pulled away. "Don't you ever do that kind of thing again without my knowledge or permission. Do you know how dangerous that was? Sometimes bad people ride the buses. You could have been hurt or kidnapped!"

Izzy hung her head. "I know, Mom. I know. I'm sorry, I won't do anything like that ever again. I'm just so glad you came."

"You're glad I came? The show is half over."

Izzy shrugged. "You're here now and we can still see the other half."

Stella sighed and squeezed her girl's shoulders, taking a good look at her. She wore her black velvet recital dress with the ruched sleeves and high waist. She'd managed to find her one good pair of tights and favorite patent leather Mary Janes, one of which had been missing for months. Her hair was combed into smooth copper waves and put back with sparkly silver barrettes.

"Did Gigi help you get dressed? You look pretty."

Izzy shook her head. The effort the child had gone to, even the rebellious trip alone, made her ribs ache. How much else could Izzy do without her?

Lights came on in the ornate lobby, and well-dressed people emerged in clouds of conversation from the theater.

"Do you want to find our seats during this intermission?"

Izzy shook her head. "No, let's go sit in the courtyard first. Sacha told me there's a waterfall and a rose garden."

"Won't you be cold?"

Izzy shrugged. "There's fish in the fountain."

Stella gave their tickets to the attendant and followed her daughter, who walked with the straight-backed posture of happiness out through gold Art Deco doors to a trellised patio. There they found a mostly withered rose garden, stone benches, and an elaborate fountain featuring Desdemona cowering from Othello's wrath.

One man stood with his back to them, fingering the last bloom on an otherwise dormant red rosebush. He was tall and had the unusually erect posture she recognized as a dancer's. And in the moment he bent to sniff the flower, his angular jaw and copper hair merged into a picture of familiarity that set her head spinning.

Stella turned quickly to Izzy. "Go find our seats, now!" She whisper-hissed.

"But—"

"Go. You're already in trouble. Go!"

Izzy scuffed a dejected foot but turned, her shoulders folding in on themselves, and scuttled off.

When Stella turned around Dylan Wheeler stood staring at her. The courtyard was dim, so he squinted, as though not sure of what he was seeing, either. So surreal was the moment she half-expected a cardboard set to come shooting down behind them, the spotlight to flash on.

"Stella?" He walked toward her with the graceful gait of a dancer. "Ye look like you're dressed to be *in* my show." Though he'd been raised mostly in the United States, his words were still tinged with the lilt of his parents' Irish accent, just one of many things that, when she was a girl, had convinced her of his superiority to all other men.

She looked down at herself, now self-conscious of the leotard and tights with the barest hint of a skirt beneath her jacket. Her eye shadow, rouge, and lipstick were about three times as thick as she'd wear on any normal evening out. She'd thrown on her black Converse too, which completed a bizarre ensemble.

"Yeah, I came straight from, uh, work."

"Ye'r dancing?" he asked. Was that a touch of hurt in his voice?

"Oh, well, not ballet. It's more like theater."

"Ah." He shoved his hands into his pants pockets.

"This is *your* show?"

He nodded. "Yeah, ever expect me to end up directing?"

She smiled, partly because the sight of him was so unexpectedly pleasant, so right, that she was back in time ten years, on stage, whirling into his arms, and partly out of nervousness.

"I'd expected you'd be the next Baryshnikov by now." She had kept her pregnancy from him in the hopes that he would be free to pursue his dreams.

He grinned deeply enough for an old dimple-like scar on his cheek to open up. "Double knee blow-out." He frowned. "I still dance to teach, but not to perform."

"I'm so sorry." Her hands felt awkward with nowhere to put them, so she folded them across her chest.

"That child ye were talking to—"

"My niece," she said quickly. And when his eyes narrowed, she pushed deeper into the lie. "Sorry, that's just what I call her, since her mother is like a sister to me." She nodded, as though convincing herself. "Lina," she added, thinking of her colleague's strawberry hair, and wondered exactly why she was going to such lengths.

"I see."

She ached at the way he chewed his lip, which Izzy also did when nervous, the natural turned-out stance that Izzy shared, which often led others to ask if her daughter was a dancer, the high collarbones, the green eyes, the long fingers. She shut her eyes for a moment; to look at him was to see Izzy through and through.

"How are you . . . now?" he asked when she didn't open her eyes.

"I'm fine," she said quickly. "Better." A mental breakdown had been a much easier sell than the truth—since she had no other lovers.

It left him off the hook, and she was glad for it now. He had done well for himself, unencumbered by a wife and child.

"I feel like there's something else we should say, or do," he said. "But I don't know what."

"We could have dinner sometime. If you're around for a while." Almost instantly her hands went to her throat as though she could choke back the words. What was she thinking just inviting him into their lives now? He was probably too busy.

"I'd love to." His smile was easy, big, as though this wasn't the most awkward moment imaginable. "It's really something to see you."

She smelled manipulation in all of this—she'd be having words with her mother tonight—but tried to enjoy this fleeting moment.

They both froze into postures of uncertainty and then, at nearly the same time, stepped into a hug that started out awkward, her lips smashed against his top buttons, but quickly felt familiar as that old scent of his—like baby powder and amber—drifted off his collar.

"I feel like I could do that lift from Swan Lake," he said into her neck. "Like my body remembers exactly how to dance with ye."

She hugged him tighter, embarrassed by tears leaking onto his shirt. "I'm going to ruin your shirt."

"Who cares?" He sighed. "Ye know what? I'm glad your date tonight is a little girl. I'm sorry if that sounds weird, but I am."

She was dizzy with grief and joy and desire. To think that she'd deprived Izzy of this man all these years. All of a sudden she was more grateful than ever that she'd ended things with Jason. And yet, what the hell was she thinking?

"Mr. Wheeler, you're needed backstage," came a woman's voice from the golden doors.

They pulled away as if they'd been caught having a tryst. A short, black-haired usher stood just outside the door.

"Of course." Dylan's voice stiffened into a wall of formality.

He pulled a card out of his shirt, and a pen from his back pocket, and wrote on it. "Stella, this is where I'm staying until the show finishes. Please call me."

"I will." She leaned in and gave him a quick kiss on the cheek. They lingered a moment longer before he strode off, his dash the loping canter of a man who once leapt across a stage with deer-like abandon.

When he was gone, she sank into the stone bench feeling like she couldn't breathe. It took five more minutes, until she heard the call for intermission's end to get up and back into the theater, where Izzy stood in her seat waving at her frantically as though she might miss her.

The show was a breathtaking rush of color and joy. Even though she was performing again, she couldn't help but envy the dancers onstage. She had to stop herself from mimicking their movements in her seat, her arms twitching to lift and straighten with that same grace. Dylan's choreography was good, too—lyrical and modern, but with all the force of technical training beneath it. She was glad not to have to watch him onstage and dancing; she wasn't sure she could stand the sight of those young, exquisite women moving purposefully into his arms.

When the show was over, before the dancers made their final bow, she grabbed Izzy's hand and rushed her out in case they should run into Dylan again in better light, where he could take stock of their daughter and see the truth plainly.

"Who was that man you talked to?" Izzy asked when they were on the street, shivering against the sharp chill of night.

"Just an old friend I used to dance with."

"He looked familiar," Izzy's tone was insistent. "Like I'd seen him before."

Stella sighed. "Maybe in some old photo album of mine."

"It's something else," Izzy said.

Stella shook her head, wondering if there was some genetic spark that Izzy intuited in meeting her own father. "I'm sorry, honey. Sometimes people just look familiar."

They reached the line of cars where she'd parked, but hers was not there. She did a double take, then pulled her daughter along to another row of cars, just in case she'd forgotten where she parked, but it wasn't there either.

"Oh shit!" she heard herself say.

"Mo-ommm . . . a dollar in the swear jar!" Izzy clucked.

"I parked in a twenty-minute spot." Her voice rose into a falsetto of frustration. "They towed me! They freaking towed me."

"Maybe we can go back and ask your *friend* if he can drive us home," Izzy said.

"No! He's the director of that show. I can't ask him to do such a thing."
She realized that her purse was in the car, too, so she had no ID, no money, and no credit card.

She took her head in her hands and slapped it. "What an idiot I am." Izzy took her hand. "It's okay, Mom. We'll figure it out."

Stella spun around in a circle, closing her eyes and opening them, as if her car might magically appear between blinks. Several fat wet drops hit her shoulders and head.

"Rain? Goddamn rain? Is this some kind of joke?"

She ushered Izzy back under the awning of a now-closed delicatessen. There was only one person she could think to call, whose number she had memorized, and who would, she hoped, take a collect call. Her mother was no help—she could call them a cab, but there wasn't any cash in the house.

"We have to find a phone, honey. Let's try a restaurant. We have to run, though."

They dashed off up the street to a diner, dodging the rain, which came steadily enough to wet their hair and shoes. The diner, a retro fifties establishment, actually had a pay phone booth, such a rarity that Stella felt a moment of grace before panic cinched her waist.

Julien answered the operator right away and accepted her call. She launched in as quickly as possible to her situation.

"Where are you?" It was impossible to tell by his tone of voice if he was angry at her for her abrupt departure earlier.

"It's called Hallie's," she said.

"What was so urgent?" he asked, "That you had to rush away from the spectacle?"

"My daughter," she said simply. "She's with me."

16

JULIEN PULLED UP not even ten minutes later, in a sleek silver BMW. Stella ushered Izzy in—the two of them were probably a bedraggled sight after hauling themselves across several blocks in the rain.

"Hi." Izzy sounded surprisingly cheerful from the backseat. "Thanks for picking us up!"

Julien merely nodded and held his arms stiffly on the wheel, barely turning to look at her. He drove them home in silence, and when they pulled up in front of her condo, he said, "Can you send the girl on ahead? I'd like to talk with you alone."

Stella had grown up fatherless, but the tone of his voice made her feel as though she was about to receive a whipping, a punishment.

"Go inside, honey. Tell Gigi I'll be inside in a few minutes."

Izzy lingered a moment unbuckling her seat belt, and shot Julien a nakedly open scowl of distrust, commonly given to those who didn't greet her natural enthusiasm with a similar response. Julien didn't register it, however.

Once Stella's back had disappeared inside the front door, Julien turned off the engine and put the car in park. He didn't look at her.

"I know you went to see the show at the Phoenician."

"My daughter won tickets."

"Why the subterfuge, Stella? You didn't have to sneak away . . ."

"I didn't *sneak*. I was already an hour late, because the spectacle ran late, not to mention whatever that scene was with that woman. . . My ten-year-old daughter took a bus by herself across town."

She could feel his breathing deepen at the mention of the woman the girls had called Brooke, and she had a flash of the dark-eyed, bloody-armed woman again. Her clothing was suddenly clammy against her skin; she shivered.

"Your daughter's very independent, Stella."

"No, she's not. And she doesn't need to be."

"You sound angry at me that the spectacle ran late."

How could he remain so still; she could feel anger seething just below the surface—his rapid breathing, the set of his jaw. She would almost welcome an explosion over this cold calm.

"I made my daughter a promise, Julien. One of many I haven't been able to come through on lately."

He tented his fingers together. "Do you remember your first night dancing at the string factory spectacle? Your vows?"

She felt defiant. "I remember being tipsy and . . . in a kind of fog that night."

He turned to look at her directly, his eyes like nails pinning her. "Well let me remind you. *This* is what you vowed: 'I treat the company of Frivolity like my family. It comes first, but for every sacrifice I make, there is a greater reward.'"

Fear nipped between her ribs, but she wouldn't be intimidated. "I didn't *marry* your company." The words sounded shakier than she hoped. "And I don't remember signing any contract."

Julien just looked at her for a long moment—long enough that she began to fidget; if they were playing poker, she'd be showing one tell after another. And then he laughed, harsh and braying. "So either you're telling me you don't take your commitments very seriously, which I could have deduced by the fact that you don't have a husband, and shed lovers like old hair, or you're just in a fighting mood."

She fought the urge to tell him to go to hell and toss this job with the same passion that had her throwing her apron at Jason's feet. "My daughter comes first. "No contest. No question. Always. She's *why* I took this job."

"Oh really? You took this job, the one that has you breaking promises to her, *for* her? You didn't do it because you hungered for your audience, to be a star again?"

Stella couldn't unbuckle her seat belt fast enough. She tasted copper where she'd bit the inside of her cheek to keep from telling him to fuck off. "What do you want from me?"

"I want you to take *me* seriously. To treat my family with the same—no, better—regard than you hold for your own daughter. If you don't want to let her down, then don't make promises you can't keep. A spectacle has a life and a time of its own. I can't give you a perfect window of time. Like anything brand new, it's hungry when it's hungry, it grows at its own pace, and those parameters can't be mapped."

Stella thought she saw beads of sweat on his brow, as though he had worked himself up into a fervor. And though one part of her was taut with fury at being told how to live her life and parent her child, she had to admit that he was right about one thing; she didn't want to give it up.

"Okay." She jabbed a fingernail into her palm so she didn't say something she regretted. "Okay. I'll do a better job of scheduling things more loosely. Do you want to talk about the woman?"

To his credit, he sighed in a full bodied, slump-shouldered way, as though the very thought of "the woman" hurt him deeply.

"One of my greatest regrets."

"Yours? As in you're personally responsible for her?"

"Well, she was one of ours, so in a sense yes. But I have learned the hard way that for an addict, her drugs will always come first. There is no other loyalty. What hurts me most is that her behavior hurts the other girls. They love her like a sister, and she only cares about herself."

She was familiar with the whittling down of meth—she'd gotten close to a waitress named Allison who fell to its promise of unending energy before it emptied her down to a husk.

"I ran into my ex tonight." She tried to meet his vulnerability with some of her own.

"Ex what?" He sounded almost amused.

"Ex everything. Dance partner, lover. Isadora's father."

"He's a dancer?"

"Well, mostly a director now. Has his own dance company. That was his show."

"I see." Julien tapped a finger to his top lip. "You *ran* into him?"

Stella didn't want to go into the details of how this was most likely engineered by her meddling mother. "I did. It was a total shock. But good too. Sort of reminded me who I used to be."

"And why should you be unexpectedly running into the father of your child? Surely you have arranged custody dates?"

Stella sighed, feeling weighted down by the possible answers. "He doesn't know about her."

"Ahh." He nodded gently, and some of the tension that had been there a moment before dissipated between them. "Lina is my daughter, you know."

She laughed. "That's kind of a relief, because frankly I thought the two of you behaved like you were married."

He chuckled. "I'm sure she would claim to feel like an underappreciated housewife. She doesn't look much like me, I don't think. Except maybe around the eyes and cheeks—very much like my mother. Her mother died when she was very young."

"That's terrible."

"Yes." he pursed his lips.

"Do you still have feelings for your ex?" His change of topic was so sudden that Stella didn't answer right away.

"Uh, well, there're always feelings," she said dumbly.

Julien leaned back against his seat and exhaled heavily. "Yes. And most of the time they just complicate things."

Stella shrugged, unwilling to reveal, or admit, more.

"Well, don't let me hear he's trying to recruit you away from me. That would make me very unhappy." Though Julien was smiling, his neck muscles had pinched into taut ropes.

"Of course not." Stella opened the car door. "I work for you. I promise."

"I will take you at your word." He made a little flourish with his hand, a courtly gesture. "Good night Stella."

She was almost inside when she heard him call out, "I'll be here at eight a.m. to take you to get your car out of impound."

And then he was gone before she could think of telling him that she didn't need his help for everything.

When she went inside, Izzy was eating vanilla ice cream with chocolate sauce at the kitchen table, with Margaret sitting watch beside her, her eyes daring Stella to call her out for sugaring her daughter up before bedtime.

But Stella didn't have it in her to argue with either of them.

"That's your boss?" Izzy asked between sticky lips, wiping errant whorls of chocolate sauce from her mouth to her hand.

"Yes, that's him."

"Lucky he was there to pick you up." Margaret's tight lips and sharp tone suggested she didn't really think so.

"Your boss is kind of a jerk," Izzy scraped the bowl with her spoon. "He didn't even say hi to me."

Stella frowned. "I just don't think he's very good with children."

"Mom ran into an old friend of hers at the ballet tonight," Izzy said, then drank the last puddle of her ice cream from the bowl.

Stella whipped around; it was too late to pretend it was no one of consequence—she could tell her mother had seen something in her face.

"Oh?" Margaret said. "Someone I used to know?"

"He was tall, with red hair," Izzy said. Stella glanced at her daughter too sharply to go unnoticed. She hadn't thought Izzy had been able to see him so clearly.

Margaret raised an eyebrow. "Was he now?"

Stella glared at her mother, tried to make her voice cut. "Yes, it sure was a surprise."

"He was cute." Izzy propped her chin on her fists. "Maybe you should date him, Mama."

Stella snorted with frustrated laughter. "Maybe you should go take a bath and then get into bed."

"Your mother was in the habit of sneaking out of the house, too, you know, when she was not much older than you." Margaret shot Stella a hard look, her fair eyebrow sharp.

Stella slapped her hands down on the table harder than she intended, rattling Izzy's ice cream bowl and spoon. "I was a *teen-ager*, a hell of a lot older than her, and you were never home!" Her tone came out shriller than she'd intended. "I'm not talking about just seeing you in the evenings, either. Never. I went whole weeks without seeing you at all. You didn't come to any of my rehearsals. Tasha Baron's mom was always driving me to and from school and home, feeding me, and taking pity on me. I hated that."

Margaret and Izzy both stared up at her, as though they didn't recognize this madwoman. Izzy slid out from her chair quickly and put her bowl in the sink without another word.

Margaret tipped her head toward her hands and exhaled loudly.

Stella was caught on the edge of an apology, hating the way she'd begun to snipe at her mother lately, and yet unable to stop the bitterness from seeping out now that she was finally getting a chance to reclaim something for herself.

Stella watched Izzy creep off to her room, her body hunkered in on itself as though she felt responsible for the fight.

"You're right," Margaret said at last. "I put ballet before you, before everything and everyone. And I am so much sorrier for that than I have ever expressed to you."

Stella exhaled breath that would turn to tears if she didn't let it out. It felt good to hear her mother apologize, though.

Margaret smoothed blonde hair out of her eyes. "And then there was the accident, and I lost the use of my legs, and I don't know what you want to call it, but I can't help but see it as payback for my selfishness, my obsession. So forgive me if I'm just afraid of the same thing happening to you and Isadora."

When Stella was young she would sneak up on her mother sleeping, on those rare occasions she was home for more than a perfumed breath, and stare at her, memorize the high cheekbones, the perfect bow of a mouth, carefully plucked eyebrows arching over dark eyes, the tiny mole above her right eye. That beauty was still there in her mother's face, but softened and worn around the edges.

Stella inhaled to keep herself from shouting or crying. "I'm just the new girl right now, and that means I have to put in a little more effort than anyone else. And it's not all about me fulfilling a selfish desire—I'm making three times as much money as I have at any job. I can put money for Izzy away, pay for violin lessons. Maybe save for a real house. And now, when I wake up in the morning I don't look at myself in the mirror and see a failure."

Margaret shook her head. "I don't understand how you could ever see yourself as a failure . . ."

"That's what makes us different, Mom. I did put Izzy before ballet. But I also gave up on making myself even remotely happy."

Margaret nodded. "What prompted your meeting with Dylan, then?"

Stella crossed her arms. "Oh you have some nerve. You really think I'm going to believe that Izzy won tickets. What the hell were you thinking?"

Margaret still had a diva's power to make her wide eyes and bowed mouth look like the world's most surprised woman. "Before you go accusing a person of a thing, you should get proof to back you up."

"What are you talking about? How else would Izzy have gotten tickets to that show?"

Margaret unlocked her wheels and backed slightly away from the table. "Maybe you should ask her."

"What are you saying?" Stella dropped her voice to a whisper, though the noise of the running bathtub was probably drowning out their conversation. "That she somehow engineered the meeting? She doesn't even know who he is."

"She's a sharp girl."

Stella stood up, her spine a heavy lattice drooping under sagging supports. The effort of a performance had always come on delay, several hours later. "I don't think she's that manipulative."

Margaret pursed her lips. "We are fools to underestimate our children."

All of Stella's overtired muscles made a last effort at tensing, which turned to cramping in her thighs and calves; her body as familiar with the postures of defense as those of dance.

Her mother held up her hands. "I'm not itching for a fight; I'm just pointing out that mothers don't always know everything they think they do about their own children."

Stella tilted her head back and closed her eyes. "I think I need a break from these late night heart-to-hearts."

Margaret nodded as though coming to some sort of understanding with herself. "I wish we'd had more of them a long time ago."

17

"OW!" YVETTE'S LAST HEAVE on the corset strings punched Stella's breath out of her midsection. "I feel like you just broke my ribs."

"Then eet's on right." Yvette exhaled a ribbon of smoke straight into Stella's nose from the cigarette that dangled precariously from the corner of her mouth.

Stella coughed and waved it away. "How am I supposed to walk in this, much less dance?"

Lina surveyed with her discriminating eye. "That's why you're practicing."

The back door slammed open, and Aja and Chloe staggered in beneath a small red velvet couch, which they dumped to the living room floor. "Seven dollars!" Chloe exclaimed proudly. "Good-will rocks."

Aja's long black hair was loose and wild around her shoulders. Her perpetual scowl kept her face just this side of pretty. *Resting bitch face*, Stella had heard it called.

"What's wrong?" Lina's words came out as a sigh, as though she didn't really want to know but felt it her duty to ask.

Chloe shook her head and sent beseeching glance at Aja. "Nothing."

Aja's eyes glittered with emotion. "Not nothing."

Chloe rounded on Aja, her usually sunny demeanor dropped. "You on the rag again or something? Go upstairs before you bring everyone down with you."

Even Stella felt the change in the air as Aja drew herself up taller and set her face in a hard line. "Maybe you don't give a fuck that one of our friends just up and disappeared, but I sure as fuck do, and I'm not gonna keep quiet about it."

Lina rubbed her thumb across her nose. "Brooke had problems, Ayj. Big problems that none of us could fix."

Aja sneered and muttered something under her breath. She bent down to tie the loose laces of one of her tall black Docs. "He said he could help her, that he would help her, and then what happens? She's gone. Nobody hears shit from her. Is that what would happen if I suddenly went missing? None of you will ever come looking for me? I just dissolve into thin air?"

Lina strode right over to Aja and took her by the shoulders. Stella held her breath, waiting for a physical fight, but Aja just stared at Lina for a beat, eyes wide and bright with anger. "You're not my fucking mom."

"And Julien's not your father. We're all adults here. We all miss Brooke, okay? I know you girls were especially close. But she had a drug problem. And you go read me the statistics on meth and tell me what happens to most users, okay?"

Chloe plunked herself down on the red velvet couch and smoothed her hands along it as though she could brush away the tension between them.

Aja kicked one leg of the couch. "I know the fucking statistics. Cuz all I ever see when I close my eyes is my mother's blue face and the needle jammed into her throat because her arm veins and leg veins and the spaces between her toes were too shot to use. Don't lecture me. What I think is interesting is that our Big Daddy Jules and Brooke had a pretty nasty fight that day after the spectacle— and nobody has seen or heard from her since."

Lina shook her head. "Go take a hot bath or have a stiff drink, Aja. You're getting ugly."

Aja held out her hands. "Better watch what I say, you mean? Or maybe something will happen to me, too?"

"More like, remember where you come from, little girl." Lina spoke in such a gravelly, hard voice, Stella felt as chastised as Aja looked, who turned away, a hand to her pale face as though she'd been slapped.

"Stella, come here, let me fix that corset," Lina commanded. "Yvette, you've got the laces crossed. She probably can't breathe." Aja made a rude snort and stomped upstairs like a sullen teenager. The tension drifted apart like more of Yvette's cigarette smoke. "Yvie, come here and help me move my couch." Chloe lifted one of its ratty sides with a reverent gaze, as though she saw the couch's true potential already manifested rather than its shredded edges and worn cushions. "We got this fantastic lamp too. This dump needed some improvements."

Lina reworked the laces on the corset and Stella gained an inch or so of breathing room. While Chloe and Yvette were preoccupied with their refurnishing, Lina whispered to Stella, "Aja gets overwrought. She's had a very fucked-up life, and Brooke was really special to her. Brooke was very sick, though. Julien tried to dry her out several times, and she repaid him by stealing money and clothes and disappearing."

Stella nodded, unsure of what to say. She'd seen a few fellow dancers get hooked on cocaine, but she'd been spared that kind of tragedy. "Aja sure does know how to throw a snit."

Lina sighed. "I know. Julien's got great instincts for talent, but not always so great with the diva radar. There. Feel better?"

Stella exhaled and turned around. "Yeah. Hey, can I ask you something? Why don't you call Julien 'Dad'?"

Lina's chiseled right eyebrow shot up. "Excuse me?"

"He told me . . ."

Lina's face went pale, as though Stella had said something deeply offensive. She took a step back. "I don't know, that's, well, Stella that's not true. He meant figuratively, like a father figure."

Stella grasped for some way out of her blunder. "I'm sure that's what he meant. I misinterpreted it, is all."

Lina smiled tightly. "Yes, clearly." Then she turned and walked off.

Stella stood there, squeezed into the fist of material that, even loosened, made breathing feel as though someone was digging sharp knuckles between each of her ribs. It was as though she'd failed some test or broken something irreparable.

Chloe looked up from her loveseat perch with her full lips pouted out. "Everyone's testy today, don't take it personally."

Stella did her best to take a deep breath. "Any reason why?"

Chloe cocked her head. "You don't know? Oh, that's right, you left to go after your kid."

"What happened?" Stella tried to ignore the disdain in Chloe's voice about having tended to her child. "Julien didn't say anything to me."

Chloe glanced over at Yvette, who was crouched on the floor rearranging the carpet. Chloe pointed toward the backdoor. "Come outside with me."

"I'll try to walk, but I make no guarantees," Stella said. "I might keel straight over in this thing."

"Ah, in about ten minutes the agony will have quelled to a gentle throb," Chloe chucked her lightly on the shoulder. "You're tinier than me and I wore that thing for seven hours once." She raised her brows in pride.

Stella hobbled alongside her through the kitchen that seemed permanently forged in the scent of apple and cinnamon. It was a homey kitchen, one that made Stella nostalgic for a kind of child-hood she'd never had, with an aproned mother who stayed home with her, and a father who came home at the end of the night.

Chloe pulled Stella over to a dubiously stable wooden bench so weathered it was gray.

"Look, someone at that Ernestine mansion spectacle is accusing Frivolity Inc. of theft. There were several hundred wedding guests there that night, and the eight of us, but they have the audacity to finger us! Right after you left, right out front of that mansion for the spoiled little Sweet Sixteen, this dude who works for Ernestine hand-delivered a letter with the accusation to Julien, as a message, I guess. Cops are coming to talk to us any minute now. Julien went ballistic on our way home in the van." Chloe looked around, as though someone might be eavesdropping and lowered her voice to a whisper. "I've never heard him yell like that. Anyway, Julien feels we have to be especially careful since Ernestine has a lot of sway not just in town but in the state, you know. He's like major money and power—so he's worried that it's going to ruin our business. Naturally all the girls get nervous because none of us have ever had this kind of a job before, you know?"

Stella nodded, wondering why Julien hadn't mentioned any of this when he picked her up. "What did they accuse us of stealing?"

"Some really valuable ancient jewelry Ernestine has in a collection—belonged to some queen or something. I don't know why anyone would have that shit on display anyway—it's asking for something bad to happen. Anyway, I don't know the details, but I do know that none of us would pull that kind of petty crap, not even Aja." Chloe looked around again, and flipped her blonde hair over one shoulder.

"Okay, well . . . duly noted," Stella said.

Chloe nodded, nudging her toe into the hard dirt at their feet. "Something else I've been wanting to say, Stella."

Stella tried to take a deep breath but her corset made it too painful.

"Well, I guess this is the kind of job that asks more of a person than a regular job, and it attracts a different kind of person. Creative types, you know—code for especially fucked-up and not rule-abiding."

Stella laughed and then regretted the stabbing pain it caused. "Ow, don't make me laugh in this thing."

Chloe winked. "All I want to say is that Isis is an amazing artist and choreographer and maybe you could say her biggest talent is bringing out the best talent in others. Like she can make you feel more of what you are, better than you think you are, than ever in your life. But . . . I don't know . . . I don't think she's really got any of our backs. I wouldn't put any trust in her."

Stella nodded. "Ah yes, the choreographers are often the biggest divas of all."

Chloe smiled. "I don't think you've quite fallen under her spell yet. But when you do, remember what I said. She gave herself the name of the Queen of the Underworld, after all."

Stella chuckled, more nervously than anything. "I suspected that wasn't her birth name. Okay, I shall heed your warning. Now speaking of the Great and Powerful Isis, aren't we supposed to be lining up for rehearsal soon?"

"Sort of. We're meeting onsite."

"Which is where?"

"Respect the revelation!" Chloe intoned, lifting her hands in the air, mimicking Julien. "All I know is that we meet at the seminary down in San Anselmo."

"Oh please tell me we're not going to be interrupting someone's church service!"

"No, actually I think it's another wedding. We're getting really popular at weddings."

Stella looked down at her black corset. "Really? In this?"

Chloe raised an eyebrow. "You should see what I'm wearing. Black leather cat suit. Fuck-me pumps. No wedding I've ever been to, but hell, why not."

*   *   *

The bride, Susan, sat demurely in a simple, strapless, white satin gown with a tiny veil and simple pearls—her grandmother's, the something "old" part of the equation, she told them when they arrived. Her pumps were white satin, brand new. She also wore a blue garter belt, which she'd flashed with a silly grin when they'd helped her into her dress, and a borrowed pearl bracelet. Her demeanor and attitude said: good girl. Traditional girl.

So Stella had a hard time reconciling the pretty woman seated at the vanity mirror with the ten of them, dressed in black corsets and cat suits, stilettos, and "whore heels," as Aja called them, not a single pair less than three inches high. Teased hair, black lipstick, purple eye shadow, and red nails.

Susan talked to them as she touched up her lipstick. "Tom and I have worked really hard to appease each other's families with things. He converted to Judaism for me, but we agreed to get married in a church; I waited until we were engaged to move in with him; we trade off holidays, and didn't get the Labrador puppy we wanted because his mom's allergic. There are a thousand things we've done to make our, and each other's, parents happy. But we're doing our wedding our way."

Stella nodded, impressed. Isis assumed center stage then, while Julien hung back, looking proud and important in a black suit.

Susan and Tom, looking as cookie-cutter as possible up there at the altar, elicited sweet murmurs from the crowd. Stella could just make out Susan's moon-shaped face from where she stood in the eaves, and though she knew her nerves would still when she entered character, a part of her trembled at the illusion of the sanctity of marriage inside a church and what they were about to do to it.

The rabbi read a blessing and welcomed the family and friends, and then, as he was about to launch into a prayer, Isis pointed her finger and Stella and the rest of them rushed out through the little room where they'd been hiding and took hold of the bridesmaids and groomsmen, wrestling them back into the room where they'd come. Stella had the job of grabbing hold of the tender bride, who did her part very well, screaming.

People in the audience stood up, but before anyone could rush the dais, Stella grasped the two Velcro seams of the back of Susan's dress and pulled. It came away easily to reveal a skin-tight black sequined dress as the first strains of "Bohemian Rhapsody" burst out of the overhead speakers.

Tom played air guitar, now poured into black leather pants and a torn tank top.

Family members murmured to each other loudly, waving hands and blinking wide eyes of disbelief at each other, while Susan and Tom dissolved into giggles at the altar.

Tom then touched the rabbi on the shoulder and pushed him lightly out of the way and took up a microphone and switched it on.

They read their vows to each other, accepted each other's rings, and when they'd kissed, turned to their audience and said, "We just want to make sure you know that we'll be doing things our way from now on."

To Stella's surprise, a large contingent of the audience clapped and whistled, and Tom threw Susan over his shoulder and flounced down the aisle rocking out head-banger style to AC/DC's "You Shook Me All Night Long."

Stella and company stayed at the periphery of the wedding, where Susan and Tom had asked them to remain, but none of them wanted to mingle with strangers.

Stella stood outside on the stone ledge that overlooked a mass of orange and yellow trees. The air was perfumed by the decaying scent of trees and earth, of fresh rain and something the old seminary itself seemed to put off.

A passing waiter placed a glass of champagne in Stella's hand, and then an arm suddenly wrapped around her shoulder. She jumped slightly and turned to catch a gleam of turquoise at her side.

"Isis, you scared me." Isis was squeezed into a tight black silk dress with a velvet stole and spiked boots that made her tower over Stella. Her turquoise hair a sea of gelled finger waves, she looked like a modern Marlene Dietrich in Technicolor.

Isis smiled. "That has got to be my favorite wedding of all time. Did you see the look on the mothers' faces?"

Stella nodded. "I felt a little sorry for the one in lime green—I think that was the mother of the bride. She looked so disappointed. You could tell she'd been dreaming of this day for a long time."

Isis chortled. "Ironic, really. Usually it's the little girls who dream of the white wedding. But if that mother has gotten this far in her daughter's life without that level of disappointment, then I'd say they're an unusual pair."

"You have children?"

Isis went silent, then plucked the champagne out of Stella's hand, and downed it in three sips. "One never really *has* children."

Stella felt the same bewilderment she had when Lina refuted Julien's paternity, so she stared out at the night sky, with its thousand tiny pinhole stars weakly asserting their light, trying not to think how well this applied to her own daughter. Her *independent* daughter who took buses across town without any help.

"I'm not anti-marriage, you know," Isis offered. "I don't believe that marriage and love are synonymous, or even all that commonly found together, but I'm not as jaded as you might think."

"I didn't think that," Stella said, realizing she didn't know what she thought; Isis and Julien both kept their cards very close.

"Julien and I didn't marry because we never could really trust another person wholeheartedly."

Stella turned sharply to look at Isis, who continued to stare out at the night sky. "You and Julien . . .?"

"Oh I don't mean together, darling, I mean each of us never married anyone. We've known each other since the beginning of time, though."

Did you know Lina's mother?" Isis grimaced as though Stella's words were painful, and Stella made herself a promise never to mention Lina's family line again.

Isis turned to Stella with a curious smile. "He told you about her, did he? He must really find you trustworthy. Maybe you can be the one to keep that ego of his propped up high then, give me a much needed break."

Stella wasn't sure what Isis was driving at, and chose to ignore it. "He told me Lina was his daughter, and she denied it, so I'm thinking I should just keep my mouth shut."

"Generally that's a wise plan," Isis said. "But yes, I knew Lina's mother. Lina's got good reason to be . . . quiet on the subject. I'm quite sure she doesn't want that topic discussed at large with the other girls."

Stella nodded, craning her head for the drink-toting waiter. "I think I'm going to have some champagne."

Isis turned and gripped her by the shoulders, surveying her. "I think we need to do something about that red. It clashes with your skin color. You need something darker. I'm thinking maybe . . ." A tip of her tongue appeared at the edge of her mouth like a painter assessing a canvas. "Indigo. Violet."

Stella touched her head self-consciously. "Okay."

"Tomorrow. We might not even have to bleach you—adding blue might just do the job."

"Thanks." Isis looked down at her with her warm, dark eyes with a tenderness she'd rarely even received from her own mother. Stella's words were muted by a sudden shyness.

"Don't thank me," Isis stroked her cheek. "I haven't even gone to work on you yet." She strode off, commanding her high-heeled boots and dress like a woman half her age.

On the way home, crushed between the knees of her new "sisters"—Lina and Chloe—Stella reveled in the warmth of camaraderie as they headed back to Headquarters; almost as if they'd accepted her. But the moment they piled out of the van laughing and discussing the highlights of the evening, Stella spied a cop picking his fingernails on their porch. All good will drained instantly away.

18

"HELLO LADIES!" The cop who sat on the porch was of that indeterminate age of men in their thirties who don't age very well—bad skin, thinning hair, a little overweight, and unkempt but possibly just because he didn't exercise enough or eat well.

"He's really let himself go," Aja whispered to Chloe.

Stella wanted to ask if they knew this man, and why—he didn't look like someone they should be acquainted with.

When Julien laid eyes on him, his face settled into a grimace of displeasure. "Detective Schultz."

"Mister Grant. You brought just the pretty ladies I wanted to talk to!"

Julien stood where he was just out of the van, not moving a step toward the detective. The girls glanced at each other out of the corners of their eyes, as if afraid that direct eye contact would reveal guilt.

"Well, you better come on in, Detective." Isis broke the silence. "I'll go hide the drugs and hookers while the ladies make you some coffee."

There was a beat of held breath; even Stella felt anxious that Isis would toy with a man of the law when they were under suspicion for a very real crime. But Detective Schultz laughed, a phlegm-filled garble that made Stella want to give him a glass of water and a lozenge. "Don't hide them, honey, that's half the fun of my job."

Julien laughed too, and his neck and shoulder muscles sank several inches lower. "Yep, come on in. The girls are happy to cooperate, right?" He opened his arms wide and swept them toward his company who, Stella decided by their frowns and narrowed eyes, were not enjoying being referred to as either "girls" or "ladies."

Stella gulped and faked a smile and they all moved into the house—where haphazardly framed photographs now appeared on the hallway walls, which had not been there before. Chloe had worked some magic in the living room as well: the couch was covered in silky brocade fabrics and a new lampshade graced the ratty lamp Stella had thought there was no hope for. A clean knotted throw rug replaced the stained one that had looked a victim of a very toothy dog. It was as if all the girls but she had known the detective was coming that evening.

Detective Schultz camped out in the big armchair and stuck a foot up on the edge of the coffee table. Chloe shot a hostile look at his foot, as though it was smeared in dog-shit. Stella knew the table hadn't cost more than a few bucks, but she understood the principle of not wanting a man's dirty shoe up on it. The girls scattered between couch and loveseat slowly and sat quietly.

"Ladies . . . that must have been some show you put on this afternoon." Schultz's eyebrow stayed at full mast as he surveyed their black leather ensembles, stilettos, teased hair. Stella's ribs were sore and her breathing short. She needed to get out of the corset and soon.

None of them spoke.

"So I just want to ask a few questions of you all, then I'm gonna talk to you individually."

Aja made a throat-clearing sound and the detective homed straight in on her. "How long since you've been in a gang, little miss?"

Aja uncrossed her legs and sat up and forward. "Excuse me?"

"Tattoo on your cheek. Gang related, usually. Did you have to kill someone, or just destroy a little personal property?"

"Fuck you. Maybe somebody I loved died."

Lina put a hand on Aja's knee. "Easy, girl."

Schultz bared his teeth. "I bet that fancy necklace of Mr. Ernestine's looked good on your pretty neck. Probably was a little uncomfortable though, not too accustomed to that level of quality. I bet you could buy a lot of crack for something that valuable."

"You don't know what the fu—"

Lina nudged Aja sharply before she spit out another F-bomb. "You don't know what you're talking about, Detective." Aja's voice was flint against stone. "You're profiling me because I look hard, like I lived on the streets once, which maybe I did. But I never killed nobody or stole anything. I'm probably the cleanest person in this room. She glanced peripherally at Lina, whose brows briefly furrowed. You want to know what I think? I think that the only one in this room that none of us can vouch for is her—" Aja pointed directly at Stella.

Stella heard herself gasp, then wished she could have taken it back, such a guilty sound. She knew Aja didn't like her but she hadn't seen *that* coming.

Detective Shultz looked at Stella with his puffy late-night eyes, taking her measure. She wished she could say she looked more upstanding than Aja, but in her current getup, with the mad red hair and black corset, she probably looked as capable of stealing a piece of jewelry as any of them.

"Can't vouch for her, huh?" he asked.

Aja leaned forward, all teeth and red-rimmed eyes. In her black vinyl bodysuit and lace-up thick soled boots she looked demonic. "We all finished up our routine in the pool and changed together in the same cramped little room. But not her. She disappeared. Don't know where she went."

"I was in my own dressing room!" Stella cried, half-aware that she was admitting to getting special treatment. The corset edges were poking tiny wounds into her chest and constricting her breath to short gasps.

Aja shrugged. "I don't know anything about that. All I know is you were there, then you were gone."

Stella scoffed loudly. "You saw me get in the van with you. Did you see me holding any big, ostentatious piece of jewelry? No. Because I didn't take it." She looked around for Julien, to corroborate the story about the dressing room—he'd come to her there in that awkward moment, after all. But he was off making coffee in the kitchen.

"Isis, please, you don't think I'm capable of this, do you?" If she wasn't in so much pain she would sound a lot less desperate. "Can someone please get me out of this damn corset? I can't breathe, or think."

The detective smiled, showing surprisingly white, anachronistic teeth. "Ms. Russo, why don't we go talk in the kitchen alone, hmmm?"

Stella looked at Isis, who opened her mouth and stuck out her hands helplessly, as though she didn't know what to say or do.

Stella stood up, wincing. "Please, Detective, I've been in this thing for hours and I can't even think straight in it. See, it's digging into my ribs."

Detective Schultz smiled, a gesture that gave him a double chin. "You just tell me what you know and then your ladies here can get you out of that thing. I'm sure they'd be happy to help."

He nodded at the rest of the company. Stella couldn't help herself, she turned back to Aja and glared, shaking her head slightly. *How could you, you bitch,* she thought silently, hoping the message shot through her eyes.

The entire conversation with the detective was a blur of pain—she'd begun to sweat halfway through with discomfort and then the bursting pressure of her bladder ballooned. She told him over and over again what she knew, until, after he'd made her repeat in detail her every step and memory of that night, he finally stood up and thanked her, as though she'd just served him a great meal and was about to throw down a tip. None of the others would talk to him without a lawyer—something Stella hadn't even considered an option, and now she felt like an idiot.

Stella hunched on the porch shivering and gasping in her corset, but unwilling to go inside where to even look at Aja was dangerous; she could feel the spines of words she'd regret lodged beneath her tongue.

Lina emerged from the house with a lit cigarette, and suddenly Stella's whole body quivered with the desire she hadn't had since she was eighteen.

"Can I have one?" She pointed at the smoke trail drifting from Lina's fingers. Lina had scrubbed away all her makeup and looked younger, and more tired, than Stella had seen her.

Lina plucked the cigarette from her mouth and handed it over, plopping down next to Stella so close their tights made a scratching sound as they rubbed together. Then she leaned behind Stella and worked open the laces of the corset.

The nicotine greeted long dormant centers in Stella's brain, and endorphins rushed in like ladies at a spa tending her nerves, soothing away the angry jangled-cat feeling. Once the corset was open, blood rushed painfully back into her ribs and back muscles, but she shrugged out of it with a feeling of relief bordering on orgasmic.

Lina sniffed, tilted her head back. "I know you want to blame her, hate her, even, but Aja sees you as someone who doesn't know how good she has it."

Stella slapped the wooden deck, regretting it as a splinter slid into her palm with a sharp stab.

"Then she's even less mature than I thought." Stella pried at the tiny piece of wood jammed into the meat of her palm.

"I think it's something in the Olympian spirit." Lina pressed her lips together.

"What do you mean?" Stella was distracted by thoughts that she had better shower before she got home and her mother smelled smoke on her.

Lina lay back on the deck. "That girl spent the first decade of her life training to be the next Mary Lou Retton in gymnastics. She can do stuff with a ball, a hoop, and a balance bar you didn't even know were physically possible. She was in, going, signed-sealed-delivered. Then poor junkie mama made good on an O.D. Aja lost focus and was left without a legal guardian. Her coach decided she wasn't ready. Took her out. Pretty much broke her I think. She hit the streets after that. Teen runaway."

Stella sucked in the sweet burning smoke to hide her big sigh. A shitty thing to happen to a kid with dreams. She would know.

"So her childhood tragedy is why she threw me under the bus tonight? How is that not immature?"

Lina's hand suddenly shot out, making Stella jump, and grasped the remains of the cigarette straight out of Stella's mouth, then smoked it down to its embers. "I'm telling you that she holds a grudge against fate or God or life for taking away her happiness. And here you come, breezing into her life, Julien's new pet, who lives with your mother still and already had her day in the sun . . ."

Stella began to protest that her day had, in fact, been cut quite short, but Lina held up a hand. She flicked the dead butt onto the lawn. "I know, you've got your tragedy too, darlin'. I'm saying don't expect Aja to give a fuck. Don't expect her to form any loyalty to you."

Stella shook her head. Just when she'd been feeling so warm, so included. "How'd she manage to bond with the rest of you?"

Lina's smile was somewhat rueful, crimped. "Julien offered her salvation. We've been her family for a long time. Years."

"Years?" Stella had pictured each girl as a breezing in and out of the company for no more than a couple of months, maybe a year, wanderers on their way to something bigger. "So I'm like the kid sister nobody wanted."

"Yeah," Lina laughed. "And you're adopted." Her belly laughter was contagious, and soon, as a release from the night's tension, Stella and Lina were both in hysterics, the kind that had them gasping for breath.

It was then that Aja slammed her way out of the kitchen, walking with her usual brusque strides past them. This time, though, she stopped, turned, and glared at Lina for a long moment. Then, to Stella's surprise, she smiled—a smile that revealed more teeth than lip, one that harbored information. "She's not your fucking friend." Aja's words hung sharp in the air.

Stella couldn't tell which of them Aja was addressing before she tromped off.

Lina snorted. "Does not play well with others," she whispered, grimacing at Aja's back, which caused them both to fall into a fit of laughter again, despite knowing better.

19

FOR ONCE, STELLA'S ABSENCE worked in Margaret's favor. Izzy was at her best friend's house for the night. Margaret leaned into the mirror, with its obscene fluorescent lighting that showed the coarse truth of wrinkles and sunspots, to touch up her mascara. There'd been a time where she didn't recognize her own face without its layers of thick performance-ready cake makeup that smothered her pores and melted under the hot lights and exertion of ballet. Even now, it felt a wee bit wrong to stop at just one layer of concealer and powder, to merely dust her ever paling eyebrows with charcoal eye shadow where once she'd have drawn dark storm clouds with eye liner, made her lips twice as full with pencil and brick red lipstick.

Now, what she saw in the mirror was a ghost of her mother made up for church. But she would not be going to glory the Lord or save her own soul; it was too late for that. This was her last opportunity to feel like a woman, and she dressed the part. Her breasts were still remarkably firm—perhaps, as she'd sat in a wheelchair for more than fifteen years, they'd suffered less pull from gravity. She still had beautiful clothes from designers and fans. She selected a red silk V-neck blouse that draped into her ample cleavage, revealed her strong shoulders, sculpted from years of pushing herself around in this damned chair. She pulled her hair into a simple twist at the back of her head, left a few tendrils to drape invitingly around her long neck, added jewelry that Max himself had given her: gaudy but gorgeous webbed diamond earrings and a necklace that fanned out across her chest like a bejeweled spider web. Black faux-fur coat, and on her useless lower half, a long black skirt she put on over her head and slid down to her waist—a trick she'd learned to avoid having Stella help her with everything. Finally, elegant black pumps. She could wear all the high heels she wanted now without ever causing a bunion or a charley horse in her calf.

The special access cab picked her up and took her to Max's hotel. She had refused to let him pick her up, make judgments about her based on the state of her house—Stella's house, really—with its clutter and shabbiness. When Max had known her she'd lived in something close to splendor in San Francisco in a spacious two-story apartment with hardwood floors and huge windows. So many things had changed.

The bar was more populated than she liked by a bevy of young people with their smooth skin and tiny waists—too young to be Stella's peers. Young girls in slip dresses too short for the cool weather, young men with expensive watches and silk shirts. Where did these rich young people come from? And what were they doing on her Friday night date?

By the time she'd selected a table near the window, which looked out on the river—the pretty twinkling white lights casting delicate light on the surface of the water—beads of sweat had formed in her armpits and at the back of her neck and she cursed her choice of silk after all. She extracted and dry-swallowed the one and only pain pill she would take that night, almost fond of those strange new pulses of pain in her allegedly dead legs. She wasn't getting too hopeful about it; pain lived in the brain, not necessarily the body, but one thing was for certain: when she had touched herself, right at the center of her womanhood, she wasn't numb.

She ordered a Cosmopolitan and checked her watch. Max had been notoriously prompt back in the day. But back then she'd run late; it didn't bother her they called her a diva; she was, and she loved it. Age changed everyone. Fifteen minutes passed. Twenty. She ordered a second drink. She heard people speaking in Russian and, despite herself, her heart thudded with anxiety, palpitated, and she had to take steadying breaths.

Nearly thirty years before she'd sat in a hotel bar not so different from this one trying to work up the nerve to go up to the room of the world's most desired male dancer — "Call me Mik," he'd said — to see if he'd meant what he said when he leaned into her ear after directing her company through the piece they'd be performing together and said, "Come to my room after ten. Six twenty-five." All the suspicions of him being gay dissolved the minute she stood in his presence. He was small, shorter than she by a couple of inches, light on his feet. He moved like a jungle cat, with his Russian seriousness. His facility for dance wasn't feminine, it was European — where men were not so self-conscious about appearing weak or artistic. On the studio floor he constantly touched her — fingertips guiding her arm, palms gripping her hips, buttocks to show the proper lift. Her sister dancers took notice, pursed their lips, narrowed their eyes at her, which only bolstered her determination to claim his bed even though there was Max back home. Max, who brought her wine and flowers and rubbed her sore legs at night. Max, who could get her those little magic pain pills when her aches would not go away. Max, who didn't care if she called at three a.m. or not for three days. But this was possibly the world's greatest dancer.

She'd gotten drunker than she liked, to build courage, and the elevator's sudden ascent left her dizzy. She stumbled off it, tripped, banging her knee painfully, anticipation burning holes in her gut. His room was a suite at the end of a long hall and around a corner, as close a thing to a private floor as possible. It was ten exactly on the nose when she arrived, and his door opened as though he felt her presence in the hall. A young woman slipped out of his room. She was dark-haired and dressed impeccably, though she wore no shoes; she was not one of the dancers. But then his face filled the doorway — hair a mop of wild dark blond hair, eyes shining at her over that adorable chin cleft.

"My assistant." He pointed after the back of the woman. Relief flooded Margaret.

He extended his hand, and she let him draw her into the room. His slender fingers were strong, and she couldn't help herself — she twirled into the room at his arm in a slow pirouette and then he used the momentum to push her a little apart from him, while still holding onto her and they leaned apart from one another like two reeds bending just slightly in a breeze.

"I love that you are strong." He pulled her back in so that his arm crossed over her breasts as he stood behind her, chin pressed into the back of her neck, his lithe, sculpted thighs pressed into the backs of hers. "Some dancers, they are wisps." He pronounced it *weesps*. "They are all beauty and no strength, and when they dance, there is no power."

She didn't know what to say. Every word she'd liked to have said would sound fawning. *You are amazing. I've never seen such a beautiful man.* "I'm a little drunk." A burp escaped as if to prove this true, and she clapped a hand to her mouth. He unrolled from her, spun her around. The room kept spinning for a moment after as he looked at her with much the same assessing gaze as when he'd been directing her earlier this afternoon.

He threw up his hands. "We are all a little drunk!" He leapt in place and she burst out giggling. "Tonight, we are Hermia and Lysander."

"Ah, *A Midsummer's Night Dream*. Yes, perfect."

He took her hand and spun her to the bed. Then he slipped off her shoes, slowly worked her tights off. She'd put them on for this very reason—to watch him peel her out of these clothes. Out of the wraparound skirt, the corset-like bustier top and tiny sparkling half-sweater. When she was peeled back and naked at last, he sighed as though he'd tasted the most delicious dessert. He kissed her belly button, traced her thighs with his finger, circled her nipples.

And the phone rang—a loud, harsh jangling. She shrieked at the noise. He raised his eyebrows and laughed. "Just a moment darling. Go nowhere. Here, have more champagne." He poured her a glass and she took it, giggling as she imagined herself streaking nude through the lobby.

She lay back on the bed, naked and dizzy. The room spun slowly if she closed her eyes so she opened them and stared out the window that looked down on New York City—truly a city that never slept.

He spoke in agitated-sounding Russian to the person on the phone. She shifted onto her side, closed her eyes a moment. Just a long, drifting, dizzy perfect moment that stretched on and on. She fell in and out of dreams of their bodies entwined, first making love, then dancing, then strange hybrid variations of both at once.

Her eyes popped open. There was a warm, unclothed body behind her. All the lights in the room were off. "Darling you must go now. We must get our sleep!" he whispered.

A rush of humiliation flushed her. She sat up, vaguely aware of a wet spot between her legs. She suffered a stab of panic. Her memory wouldn't offer up to her the singular moment, the whole reason she'd come here, to watch his eyes as he entered her, to absorb some of his talent and grace. What had happened?

He patted her behind. "Come, come, darling."

Had she?

She squeezed herself into her clothes, grateful at least for the dark so he couldn't see the shame on her cheeks as she scurried off into the night.

* * *

Margaret was two drinks in, staring out at the river, when a man's reflection appeared beside her at the table.

"That beautiful neck." He drew a finger down the length of it. Goosebumps bloomed on her arms and heat twinkled between her thighs. He still knew her erogenous zones.

She turned slowly to look at him, almost afraid of what time might have done to him. But it had been kinder to him than it had to her. He was not completely gray, and not terribly wrinkled either. Same strong features, only slightly softened by time. He dressed with dignity, his posture straight and strong.

"Max. Well, here we are again."

He tipped his head back, smiled. "You are still a beauty, Margie."

"Margie, ha. Haven't been called that in forever."

"Not as long as forever. Don't make me feel ancient."

She took him in again. He looked anything but ancient. He had the lightness of a man ten years younger; a man who had had the freedom to do what he liked, who wasn't burdened by wife and child.

"And how is that daughter of yours?" The question came so suddenly she nearly choked on a sip of water. Margaret bowed her head, her feelings like a tangled necklace, though she could tease out the iron weight of dread, the silver of anxiety. But he rushed on.

"It's okay, you know? You were a woman in demand, my dear, a woman not to be possessed, but adored. I know she could have been anyone's."

Margaret was surprised by the way her spine stiffened at his words. Not anyone's. *His.* Beautiful Mik. But what kind of a life would it have been for them, Stella his bastard shadow, Margaret just another whore? None. Though there were times she suffered pangs of desire for the financial backing it might have brought. A little extra to pad the empty spaces.

"Stella is well. In fact, she's back to dancing. Can't say that I approve."

Max's pale eyebrow rose over his pale eyes. "Oh no, that's not jealousy I hear?"

Margaret laughed, but it came out sounding like a bray. She finished the remains of her drink. "It's concern you hear. She works for this megalomaniac, so far as I can tell, who thinks the world revolves around his little ragtag group of misfits. They're barely more than lounge entertainers, no technique, no real talent."

"Ah, I see. That does sound sketchy." He slid his hand over hers. His palm was cool—he'd always had slightly poor circulation, his feet icicles in their bed.

"But the thing is, she seems happy. Sort of. Purposeful, I think. But she's not spending enough time with Izzy. I have a vague sense of unease about it that I can't explain."

He nodded as though he understood all too well. "She's been your world for a long time. It's sort of as if she's a teenager again, and you're having to let her go, grow up."

Margaret sighed. "Yes, I suppose. Though when she was a teenager I was . . . well I was lamed, all tragedy and woe over what I'd lost. I went from star to invalid and there was nothing in between. Anyways, this is all very dull. Tell me about you—about this business of yours. That sounds exciting. L.A., Hollywood, all that good stuff. It must be thrilling."

Max laughed vigorously, contagiously. Soon she was laughing with him. "I don't think anyone who's been in the business of Hollywood long enough would ever describe it as thrilling. Ha, no. I manage talent. I'm like a real estate agent for actors. And actors are notoriously full of themselves. I specialize in new talent precisely because I like to get them when they're still hopeful and grateful for every job they take."

"So you like to pop their cherries." Max's eyes widened as though she'd offended him. "Their acting cherries, I mean."

He shook his head. "I'm glad you clarified. If there's one thing a man of my age doesn't need it's to be reminded of how old and out of my prime I am by chasing much younger women."

He entwined his fingers into hers.

"I'm glad to hear that," she said.

He whisked the waiter over and ordered a glass of Merlot, which he sniffed like a connoisseur with eyes closed.

"We were good together, Margie."

She sighed. "I know."

"We could be again."

She wished she had another drink to guzzle to drench the elated shock that produced a sudden streak of pain down her leg, far past where any nerves were still alive. These phantom pains were becoming a lot less phantom. "I can't live in L.A.. And look at me, Max, I'm stuck in this damn chair."

Max's eyes pinched, as though it hurt him to see her in it. "I travel all the time. I'm up here twice a month."

She couldn't believe he was talking like this, making plans as though they were thirty again.

"Stella wouldn't like it. She needs me."

He sipped his wine slowly, held it in his mouth before swallowing.

"She needs you? Or the other way around? She's a big girl. A woman with her own needs, I imagine. Eventually, she'll want a man to fill the space."

Indignation cinched the base of her spine up, like a zipper straining to close. But she couldn't deny it.

"Max, come on, this is just a tease, right, a tryst? You don't want to be saddled with an invalid. Everything you loved about me is gone." She heard the quiver in her voice before her chest contracted, her eyes burned with tears.

He squeezed her hand even tighter and his eyes narrowed to slits. "Margie, my dear, I will not deny that I was angry once, for a while, a long time even. Angry enough that when I heard about your accident I indulged in a brief moment of satisfaction that something had been taken from you equal to what I lost."

She inhaled hard, his words as painful as fingers squeezing her throat.

He shook his head. "But that moment gave way to grief, to loss. For you. For me." He shook a finger at her, his eyes softening. "I know your kind. You're not meant to walk among mere mortals. I could make you happy again, Margie."

Whether it was the wine, or his words, she didn't know, but warmth crept up her spine, lit her from within, a sensation she hadn't had in years. Too many years.

"And how do we go about this arrangement, you making me happy?"

His eyes drooped to her breasts only briefly, his mouth parted. "Come up to my hotel room tonight, for starters."

A giggle welled up almost like a burp, as though her much younger self had awakened inside her. "Show me the way."

His smile was feral, intense—it reminded her of the man he'd been when she'd been in her prime, the dogged way he'd pursued her.

When he stood up and took the handles of her wheelchair there was a slight slipping of the moment, a downward shift into the reality that no matter what spark still existed between them, she no longer had the same agency over her body.

He left cash on the table. The lights outside reflected on the water, twinkling in the faces of the young people laughing and drinking in the bar. Her head swam, giddy, as he pushed her a little too fast down the hall to the elevators and she laughed like a much younger woman.

Her wheel got stuck on the lip of the elevator door and he nearly jounced her onto the floor but she held on tightly to her handles and shrieked, sweat beading down her neck.

"This is fun, isn't it, Margie?"

She sighed and tilted her head back, exposing her throat. "Kiss me."

He leaned down and nibbled up her neck, then sucked lightly, then harder. She knew the blood vessels were straining to the point of breaking beneath his tongue, that she would wear an unsightly mark of passion there tomorrow but she didn't care. Who would care, Stella? If she even noticed.

Then he kissed her hard and hot on the mouth, his tongue plunging in, sudden, urgent. She suddenly remembered that he'd been a vigorous, intense lover. That he liked to thrust himself roughly against her, pull her onto his lap, take her from behind and pull lightly on her hair. It had been thrilling then, but now?

The doors dinged open and they parted like teens caught at the sight of another young couple, hands entwined, who stared at them.

"You kids haven't cornered the market on lust," Max said with a laugh and the kids looked awkwardly at each other as he swooped her off down the hall to his room.

Her lips were slightly bruised from his kiss but now that slowly reawakening dead part of her was more awake than ever. His spare room overlooked the river. Other than a half-full glass of water by the bedstand there were no personal effects, no clothing draped over chairs or pajamas crumpled on the bed. She imagined all of his shirts and pants neatly hung in the little closet.

He wheeled her close to the window, facing her out. "It's lovely."

She twisted around to look at him. "I don't need any foreplay, Max. Take me to bed."

His grin was lopsided and dragged up one side of his face before the other. "Still as commanding as ever."

But he wheeled her over, propped her chair up at the soft edge of the bed then looked down at her a little helplessly. "What now?"

"Lift me onto the bed. Undress me."

He was surprisingly strong, didn't groan or strain with the effort of lifting her. Though she supposed she weighed a fraction of her former self, muscles atrophied to noodles, bones unaccustomed to weight-bearing.

He thrust her back onto the bed a little roughly, her head bouncing. "Sorry."

But he undressed her slowly. She clapped a hand over her eyes when he pulled off her skirt. "Don't look too closely."

"Don't be vain." She felt the tugging sensation of her skirt's removal—she hadn't bothered with underwear—but no other sensation until his mouth was hot between her legs and there was, undeniably, sensation, heat and tiny zapping tingles and rolling, near forgotten, waves of pleasure. She moaned aloud, then clapped a hand to her mouth, embarrassed. He helped her out of her top, stroked her breasts, squeezed each nipple as though testing it somehow.

And then he undressed himself, quickly and with no preamble— she had denied foreplay after all—entered her. It came with equal parts pain and pleasure, like being a virgin. She gasped. The weight of him was sudden, a shock, and strange, as she could only feel his body from waist up. But she could feel him!

It lasted a good deal longer than she had anticipated, too, for a man of his age. He gazed into her eyes and kissed her and moved slowly, tenderly and then, with a sensation of climbing to the near summit of a peak, heart beating with extra work, her body released itself into the first orgasm she had had in nineteen years.

She cried out, and then was crying, hard tears, big tears. He rolled away, lay next to her, put his arms behind his head. He didn't attempt to comfort her, just lay next to her silently.

When she was done crying he wiped her face with an edge of the blanket. Then he sat up, strode naked across the room, extracted a robe from the bathroom, put it on, and then fumbled in a drawer. At last he lit up a cigarette and then sank into one of the chairs near the bed.

"I'd like the test."

With a great deal of effort, she scooted herself back and up, leaning against the bed. She wasn't sure she'd heard him correctly. "What test?"

"I'm no good at pretenses, Margie. I want the test. I was patient all these years."

Understanding docked slowly in her brain. The test, the test she'd talked him out of years ago, and then he'd just gone away and dropped the matter so there was no point.

She laughed, though not out of humor. "I should have known this was all too good to be true. I thought you'd at least have tried to fuck me a couple more times first."

He inhaled sharply. "She'll take it better coming from you, I presume. She doesn't know me."

She almost cried again. "Why now? For god's sake, Max. She's twenty-nine years old. Her daughter is ten—"

He inhaled. "Ah yes, my granddaughter. The violin prodigy."

"What is wrong with you?" A shiver of fear walked coldly over her. She was helpless here. Couldn't run, couldn't even walk herself to the bathroom to clean up.

"She's never asked about her father. She doesn't care. She isn't beholden to men." Margaret wasn't sure where this urgency was coming from to keep this truth from Stella. What did it matter, in the end? But something inside her clenched.

He leaned forward. "We could be a family, Margie. We could all take care of one another."

It hit her all of a sudden, adding up the pieces. "You stay away from the child. She's not some commodity to pick up and make you rich."

He laughed then, a harsh sound in the still room. "You're so suspicious of me. I'm a man past his prime, Margie, and I want what I have always wanted. You. Our daughter. A family. Why do you presume my intentions to be diabolical?"

She shivered and clutched the blankets to her. "Because you are the most persistent, manipulative man I've ever known."

"Oh, more persistent than you? I seem to recall a restraining order . . ."

"You know nothing."

"I know more than you think I do. I forgave you for fucking *him* when I was waiting for you back in your cold bed in San Francisco. And you repaid me with abandonment. Betrayal. Refusing me my own child."

Margaret sat up as tall as was possible. "If you were so sure she was yours, why did you disappear? Maybe you were actually in love with that little twit Sarafina?"

Max dropped his chin, his voice grew soft. "Because I knew you'd poison her against me if I kept pushing."

"So you've spent the last years buttering me up with love letters, have you?"

"May I remind you that you contacted me, Margie?"

He stood up suddenly—had she forgotten how tall he was or did her own lowered gravity simply make him seem so much taller, looming? A man who could lift her without breaking a sweat even now, nearly sixty. Sudden fright made her blood thud against her veins as it traveled, adrenalized sweat prickle at the base of her neck. She had to remember that she was, essentially, helpless here.

He didn't come for her though, merely walked to the window and looked out.

"I sent you letters expressing how I feel. How I've always felt, Margie. You are the one, have always been the one, pushing me away, as women seem to love to do with men." Now he turned back to look at her, his pale eyes drooping, and despite her weak lower half, she swelled with momentary power. Until a foolishness slithered down her neck.

She exhaled loudly. "I'm sorry." Her voice was a rasp. "My life is so small, I don't know how to do this, anything, anymore."

He sat down at the edge of the bed and laid his hand on her leg. She had to look away, the sight of his strong hand, her shriveled foot; it mortified her.

"There's really nothing to do. I'm just asking you, begging you gently, really, to do this thing for me. If Stella rejects me, if she wants nothing to do with me, I will go away."

The irony wasn't lost on her; that here she was encouraging Stella to tell Izzy about her own father. But this was different. Izzy was a child; there was still time to bond to Dylan. Stella was her own creature, with moods that Margaret knew were her own legacy steeped in her daughter. *And beyond Stella, what about me?* Margaret thought. *What if I want more of this?*

"Just give me a little time to gather my thoughts on how to tell her. That's all I ask."

Max's smile was a sudden sun in his gloomy face. "I have to go back to L.A. tomorrow, but I'm back in a couple weeks. Will that give you enough time?"

She nodded. She tried to push herself back up against the bed— her lower back was starting to ache, and the not-numb edges of her haunches tingled as though going to sleep.

"Can you hand me my skirt there? Then help me back into my chair?"

He followed her pointing finger to the crumpled black heap on the floor with a glazy gaze, as though not really seeing it, as if caught somewhere else in time.

"Max?"

His eyes snapped up to her and he shook free of the reverie. "Of course, my darling." He brought her the soft material, thumbing it as though it were a small animal to pet. "And I must say, I don't believe you are dead of feeling in very many places."

20

IT WAS A SIMPLE REQUEST. "Can you please go and get me some more flour from the basement cupboard." The girls were making more pies, which Stella now knew meant Julien was anxious; in lieu of offering other more obvious feminine comforts, the girls settled on a domestic peace offering. And there were several reasons for Julien's anxiety. The specter of theft. The drug-addled former dancer and her brash appearance. Aja's persistent mood that had fouled up the air in the company. Stella didn't expect this job to be free of complications, but these were a little more than she would have liked.

Aja looked up from the sink, where she was washing berries. She didn't repeat her request, merely raised one eyebrow and gave Stella a look that she'd begun seeing on her own daughter's face. Something between *Are you serious* and *What are you waiting for?* There was no one else around, and Aja still had not warmed to her, so Stella turned toward the basement door.

Yet she hesitated. It didn't matter how old she got, basements would always be a place to dart in and out, fumbling for a light with a sweaty hand, heart choking her throat. The theater basement where she'd been sent often as a girl to fetch gauzy skirts or scuffed shoes, most of them fool's errands to get her out of their hair, she realized later, had made terrible creaking sounds as the dancers practiced above, and she was always half convinced the ceiling would fall on her head. She recalled pressing the musty fabric to her cheeks; and worse, the basement of the house she'd lived in with her mother and grandmother, where once she'd encountered a tall, slender man smoking when she had thought no one was home. His silence, the way he stood there so still that only the smoke curling up around his leonine face moved, had iced her with fear more than the place itself, like he was the basement's dark agent, waiting to take her soul.

Later, she would see this dread as her body's instinct, a knowledge of the most terrible thing. Now, she took the stairs two at a time. Someone had left the curtains open, so it wasn't as dark as she feared—weak sunlight revealed streams of dust motes on parade. Her immediate thought was "Oh no, will we have to do that?"—a flash to those circus women spinning by their chins from a wire.

Her second thought came with a strange numbness in her legs, like the shock of stepping into a puddle that is deeper than you think, cold water wicking over the edge of your shoe into your socks, squishing unpleasantly between your toes. The woman was not swinging by her chin as some kind of preparation for a spectacle; she was hanging by her neck, which was limp and tilted back at a slightly wrong angle. Desperately, horribly she thought: *Shoulders back. Neck long.* The woman was dressed in one of the green leotards Stella recognized, had probably worn herself. One arm was tangled in a nearby strap as though she'd tried to reach for her neck, had second thoughts before her last breath left her. The way her limbs hung was almost graceful.

Stella's body managed to work despite the blackout that had taken place in her brain. She simply found herself at the top of the stairs, out of breath—panting, really—on the threshold of the kitchen. A name worked its way through this shock. *Brooke.* This must be Brooke—even though she had only glimpsed her briefly at the Sweet Sixteen spectacle, a certainty slammed down with finality like a metal door inside her. She couldn't let Aja see; she knew they had been close. But Stella couldn't soften her face, couldn't close down the horror that must have been plain there, as though she carried death upstairs with her. Aja was in the kitchen, alone, stretching, one strong, lean leg planted on the floor, the other leg and arms floating in space, making her a human letter T.

"Where's Lina?" Stella asked in a casual tone, or tried to, but Aja's eyes cut to Stella's empty hands and her thin brows made a sudden V. She asked no questions but bustled right past Stella down toward the basement.

Stella made a weak attempt to clutch at Aja, but the taller woman moved with too much purpose, a crackle of energy as she bounded down the steps. After an agonizing beat of silence, the wail that rose up was so loud, a thunderstorm of emotion, Stella had no need of alerting the other women in the house—they all came running.

Lina was the only one who paused at the lip of the stairs, as Stella had before she knew what horrors lurked there. "What?" she asked, tilting her head toward the caterwauling.

"Brooke is. . . ." is all Stella could say, then shook her head.

Lina stuck her face into her palm. "Shit. Shit, motherfucking shit." Stella stared.

"This is not good," Lina said. Stella couldn't argue with that, but she wondered if Lina meant for business, or something else.

Stella glanced down the stairs again, half-afraid to see the hanging dead girl, but debating whether she should try to offer Aja some comfort. Aja tossed her head back and forth, a kind of grief-borne head banging. Stella took a step back but Aja whipped up to look at her.

"*You!*" she pointed a dark-painted nail at Stella, who instinctively touched her own throat as if for protection.

"Don't start—"

Aja's voice rose to a shriek, overpowering Ina. "He replaced her with *you*. You think she didn't notice? You think it didn't dawn on her what he was doing?"

Stella couldn't breathe. The room was hot and too small for the wildness in Aja's limbs. Suddenly she was up the stairs in a flash and on Stella, firm, sharp fingers grasping her shoulders and shaking, hard, Stella's head snapping back and forth. Stella was suddenly eight years old again, caught in the grips of a wild young dancer who'd been understudying her mother. *You little brat, don't you fucking ruin this for me*, the dancer said, cornering her backstage. Stella had fallen into sobs, a fully-fledged tantrum when her mother had told her she wouldn't be taking her to the drive-in for dinner, she had work to do. *Don't you have a father who can take you out of the way?*

"Stop it Ayj!" Lina tried to step in to pry Aja off Stella, but Aja tossed back an elbow and Lina was forced to dodge, though not very successfully, and Aja grazed Lina's cheek hard enough for a red welt to appear. Lina clutched her cheek with an outraged widening of the eyes.

There were a series of slams—Stella's back up against the doorway to the basement, pushed there at Aja's hand, where she teetered precariously for a long, terrifying moment, with a bleak feeling that the dead woman at the bottom was pulling her down, calling her to the black depths; then the slam of the front door. Stella fell back painfully onto her ankle and caught herself at the second step as Julien barreled in, steps firm and full of force.

Aja shrank back, folding in like a hermit crab into the nearest kitchen chair, where she dissolved into hiccupping sobs.

Stella stood up, took a deep breath. "Don't go down there, Julien," she said softly. "Please."

His face was so serious, his jaw squared and stoic, his eyes flashing cool green and blue, and then—as Lina's voice on the phone to the police drifted to their ears, "There's been a death . . ." Julien slipped to his knees. To Stella's surprise he half-crawled to Aja and took the weeping girl in his arms. "*Nooooo*," he said, his voice thick . . . their voices merging in a mutual aria of sorrow.

21

STELLA FELT SCOOPED OUT, hollow as she primped in the mirror—the face staring back at her someone else's face, ringed in dark eyeliner, blushed and painted to her prettiest edge. Izzy was all but doing dance steps at the door. Stella was relieved that she would get to do something to take her mind off Brooke, if such a thing were possible—the woman's last death pose was affixed in her mind's eye, grotesquely beautiful—and eaten up with an acid anxiety that was equal parts thrill and dread at spending time with Dylan again, not unlike stage fright.

"Well? Too much, too little?" Stella nervously patted her body. Her mother winced slightly at Stella's new violet hair, which she'd swept up with a big black clip, allowing her newly shortened bangs and some soft tendrils to drift down and frame her cheeks. She hadn't been sure at first about the color, Isis's suggestion, thought it looked too dramatic, attracted too much attention, but suddenly, as she peered at herself in the hallway mirror, she felt as though for the first time in a while, the outside matched the inside.

She settled for dressed-up comfort. Her nicest pair of dark-wash jeans with a tightly fitting teal crushed silk top, V-necked, fitted at the waist, and black high-heeled boots.

"I think you look beautiful," Izzy said, her voice full of breathy hope that would have bothered Stella if she weren't so full of anxiety about the impending meeting.

Margaret frowned at Stella as she grabbed her keys and headed out the door. "Be careful."

Stella threw her mother an "I don't need your advice" grimace, and jumped in her car.

Dylan waited outside the restaurant, pacing slightly. She stood across the street for a minute, relishing watching him: the way he gnawed at his thumb cuticle, tilted his head back just slightly, and inhaled. Then she dashed across the street, feeling warmed by his delighted gaze at the sight of her.

"Wow, ye . . . look so different than just a week ago." His hand went in such a familiar way to her temple, where he smoothed away one of her violet tendrils, that she froze in place.

"Bad? Should I go back?" She pulled at one of the violet strands self-consciously.

He smiled. "No, no, I didn't say that. Though, my god, is it possible ye used to be blonde once?"

She frowned. "I believe they call that dishwater. Yuck."

"Hmm, I remember liking it." He smiled. "It smelled good too—whatever that shampoo was . . ." He leaned in then and, to her amusement, sniffed her head. "Still using it."

She shrugged. Not much of a first impression. Other than her hair, he'd all but told her she hadn't changed. "Prell. Cheap and predictable, that's me. Why change what's working?"

He frowned. "That was a compliment, ye know?"

Stella followed him into the restaurant. "It's true, once a woman changes her shampoo, everything else follows suit. Pretty soon she's eating different cereal and forgetting where she parked her car."

Now he laughed as he opened the door for her. "Ah, good to see yer sense of humor is intact."

She'd suggested a Cuban place in town, owned by her former boss/lover Jason's nemesis, a one-armed Greek who was notorious for holding people hostage with his annoying banter. But the food was good in a predictable sort of way, and affordable.

"Tell me about yer new company," he said.

She'd ordered a glass of Cabernet, but he was only drinking iced tea, and she felt self-conscious suddenly of her wine.

She shook her head. "It's been a very bad week." As soon as she said it, she wished she hadn't; she knew she'd have to tell him about

Brooke now, thus ruining the illusion that she had a grand life and a grand job.

"Well, not all bad, right? Ye ran into me." His gaze held an intimacy she hadn't experienced in so long it left her giddy and stupid. Suddenly, bringing up Brooke seemed like a good thing.

"One of the former dancers, I never knew her, was found . . ." Her voice choked off mid-sentence and for a horrifying moment her stomach squeezed like she might throw up.

"Y'okay?" His eyes squeezed together.

"She was found dead today at my job. She is, she was, uh, a terrible drug addict—Julien, my boss, he asked her to leave the company some months before I was ever brought on. So, I guess, I guess she wanted to send a message."

Dylan sat back hard in his chair, let out a soft sound. "What a terrible, terrible thing."

"I found her," Stella added softly. He eyed her warily, as though he wondered if finding Brooke had awakened her fragility, and she felt she might wilt under his studying gaze. She suddenly wanted to set it all straight—reset the lie of her alleged mental breakdown. But how could she?

He reached across the table and grabbed her fingers, the way she'd seen men who'd been married for years do with their wives, as though reassuring themselves, that they were not alone, that their life partner was always there, just within reach.

"I'm okay. I've been okay for a long time." She took a gulping sip of her Cabernet. "You can take that 'I've only got six months to live' look off your face."

His mouth twisted into a half-smile, half-grimace. When he spoke again, his accent was thicker, a sign of emotion. "I've spent a lot of time thinking about ye in the last ten years, Stella, hoping ye were okay. Tried not to take it personally when your mum told me that your mental health was better off without me in your life."

Stella let herself look at him, though she was afraid of what it would conjure. A groove right between his eyebrows deepened when he grew emotional. She remembered watching it appear when they made love. There were pale freckles across both his cheeks. His jaw was strong, marked by a tiny cleft she had liked to press the tip of her tongue into. Her desire to tell him about Izzy was suddenly so overpowering, she was afraid if she opened her mouth at all, they would be the next words she'd say. Shouldn't she give him the chance to decide? He might hate her for it, too. She sipped her wine to wash the urge away.

"I've thought way more about you than you know." She tried to remember the full scope of the lie they'd sold him. "I couldn't handle the pressure of success, the workload, and my mom always needed help. I cracked. But I'm not permanently cracked. I just didn't know how to get in touch with you again after all this time."

"So why did ye?"

Stella shook her head. "It was a coincidence that I ran into you at the show. I didn't even know it was your show."

He raised an eyebrow. "Sure ye don't have a split personality? Ye sent me that message on Facebook."

Information all slammed together in a train-wreck of understanding. It smacked of Izzy, which meant that her mother was right; Izzy already knew the truth and had somehow arranged their meeting.

She choked down the bile of frustration at having to make more fabrications. She tried to imagine what was going through Izzy's head—the hope of it crushed her, made it hard to feel anything but a muddy guilt.

"That's what all the cool kids are doing these days," she said, buying time. "Okay . . . the truth is, my mom sent that first message," she fibbed. "I don't even use a computer most of the time, and I was . . . um, mad at first when she told me. But I'm glad she did. It's nosy, but look at the results."

"Why were ye mad?" He pushed his plate away.

"Maybe I wasn't so much mad as guilty . . . that I wasn't the one to do it first."

Dylan smiled. "So what now?"

"Does there need to be a game plan?"

"Can we see more of each other?"

"Um" came fumbling out of Stella's lips at the same time as Aja, Chloe, Lucy, and Yvette powered in the front door of the restaurant dressed in black cat suits and big, hairy wolf masks. She could make them out by their body language and leftover leather remnants of the "Back in Black" wedding.

Sweat broke out on every surface of her body. She scanned the exits, but the girls now surrounded their table. Aja held a tiny pair of speakers attached to a tiny iPod in her pocket. The music to Hall and Oates's eighties hit "Maneater" came blaring out. Aja began to sing in such a disarmingly gorgeous, husky voice, like the lovechild of Billie Holiday and Adele, that Stella momentarily forgot to be stunned that they'd followed her here and were interrupting her date.

The foursome pranced and loped around the table, and Aja drew a finger, capped with a long, false black nail, down the side of Dylan's face as she sang, "Watch out boy, she'll chew you up!" She looked like she was enjoying every minute of it.

To his credit, Dylan was smiling, as though he thought this was just a good time, another show.

The music was too loud for Stella to talk over. So she folded her arms tightly across her chest and frowned at them. Then Yvette shrugged at Dylan as Lucy leaned almost into his lap at one point, shook her wolf mane, and the music came to an abrupt halt. They all took a wolfish bow, hands arched into claws.

Stella was ready to clap and pat them on the back if only to get them out of there when Aja pulled a piece of paper out of her pocket and read aloud: "Dear Stella, thanks so much for chewing me up and spitting me out. Hope the next one breaks your heart.—Jason."

Stella shook her head and stood up, rage strangling the words in her throat. She caught Aja's eye just long enough to mouth the words, "What the fuck?" before Aja spun away.

Dylan raised an eyebrow as the ladies made for the door without another word, but Stella was on her feet and had hold of Chloe's hand.

"What the hell was that?" she whispered.

Chloe's eyes drooped as though she felt sorry. "Just doing my job, sweetie." She pulled her hand out of Stella's grip and followed the others out of the restaurant. It was in almost every way the opposite of the very first time she'd seen them perform at the Fuse—no elation this time, no sense of wonder; only cold, blistering hate.

She stomped back to Dylan. "Okay, please let me explain. I work with them, they think it's funny to mess with me. That was not a real message from anyone. The guy they're talking about, we weren't even a couple, or dating, you know it was just . . ." She realized she was admitting to having casual sex and so derailed that train of thought. "I just don't want you to think . . ."

"I don't think anything," he said quickly, standing up. He'd thrown down cash on the table. "It looked like fun, it was a show, and that's all. Don't stress."

Stella breathed deeply. On their way out she apologized to the hostess for the interruption.

"Oh that was a blast," the hostess said. "They're welcome back. Could be good for business."

Stella's jaw muscles screamed in agony as she ground her teeth together.

The cool air did nothing to reduce the steam in her heart. She walked without knowing where to, feeling her shoulders bunched up at her ears until Dylan took her hand.

"They really upset ye, huh?"

She stopped and exhaled loudly. "Not them, it's . . . they just did what our boss told them to do . . ."

"Your boss? Why?"

Stella shook her head. "I don't know. He's odd. Kind of possessive about his employees."

The night air smelled like hearth fires and coffee from a nearby café. When he pulled her against him, so tightly she could feel the sinews of his abdominal muscles, the press of his ribs against hers, she almost let herself curve neatly against him. But she kept herself held just slightly away. If she let herself go she would make mistakes, say and do things she regretted.

"He's possessive, as in he thinks you're his property?" He spoke into her hair.

His words made something catch inside her, like two halves of a broken mirror momentarily pressed back together again. "Hell, I have to talk to him. That was totally uncool. I can't let him get away with that!"

"Yeah, ye should do that."

She pulled out of Dylan's arm. "I should do it now. That was like something a jealous teenager would do. It was not right."

Dylan stared down at her. They were standing at the edge of one of the small footbridges that you could cross the river on, and the moon was swollen yellow, almost full. She could vaguely make out the edges in her memory of that first night when Julien had taken her to the rusty bridge down by the string factory and made her feel full of possibility. Now he was forcing his way into her life.

"Ye really have to talk to him tonight?" He touched her temple, brushed his finger down her cheek.

She kissed him, just gently at first, then firmly, ten years of longing worked into it. They stood kissing for a long time, until her body began to thrum, to ask for more, and so she forced herself to pull away.

He stared down at her, confusion full in his eyes.

"I do want to see you again." She squeezed his hand. "But first I need to take care of something. Can I call you?"

"Jaysus, Stella—it's like all ye know how to do is disappear."

The unfairness of his words made her nauseated. If he only knew.

"That's not fair. You just tumbled back into my world at a time when it happens to be complicated."

He inhaled through his nose, his eyes gone cold. "Okay, I'll take ye home."

"I don't think you should drive me home," she said.

He stepped backwards, threw his head back in surprise. "Was it that bad seeing each other again? Did I misread the signals?"

"No, it's just . . . I don't want to involve you in this mess. And my boss is, he's kind of bipolar in his moods, you know? If I don't call him on this tonight, he wins—he gets away with it and then I'll never have another chance."

"I'm not just going to leave ye on the street." He pressed his lips together. She could all but read his thoughts: *Mentally unstable. Is she really well again?*

"Don't worry," she nodded firmly. "I'll be fine."

His eyes were slits folded between creased brows. "Ye look like some kind of mythological creature right now in the full moon, with your violet hair. Like *Cliodhna*, Irish fairy of beauty."

"A fairy?" She wasn't sure if he was flattering her or not.

He frowned. "Or maybe more like Goddess of the Underworld."

She shivered at the echo of Isis's title for herself. "I will call you, you know. I'm not just saying that."

He shrugged, his furrow deepening. "I just hope it's not another ten years."

She shook her head, but when she tried to reach for his fingers he pulled his hand away. "Let's save the touchy-feely stuff for the next time . . . if there is a next time." Then he pulled the collar of his jacket up tightly around his neck and walked away. It was agony watching his easy lope, an echo of Izzy.

* * *

In something of a daze, when she was sure that Dylan had driven off, she walked down the cobbled back alley behind the Cuban restaurant and dialed Julien's number.

"Frivolity Inc.?"

For the first time, Stella considered the absurdity of his company name; she'd never had a job that felt less frivolous.

"What the fuck was that about?" she spat into the phone.

"Excuse me?" Julien managed to sound amused, which only increased her rage. "You ruined my dinner."

"I did? Where are you?"

"Yes, you *better* come over here in person and talk to me like a man." She gave him the location of a café a few blocks up and walked there, waited outside, tapping her foot in frustrated impatience, growing more and more angry. *The fucking nerve. What right does he have?*

When he finally pulled up she threw herself into the passenger seat like a self-righteous teenager and turned to glare at him. His expression was smooth and guileless. He was as dressed down as she'd ever seen him, in a long-sleeved purple T-shirt and faded jeans and tennis shoes.

"That was unfair, and juvenile." She wanted to slam her hand against the dash but thought better of it. "And what about your separation-of-church-and-state line to me? I get raked over the coals for leaving a spectacle a few minutes early to make sure my child hasn't been kidnapped or molested, but *you* infiltrate *my* personal life whenever you want? This may be the best job, the most creative job, the most satisfying job I've had, but that does not give you the right to interfere."

Julien kept his eyes on the road as she talked, but didn't speak.

"I haven't talked to him in ten years! What do you think that little mini-spectacle did to him? The last thing he knew about me was that I'd had a mental breakdown—"

"But that was a lie," Julien piped in, as he turned down a long driveway toward an enormous white shingled house that all but glowed in the night.

"Well yes, but he doesn't know that."

"Because you kept your daughter a secret."

"Don't lecture me," Stella said. "It was the right thing to do." She glanced up at the house before them, which looked old and enormous. "You live here? I thought you stayed at Headquarters."

He smirked. "I'm not safe in that haven of wenches."

"Nice to know what you really think of us."

Julien laughed and unbuckled his seat belt. Stella jumped out of the car, unsure of why she was getting out except that she felt caged in the small space of the car and wanted room to berate him.

His eyes were dark-rimmed and his cheeks seemed to hang with the weight of fatigue. "You're different from them, Stella. It's why I don't require you to live on premises, just like Lina. You're older, you're less, shall we say, damaged, and don't need the same kind of guidance."

Stella walked toward the porch of the house, away from him. "Don't try to compliment me, I'm not done being angry at you."

His feet crunched on the gravel drive behind her. She leapt up the stairs lightly and wandered the porch, which was hung with long trailing green plants and decorative pots full of colorful little flowers. Its decoration seemed to cry out for a woman's touch.

"Okay, so let me have it some more." Amusement in his voice made her turn around. He was standing at the bottom of the stairs with none of his usual grandeur, arms relaxed at his sides, head tilted. "I must admit I'm curious what made you run away from your magnificent date with your lost soul mate to call me."

Stella wanted to throw one of the pots of flowers at him. "No, it's not because . . . I wanted to make sure you understood that I am . . ." She pursed her lips and thought about what she was going to say. "That I'm not your property, no matter how seriously I take this job. And I didn't want to waste any time telling you."

Julien took the steps slowly, one at a time, until he was close enough to reach out and pull her into his arms if he wanted to. His eyes gleamed in the moonlight, amused and something else that she couldn't read. "Is that all?"

Stella didn't like the way he looked so satisfied, like she was just where he wanted her.

"No, I want an explanation. And a promise that you won't pull that bullshit again."

"An explanation?"

"Yes, you know, taking a good hard look at your motivations and asking why."

"Easy. I didn't do it, Stella."

"What?" She tilted her head at him, hoping the violet hair made her look fiercer than usual.

"It wasn't me. I suggest you look to the source."

"But they wouldn't . . . without your permission, and why . . . nobody even knew where I was going tonight!"

Julien shrugged. "Do you want me to hand out punishments, or do you want to show them that you're not so easily pushed around?"

"I'm having a hard time believing you."

"Why, Stella?" His mouth tilted up in a satisfied grin. "You think that I'm in love with you?"

Embarrassment wrapped tightly around her. She had presumed. "Not . . . love."

He nodded. "Let me tell you one thing, so you don't have to think too much about it. If I wanted to fuck you, I would have made that clear from the beginning. I hired you for your talent, and that's all I care about, no matter what ideas you may have about yourself, and me."

She wanted to protest—hadn't he been the one to make advances on her, to touch her, to put himself physically in her space? He had come on to her. Hadn't he? Or had she just read what she thought she saw into in his gestures?

"I'm sorry." She exhaled, deflated. "I guess after our last conversation, I just assumed."

"It's okay." He gazed off at the bright moon. "I'm used to the female mind. Surrounded by it. Steeped in it."

She prickled at the arrogance of that statement but was now too tired for a tirade on the subject. "Well, I guess I'll take it up with the girls," she said at last. "It was so ridiculous. Wolf outfits. 'Maneater.'"

He plucked a green leaf off of one of the hanging plants and rubbed it between his fingers. "Or you could act like nothing happened, that it didn't faze you in the slightest."

"Why?"

"Think back to high school, Stella."

"You think they were testing me?"

"See it happen every time we bring a new girl into the fold."

"And what about when you lose a girl, like Brooke?"

His eyes filled with tears, and she mentally slapped herself; she'd sounded accusing. Why couldn't she stop from asking these kinds of questions?

"Then we mourn her no less than we would a true daughter, Stella. And some of us mourn in more overt ways than others, like Aja. I grieve privately, so nobody sees what it does to me, how hard it is for me to lose . . ." His voice cracked and tears filled his eyes.

Stella's shoulders drooped with something like relief. "I'm sorry. I'm a callous idiot. I guess . . . you know, in the years since I danced, I've always had jobs where I'm sort of my own woman. I don't really remember what it's like to be part of something like this. I'm out of my element. I don't do all the games well."

"Neither do I, Stella." He wiped his eyes.

She reached out and squeezed his shoulder, and when he didn't move, she leaned in and hugged him.

Into his shoulder she said, "I was raised only by my mother, who led me to believe that men were either to be distrusted or manipulated . . . so, I'm not too good at this either."

He pulled out of the hug first. "Well that's something we have in common, Stella. I, too, was raised by a mother who thought men were good for little more than the contribution of DNA. It's forgotten already. Let me drive you home. Or you could stay here—in one of several guest rooms. I won't tell anyone."

Stella thought about going home, how she couldn't avoid the fact that Izzy knew about her father, and the questions that would ensue.

"You know, I think I would like to stay here, if it's not an imposition."

Julien shrugged. "Not at all. Oh, and Stella, I'm making a special trip to meet with a client who could be big for us down in Cambria for a really great gig at an expensive winery. I wonder if you'd consider going with me—you could be my demonstration, in essence. I feel like you're the only one I can trust to have her head about her on such short notice."

Stella felt pressure in her chest, the familiar panicky sense of having to choose between things. "Oh wow, Julien, I'm touched you'd ask me."

He frowned. "But . . .?"

"Is this one of those situations where you'll be mad at me that I have a family, a daughter? I really can't leave Izzy for a couple days right now—my mom doesn't seem like she's doing super well. What about Lina? She's level-headed, too."

He exhaled heavily, crossed his arms. "Lina and I get a little tired of each other's company, to tell you the truth. So there's nothing I can do to convince you?"

She shook her head. "I'm sorry. I understand if you don't want me to stay here."

He made a twisted smile, like he was about to say something sarcastic. "Of course you can stay. I never rescind an invitation."

In the room he pointed her to stood a massive four-poster bed mounded by a frilly white eyelet duvet and pillows. Nothing Stella had seen yet gave her a firm impression of Julien's style or taste. Everything about him seemed to be haphazardly poised or staged.

The room was otherwise nearly empty besides a chest of drawers and a lamp. She tiptoed to the closet and opened it. Two more blankets, a quilt made of American flags, a dull beige blanket like you might find in a hotel, and nothing more but a poster tacked up on the inside wall. She could barely make it out, and fumbled for a switch. When the bulb sprang on she jumped back. A mouth formed into a rictus leered back at her. It took her a moment to determine what she was seeing: it was a poster from the movie *Oh Mother*, starring forties silent-screen actress Faye Harlowe staring. Faye's dark-lipsticked mouth had been drawn over in crude sharpie so that she bore a clown's nightmarish grin, the eyes blacked out.

Stella shivered and shut the door. Clearly whoever had done this had mommy issues.

That night she dreamt that she was woven into a giant loom by Isis, who was actually Nemesis, one of the Furies and controllers of the Greek tapestry of life. When she woke with a start in the middle of the night and choked back a scream, Faye Harlowe's demonic smile loomed out at her in the darkness of her bedroom door, before she realized she was still dreaming.

22

IZZY SAT AT THE EDGE of her bed, her violin in her lap. The sky was still dark, but it was morning, and the house was lonely, the now familiar hollow strangeness of when her mother was not home. Stella hadn't come home last night. Izzy sat there, plucking the violin strings so lightly that it wouldn't wake Gigi, trying to decide if it was a good thing that her mother had stayed over at her dad's. That word sounded weird in her head. It couldn't be a bad thing, although her mom had spent other nights with another man, and nothing had come of that. But Dylan, he was different. She could tell, by the way her mom had flittered around the house getting ready, that she cared about the date, that it made her nervous. And if she'd figured out one thing about grownup women, it was that love and nervousness went together.

She was deep into imagining what her room would look like in their new house once her parents got married and moved in together when she heard the soft click of the front door opening and closing, and her mother's stealthy attempt to slip into the house unheard.

She met her in the hallway, her mother's hair a mess of purple tangles.

"Oh sheesh, babe, you scared me." Stella's hand went to her heart and she breathed heavily.

"You just got home?"

Her mom shook her head. "No, I mean, yes, but it's not—I didn't stay . . ."

Izzy tucked the violin under one arm and gave her mother a look she hoped conveyed that she didn't believe her. A rare wave of power washed over her at the way her mother looked stumped, caught, as though Izzy was the mother and Stella the child.

"I didn't stay with him. With Dylan. I stayed at Headquarters for my job, as we call the place where all the girls live."

"Why don't you live there, too?"

"Because I live here, with you and Gigi."

"So you had a bad time with him?" Izzy asked. "That's why you didn't stay?"

Her mom tossed her jacket onto the couch. Her mom's rumpled hair and smeared makeup said she had not showered yet that morning, but she smelled clean, like laundry detergent and perfume.

"Come here, let's sit down together and talk." Her mom opened her arms as though to guide Izzy to the couch.

Izzy stood where she was.

Her mom raised an eyebrow and then went and sat on the couch with a big exhale. Izzy legs were as heavy as tree trunks, and she didn't want to sit next to her mom and have all her dreams of a family crushed in one sentence.

Stella sighed again. "I know you arranged that meeting with Dylan."

Izzy felt her own eyebrow rise, and she shifted her violin to the other hand, since her grip was getting sweaty.

"I really wish you'd come over here and sit down where I can look at you. This is important."

Izzy looked around the cluttered living room, with its stacks of books and loose music pages and her own art projects posted up on the walls with no order, like they'd just been flung there to keep them off the floor. The gray couch looked tattered, the pillows shabby. The room felt suddenly small and dingy, and she had an urge to clear the books and clutter off the end tables and the top of the TV.

But her mother was looking at her with a tight-eyed, pinch-lipped expression she knew. It meant there would be a Serious Talk whether she liked it or not. The same one she'd had about Menstruation and Where Babies Come From and Not Talking to Strangers.

She shuffled over to the big puffy yellow chair that she'd once loved to fall asleep in as a little girl and flung herself into it, setting her violin on the footstool.

"What do you want to know about him? About Dylan."

Izzy bit her lower lip. Why was her mom making her ask it? Maybe she was wrong and Dylan wasn't her dad, and she had gotten her mother and this guy involved for no reason.

"Iz?"

"I don't know!" Izzy twanged her violin strings again.

"You'll wake Gigi," Stella chastised. "Well . . . okay, so I haven't been totally honest with you over the years. When I got pregnant, Dylan and I were both just accepted into a very prestigious dance company. We were nineteen years old . . ."

"Did you guys . . . were you in love?"

Stella blew air out heavily. "We were so young and we didn't have a lot of experience, but yeah. It was love."

"Okay, so, you loved each other but you loved dance more?"

Stella's eyes went glazy, as though she was focused on something very far away. "Dylan was, is, extremely talented. The kind of talent, well, like you. It's like it's just born in you, and classes and teachers can sculpt it, but ultimately your talent will carry you—it's got no choice but to come out. He was like that. I knew that he had a very, very important future in dance, that it was his destiny."

Izzy felt a froth of confusion. "I thought it was your, uh, destiny, too?"

"Me." Her mom folded her hands together as though cupping something wild that might escape between her palms. "In all honesty Iz, I'm not sure if I was ever that talented or if I was just driven to succeed. I mean, Gigi, well, she was one of the most renowned ballerinas in the country at one time. And everyone always told me that they saw her in me, that I was a mirror of her and her talent. I sort of ran with that for long enough that I believed it, too. And then I fell in love, and you came along."

"And you gave up on everything, I know."

Her mother bit her lip and leaned forward. "No, I didn't give up on everything. I gave my energy to you. I *chose* to do that. Lots of people tried to talk me out of it, actually, but I had this feeling. Honey, I had this feeling that Dylan and I had made someone very special, and that it was my greater destiny to bring that, to bring *you* into the world. That you were more important than my ambition. Maybe I already knew that success only lasts so long. It was a very complicated time in my life."

A warm feeling at her mother's words filled her, but something else, too. An achy, dark feeling.

"I don't know if I could ever give up playing the violin," Izzy said, a sensation like seasickness coming over her. "I think I might just want to curl up in a ball and never get up again."

Stella smiled. "You see, you're just proving me right. I *was* able to give up ballet. I'm not saying I never missed it, or that it wasn't hard, but I did it and was plenty able to get out of bed every day. And the reason is so that you could be here and make your otherworldly music. That's *your* purpose."

Her mother's eyes were moist and soft, and Izzy could tell she wanted to hug her, but she didn't feel it yet. There was something else.

"So Dylan is my dad."

Stella took several deep breaths, but finally nodded.

"But he wasn't willing to give up dance . . . for me?"

Stella bowed her head. "I never figured out how to tell him. He doesn't know."

She reared back as though her mom had slapped her against the cheek. "Why not? Were you ashamed?" She took up her violin against her chest as though it could protect her from the truth.

Stella's eyes were wide now, sharp and shiny. "No! Honey, you have to understand that I didn't have a lot of guidance through all of this. I just knew that if there were going to be sacrifices, that I was willing to be the one to make them, but I wasn't going to ask Dylan to do the same. The same way I don't want to have to make you sacrifice your talent. That's why I'm working so hard at this new job. I want to give you everything to make sure you have all the chances I didn't."

"But what if—" Izzy couldn't find the words. Tears were already pricking at her eyes, and this made her want to kick something at the same time. "What if he wanted to give it up, too? You never let him have a chance."

Her mom was crying now too. She nodded over and over, her brows creased. "I know."

"You didn't tell him last night either, did you?" Izzy asked. She could tell all of a sudden that nothing was changed, that her mom was still a liar and that she probably had no intention of telling him.

"Honey, how could I? What if he's angry? What if it means he doesn't . . ."

"Doesn't want to be my dad?" Izzy was shocked to hear how loud her voice had gotten.

"No, it's just I want to give it time, let him get to know me again before I spring it on him. Let me remind you that you are the one who made contact with him without my knowledge or permission."

"You are so selfish!" Izzy shouted. She knew by the way her mother's face went pale that she'd said something mean but she didn't feel like taking it back. She kicked the yellow footstool and inside her rose the heat and indignation that scared her, as if she might smash her new violin in the same way she'd done with the old one. But somehow she held it together long enough to stomp off to her room, where she slammed the door, set the violin down on her desk, and flung herself onto her bed, not caring if she woke Gigi.

23

STELLA CRINGED at the sound of her mother's wheelchair squeaking out of her room behind her. Her body was hot with emotion, her head pounding.

"I don't really feel like a lecture right now." Her hands muffled her voice.

Margaret put a hand on Stella's shoulder and she cringed away. "I'm not going to lecture you. I was just going to see if you're all right."

Stella looked up at her mother—Margaret looked flushed, sweaty. "Izzy set the whole thing up. Did you know that? She made some kind of page on Facebook and sent him a message and responded as me. She's ten years old and she's taking buses across town and figuring out her parentage. How the hell did she pull all that together?"

Margaret raised an eyebrow as though impressed. "I might have inadvertently pointed her in the right direction."

"What the hell, Mom? I thought we agreed you would never meddle. You understood my choice, you said."

"I did. I felt sorry for Izzy. Anyway, I didn't tell her who he was, the only thing I did was tell her the name of the dance company and that her father had been a dancer too."

Stella shook her head. "You might as well have told her his address. Thanks to the Internet age apparently anything is possible to find."

Margaret stared at Stella for a long moment. "I'm not sure I like the hair."

"Boy you really know how to pick your moments."

"I'm sorry, I just think it makes you look . . . like someone else."

"Like someone who's finally getting an identity back after ten years? She called me selfish. And that's the fucked-up part of motherhood, isn't it? All the days and nights I gave everything to her—went without sleep, breastfed her until my nipples bled, took two jobs to support all of us—she'll never see any of that, never appreciate it. She's going to hate me the rest of her life because I didn't tell her father about her. She's not going to appreciate that I chose to give her life."

Margaret's mouth slid into an amused smile.

"What?"

Margaret shook her head. "Believe it or not, I did all those things, too. But by the time you were old enough to notice, I was dancing full time. Gone."

"I'm not trying to say anything about your mothering right now. I'm a little preoccupied with my own."

"I know. You're different from Izzy, too. Why is it that you never cared to know about your father?" Her mother chewed her lip in a strangely self-conscious way.

Stella sat back against the too-soft couch cushion. "I guess I was too busy always longing for you."

Margaret slid her arms around Stella from behind the couch. "I know. And when you finally got me, I was this lame horse." Her mother squeezed her, much harder than usual. It made Stella wonder if her mother was feeling all right.

"So am I supposed to be interested now? Go hunting for my dear old dad?"

Margaret's lips twitched a little, and then she shrugged. "I couldn't tell you if I tried, Stella. Or rather, your guess would be as good as mine."

"It's okay, Mom. I'm happy imagining myself having popped out of your head like some goddess."

Margaret's face relaxed in such obvious relief Stella made a footnote that Margaret might actually be ashamed of her promiscuous behavior at the time she'd conceived Stella. "Tell me one thing, sweetie. Did you have a good time tonight?"

Stella tilted her head, relived the good parts of the night before the frivolity girls ruined things. "Yes. There's definitely still a spark. I want to see him again."

"Will you tell him?"

Stella looked toward her daughter's shut door with a sinking feeling. "I don't know. I want to protect her. And if he's not just one hundred percent delighted with the knowledge of her, what do I do with that?"

Margaret folded her robe tighter around her. "You don't breathe a word of it to her. But don't you think you better decide soon whether you're going to tell him? It's not fair to her for you to get more deeply involved with him if you don't know where he stands on the issue."

Stella chewed on the cuticle of her right thumb. That *would* be selfish, she thought, heart heavy.

24

STELLA ARRIVED to Headquarters feeling emotionally hung over. She decided on the drive in that she would take Julien's advice and not allow the girls to think she had been riled by their ridiculous Maneater performance.

All the doors of the house were flung open and clouds of dust were issuing forth from them. Bob Marley blared from its guts, and when she entered the yard, she found the dirt freshly tilled and Yvette and Chloe in grubby looking shirts and pants raking and digging.

"Spring cleaning?" Stella asked, standing with hand on hip.

Chloe looked up sharply, looked back down and then composed her face into her usual pleasant smile. "Oh, no. We're just all tired of living in a pit, so we decided to clean things up. Going to plant flowers, pretty it up around here."

"I thought we had a rehearsal now?"

Yvette shot Chloe a dark look. "Julien's gone away for a couple days. We're on hiatus."

Stella's vision tilted slight, dizzy with guilt. She should have gone with him to Cambria. Could have been fun, and probably would have made for some job security.

"What about Isis? Doesn't she take over in his absence?"

Again the girls exchanged knowing looks. "Ah, Christ, what's with the weighted glances. Either tell me or don't."

Chloe brushed dirt off her gloves and peeled them off her hands. "Isis doesn't tell us her schedule. She comes and goes as she pleases, and when the boss is away, so, often is the Queen of the Underworld."

"He's interviewing for a new gig, right? Down south a ways?"

Yvette muttered something under her breath and Chloe, trying to be subtle, but not succeeding, nudged her with a toe.

"Uh, is that what he told you? He's gone to deal with the shit-storm before it gets worse."

Confusion settled over her. "You mean Brooke?"

"You really are a persistent one, aren't you?" Lina's voice came from the open back door. She stood on the porch smoking a small white cigarette. When a wind brought the stink of the smoke to Stella's noise, she realized it was a joint.

"Let me see if I can close that case for you. Brooke. Drug addict. Suicide. Done. Any questions? Julien tells everyone a different story when he goes away. It's his attempt to stay mysterious, I think."

Now Stella was really confused. He'd asked her to go with him to Cambria. Did he really did trust her more than the others? Maybe he had actually told her the truth and lied to them. But why? "So, do I need to be here today or not? If not, I've got a ten-year-old who could really use her mother."

Lina raised an eyebrow. "I need help cleaning up and sorting the costume closet, and there are some toilets that need bleaching."

"Toilets?" Stella knew she sounded indignant, superior, but she couldn't help it.

"Yeah." Lina pursed her lips. "You're still getting paid. Are you too good for toilets?"

She sighed and walked up the steps of the porch. "Nope. Show me the way."

Lina laughed. "Nah, I'll put Aja on toilets. Come help me with the costumes. You can tell me what should stay and what we should donate to the Homeless Circus Freaks Foundation." Lina busted up into stoned peals of laughter.

Stella moved warily through the house, looking for signs of Lucy and Aja, who had been part of her public humiliation the night before. "Where's everyone else?"

"Grocery shopping," Ina said. "Gotta get the bitches out of the house sometimes or we will have bloodshed."

She grabbed Stella's hand and pulled her upstairs. Stella peered into the rooms they rarely used, noticed mismatched pieces of furniture—gingham couch next to a rattan chair in one room, with a wild Tiffany-style lamp. A mattress on the floor in another room next to an unassembled metal bed frame.

"What is with the furniture in the house? It's like someone upended a couple of Salvation Armies in here," Stella said.

Lina still had hold of her arm and dragged her into a large room full of standing clothes racks, all draped with costumes, many of which Stella had already worn herself. By daylight she realized that many of them were shabby and threadbare.

Lina inhaled again on her joint and offered it to Stella, who shook her head. "No, sorry. Makes me paranoid. The last time I got stoned, I spent the first fifteen minutes paranoid I'd be stoned all night, several hours communing with a moth on a lightbulb, and the last stretch collapsing into inertia."

Lina didn't laugh; instead her face had grown into a lank mask of seriousness. She dropped her voice to a whisper, "Listen to me, we only have a few minutes before the girls get back. I need your help, okay? We're in trouble."

"Who is?" Stella asked, her eye on the red ember of the joint that was burning perilously close to Lina's fingers.

"Julien, the company, all of us, really. Look, the theft incident at the mansion—this is not the first accusation. And Julien doesn't know who's doing it. The bitchier girls want to point the finger at Aja because she has a record, but I know her. She's not interested in going back to jail. She's got integrity."

Stella thought of the glee in Aja's eyes over the Maneater performance with some doubt, but nodded. "My bet is on Yvette, because she's got that poor-girl-deprivation mentality. But Brooke's parents tracked Julien down. You really have to shut the fuck up about her, okay? But since you know, and since I think you might be one of the few among us with an actual rational brain in her head, I'm telling you: it just looks bad for us."

"Why?" Stella asked. "If she was a drug addict, and there's no doubt that was a suicide . . ."

"Because," Lina yelped as the joint burned her fingers and dropped it on the carpet. Stella stomped it out. Lina's eyes were glazy. She turned suddenly and cleared an entire rack of sparkly bodysuits and tutus right onto the floor. "Her parents don't believe it was a suicide and they are going to hound us and make life difficult for Julien. And the cops are going to keep up with the investigation of the jewelry."

"So you think someone in the company did steal the jewelry?"

Lina shrugged. "I guess the thing is, I don't know that someone didn't, if that makes sense. I don't have a sense of ease about the situation."

Stella stared at the pile of clothes on the floor and back at Lina, whose hair was loose and wild. She was wearing a man's button-up white shirt and short black leggings, like some fifties Bohemian. She had none of her usual composure. Stella tried and failed to keep at bay the image of Brooke's unnaturally elegant body suspended in the air, heralded by a stream of dust. Nausea made a quick dart through her stomach. "Do they suspect Julien in Brooke's death?"

"She was pregnant." Lina sank onto the floor. "When she ran off she was almost twelve weeks. I was the only one who knew."

Stella remembered the way her eyes had been drawn to Brooke's slightly taut belly that day she bustled into the Sweet Sixteen party. "And the baby . . ."

"His."

"Julien's?"

Lina nodded.

Shock tore through her like she was made of paper. "You're positive? Do the police know, her parents? Couldn't Brooke have been lying?" All of Julien's protests that he didn't want to fuck her, that he couldn't live in the "house of wenches." Was he just another pigheaded man?

Lina shook her head. "She wasn't lying."

Stella sank to the floor next to Lina, picked up the squashed remains of a joint and unrolled its ashy contents into her hand.

"So is that why Julien's gone out of town? Doesn't that look more suspicious?"

Lina looked up at Stella suddenly as though she'd only just realized all that she'd said. "Oh god, no, he didn't run away from the cops. He went to grieve. He loved her. He's devastated."

Stella shook her head. She didn't understand Lina, who maybe was Julien's daughter, who defended or protected him in one breath and seemed ready to call him out on the other, who confided in a stranger and kept secrets from the girls she lived with every day. Stella didn't understand Julien, for that matter, who was half the time forbidding father figure/maestro and then tempestuous lover to a drug addict.

"I really wish you weren't stoned right now so you could explain all of this to me clearly. What I'm hearing are a lot of accusations," Stella said, flouncing the tulle of a pink skirt at her side. "But nobody appears to have pressed charges, and Julien hasn't been arrested. So what are you all worried about?"

Lina put her face into her hands and began to sob, her thin shoulders heaving. Stella put an arm around her and sat there, befuddled.

When she could finally talk, Lina pressed her wet face into Stella's neck, whispering into her ear. "I like it here. I like this town, I like these girls. I like how calm Julien is. I like you. Promise me that you won't let anyone drive you away. They're just idiot girls who don't know better. I need someone like you around, Stella."

Stella patted Lina's shoulder, prickling with anxiety. "Lina, I'm here. Everything is okay right now. I'm not going anywhere."

She nodded. "Right now. But for how long?"

Stella sighed and leaned into her friend. "Nobody knows that. Shit, even I don't know that. Do you know that in the decade since I became a mother all I've done is work and read? I don't even have any friends. I mean, there are acquaintances—other moms, the ones who don't read my hair color and clothing choice to mean I'm not in the Blonde Soccer Mom Club and shun me. This job is the first thing I've had in years that has made me remember what it's like to be something other than Izzy's mom."

Lina was staring at her when she looked back.

"What?"

"Well you have us now. We're your friends, even those of us who are petty little bitches from time to time. Julien means what he says about us being like a family."

"Okay." Stella patted Lina's knee. "So then, there's nothing to do until there's something to do. That's what I tell Izzy when she works herself up into some kind of a fret. There aren't any cops banging down our door. What really happened to Brooke will come out in time, and everyone can have their feelings about it. Right now, all we have to do is open those windows, crank up the music, and decide which of these outfits needs to go, like this one!" Stella pulled a hole-riddled blue body suit made of vinyl off a hanger. "What the hell was this even for?"

Lina giggled. "Some sort of blue-man routine, I think. Not one of our finer moments."

"So we're really just going to clean house today?"

Lina sighed. "No, it's really okay if you want to go be with your baby. We rarely get days off; might as well take it where you can."

Stella hugged Lina tighter. "Thanks." For a moment, the way Lina looked up at her from the ground with pitiful eyes, she was tempted to stay, but thoughts of Izzy had a greater pull.

Chloe and Yvette looked at her curiously on her way out.

"Must be nice." When Yvette whispered, you could hardly hear her accent. "To come and go as you like."

Stella was unsure how to reply for a moment, but then she thought of Yvette's smug little face during her Maneater routine and her response came freely. "Well last I checked it was a free country. No shackles on your arms, either."

Chloe raised a pale eyebrow and her cheeks colored in a way that Stella thought looked angry, but then she just shrugged. "See you on the flip side."

As Stella was getting into her car, Aja pulled past her, into the driveway and shot Stella a look so heavy with loathing Stella felt slapped. She sat for a moment in her car, weighing all the information. If it hadn't been for Lina's plea to stay, she had to ask herself if it was all worth it.

25

AT FIRST WHEN MARGARET stopped taking all the nerve dulling medications and reduced her Vicodin to a bare minimum in the hopes of waking up the old pleasure centers, she wasn't sure what she'd expected—would pain return in gentle waves, like those first tiny labor pains that are so small you tell yourself it can't possibly be the real thing since you can still walk and talk after all?

And it *had* been fine for the last couple weeks, nothing major, those electric impulses, those phantom stabs down the imagined pain pathways to her legs.

One minute she was sleeping and the next she was awake, twisted in iron clamps, with compressed nerves that had been lulled into complacency now proving that they did, in fact, remember their purpose—*to feel.* And yet the strangest thing of all was that with the pain, which felt as though her lower back and buttocks were being pressed against an electric fence, seemed to travel the full length of her legs to places that had long since lost sensation. Pain was mapping out the lost terrain of her legs in space again, if only temporarily. She knew it was a trick of the brain—that some people who truly lost limbs still experienced their presence long after they were gone—and it was the only thing that made the pain tolerable for a little while. In between pulses of agony she felt as though she could leap off the bed, push past the agony in her limbs to become a swan, a dying woman, a creature of fierce grace. It had always been a source of pride that she could bear so much pain and look beautiful doing it.

But grace and beauty weren't going to get her through the rest of the day, not when Izzy came home from school and wanted to chat about music or Stella came flouncing in to brag about the big show they had next; spectacles, she called them, which eased only slightly the feeling that Stella was somehow better than she had been. A spectacle was a circus show, a tawdry act, something to shock or surprise. Margaret had been a prima ballerina, a finely tuned machine.

And now there was this decision sitting like a knot at the base of her throat. To tell Stella what Max wanted her to say. And what would he do when the test came back negative? He would probably abandon all entreaties of love and pleasure. What would Stella do? She couldn't fathom finding the words to tell her daughter the truth.

The only thing she had left was an old bottle of Percoset that she'd saved for a just-in-case occasion. In truth, and it was rare that she even let herself think it, it was a bottle she'd saved in case it all became too much. A someday out in case she could no longer live in the wretched shell of her body.

Today it would help her *stay* in this wretched body. Getting herself into the wheelchair took nearly twenty minutes, in which the pain was sharp, as though a butcher's knife flayed the skin right off her body. And the pain wasn't consistent, not a nice steady throb or burning, but a series of hot, needle-like pulses all up and down her backside. She was drenched in sweat by the time her aching back side met the hard vinyl of the chair. And though her arms had always stayed strong as she'd insisted on a hand-controlled chair, they now felt inadequate to the task of pushing herself a mere few feet to the bathroom cabinet. Daylight so harsh and yellow, it stung her eyes.

By the time she rolled herself to the cabinet, her clothing was plastered to her skin, her heart racing. And of course, to add the most insult to all this injury, she could not open the bottle. It was an older prescription, the only bottle left in a now mostly empty row of spaces that should hold her medications. But she didn't feel regret yet. Pain meant you were alive, that you were not beaten. Still, she could dull it a little—and with a great wrenching, twisting motion that tore one of her thin fingernails down to the quick, beautifully red blood beading up at the corner of her thumb, the bottle flung open, scattering all over the bathroom, pinging off the tile in an almost musical manner. But there were exactly five left in her lap when all was said and done, and though it was a lot, five, it wasn't too much, not dangerously much, and it would do the job.

Margaret had no sense of how long had passed since she took the drugs, but with the sweet, sudden numbing of the pain came the urge to doze. She didn't even bother getting back into bed, just let her head loll where she was, slipping away.

She fell into something like a dream. There was her old house, a two-story apartment in Ocean Beach—just two blocks from the shore. But in this dream that didn't feel like a dream—the rust color of the house was too vivid; the pale blue swatch of sea so clear—the house floated just above the ground, in a little bank of clouds.

And she was walking—yes, walking—with purpose, on tired legs, but it was that good kind of tired where you have worked so hard and deserve the moment when you slump onto the soft couch with a glass of Cabernet to your lips. She'd put on Joni Mitchell or maybe Miles Davis and just go out.

The house seems to walk toward her as much as she moves its way—like the house wants her, wants something of her, which is ridiculous but also makes perfect sense. And she doesn't have to take the stairs two at a time, she is simply at the top. And there is no door to open, she is just inside. But Sarafina isn't with her baby girl as usual. Instead it's *him*, and he doesn't even look up from the *Grimm's Fairy Tales* he's reading her, her daughter's soft little toddler limbs tangled in a just-awakened-from-nap pile in his lap.

And she can entertain for a moment an illusion of his love for the child, for her, but when he looks up from the book at last, and plants a kiss on little Stella's forehead, his gaze is loaded and dark; there are creatures in the deep of those unusual eyes and she wants to wrench her daughter from his arms.

But Sarafina is there after all, dancing out of the kitchen with two glasses of wine, her eyes cages of terror at the sight of Margaret, home early.

There are barked, angry instructions to Sarafina, though her mouth does not move, and the girl collects up baby Stella in a rush and whisks her out in the stroller for a walk to the beach, and suddenly the ocean is in the room; the room is the ocean and it is broiling, a storm, and she plunges in, she flails her way through its salty madness to get to him, and when she reaches him, she slaps him, her flat palm making repeated contact with his soft skin. He's a shark, he's a merman, he's half fish and half human. She wants to hurt him, consume him. They are fighting, they are making love, angry and with gnashed teeth and nails and rage. She hates him, is what she realizes. She hates him for thinking he could possess her and then treating her so carelessly.

She calls him a starfucker and then he becomes a starfish, just a tiny weak orange thing, dried and desiccated on a blinding beach, and she is spent, bruised, aware that the last words she has said to him are: *she is not your child, you have no right to her, to us.* And the starfish blinks its eyes, and once again she sees the menace, knows he will not leave it at this. He will come again. He will take what he wants.

*   *   *

"Gigi, Gigi?"

Izzy's voice was very far away, but the yeasty, peanut butter scent of her was strong in Margaret's nostrils, and so she knew the girl was near. It took a great effort to pry open her eyes, and when she did, for a second it was like seeing Sarafina again, understudy, babysitter, with that red hair, those big bright eyes. But Izzy was just a child, and Sarafina was dead, and the dream with all its mad tragedy filled her with a feeling so bleak that she couldn't stop the tears, couldn't hide from Izzy.

"What's wrong, why are you crying? And bleeding? Did you hurt yourself?"

Margaret shook her head. She blinked like a newborn against the effects of the drugs, but caught a glimpse of herself in the mirror and saw her face, streaks of blood—she remembered tearing the fingernail.

"I'm okay," she said, though it wasn't entirely true. She could either live in dulled complacence, or in agony relieved only briefly, if it could be called relief.

"I just need to rest today."

She tried not to react to the way Izzy's whole face frowned, dragged downward, a gaze she remembered Stella making, a bitterness in accepting that the person you count on is useless to you, a helpless, worrisome heap of flesh.

26

STELLA'S GOOSEBUMPS competed in size with the rhinestones plastered to her body. Other than a sheer body suit, that was her entire costume. Albeit the rhinestones were strategically placed on a thin, nude mesh bodysuit, and she was one of five girls posing between white frosted Christmas trees, but she felt naked, and cold.

"They can't afford to heat this place?" she whispered to Lina, who stood beside her.

"Be a tree, Stella. You're an ornament, ornaments don't feel heat or cold," Lina whispered back with a sly grin.

"I don't know how you get used to this." She shivered. "If I catch pneumonia, it'll be your fault."

They were lined up against the back wall of an art gallery that was hosting a Christmas party and a show for a new artist, a photographer whose subject, as far as Stella could see—rearranged bones, organs and feathers of roadkill into everyday objects—was awfully grotesque for a Christmas party.

In contrast, the sparkly costumes were starkly optimistic. They were to strike a series of poses for the next hour, moving only every fifteen minutes—on Lina's command—in unison, so that they moved, as Isis said, "like the gears in a human clock." After that they would mingle through the crowd, choose a person to "shadow" and walk behind this person, mimicking their body language until the person grew annoyed or walked off.

Stella was fine holding the poses—Isis had modeled them after yoga poses so that they would be relatively easy to hold for lengths of time—but she didn't relish the idea of tagging along behind strangers who weren't in on it. Yet this was her job. It was better than listening to some overweight regular bitch about his food order, or have to find a polite way to cut off one of the drunker patrons at the end of a shift.

The hour of poses passed with agonizing slowness, and Stella had to breathe through a cramp in her hip at the end, but at last Lina gave the cue for them to mingle among the finely dressed people who had amassed. The young artist, who was thin and pale in a pretentiously staged sort of way, leaned in close to talk to an older woman in a leopard-print bustier and bright red lipstick that had feathered out above her top lip. Stella thought of rescuing him by mimicking the woman but then, taking a second look at his reconstituted images of death, she thought maybe he was thicker-skinned than he looked.

She settled upon a heavily gesticulating woman with long dark hair, dressed in a tight black dress slit up the thighs. The woman conducted orchestras with her hands, and Stella fell right in behind her, adding a balletic flair to her arms as she paralleled the woman. It took a moment for the woman to see why her conversational partner—a man with John Lennon glasses and a tweed jacket—was giggling and looking over her shoulder. When she flipped around, Stella froze in place and looked off to the right. The woman smirked and cocked her head at Stella. "Performance art, I like that." Stella raised an eyebrow but said nothing, and when the woman turned back around, she began her act again.

She tagged after several different people, and was in the process of lumbering slightly after an elderly man with a cane when a hand pressed against her lower back and she turned to find Jason, former boss and lover, smiling at her incredulously. He looked different in his dark blue suit, more mature, the pale blue of his shirt setting off his dark skin.

"Wow, I'm sort of surprised to see you here . . . like this."

She didn't like his tone, as though he'd turned up at a strip club and found her dancing on the pole.

She smiled. They were under strict orders not to talk to any of the patrons, but only to smile politely. She shrugged and raised her eyebrows.

"You look amazing." He stood close to her, familiar in his quick and easy touch and smile. "Doing well, I gather?"

She nodded and scanned the room of the rest of the girls to see if she was under any surveillance.

"Can't talk," she whispered between gritted teeth and pivoted away fast, making for the restrooms, where she knew she could hide out long enough to figure out how to avoid him.

But he followed after her. Just as she slipped through the partition, a curtain made of Christmas lights, his hand gripped her arm, and as she turned back to him to protest, his mouth was suddenly on hers.

He was so familiar, the bay rum smell and low heat feel of him, that she found herself kissing him back, and then letting him open the bathroom door and pull her inside. He groped her all over, looking for a zipper. "How do you get this thing open?" he said.

All manner of protests formed on her lips, but she was intoxicated by the act of having walked nearly naked through a crowd of admiring visitors. Lonely. And the remnants of anger she felt at Jason for having not stood up for her at her job boiled nicely into an erotic mix that made her feel like someone much bolder. She showed him how to slide the nearly second skin down around her shoulders, and peel the sheer fabric right down to nothing.

He made a murmur of appreciation once she was truly naked, as though he hadn't essentially been looking at her in the flesh just moments before, and she unbuckled him quickly. There was very little time for anything but a quick and intense rush of pleasure, her back pressed uncomfortably against the sink, one leg up around him.

When it was over she said, "Look the other way," and then cleaned herself up before pulling the bodysuit back on. Some of the adhesive rhinestones had moved slightly, and she had to reposition them.

"What kind of a job is this?" He squinted at her. "Hope you don't do that with all the guys."

She slapped his chest. "Jeez, what the hell do you think I am? I can't stay in here, I'll get in trouble. I'm on the clock."

He reached out for her. "But Stella, we need to catch up . . ."

"We can't do it here. Later."

But even as she said it she knew there wasn't going to be a later, that they'd used each other for something fleeting, and by the time she opened the bathroom door, she'd deflated, like she'd spent something she'd meant to save.

She barely made it through the curtain of lights when her arm was tugged on again, and when she turned to chastise Jason to leave her alone, she was mortified to find Julien frowning at her, her arm gripped in his hand.

"What the hell was that?"

Stella wrenched her arm away from him and stepped back through the curtain. Jason was still in the bathroom. "Excuse me, were you spying on me? I have a right to privacy."

Julien's eyes narrowed. "You're on the job. You have a right to do as I tell you and nothing more. You will not behave like that again. It's my job to ensure we have happy patrons, and if they find out my girls are in there fucking the guests . . ."

"He's my ex . . ." She couldn't exactly say boyfriend, but she figured she'd gotten the point across by the look of relief that crossed Julien's face.

"It doesn't matter if he's your paid sex slave—never again while you're at work."

Stella was torn between humiliation and rage that her most private actions had been monitored in some way. But she couldn't argue with him.

"Your lipstick needs reapplying." He handed her a tube.

She put it on and looked away as he fidgeted with the material at her shoulder. "You're better than this, Stella." His tone was disapproving, paternal.

She pursed her lips and stared at him coolly, unwilling to admit how badly she'd behaved.

Jason emerged from the bathroom then and stopped to stare at them as he passed. Stella shot him a look that meant to convey he should keep on walking. But his eyes fell on Julien's hand, which was once again proprietarily back on her arm.

"Are you—?"

"My employee isn't feeling well." Julien's tone claimed Stella. "Please return to the gallery."

Jason shot Stella one last confused look before shaking his head and hurrying past.

"I know you didn't use protection," Julien had glanced in the bathroom, into the waste basket where there would have been no evidence of any.

Stella shrugged off his arm. "For fuck's sake, Julien. I'm on the pill and we both had clean bills of health when we started sleeping together. And why am I even telling you this? Do I go back to work or are you going to fire me?"

Julien appraised her for a long moment, his furrowed brows and pursed lips finally relaxing. "Take fifteen, and then go back. Sometimes, Stella, I don't think you have any true appreciation for what you've been given."

Stella returned to the gallery torn by competing stabs of humiliation and indignation.

27

DYLAN'S NUMBER FLASHED on Stella's cell phone, and shame twisted up her throat. Why had she slept with Jason? There was something about a spectacle that created a heightened sense of reality, as though she were immune to consequences. But now in the dull light after the endorphins and adrenaline wore off, she felt foolish and trashy.

And the girls, like wolves, seemed to smell her weakness.

Aja's expression was a variation on a sneer each time she looked at Stella, who found herself in the awkward position every time of appearing to be staring at Aja just when she looked up. "What?" Aja finally spat out.

Stella shook her head. "Nothing." *I owe you nothing after you threw me to the cops, blamed me for Brooke's death, and have been a royal pain in my ass ever since.*

"When's Isis going to fucking get here?" Aja grumbled.

Lina rested her feet up on the chipped tile coffee table that had appeared mysteriously on its own since the last time Stella had been at Headquarters.

"She moves een mysterious ways," Yvette exaggerated her own accent and waved her hands in the air.

Chloe gnawed her cuticles ragged and the entire room had a charged, silent air of a legal proceeding about to begin.

As if in answer the front door slammed open, letting in welcome wisps of fresh air. The person was not Isis, for the footsteps were heavy and ponderous, yet Stella was surprised to see Julien enter the room, for he normally walked with a slow and calm gait.

"Lina, sit like a lady," he barked. Lina's head snapped up in surprise as she dropped her feet to the floor, cheeks flushing.

Julien ran his hand over his scalp several times, as if smoothing out his thoughts that collected just below his cropped hair. "Isis won't be coming tonight. We are on our own, ladies. And this one has to be full stops, because not only are we still rebuilding our reputation after the Ernestine fiasco—" he lasered in on Aja for a moment, as though accusing her, and her pretty face scrunched up on itself into a tight mask of indignation or hatred. Stella had the urge to put a soothing hand on her shoulder, but Aja would probably try to bite her fingers.

"—we are also becoming predictable. This town is too damn small."

"Ah, Jules, it's not that small," Lina piped up, eyes suddenly red and wide. Stella remembered her stoned panic attack, begging Stella not to leave, saying how much she liked this town.

All of Julien's customary charm and calm had eroded into this jittery man who paced the room, pawing at the skin of his face and neck, eyes darting back and forth.

"Is Isis coming back?" Chloe ventured, so quietly Stella barely heard her, though Julien's sharp ears missed nothing.

"When she damn well pleases!" he all but shouted. "Lina, you're going to have to work on the choreography. Here's the deal—it's a kind of wake, though the family isn't Irish, so no Gaelic poetry or folkloric crap. They don't do funerals: they celebrate the life, not dwell on the past—a sentiment I appreciate, frankly."

"A spectacle for a dead person?" Chloe said in a grim tone. "How are we supposed to sell that?"

Julien inhaled a harsh breath, the kind mothers take after they put the baby down so that it doesn't end up tossed out a window or locked in a closet. "The deceased was ninety, lived a full life—traveling, adventuring, even taking lovers in her later years. Her family wants a celebration of her life—they want to stun the party with joy, not grief."

Stella felt that wizard-behind-the-curtain pang of disappointment. Julien's tone was desperate and his body language distracted, as though he'd only just remembered that he ran a company of performers.

"I'm not good on the fly," Lina whined. Julien's nostrils actually flared as though he would paw the ground next and charge. He pulled himself up straight and stared at her with such hard focus the room seemed to tighten around them. Stella couldn't breathe, and for a moment she feared Julien was going to rush at Lina and slap her. "You're better than most," he said at last.

"I am, I mean, I could do it," Stella heard herself say then, her words coming out half-smothered in the breath she'd been holding.

"Of course," Aja muttered. "You can probably make money fly out your ass if you want."

"Yes, I can, actually," Stella said, standing up, feeling momentarily full with something like power. "So watch and learn." She waited a beat, expecting to hear some defense from either Lina or Julien, but she was on her own—they were both looking off into space, wild-eyed.

Aja scoffed but said nothing more, and Stella took it as a small victory.

Lina nodded a little too eagerly, a bobblehead on a dashboard. "Yes, great, Stella, that's great."

"Joyful death, it is." Now the panic swelled inside her, crowding out all feeling in her body until she was practically numb from the waist down. How the hell was she going to pull this off?

Aja shook her head. "Can't wait to see this shit." She plunked her big Doc Martens-clad feet up on the coffee table.

Julien, staring off out the window, didn't even seem to notice, for he simply mumbled something to himself and began to walk away. "Twenty-four hours till go time," he said. "And not a one of you leaves here until then."

"But my . . ." Stella began. Izzy's recital. Julien had promised she could go, but now it could mean the loss of her job. And since she'd been so stupidly casual with Jason she couldn't go slinking back for her old job. Her only hope was that she could distract the girls enough to sneak out for the second half.

*   *   *

Standing before the group of them, their eyes at suspicious tilt, chewing their lips or cuticles, Stella choked down the greasy roil of pre-show anxiety. Her tongue stuck to the top of her mouth as she opened it; her voice came out like a squeak at first. "So I have this idea that we could play with the idea of rebirth, reincarnation, even, in the spectacle. Since they're not religious I thought we could sort of give a nod to the whole Tibetan Book of the Dead sort of thing: souls leaving the body, entering the bardos, facing the light of truth, then reincarnating into a new body."

Aja snorted. "You're kidding, right? We have twenty-four, no, wait—" she looked at a chunky silver watch on her arm that resembled something Izzy would have gotten at the cheap boutique at the mall—"twenty-two hours till go time, and the same shit wardrobe as usual."

Chloe released the lower lip she'd been gnawing on. "Is this ensemble work or is someone going to be center stage?"

Stella shrugged. "I think it would be cool if we focused on one main player—to represent the dead woman—and then the rest of us could be supporting."

"Oh, thought for sure you'd want to be the star again," Aja said, wiry arms folded across her chest as usual.

Yvette raised a sculpted brow. "So who ees the dead woman?"

Stella gazed around at her motley company—Yvette, Chloe, and even Aja were all too young and nubile in one way or another; youth had a way of busting out the seams of even the hardest life. But Lina, she looked frazzled around the edges, the skin around her nose chafed and peeling, her eyes glazed and weary. Stella pointed at her. "Lina."

Lina's eyes shot up to meet Stella's with the surprise of someone who'd been awakened rudely from sleep. "Me? No, I'm not center stage material."

Aja nodded slightly though made no pretense of hiding it.

"You'll do great," Stella insisted. From what she'd seen so far, Lina, though not always the most creative or fluid in her movements, never forgot the choreography and could, with just a gesture, remind one of the others of a forgotten step and pull them into her orbit. She was natural glue, the kind of dancer no one remembers on her own, but without whom the company would fall to shambles.

Lina shook her head again, but none of the other girls made a move to offer themselves.

"Listen, ladies," Stella said, buzzy with impatience. "Every minute we spend talking about this, we waste more time, get closer to screwing up, pissing Julien off, and threatening our jobs."

There was a sudden shifting of limbs, necks elongating, focusing of eyes. It was the first time Stella really saw how much these girls needed this job—and direction.

"Lina's lead," Stella said forcefully, as though she really was in charge. She liked the zing of it, not being the bewildered new girl for a moment. "The rest of us are ensemble, and we're now going to get down to brass tacks."

Aja stood up, nodding as though she was, for once, on Stella's side, though of course Stella knew better than to hope for solidarity. "Yeah, ladies, no big deal, just figure out how to represent death and reincarnation in less than a day!"

Stella bit her lip. She was used to just letting Aja's nastiness roll over her, but tonight, when she was not only picking up the slack but the only one with any working idea, her self-control eroded.

"You can be in back," she said to Aja, who opened and then closed her mouth as though biting back an insult, and turned away with a brief sense of power, the way it felt to offer an appropriate punishment to a misbehaving toddler.

*   *   *

"Okay, let's break, catch some food, catnap, and then we'll reconvene in an hour," Stella said, frustration taking small nips of her flesh. Though she'd been only a girl herself last she'd danced in a company, she remembered the small, petty ways the dancers had poked at each other, undermined one another's talent, competition a parasite driving each of them to feed off the insecurities of others. And now, gathered among women once again, and these ones perhaps more damaged than any, she remembered why she hadn't been completely devastated to give it up when she found herself pregnant. Though she had missed the rush of praise, and the feeling of performance, there had been relief in taking up a life that didn't involve always trying to be better than everyone else.

Her only hope was to catch Izzy's solo at this stage. And all the while, Izzy had probably been scanning the crowd for her, eyebrows frowning, not putting her full effort into her playing.

She rushed out of Headquarters without a coat, to attract the least amount of attention. The night was moonless and grim, the world rendered a flat black series of silhouettes, like night in a child's diorama—hulking black shapes at every corner. The wind rushed in, loud and chill, and bit at all her uncovered edges, and she cursed herself for parking so far away, but she had needed to be able to get out on foot.

Heart beating the frantic message of impending failure, she could see her car, or its squat little outline, under a streetlight. As her right foot stepped forward, something tangled with her legs, and then a bright pain shot up the side of her hip, radiant in its intensity. It was another dazed moment before she thought to begin to defend herself against the now obviously human-shaped presence that was grasping at her. She batted the person away with wild hands, tried crawling backwards on the cement, which ripped at her tights and ground more agony into her bruised side.

"Stella!" Her name broke the fog of panic long enough to still her.

She looked up to find Lina, wild-haired and red-eyed, staring at her, mouth a twisted gash.

"What the hell, Lina? You scared me half to death."

"You can't leave, Stella. You just can't." Lina's voice was a rasp, harsh with tears that would follow.

"I'm just running to my daughter's goddamn violin solo—not even an hour! The other girls are napping and eating, okay, so what does it fucking matter?" Indignation had settled itself in all her bones.

Lina shook her head. "It's not just about you anymore, okay? Julien finds out you're gone and he will lose his shit."

Stella heaved herself to standing, brushing off particles of dirt, and winced at the tender feeling in her leg and hip. "I can't be Julien's keeper, all the time, Lina. I've got an actual child to take care of. Nothing is going to happen if I'm gone an hour. You can all deal with it."

Stella turned to get into her car, but Lina grasped her from behind like a mugger. "No, Stella, you don't get it."

Stella shrugged her off easily. "Fine, then make me get it!"

Lina stood, panting, looking every bit a crazy person. "All of this—the company, the great money you're making, the welfare of these fucked-up girls, hinges on Julien keeping his shit together. And that means that he doesn't have too many things on his plate to stress about. Isis disappearing and the Ernestine case following him . . . Brooke."

A sob emerged from Lina like a disembodied voice, ghostly. "Brooke. Fuck. Why does it always have to be like this?"

Stella checked her watch—she had ten minutes to make it for solo time and she was not going to waste it. She grabbed Lina's shoulders. "Be like what? Tell me now, or save it for later, but I'm going to my daughter's solo."

Lina's lip began to quiver then. "Your daughter is so lucky. To have a mother like you. I never knew mine. Died when I was too young to remember, and Julien—dragging me from place to place, calling himself Dad even though I knew he wasn't really. I mean, he's the only one I've ever known, but . . ."

Stella took a deep gulp of the cold air and squeezed hard on Lina's shoulders. "You'll tell me later, I'm going now."

Lina shook her head. "No, Stella, I'm afraid you can't."

Stella stifled a shout and opened her car door, but before she could even get the keys into the ignition, Lina had shoved something hard and cold just below her clavicle. It had the solid feeling of a gun but she was afraid to look down and confirm.

Rather than fear, what crystallized inside her was a cold feeling of resignation. Despite all her best efforts, she would fail Izzy, one way or another. It all came down to this: her one attempt to give back to herself had been just another selfish grasping at a temporary high. Izzy would suffer. She had already failed.

"You can put the gun away, Lina."

"I'm not going to put the gun away until we get back to Headquarters," Lina said.

And so they walked back in the now even colder wind, Stella's hip throbbing, walking like two people in a trust-exercise, one behind the other, except all Stella felt for Lina was a dull sense of dread.

They walked up the driveway to the house, which was lit cheerfully from within like some false advertising for a life insurance policy or a pill that would solve all your problems. Stella had never wanted to go back inside less than she did at that moment.

"This is all a big sham, isn't it?" Stella asked in a whisper.

Lina sighed. "Don't be ungrateful, you bitch," she said. Despite that her former friend was holding a gun on her now, this sudden change in tone made Stella feel as though she'd been slapped. "We have given you so much, and all you can think about is yourself."

"Did he kill Brooke?" She was emboldened by the fact that they were now back in a residential area with streetlights. She could make out Chloe in one of the windows.

Lina made a scoffing noise. "He should have," she said. "But she didn't need his help."

Stella began another question, but Lina jabbed the gun painfully between her shoulder blades. "You're going to go in. You don't answer any questions if they notice you were gone. You go change your tights, you act like you are in charge, like Isis would do, and then we go and do our spectacle. You can go home after that."

Stella had all kinds of other questions, like what if she went to the police about Lina's threats with a gun, or left the company, but a sudden terror spread wings inside her: Lina, through Julien, knew where she lived, where her daughter went to school, that her mother was paralyzed. She would have to make her moves very carefully from here on out.

"I'm on it, boss," she said instead, and took a step toward the house.

28

AS WAS HIS CUSTOM, Julien made himself scarce during their practice—as though he, too, wanted to be surprised by their show, and then reappeared at go time. He drove them in the big van that made Stella feel like a lobotomy patient taken out for a day of sun to a condo complex on the east side of town, all the homes one of three varying mute shades of beige or tan, the same hegemonic greenery sculpted in identical mini-lawns. Julien parked beside a big clubhouse that spilled out sparkly light, disgorged wandering children. The people Stella could see were all smiling—it didn't feel anything like a death, and she supposed there was something lovely about that, if not for the nauseous knot of anxiety stewing inside her.

And then there was the fact that that this was the kind of room in which people threw baby showers and potlucks—not a theater, not a stage.

They were all wearing two leotards—pink layered closest to the skin, and dark gray. The fabric dug into the flesh of her crotch, beneath her armpits, making her feel bound and sensitive. They carried soft scarves, each a different color. Julien led them around to a back door that led into a hallway that attached to the clubhouse, where the bathrooms were.

Lina would not look at her. She excused herself to get her makeup bag from the car, and Stella encouraged the rest of the girls into a circle around her.

"Remember to be light, ethereal, loose in your bodies out there. Even in the first part, in death, we're not in pain, we're not in agony, we're freed, we're shedding a body.

Aja looked up sharply at Stella then with an unusually open face, as though this thought terrified her. "That would be nice," she said, then shut up when Chloe grasped Aja and Yvette's hands, a starting ritual Stella rather liked.

"Shit, where's Lina?" Aja asked.

"She went to get her makeup," Stella said, her heart tapping out a Morse code of anxiety beneath her ribs.

"Yeah, like ten minutes ago. What the fuck?" Aja's eyes were wild.

"Don't freak," Stella said. *I am so far beyond freaking.* She spotted Julien in the other room glancing at his watch and then looking in her direction.

"I'm freaking—we have five minutes, and Julien is not copacetic with lateness," Aja said.

"It's true," Chloe said. "You do not want to see Julien give his timeliness spiel. There is yelling, and hand waving, and occasionally throwing things."

"I'll go find her," Stella sighed. *Oh, what I'd like to do with her when I find her,* she thought. She moved to exit the doors, but Aja grasped her by the waist. It was so much like the way Lina had accosted her earlier that she shoved Aja's hands off her.

"You don't leave either," Aja growled. "One down is bad enough. You don't fuck this up for us!"

The tattoos on her cheek seemed to writhe, and veins pulsed at her temples. "Fine," Stella said. "I'll take Lina's part."

"I'm sure you will."

"Well, somebody has to keep their shit together," Stella said, holding Aja's gaze. She had had her share of being pushed around.

Aja blinked fast but said nothing more.

And then Julien gave the "go time" thumbs up and Stella took the deepest breath she'd managed in hours, assumed the lead, and led the girls out like they were beads coiled on a perfect wire.

And it worked. It wasn't perfect, but the audience was comprised of grieving people—they watched with generosity in their hearts.

When it was over, Julien didn't let them linger. He hurried them out the door and into the van. His silence weighed pounds as they loaded up.

"What the fuck happened to Lina?" Aja asked, sullen in the backseat. The van smelled like sweat and rotting apples. Stella was shoved up against the window, with Chloe in the middle and Aja to the left. Yvette took shotgun.

"She let you down," he said grimly.

"Oh right, we're supposed to believe that shit?" Aja shouted.

"You have an alternate theory?" His voice was tight, strained.

Aja scoffed.

"No, please, go ahead." He slapped the steering wheel. "I'd love to hear what you really think." His driving was erratic, too fast in the residential area, too slow once he hit the freeway, glancing back at Aja in the rearview mirror.

"I think that some of your girls get afraid of you." Aja's voice quivered as though to prove her point.

Chloe reached over and patted Aja's knee. "Hush," she said softly.

"Are *you* afraid of me?" His eyes searched her out in the mirror.

"No." She sounded so much like a petulant child that Stella turned to look at Aja to be sure the words had come out of her.

"Doesn't sound that way to me." He swerved suddenly into the left lane, sending all three of them into each other, the hard point of their hips slamming together. Aja screamed. "Fuck, don't do that!"

"You think I would jeopardize the very people I rely on to work for me? People I might as well have found in gutters and alleys, whose lives were worth so little to them or the people around them that if you did happen to come to some kind of harm, you'd be lucky if anyone noticed?"

Aja made a strangled sound, and Stella was surprised to look over and see her crying—hard tears falling down her cheeks, tracing lines of pain in her powdered cheeks. Stella tried not to take his words personally; he was angry and he had a right to be. If he only knew how much. Her flesh had a sense memory of the cold gun metal pressed to it.

The final few minutes before arriving back at Headquuarters were full of a tension that had body, took the shape of the missing Lina. Stella could barely move, stiffened with rage at Lina's gun-toting behavior from earlier, and now crawling with fear that she'd done something stupid, crazy; guilt over Izzy, and a low buzzing sort of tension that drilled right inside her skull about whatever was going on between Julien and Aja.

Julien pulled the van into the parking lot and Aja all but threw herself out of the van and stalked toward the house. As Julien stepped out, his movements soft and boneless, exhausted, Aja suddenly turned and came at him, arms making blurred windmills in the weak night light. She was at him before any of them could stop it—screaming, "You're a fucking liar, you're a madman, I know it. Why don't you take me back to the shithole you found me in and leave me there, I was better off."

It took Stella and Chloe both to restrain her, but by the time they pulled her off Julien, his face lacerated with dripping red streaks where she'd sunk her nails into his pale cheeks, she wasn't fighting anymore. Chloe and Yvette dragged her dead weight into the house and Stella stood outside feeling as though the curtain had come down revealing the ugly bones, the false seams of what had once been a beautiful show.

Julien stood there, shoulders slumped forward, face drooping in the meager light that seeped out from Headquarters. The house itself looked more rundown and sad in the light—a metaphor, Stella thought.

"I don't know what to do," he said simply. Blood dripped down his cheek and onto the collar of his shirt. Stella couldn't help herself; she pulled her handkerchief from her handbag and leaned in to mop it up. He clutched her hand as it made contact and pulled her in so close she could smell garlic on his breath. "You don't think I'm a madman, do you?"

His tone was so nakedly wretched that Stella wasn't sure whether to walk away from the pitiful sight, or console him. The entire drive back from the spectacle she'd been thinking of only one thing: how to quit, how to escape this tangle of damaged people. No money, no flexibility—and really, that was mostly a joke—was worth this drama.

"No, Julien, I don't think you're a madman, but you've assembled this cast of unstable girls who are not handling recent events very well. It's a miracle I'm holding together at all, and from what I can tell, I'm the toughest of the bunch. Is there anything you want to tell me, Julien?"

His eyebrows softened into grief-stricken peaks. "Everyone I've loved has gone away, Stella. Eventually, they all go away."

Stella searched for words of comfort, but she was hesitant. "Lina will come back."

He gazed at her hard then, pressing her hand, which clutched the now crimson handkerchief, against his cheek like he would die if he released either. "You're so strong," he said, then. "So much stronger than any of us."

She flushed hot with embarrassment, his tone making her nervous. "Please. I just . . . I just want everyone to be happy. Nobody seems happy right now."

"I know." He nodded. "You're right. I haven't been taking care of my company the way it needs me to. I'm going to set things right, I promise. Oh Stella, you have no idea how glad I am you came to be with us. You're our rock right now, do you understand that? We'd be lost without you."

She kept her face as blank as possible. Words about quitting dissolved on her tongue. Should she tell him about Lina, or would that send him over the edge?

"Did Isis really leave or is she also just taking some sort of sabbatical?"

He sighed. "We're having artistic differences," he said. "But she'll be back. She always is. Lina, though . . . I haven't been good enough to her in a long time. For years she was my main priority. I think she gets jealous of the girls. I don't mean to let it happen . . ."

"Her mother died when she was young?" It came out a question when she meant to make it a bold statement, to assert that she knew something he had not revealed to her.

Julien released her hand, and the bloody handkerchief fluttered like a dying moth to the ground between them. Stella didn't dare move to pick it up.

"A terrible thing, to lose a mother so young." He shook his head. "I'm sure I was a paltry substitute."

Suddenly he slapped his face so hard it sent the blood from Aja's scratches splattering; the bloody spatter settled wetly on her own face but she was too afraid to wipe it away. "This is not right, not fucking right! I give these girls everything. They get their one week out of the month to behave like little witches, but the rest of the time, I've given them my life blood!"

Stella took an involuntary step back. He stared past her as though she wasn't there. "You know what it's like, Stella, you have a child—you give everything, and all you get back in return is whining and ingratitude!"

Stella opened her mouth, words sucked into a whirlwind of uncertainty. Suddenly the entire day and a half hit her like the end of a long training—her body felt as though it would collapse, a weighty, noodle-like thing, barely human. She staggered backwards onto the porch and sat because the other option would be to drop to the dirt. "I'm tired, Julien, really tired. I just need to get some sleep, okay?"

Julien's eyes were wide, wild, pupils dilated, his body tensed, hands jittering. Aja's scratches in his cheek were livid in the pale light, and it made him look half monstrous. He seemed to be panting as he stood there, and then, with one deep inhale, it all relaxed. His shoulders dropped, his head tilted, his mouth softened. He walked over, sat down next to Stella, and clapped a hand onto her shoulder, like they were old drinking buddies.

"You've earned some time off. Go spend a few days with your daughter. I think Isis will be back soon, and then we'll get back to work, whip these good-for-nothings into shape, eh?" He leaned into her like they were best friends, pals in cahoots, and Stella, terrified by the swiftness of his mood change, faked nonchalance.

"Absolutely." Suddenly she wanted nothing more than to clutch her daughter to her body like when she was a toddler, warm corners pressed against her, little heart beating a rhythm that always begged for protection. She wanted away from Julien's flimsy company and the paper people who lived half-lives under his spell.

She patted her knees, stood up as though this had been nothing more than a post-mortem of how a show had gone. "Three days sound good?" she said.

He nodded. From behind them, inside, came a muffled cry of indignation followed by Chloe's voice, loud and clear: "You're not coming out until you get your shit together."

Stella took a few steps away from Julien, in case the reminder of the drama would convince him to keep her there.

She nodded at him, kept walking away, and had nearly exited the parabola of light cast by the porch light when Julien called her name. "Stella," he said, his voice hard to read.

"Hmmm?" she lifted only her face into the light, already seeking with her body for the invisibility of darkness, as if she could become shadow and melt away.

"I trust you'll keep confidential anything you've seen or heard at any time in the company Headquarters or on the scene of a spectacle."

Saliva gathered at the back of her mouth, but she choked it down. "Of course, Julien. Of course I will."

He nodded, let her go, and she could barely keep herself from running the distance to her car. She stalked up on it when she found it, expecting to find Lina crouched in the backseat with her tiny weapon, but it was empty. Still, she flung herself into it and locked the doors with a nameless terror she couldn't shake off.

29

EVERY STEP TOWARD her own door was harder than the last. The lights were on inside, and though it was an hour past Izzy's bedtime, Stella knew she'd be up, Margaret stony-faced behind her, meting out judgment for her failures. Dread lodged itself just below her breastbone. She braced herself, inhaled, and inserted her key in the door.

They were seated together in front of the TV—her mom in her wheelchair, Izzy half-curled, like a cat startled awake, watching *Glee*. Izzy snapped her head up, leapt off the couch, and made for her room the moment she caught sight of Stella. The blue chenille blanket that had been on her lap caught on the edge of the coffee table, stretched between there and the couch like a burial shroud.

Izzy slammed her door, and Stella leaned into the wall of the hallway. She didn't think she could lift even one foot and go to her daughter's room to beg forgiveness, or walk to the couch where she wished to collapse. Her mother's face was unreadable—a blank mask, a momentary reprieve in casting blame, though it lurked there in the shadow. It must be nice, Stella thought, to be the perpetual victim of a tragedy one could use to always act superior, always claim to have the advantage of hindsight, lessons long since learned, since there were no more goals or dreams to strive for.

"I'd like to say I'm sorry, but then you'd just get to sit there and judge me and that would make me feel even shittier than I already do," Stella managed. She slid down the wall, pressed the ridge of the wall into the aching knobs of her vertebrae.

Margaret took a very big breath. She looked frazzled this evening—hair half out of a ponytail, a trace of mascara smudged beneath her eyes.

"Did you two go out afterwards?" Stella asked.

Margaret cocked her head and was quiet so long, Stella didn't know if she was going to answer her question or not. When she did, it was as though to a question Stella hadn't asked. "I missed it too, Stel. I fell asleep. Couldn't wake me." Margaret shook her head. "She's none too happy with us tonight."

Stella eased her head into her hands, trying to look just tired, not despairing, but it was too much. The weight of it all—Julien's arrogance and Lina's madness, Aja's hatred, a dead girl, the letdown of her prodigy child who would be lucky to keep playing at the rate her job prospects were going, and the reunion with Dylan—Stella was crying before she could stop herself.

Tears had never particularly moved Margaret before, and so she didn't expect much more than a sturdy pat on the back from her mother, a piece of advice to buck up, take a stiff drink. So she was more than surprised, even a little embarrassed, when the squeak of her mother's wheelchair wheels came closer.

Margaret's soft, dry hands were suddenly warm and light on her scalp, cradling it. When Stella raised her head, Margaret gasped. "Baby, there's blood on your face, what happened?"

Stella thought about how to explain Aja's attack on Julien, Julien's strange ranting. What came out of her mouth were sobs. "I'm in over my head," she managed.

"Oh honey," Margaret said, a cool hand smoothing Stella's curved back, which heaved with sobs. She wanted to stop so that Izzy didn't hear, so that Izzy didn't put away her anger—justified as it was—and come out asking questions, too.

"I just, I'm vulnerable because I missed it so much, because I love being on stage again. God, how did I forget about performers? Every one of them a mess in a totally different way. And my boss—he's like the perfect man one minute, charming, saying all the right platitudes about how great I am, and then he's tense and angry and the girls are freaking out." *Not to mention Lina behind the gun, the murdered girl, Isis the disappearing.* "Did I just make a huge mistake?"

Margaret made soft soothing noises, vaguely like coos and continued her steady stroking of Stella's back.

"When I was at the height of my career, Stel," Margaret said, "I made a mistake, too. I let a very charming fan of mine into my bed, and thus into my life. At first it was perfection . . . and then, over time it got, well, complicated."

Stella looked up through a cloud of tears. She'd never heard this story.

"When? How old was I?"

"You weren't." Margaret sat up, grimacing as she stretched her lower back. Stella's back went cold where her mother's hands had been. "He had a sister in the company at the time, Eileen, a brooding, moody one who was always arguing with the choreographers, but within the first year she dropped out. He'd come around when we practiced while Eileen was there, and then he was coming to all our shows and bringing me massive bouquets of flowers, perfume, custom jewelry, and ballet slippers. I was not immune."

Stella shook her head — perhaps this need to be adored was born in the womb, a bright emptiness that passed straight through her mother's body into her own.

"I'm sorry if this is too much information, but after a while he became strange when we made love. I don't mean to sound full of myself, but at the time, men I went out with wanted to gaze into my eyes and possess me, you know? But he, he didn't want to look into my eyes, he preferred to be behind me . . ." Margaret looked up hurriedly as though to see if Stella was cringing like some mortified teenager, but Stella was too fascinated by this bit of her mother's history to be embarrassed.

"What happened then?"

"I stopped seeing him, and in fact began seeing another man I didn't even care for in an obvious way, so that Max would get the hint. He showed up at a few of our practices wild-eyed and irate, stating that I was making a mistake. He sent me threatening letters. Then there were things I couldn't prove he did, but I knew it in my bones: found a knife in my car tire, a window broken at my apartment. Starting getting scared, so I had a particularly large and threatening male friend of mine have some words with him, and he finally disappeared . . . for a little while."

"You must have been so scared!"

"I was. I had a lot of good male friends who made sure I never walked anywhere at night alone, but when I found myself pregnant, he came sniffing back again, convinced you were his."

Stella's heart pounded madly in her chest, dizziness taking her over. She had always left this issue untouched—when she was a child it didn't matter; there was only Margaret, larger than life and so beautiful it almost seemed as though Stella had been spawned from her head like Zeus's daughter. She had sensed that to ask the question would upset her mother. Then, when Stella'd become pregnant with Izzy and had chosen not to tell Dylan, she'd locked her curiosity away in a kind of solidarity—two mothers holding the secret of their children's paternity, a silent pact. But now . . .

"So, was he?" Her stomach lurched at the thought that her father could have been some sociopath, some stalker.

"Of course not. All these years I've told you I don't know who your father is, but I do. I know who your father is, Stella. I also had my reasons for not telling you. Not telling anyone. He was a famous dancer. I was not stupid. I look at this fact now and I think, why did I keep it from you so long? Only because you were never interested, I guess. When you were younger, I was afraid that people would believe you were lying. Then later, that you would run your mouth . . ."

"Shit, Mom, who is it? What famous dancer?"

"The most famous male ballet dancer of the 21st century, my love. He let me call him Mik." In her reminiscence she looked a decade younger, the lines falling from her face, eyes bright. "My company went to New York that year, 1987, that you were conceived, to do a workshop with the New York Ballet—he was already a star, and he knew it. He has other children, though he wasn't married then, if he is now. I doubt he would even remember me. I did not even kid myself that it meant anything, that it would go anywhere. I knew what it was between us." Her mother leaned forward, conspiratorially. "I couldn't have planned it, but did I mind? I knew that our genes would make a child of such monstrous talent."

The breath that entered Stella's throat seared, an alternate reality playing out before her. "You're not telling me that my father is . . . Baryshnikov?"

Margaret's mouth curved up at the edges in a smile that bore the shape of a truth long clutched to one's self with the agony of never revealing it. A truth savored but never shared, and therefore, left to fester. "It was like an insult after that, when Max tried to insist you were his, called me a liar about Mik. I threatened a restraining order on Max. He violated it to tell me that he would change, he would make me happy and be a good father. But I knew he could do no such thing—he liked the good life too much; to have hours of leisure and women in his bed."

"And you never told . . . Mik? He never knew?"

Margaret pursed her lips, inhaled. "I suppose I could have forced him to accept paternity, but you don't *do* that to a man in his position, and it would have done nothing for me. I was twenty-six—my star days were soon to be on the wane anyway. I'd have wound up in the tabloids as one of those gold-diggers who just wanted his money, and you'd have grown up in that pall." Margaret clasped her long fingers together. When she talked at length they moved about, mothlike and fluttering as though they were still dancing, though the rest of her could not.

Stella sat there basking in the strange possibility that she might be indeed be the spawn of talent as spectacular as that. It wasn't implausible; her mother had been a ravishing beauty, whose talent would not have gone unnoticed.

"So what about this Max character?"

Margaret shook her head. "When I rejected him, he wooed another dancer, Sarafina, or just Sara . . ." and now pain entered her voice. "She was vulnerable; her lover had just died, and she was pregnant with his child—Max took up with her, helped her raise that baby for the first few years. She and I stopped being close, of course. I wouldn't have anything to do with him, and how could I tell her that I believed he got together with her just so that he could have access to me?"

Even to Stella it sounded like the kind of thing a diva would think. It was sometimes hard to remember this grand version of her mother who dashed about in a rush of perfumed wind, moving as though every step was practice for the next big show—nothing wasted, never slowing. Such a stark contrast to this withered woman bound to a wheelchair.

Stella strained her memory. "Sara was the one, with you wasn't she . . . in the accident?"

Margaret nodded so slightly it looked as though a strong wind had merely pushed her forward a notch.

"I didn't realize she'd had a child. What happened to that child?"

"Max adopted her."

"You've always claimed the brakes wouldn't work," Stella said. She could picture her mother and her friend, trying to have a cordial conversation in Sarafina's old car. The two friends who'd been torn apart by a man. Would Sara have known that a drive down that plunging hill, Divisadero, one of the steepest in San Francisco, would be her last?

"If you weren't friends, then why were you even in that car?"

Margaret looked suddenly up at the ceiling. Her face was flushed red and beads of sweat peppered her forehead. There was a sudden electricity in her body as though she might rise up out of her wheelchair and walk for the first time in decades. "She was desperate, wanted to leave Max. He was controlling and moody, and she knew she'd made a mistake. She figured he wouldn't suspect us of being in touch, since we'd fallen out. I was taking her to a friend's house where she was going to set up a little room for her and the child who was at daycare. And Stella, though I can never prove it, I have always felt in my bones that he was watching her all along. I think he knew what she was planning. And I think that he cut those brakes."

"Wasn't there an investigation?"

Margaret shook her head slowly. "Oh honey, the car was so totaled there wasn't enough left to work with. It was an old Volkswagen Beetle, and it would not have been uncommon for brakes to fail, much less on a hill like that. They had to use the Jaws of Life to pry me out." Her hands began to stroke her legs, as though the memories were lodged somewhere in their nerveless depths.

"And Sarafina?" Stella's voice was now a whisper.

Margaret looked away, pressed the flat of her palm to her mouth. "She wasn't wearing a seat belt. They found her . . . in pieces."

"Shit," Stella said. "Why are you telling me all of this tonight? We've had years!"

Margaret nodded, chewed at her lip. "Because I want you to make smarter decisions than I did. Because I fear . . ." she inhaled a strong breath that lifted her ribcage, revealing how thin and frail she was. "I fear that you are on the precipice of something bad, my dear girl, something that could change the course of everyone's life. I know you won't tell me what's really going on, and I know that most of it is not my business, but in the hours between, I am holding Izzy's hand, and wiping away her tears, promising her that this is just a temporary phase you are in, and that I don't know anything about her father." Margaret's voice was a whisper, but lethal, like a blade that makes no sound as it plunges into an organ.

Stella held back all the defensive vitriol she wanted to spew, the teenage rage, the weight of her uncertain paternity, mostly because she did not think she could manage the energy, and simply nodded, then heaved herself to her feet, which weighed a thousand pounds. When she made it to her room, she slung herself onto her bed, and fell into a sleep that was fathoms deep, just as dark, and full of slithering beasts that moved soundlessly through her mind, chasing her with teeth and scales.

30

IT WAS A COWARD'S WAY OUT, she knew, not to face him in person. And she had entertained the notion for a couple of days—what it would be like to live as a family, to have someone to talk to, to not be alone all the time? A male presence might ground them all.

He seemed to genuinely love her, and for these couple days she considered that how he'd behaved all those years ago had, in fact, been simply a case of love so strong it had made him irrational.

As with most things, the fantasy of him was better than the reality. He was as stubborn and hard-headed as Stella—she could picture fighting and the two of them ganging up on her.

And what about the worst-case scenario? If he insisted on taking the test, the truth was revealed, and he lost his temper? No. It made no sense. She'd had her good time.

Her head and face were flushed. Her extremities felt far away and cold as she dialed his number. She didn't expect to get him on the phone, but he answered. The tin-can sound of his voice told her he was in his car; she could make out the sound of the tires on road beneath him.

"Max, it's Margaret."

"Margie, lovely Margie."

"I've thought a good long time about your request. I don't think it's a good idea. Stella's not in a good place right now. There's a lot of complexity. I think we need more time. We need to wait." A heavy silence ensued.

"Max?"

"Margie, I've waited nearly three decades, I am done waiting. She'll hate you for keeping it from her, you know."

"Why are you like this, still, after all these years? Threatening and demanding. Why would you want something you had to take by force, Max?"

"Oh, that's rich, coming from you. He didn't want you, either. And I'll tell her everything. Reveal you for all your lies."

Her pulse was jumping all over the place at his words. She had a strange feeling of having slipped into a dream, the room around her seeming both too big and too small all at once. She smelled smoke.

"Margie? Margie?"

She thought her mouth was moving to tell him to fuck off, go to hell, that by the time he got to Stella it would already be too late—she already knew the truth about this man Max who called himself her father—but her lips didn't seem to be moving. She couldn't tell him anything. Something was happening to her that made no sense. This moment felt as though it was all taking place on a faraway stage and she was way at the back of an audience. She couldn't make her mouth work.

"Goddammit, Margie, do not go silent on me. I have every advantage over you!" He was shouting. She could all but picture the spittle flying.

31

STELLA WOKE AT SIX A.M., less than five hours of sleep under her belt, but all of them hard. She made herself black coffee and sat in the silence of the morning trying to keep the tendrils of panic sprouting inside her from overlapping—she finally did some yoga poses until seven, when she crept into Izzy's room. The child was asleep on her back, limbs spread in a wide scatter as though she'd been dancing in her dreams, a swath of hair clutched between her lips, sucked into a sleek tail, the only thing about her sleeping posture that harkened to her baby years. When she slept, Stella could envision the teenager in her daughter—the way she would charge through the world on her lithe legs as though she owned it and yet resented it all the same. Hopefully Izzy would channel her anger into her music, and not rebel boys with bottles of booze and promises of backseat heat. Maybe she would even write off the opposite gender, giving in to her muses, taking seriously a career opposite of the way Stella had so casually walked away from hers. It still alarmed her now how easy it had been to let go, as though all of those years of effort had meant nothing, had been some robotic impulse inside her to do as she was expected.

Stella sat beside her daughter's body—noticed one last time the edges of the woman encapsulated in the girl's body—and kissed her daughter's forehead, then gave her the butterfly kisses of eyelashes swept against cheeks until Izzy stirred and smiled and murmured something sweet before she rolled away from Stella and pulled her knees up into her chest.

"You and me, we're going out for breakfast together, alone. You don't have to stop being angry at me just yet, but you do need to get dressed, or else I'm going to carry you to the car in your pajamas with holes in them."

Stella rose and left Izzy alone.

Ten minutes later Izzy shuffled out in jeans and a black and white San Francisco Ballet T-shirt that Stella had never seen before.

"Where'd you get that?"

"Gigi gave it to me." Her words came out clenched, reluctant.

Stella looked at it more closely, saw the way it pilled at the armpits, stretched slightly at the neck where she habitually tugged all of her shirts free, but couldn't imagine her mother having ever worn such a shirt.

She didn't try to make small talk and had no plans to. Izzy sighed a lot, dragged her feet, but she came.

Stella took her straight to Buona Torta, where a pastry cost five dollars and they hand-brewed each cup of coffee. Izzy's eyes expanded as she saw the destination. Soft classical music trickled out onto the street, and amber light drifted down from yellow crystal chandeliers. The light scent of sweet milk overlaid the deeper note of chocolaty dark coffee and burnt sugar. Izzy visibly rose on tiptoe as though to capture more of the scent from above. She made such a gasp of such childlike awe at the pastries glistening in the glass case that Stella mentally patted herself on the back for this excursion. With children, she remembered, most of fixing your mistakes was to simply show up again, be present for them, take action. Something her own mother had never learned. And even though she could afford the éclair, hot chocolate, and cappuccino just fine now, she still had a pang of resistance to laying out the fifteen dollars for things they didn't need. It was clear that she could not keep this up. Ever since Lina had pulled that gun on her, the too-good-to-be-true bubble of her fantasy job had cracked open, revealing its bleak underside.

They sat at a table in the window nook that looked out on the bustling little boulevard of boutiques across from the ancient bank, a building whose Victorian accents and ornate moldings marked it as one of the town's architectural treasures.

Izzy's mouth was full, and thick white whipped cream curled over her top lip.

"I'm sorry I missed your recital."

Izzy dropped her eyes to her plate, refusing to look at her mother.

"I know that nothing I say is going to make you feel any better about it, but I want you to know that I was on my way to you. I was on my way to the car, and . . ." her throat closed up, she forced herself to swallow. Suddenly all she saw was Lina, crouched like a bogeyman by her car. "But my boss got really angry. And this job—" Again, the sides of her throat seemed to meet. She coughed down a sticky fluid. "This job is what keeps us afloat. Pays the bills and your violin."

Izzy sighed heavily and shoved in the last bite, a bit too big for her mouth, white cream forming a mustache.

"You can be mad at me. I'm going to try to make a bigger effort."

"You don't need to tell me to be mad at you, I already am." Izzy pulled her napkin into her hands, began to fold and refold it into ever smaller triangles.

"I know. Believe it or not, I remember being a kid. Being mad at my mom for very similar reasons."

Izzy chanced a glance at her but then quickly looked out to the street. Her hair was flyaway, little red tendrils like creeping vines all over her face. It made her think of Dylan. Of what she needed to do.

"I'm going to tell him, Iz."

Now Izzy's eyes snapped to hers, though her mouth and lips hung loosely from her cheeks, the telltale sign of tears hiding just below the surface.

"And I want you to know that you are loved beyond measure, and I will always be here for you, no matter what happens."

"If he doesn't want me, you mean. If he hates you for keeping it from him?"

Her daughter's harsh tone stung but she reached across the table anyway, grasped her daughter's sticky hands.

"Dylan is a good man. No matter what he feels, he will not be unkind to you, I know that in my heart."

A swell of emotion swept up inside her—a mixture of that momentary dread she always felt before going on stage, and the crumpling relief that followed when a performance was over. Stella sighed. Now that she'd made the promise aloud it seemed like a mistake. But she couldn't take this one back.

Izzy shrugged and sipped her hot chocolate, continuing her nonchalant act of looking very curious about the people on the street. Stella followed her gaze. Across the street at the bank, a woman emerged, looked both ways as though she was going to the cross the street, but then pulled her coat lapels up higher as though to hide her face. She had black hair, but something fizzed inside Stella and before she knew it, she stood up. "Stay here, Iz, I need to talk to that woman. I'll be right back!"

Stella darted out of the shop. The cool morning air slapped her—she'd left her jacket in the café but she wasn't going back; she spotted the woman rounding the corner onto Western and put everything she had into running after her, her unwarmed knees twanging in protest.

Two sharp beeps signaled the woman was unlocking a parked silver BMW just as Stella caught up to her, panting, and placed an arm, on the woman's shoulder. The woman screamed slightly and wheeled around. Despite the black hair and the dowdy jacket, she was looking into Isis's eyes, just as she'd thought. Eyes that were huge circles of . . . terror. Isis pressed back against her car as though Stella held a knife to her throat.

"What do you want?" Her words were all breath.

Stella shook her head. "What do I want? Where have you gone? What the hell is going on with Frivolity? With Julien?"

Isis's eyes softened a moment, her beautifully high cheekbones slack. "Oh Stella, it's all a house of cards. Don't you know that by now? I thought you'd have figured it out right away, that you'd see through it all."

"What do you mean? Please don't be cryptic. This is my livelihood, my daughter's future on the line here. I don't have another job. I need this one to work out." She was embarrassed at the desperation that strained her voice to a high pitch.

Isis looked both ways again. Stella chanced a look at what Isis held in her hands. A heavy-looking black purse.

"What's in there? Money? I saw you leaving the bank."

Isis clutched it tighter. "I can't be seen here, Stella. It's time to say goodbye. *Au revoir*, sweet girl. It was a pleasure to watch you dance."

Isis opened her car door and slid inside. Stella pushed herself between the door and the car. "Where are you going?"

Isis started the car, and her face hardened. "Get out of my way, Stella. You want to know what's going on? Go ask Julien about the messes he's made."

Isis started the car and with a quick and surprising shove, pushed Stella far enough away to close her door and then peeled away.

Stella stumbled and fell into the street. A passing young man stopped. "You okay, Miss?"

Stella stood up in a daze. What had just happened? And then she remembered she'd left Izzy in the café, and all the guilt flooded in. This was the real measure of her life—always running away, always leaving her daughter behind.

Izzy wasn't in the café when she got back. She knocked on the bathroom door, found it empty, and little bolts of panic danced up her spine. She bustled rudely past the line of patrons to the woman behind the cash register, who looked up at Stella with a pinched frown of annoyance, as if she were a homeless panhandler. "Did you see where the young girl went who was sitting at the window with me?"

The woman, her hair dyed the same shade of red that Stella once wore, lip encumbered by three silver hoop piercings, frowned. "She left crying."

Stella bolted out of the café and jogged a circle around the boulevard, nausea slowly rising up from the deepest part of her belly. What had she done?

But then, suddenly, there was her girl, walking toward her. Her eyes were red, and she held something out toward Stella.

"Oh god, there you are! I was scared to death." Stella grabbed Izzy into a bear hug. "I'm so sorry."

Izzy struggled out of her grasp, held Stella's own cell phone out to her—she'd left it in the café when she dashed off. "Gigi's doctor. He says she's had a stroke." Izzy began to cry even harder. Stella took the cell phone from her and put it to her ear. "Hello?"

But there was no one there.

32

MARGARET'S NEW DOCTOR was so young Stella couldn't stop staring at him in disbelief. He barely had enough facial hair to pull off the beard he wore, clearly only grown out to add some gravitas to the edges of his smooth skin, so free of wrinkles she wanted to run her hand across it as though it were a satin sheet. She'd been letting her mother go by the pick-up transport to her appointments—well, she'd had no choice—and it had been a good few months since she'd actually accompanied her. Shame lapped at her.

"Your mother has stopped taking several of her medications. We're not sure why. She's stopped taking the nerve medications, and she says even most of her pain medication. We're honestly not sure yet if this has anything to do with the stroke. It was a mild one, thankfully, and we don't yet know what level of function she may have lost, if any."

She looked at her mother's slack-jawed, still form, skin grayish, mouth in an open swoop with a feeling of sudden chill. "Is she in a . . . coma?"

Dr. Fields shook his head, and Stella had the urge to push his bangs off his forehead and straighten his collar, like a mother would. But of course, that would be offensive. "She's just asleep right now. Exhausted. We'll do some more tests in the morning, and we'd like to keep her until we can make sure she's stable, but we think she'll be able to go home soon. I've got this fact sheet on signs to look for in future attacks."

Stella couldn't swallow a moment. It wouldn't matter if there were signs; she was never there to see them. Guilt was like a heat lamp beating into the top of her head. Sweat trickled down her neck and suddenly, as though someone had turned up a stereo too loud, her heart's vibrations pulsed in her body. Her breath clustered in her throat trying to get out.

"I can't breathe," she choked out.

"Hang on, just look at me." Dr. Fields was now very alert, dark blue eyes on her with reassurance. "You're okay. Look at me. Deep breaths. In for two, out for two. Again." He talked her down from the ledge of her panic so efficiently she wanted to hug him and apologize for her thoughts that he was too young to know what he was doing.

When she felt like herself again, though her skin was clammy and her hands shook, he patted her shoulder. "Do you want me to prescribe you some Xanax?"

She shook her head. "I'm okay." As okay as a woman who had traded a stable enough job for a flimsy chance at stardom; okay like a woman whose inner eye was imprinted with the ghostly image of a dead dancer; as okay as a mother who kept failing her daughter at every turn. Whose own mother might have lost function.

She kissed her mother's forehead. Well, there was one thing she could do right: tell Dylan the truth, face up to her lies. Start there.

* * *

When he said hello on the other end of the phone she didn't give him a chance, just launched right in: "What would you say is the halfway point between us?"

He laughed. "Stella?"

"I'm thinking Sausalito maybe? I can be there in a half hour."

"You want to visit me?"

She was still slightly winded from her meltdown, which she thought made her voice sound husky, sexy. "Yes."

"I'll come to you, Stella. You've got . . . more responsibilities than me."

Though her house was empty of people—Izzy at her friend Lily's house and her mother here in the hospital, there would be signs of her daughter everywhere, maybe a bit too in-your-face for it all. "Would you find it offensive if we met at a hotel?"

He was silent a moment. "Oh, wow. Well," he said at last.

"I'm sorry. Too much too soon?"

"Not at all. Tell me the hotel. I'll be there in the hour."

* * *

Stella loved La Lune, a little jewel of an inn that overlooked the river, with its Spartan but classic French taste. She'd only ever passed its pale red façade, neatly trimmed garden courtyard with awning, imagining the day when someone might surprise her with an intimate night out. Julien had told her in her first week at work that all Frivolity employees got a discount on rooms; it was his favorite place for entertaining relatives or out of town friends.

You could sip a cocktail and watch the lit boats at night. Only this was afternoon, and Stella felt, well, *skeezy* was the word that came to mind, sitting there waiting in the burgundy leather recliner near the bar for Dylan to arrive. She didn't want him to meet her at the room, first. This was not just a tryst, this was a moment that could never be unmarked, that would change everything for Dylan, and possibly for her and Izzy. Even if the only change was that the words were finally spoken.

Under normal circumstances she'd never have a drink in the afternoon, but she didn't know that she could face Dylan entirely sober. So she ordered a glass of cool Chardonnay and drank it too fast, so that by the time he strode in, wearing a pale blue checkered shirt and dark blue jeans, all which offset the copper of his hair and the searching certainty of his green eyes, her inhibitions had dropped like a morning robe.

His smile was full, and he took her hand in his as he slid into the leather seat next to her. "Got it all sorted with the boss man?"

She laughed, an embarrassing honking sound. "I don't know that I'd call it sorted. Turns out it wasn't him behind that little performance when we went on our date. The girls were hazing me."

"A date, was it?" He raised an eyebrow, his expression all cheek.

"I treated you badly." She squeezed his fingers. His hands were warm against her perpetually cool ones.

"I wouldn't go so far as badly. I mean, ye didn't slap or otherwise physically injure me. Maybe treated me 'inconsequentially' is more like it."

A sigh heaved out of her chest. "I'm really sorry, Dylan. I'm glad you came today. It means a lot to me."

"Stella Russo—can we just give up this bullshit talk of bits and bobs . . ." His eyes lasered in on her. Oh god, he knew why she'd called! He'd figured it out about Izzy and now she'd just have to spit it out like she was talking about a sports score.

"I'm not going to pretend to be gentlemanly any longer. I want to carry ye upstairs and toss ye down on the bed and have at ye."

A giggle escaped, but she clapped her hand to her mouth. As a young man he'd been slightly timid, not quite a virgin, but almost, always waiting for the cue that she was in the mood—which had been several times a day when they were able.

There wasn't even a final sip of wine to toss back, so she stood, buzzing with the adrenaline of anticipation, such a stark contrast to the bumblebee anxiety that had riddled her in the hospital. He slung an arm around her waist and leaned in and inhaled her neck with a slight groan. Under other circumstances she'd have been embarrassed by the public display, but it felt so long overdue. More than that, longing for his touch, that powderlike scent of him, came like a grip to the throat, all teeth and lustful fury so potent she wanted to throw him down into the burgundy chair right there at the table.

Aside from what she assumed was a palpable, almost crackling lust rising off of them like cartoon heat lines, they walked without touching like business associates down the hall to the elevator. There was an elderly couple inside when it opened, so they hung their heads and looked away from each other as they rose six floors, though she could feel his body speaking, nerves sending electrical information via pheromones in every nerve receptor on her body.

Her hand shook slightly as she inserted the flat key card for the room. He pressed in behind her and inhaled her hair. The room was quaint—some sort of peach and yellow roses theme; for a beat guilt stamped on her desire, as though a place this sweet deserved to be stayed in by a couple with a certain future, one that would wake up in the morning and notice its fine little details, the designs of the furniture, the paint colors, the dapple of light on certain corners.

Dylan pushed the door closed with his foot behind him and reached for her, pulling him hard against his chest. His heart thumped so fast she wondered if he was more nervous than he appeared. Long slender fingers slid up her shirt and pulled it off her, taking with it the ponytail holder that held her hair in a little bun atop her head, and hair spilled around her, bringing the fresh scent of shampoo, its dense wetness on her shoulders almost too cold. He kissed her neck, then her shoulder, pulled the corner of her bra strap with his teeth, while he unhooked it with his hands and before her mind caught up to his actions, he took her nipple in his mouth. She flew away on the raw shock of pleasure, how hot his tongue felt on her skin, her senses sharpening into relief as pleasure cut through the haze of wine.

The rest of their clothes came off so quickly she didn't recall the act of it, just that suddenly they were naked, panting, pressed skin to skin. And there was something startling about the fact that she wasn't looking at an eighteen-year-old's body any longer. His chest was more barrel-shaped, with the thinnest layer of belly fat, nothing like a gut but not quite the chiseled tableau of their youth. And there were scars—one across his chest that almost looked like he'd been stabbed, and the ones at his knees from the surgeries. She'd forgotten his legs and arms were freckled. And what must *he* see? She was in shape and perhaps a little more muscled from all the dancing, but there were certain things that changed with age no matter what. She was miles away from that taut girl's dancing body. She didn't give him time to inspect her body too closely. "Toss me on the bed, already."

He smiled and raised an eyebrow. "Well, actually with the bad knees, could ye do this lad a favor and hoist yourself. I promise I'll make it up to ye."

She laughed as she sat back up on the bed, pulled him by the waist toward her, whispered about being on birth control and then, their eyes trained on one another, guided him—not that he needed help—into her with a gasp.

His entry into her body opened up sudden memories, the way he'd leave a sprig of mint or lavender on her pillow; how he'd suddenly look straight at her in the middle of a rehearsal, his eyes sending a message that could have gotten them in trouble, could have also thrown her off her form. She remembered the day her shaking hand held the pregnancy test beneath her legs and prayed that it was the vigorous nature of dance and her low calorie intake that delayed her period. She remembered the day she spent crying when she realized, her mother bent over her with cold eyes, that she wanted his baby, but that it wasn't fair to make him have to choose. He was too young. She and her mom were moving anyway, to a place they could afford, out of the expensive big city.

When she hit the ledge of climax, taking him with her, she realized that she was crying.

Dylan furrowed his brows, collapsed against her throat. "I have t'admit that wasn't the response I hoped to elicit."

She laughed lightly. "You didn't. Not in the way you think."

He wiped the line of tears down one cheek and cradled up to the side of her. He traced a hand down her arm. She rolled onto her back. "I'm sorry; I didn't realize how emotional I'd feel about this."

"Eh, it's good. It means ye care about me still."

She put her hand over her eyes and he ran his fingers up and down her torso, tickling her. "You used to do that to me to help me fall asleep."

"Aye."

"You were such a sweetheart."

"It makes a man wonder how ye could give him up." He smirked and ran his hand up and down himself as though he were a prize on display. "But I know y'were going through . . . tough things." His hand stopped short on her belly and he went silent.

"Oh Stella . . ." His voice was something lower than a whisper, heavy.

She realized what he must be seeing there. The thin, silvery fissures that showed up only when you looked closely, those battle scars of what her body had been though.

"Ye've had a child, haven't ye?"

She had the stomach-dropping sensation of the downward slope of the roller coaster. She peered between her fingers at him, barely able to swallow, and nodded.

"So that wee redhead at my show . . . not your niece?"

She shook her head, which felt like a neutron star, dense and impossible to lift.

He sat up straight, withdrew his hand. "About ten years old, ye said?" He sighed, shook his head, as though he was trying to find the right fit for the pieces of information in his brain.

Stella's chest felt full of crawling, slithering things. She scooted back up against the head board and crossed her arms against her nakedness.

He glanced at her sharply. "So your mental breakdown . . ."

"Well, it was real in its own right. I was conflicted to the point of hysteria."

"Ye didn't think I might relish a choice in the matter, accept some responsibility?" His accent was suddenly pronounced, his r's rolling more than usual.

Here it was. This had to happen, his hurt. She couldn't soften it but she wished she could. "I thought you were a brilliant dancer on his way to a brilliant career . . ."

"As were ye!" His eyes narrowed to slits.

"I was very confused."

"Ye've had ten, no eleven years, to decide how you feel. And ye didn't even set up that meeting with me in the first place. Your mum did!"

"Actually, Izzy did." Her voice quaked. "She found you all on her own."

He dragged his hands down his cheeks and scooted to the edge of the bed, hung his head and grew very quiet.

"Ye could have told me this before we made love. Given me one less complex set of feelings to work through."

She felt glued to her spot on the bed, limbs heavy. "I know. I could have done so many things differently. I could have kept at dancing and never had Izzy, who is so very brilliant, a gem."

"Fucking hell, Stella! My daughter?"

She rushed past the tone in his voice. "I think she has a real shot at a professional career as a violinist. She's that good." Stella wasn't sure why she was telling him this, a last-minute sales pitch perhaps, to clinch some sort of interest in his heart. "She's afraid you'll want nothing to do with her now. She's mad at me that I haven't told you sooner."

"As she has every right to be."

He slid off the bed and pulled on his pants. "Where is she now?"

"Staying the night at her friend's house. My mother's in the hospital, had a minor stroke . . ."

Dylan focused in on her then with empathy in his green eyes. His hands dropped to his sides. "I'm sorry about yer mum. But I don't know what I'm supposed to do right now. Or feel."

She hugged herself tighter. "Me neither. But would you consent to meeting Izzy for real, getting to know her a little?"

He was silent a long time, then, when he spoke, it seemed rhetorical. "What the hell will we talk about?"

Stella said nothing, exhaling a shaky breath.

33

THE WEATHER WAS unseasonably warm for a November day. Stella and Izzy both put on short-sleeved shirts—Stella pulled on a black Ramones T-shirt with the arms cut out, and khaki cargo pants. Izzy had not escaped the American-girl hunger for a wardrobe of mostly pink, but that was the only criterion, and so she happily went with one that held an image of Joan Jett rocking her guitar that Stella had found in a secondhand store.

Stella practiced the lecture she would give, about how she'd finally told Dylan, short and sweet, and that he'd been the one to suggest this meeting. She practiced it in the shower and while getting dressed and over breakfast, but each time she tried to say it to Izzy something caught in her throat. Instead all she managed to say was, "We're going to have a picnic in the park with a friend of mine." It was a cop-out and stupid, but there it was.

Izzy brought her violin, though she was quiet and sullen the whole time. They walked to the park where Stella used to dance at night. In the daylight her sacred grove of trees looked like some sort of burned-out campsite, with beer cans and cigarette butts littering the ground.

"I made cucumber sandwiches," Stella said in a hopeful voice.

"Is it that crappy cream cheese from Walgreens?"

"What? No. This is the whipped kind you like." Stella pulled out a blanket that had once been tucked around baby Izzy in her crib, a threadbare blue with red kitties. She flapped it open and laid it on the ground and pulled out their food, wrapped hastily in plastic wrap. Izzy traced one of the kitties with her finger.

"Is it fun to dance?" she asked suddenly, extracting a green grape from its tangle and popping it into her mouth.

Stella smiled. "Yes. Sometimes it's also hard work, but it's mostly fun."

"Can I see you dance sometime?"

Another question she couldn't honestly answer. If there was even a company left to dance with. Stella shrugged. "I'll have to figure out when that's possible. Our shows are mostly private, and sort of spur-of-the-moment."

"Oh." Izzy looked down at her sandwich and picked some of the cucumbers off of it. "What about now?"

Stella laughed. "You want me to dance now, here?"

Izzy nodded. "I've never really seen you."

"I don't have any music."

"I could play."

Stella cocked her head and looked at the violin case. "I don't usually dance to classical, but what the heck . . ."

Izzy's lips turned up in a begrudging smile.

"But I might stop if anyone comes, okay? I'm not really in a big audience kind of mood."

Izzy broke out her violin, which gleamed richly in the warm afternoon light, and Stella stood up, stretching out her joints. And then Izzy launched into music that was so sweet and full of life that it seemed even the birds grew quiet to listen.

It wasn't a tune that Stella recognized, but it moved like ballet, and though Stella was neither dressed for it, nor in any kind of shape to do so, she tried to pull some grace out of herself and dance ballet.

They hadn't done any ballet at Frivolity, and it felt a little bit like learning to ride a bike, something that had at one point been so intrinsic she didn't have to think about it. Ballet was about moving in clean lines and sweeping grace and commanding one's body while making it look effortless, and Stella was sweating within minutes. But it was easier when she thought of Dylan, remembered the way she'd felt the first time they danced together, even before they were lovers, when his body seemed to understand hers, anticipate her movements.

All of a sudden a man was standing behind Izzy, whose eyes were half-lidded with the concentration of her music. Stella stopped abruptly and moved toward her daughter in one swift motion, grabbing her by the sleeve, and flinging the child behind her.

"Sorry to interrupt your picnic, Ma'am," he said. He was dressed in a black business suit, with shiny black shoes. His dark hair was cropped short and his sunglasses were mirrored. He looked like a CIA agent.

Stella stared at him expectantly.

"Well, I'm wondering if you know this man?" He pulled a photograph out of his pocket and handed it to her.

The photo was of Julien, but with dark hair rather than the silvery gray he had now, and an odd little goatee. It was hard to tell if his age was much different due to the darker hair.

"Who are you?" she asked.

"I've got a serious interest in the whereabouts of this man. I'm uh, investigating a case. A case you might know something about. A woman was found murdered . . ."

Sharp pain shot through her knees—the image of Brooke spinning in the dim light of the basement filled her with nausea. "You're a detective? Show me a badge."

She glanced behind her and whispered to Izzy, "Pack up your violin." Izzy did exactly as she was told.

"Private investigation, Ma'am. I just want some information . . ."

Stella nodded. "Well I'm sorry but I don't know that man or what you're talking about."

The man put a finger to his lips as though to keep himself from saying something he'd regret. "Maybe you just need to take a closer look?" He stepped toward her and his jacket flapped open revealing the black butt of a gun tucked into his waistband. Not holstered like a man of the law, but tucked there, as an afterthought. Stella turned to Izzy, grabbed her arm and shouted, "Run!" pulling her daughter along, whimpering. Terror ran in spikes up her spine. The man didn't seem to realize what was happening for a beat, but he was soon on their heels shouting something Stella was too panic-driven to hear. Stella knew they only had to get about a block before they'd hit businesses teeming with people, but she was already tired from dancing, and Izzy's gangly long legs made her a clumsy runner.

They ran hard, though, and Stella didn't turn back to find out how close the man was to them, or if he was there at all. By the time her breath was bursting in her lungs they'd rounded onto Mahoney Street and Stella made for the first open business she could find, which was a dry cleaners.'

When she looked back, the man was not in sight, but this didn't make her feel any safer. A startled looking young woman stood behind the counter.

"Can I please use your phone?" she asked.

The woman froze in her spot a moment, but then she produced a cell phone and handed it over. Stella had been expecting the clunky business phone—did people still have those?

Stella pulled her wallet out of her back pocket. She'd long ago eschewed carrying a purse, and was now especially grateful for that. Dylan's card was tucked in between her automobile club card and her repeat customer coffee card.

She dialed and got his voicemail.

Panting slightly, she explained that she needed to change their location. She suggested the deli up the street and apologized for any inconvenience.

She hit end and handed the phone back to the woman behind the counter.

"Mama, what's going on?" Izzy finally spoke. "Who'd you call? We left all our stuff back at the park."

"Don't worry about our stuff—"

"But my baby blanket."

"Well, honey, hopefully it will still be there, but right now we're going to go and get lunch at the deli and wait."

"Wait for what? Who was that man chasing us?"

Stella shook her head. "I don't know, but I'm not taking our chances walking home."

The deli was full of people, to Stella's relief.

Ten minutes later the door burst open with a rush of air and Dylan's copper hair peeked out from under a hip-looking gray cap. He looked tall and lean in his dark jeans and black sweater. He smiled and then frowned at the sight of her and rushed over to their table.

"Hi! Are y'okay? You sounded weird." He smiled at Izzy and put out his hand. "Dylan. You must be Izzy."

Izzy shot her mother a dark look, bit her lip, but then nodded, and Stella felt herself exhale.

"What's going on? Your message was so strange."

Stella nodded. "I know. We were just—we were followed from the park."

"Chased, you mean," Izzy muttered.

"Chased?" Dylan frowned and set his cap on the table. "Were ye hurt?"

"No, he didn't touch us, but—" She leaned in toward him and whispered, "He was holding a gun." She glanced at Izzy to see if she'd heard, but she was busy fiddling with her violin case. "I was afraid he might follow us."

Dylan nodded, though he was frowning, and he kept glancing at Izzy in a way that made Stella anxious.

"Can you describe him?"

"He looked like one of those guys that guards the President," Izzy piped in.

"Like a Secret Service agent?" Dylan's brow furrowed exceptionally deeply.

"He was well-dressed and he was looking for someone . . ." Stella cleared her throat, definitely not ready to tell Dylan that the person in question was her boss, who happened to be 'out of town' and possibly linked to a murdered girl and a stolen piece of jewelry, who had a gun-toting daughter who denied his paternity, and whose choreographer had just bolted out of town with a bag full of money and dark murmurings.

Dylan tapped a finger to the indentation above his top lip. "Well, would ye girls like to come back to my hotel room for a while, watch some TV? Stel, you could call the cops and file a report. That way ye don't have to go home, and maybe the cops could even drive you there, or meet ye."

Stella nodded. "Yeah, that would be good. You up for it, Iz?"

Izzy's expression of annoyance when she looked at Stella melted into a wide-eyed version of adoration when she glanced at Dylan and nodded.

"Okay," Dylan clapped his hands together. "We go, then."

34

IZZY SET HER VIOLIN down on a floral couch in Dylan's hotel room, a feeling churning in her sort of like jumping on the trampoline after eating too much ice cream. She and her dad (she let herself dare to use the word) and her mom were all in the same room. Warmth filled her.

"I see ye play an instrument." Dylan pointed to her violin.

"She's incredibly talented," her mother crowed, and Izzy felt her cheeks heat up.

"Would you like to play something?" he asked.

Izzy shook her head. "Not right now, thank you."

Stella frowned. "Maybe later, though; it would be nice if he could hear you play." Stella shot her a weighted glance that made Izzy feel hot and fuzzy inside.

Then her parents—her parents!—started to talk about what had happened at the park, and Izzy walked over and turned on the television because she didn't want to think about the weird man with his sunglasses and his tone of voice, the way she'd been sure for a minute that he was going to pull a gun out of his suit jacket like she'd seen on those cop shows and shoot her mom right there in front of her.

She found SpongeBob, which was too young and stupid for her, but was probably the only cartoon on. Her mom got on the phone soon after, and Dylan came over again and sat down next to her on the bed. She knew it was sort of rude, but she stared at his face from beneath her hair. All her life she'd been told she didn't look much like her mom. Stella had a rounder face, fuller lips, and dark eyes, and her hair color was always changing, but Izzy knew it had never been the kind of red as her own, as Dylan's—like holding a brand new penny up to the light. Not really red, but copper. It made her feel funny to notice things in his face that she recognized in her own—to fill in the puzzle and realize that she did look like somebody in her family after all.

"Ye two must be close, being sort of each other's only family for so long?"

"We've had Gigi—my grandmother, too." She clutched her violin case tighter against her lap.

"Of course, who could forget Gigi. Three generations of lasses."

She loved the lilt of his voice, being called a *lass*.

Izzy raised an eyebrow.

"Do ye play other instruments besides the violin?"

Izzy shrugged. "I can play the cello and bass a little. But I love the violin most."

"Why is that, do ye think?"

Izzy shifted uncomfortably on the edge of the bed where they sat. Nobody had ever asked her this kind of question. "I don't know. It just . . . fits me."

"It feels right, ye mean? Like 'twas made for you?"

She smiled and nodded. His expression was warm and kind. Dylan smiled at her, then looked over at Stella with a long stare she'd seen adults make when they were figuring something out.

"Would you believe that my mum and grandmum played, too, only we called it a fiddle?" He closed his eyes a moment, like he was remembering the sound. "I grew up hearing its music all my life. Perhaps it's why I danced, which is not one of the more manly arts, though that could have been to piss off my da."

Izzy felt herself blush. "Most of the kids at my school want to play the saxophone or the drums."

"Ah yes, the power instruments. But I love the strings myself. I got to touch a Stradivarius once. Divine experience, that was. Twanged its strings inexpertly and it still sounded like the songs of angels."

"Really?"

He nodded. ""Twas a spiritual experience, the sound on that beauty. Have y'ever heard one played? A revelation!"

Izzy loved the way his accent rolled up and down. "Only on a record that Gigi got me once. It's not the same as in-person."

"No, it's not," he said. "Do ye know that the violin is an incredibly difficult instrument to master? It's not everyone has the touch for it."

Izzy felt herself blush, and was afraid to look at him because she knew her cheeks were bright red. And she was afraid to open her mouth again for fear the truth would all come rushing out and she'd make a terrible impression and her mom would hate her and Dylan would run away. But her mom got off the phone then and she breathed a sigh of relief. "Cops say I have to go down to the station to file the report formally, though they made me give my whole spiel over the phone."

Her mother's dark eyes darted between Izzy and Dylan with a sudden look of concern. Izzy tried to communicate with her expression that she hadn't said anything she shouldn't have.

"Want me to drive ye there?" he asked. His voice became more formal suddenly.

Stella picked up on it too, because she pulled her arms in against her chest and her jaw did that little clenching thing that happened when she was upset. "Um, yeah, if you don't mind."

"Does Izzy need to be dropped off . . . with her, um, Gigi?"

Izzy saw her mom's face redden. "Oh, well . . . actually my mom is still in the hospital. Iz, do you think you could go to Lily's house for a bit?"

"She can stay with me," Dylan said, running his hands along his knees. "It's no trouble."

Izzy's chest felt like it was going to cave in from all the tension in the room. She could feel her mom wanting to spill it, and a kind of question in Dylan's voice, but nobody was talking about the thing—the fact that Izzy was their child, their creation. She wanted to cry and laugh at the same time.

"Only if you're sure?"

Izzy tried not to explode with joy, but her chest felt sharp and bright, like when she played a song without any mistakes.

"Well, come on then, Mistress Izzy," Dylan said genially.

"Isadora." She suddenly wanted to appear serious and mature in his eyes.

Her mother's face flushed even redder.

"Isadora," he repeated, raising an eyebrow. "I really hope I get the chance to hear ye play that violin soon, Isadora."

Stella came forward and pushed Izzy toward the door.

"Yes, me too."

They rode the elevator down in silence and walked back to the parking lot where Dylan's silver Prius was parked. He cried out "bloody hell" in a strange voice, which confused Izzy, until she saw that someone had smashed the back windshield in, and glass was scattered everywhere. As Dylan unlocked his car and peered inside to see if anything had been stolen, Izzy felt a hand clamp over her mouth from behind, and watched with an urge to throw up as a man wearing a black ski mask grabbed hold of her mother, and another one took some kind of a stick and brought it down on top of Dylan's—her father's—head. The scream choked too far down in her throat to come out.

35

UNLIKE THE MOVIES, where kidnapped victims got a nice needle of sedative to the throat and simply woke up several hours later, Stella was wide awake and uncomfortably shoved down on the floor of a vehicle. She hadn't been able to scream, but she'd gotten several good kicks to somebody's shins in before they'd grabbed her legs and tied them together, as well as her arms. Her shoulder was numb and her neck kinked. The floor smelled like dirt and shoes that had been worn to shreds.

She kept every bit of her focus on the image of Dylan in her mind. Responsible Dylan, who was now in charge of his own daughter. Who knew what he'd do with Izzy, what he'd know how to do. But she tried to hold in mind the girl who rode a bus across town, who was far more independent than she wanted to accept. Izzy would probably instruct Dylan on what to do.

The ride felt like hours—she couldn't tell through her haze of shock—and eventually her bladder, which was precariously squished against her knees anyway, made its presence nearly unbearable. "I have to pee," she managed. She hadn't spoken more than a handful of words after their response was to jab what felt like a gun in her side. "I'll pee on the floor if you don't stop."

There was a sigh from the front seat. "Almost there anyway," said a rough male voice.

She took deep breaths and squeezed her thighs together, praying she wouldn't piss herself, when not a few minutes later they made a sharp right turn, drove down what sounded like a gravel driveway, and the car came to an unceremonious stop. The doors opened and she was half yanked, half-shoved out of the car, then lifted to an awkwardly standing position.

Her feet were untied and the blindfold was removed from her eyes, but her hands were left as they were, and the men, still in their ski masks, began to march her toward what looked like a tangled woods.

"Where am I?" she asked, even though she doubted any serious answer would be forthcoming.

They walked her up to a wooden shed no bigger than a broom closet, and one of them freed her hands. "Go, piss, come out. We got guns, you can't go anywhere. Understand?"

She nodded and went inside the putrid-smelling door to find a crude outhouse crawling with ants and beetles. She barely squatted over the open stinkhole and peed quickly, wondering if there was any way she could use its piles of excrement to get away from these guys. But then, shit wasn't known to be an effective defense against bullets in any part of history that she could think of, and so she resigned herself to finding out who had brought her there and why.

She was marched into the copse of trees, and her knees began to feel a little weak as the light was blotted out by the heavy canopy of oaks and pines.

Just far enough into the woods to be completely out of sight from any road, stood an unassuming red-shingled house, not in terrible shape, but in need of a new roof and a good paint job. Its graying trim must once have been white, and the remnants of a vegetable garden wilted out front, most of it gone to seed.

She suspected that whoever was in there was the same person who'd sent the man to the park looking for Julien. Which meant, she decided, that they knew about Brooke. And now she wished Lina hadn't told her anything so she could honestly stare into the face of whatever criminal awaited there and tell him that she didn't know a thing.

The men behind her shoved her toward the bottom step. "Inside," one of them said, pointing the way with his handgun.

Stella scanned the area around her, but both men quickly moved to either side of her and one cocked his weapon at her. "Up you go."

Stella walked with stiff knees. The old bones of the porch groaned beneath her. The open front door led to a sunroom, where a bunch of shoes—boots, tennis shoes, men's from their sizes—lay cast off in a corner. An empty bowl of dog food butted up against the other wall beneath a tall fern. The sunroom led to a kitchen, not entirely unlike the one at Headquarters, and the smell of fresh coffee and cigarette smoke drew her in cautiously.

She entered the kitchen to find a man seated in a chair with his back to her. He wore a white T-shirt, khaki pants that were mud-spattered at the bottom, and a black baseball cap. He held a cigarette in one hand; on the table was a large French press pot of coffee. She heard the thud of her captors' feet pounding down the porch and away, the screech of tires as the car took off.

Stella cleared her throat, heart pounding high in her throat.

Without turning around the man made a flicking gesture with his fingers, signaling her to come and sit across from him.

When she did, taking in the details of the kitchen, she saw that other than the table and chairs there were no decorations or cutting board, no half-eaten loaf of bread or bowl of apples. It was as though nobody had used the kitchen in years before this day.

She was rendered almost completely speechless when she plopped down in a rickety wooden chair across from Julien.

"Stella," he said softly. His face looked more aged than just a few days before, and dark circles ringed his pale eyes.

"What. The. Fuck?" she said. "You couldn't just invite me over for a nice conversation? You had to kidnap me in front of my child?"

Julien's eyes grew wide. "You were on the line for a murder, Stella—I'm rescuing you."

"Rescuing me? Ha!" Stella's laugh was so sharp it hurt her throat. "That man in the park was no fucking detective. That's a bullshit story if ever I heard one. What the hell is going on?"

Julien flipped the hat off his head and rubbed a hand through his hair, exhaling a cloud of cigarette smoke.

"Frivolity Inc. is not my only business. I've had a number of them over the years, and some of these businesses haven't done as well as I had hoped. Entertainment is subject to the whims of the economy. People don't always have the cash to shell out for what I can offer."

He crushed the end of his cigarette out on the table and immediately lit another. "You want one?" He held the pack of Marlboros out to her, then he withdrew it almost immediately. "That's right, you don't smoke."

"How do you know that? I do on occasion. And if there was ever an occasion to smoke it's now." Stella grasped a cigarette and pulled it out, and Julien lit it with a tarnished lighter. The smoke felt harsh and foreign curling into her lungs, but she didn't cough it up, and in a moment the buzz energized her, made her sure she could find a quick and simple way out of this.

"Okay, so you have some failed businesses. Did you piss off the wrong people? Owe some money to someone other than the bank?"

Julien picked something off his lip and stared at Stella. "Has anyone every told you how much you look like your mother?"

Stella reared back slightly. "Why can't you answer a straight question?"

His slight smile was the kind she'd seen men make just after sex, as though reliving the orgasm. "Your mother was a star. Who doesn't know about her? Or didn't, at the time? Before American fucking Idol and Dancing with the Stars, people went to the ballet, to the theater. To the true places of worship, where true artists performed true magic. Your mother is one of the reasons I started Frivolity—I saw her dance *Swan Lake* and that was it. I knew I could never run a theater or be in 'the business,'—" He made air quotes around the words and stood up, that manic gleam in his eye that she'd seen on Spectacle nights. "I knew I wanted to promote performing art, to support the kind of talent that Hollywood was already capitalizing on back in the seventies, and which now our banal media culture has stripped away to the bone, made absurd."

Stella leaned toward the entryway to see if she could make out the masked gunmen who'd led them there, but all she saw were the washing machines in the sunroom.

"Julien, you're talking all kinds of pretty words but you're not telling me the most important thing. My little girl is . . ."

"With her father, I believe?"

Stella dropped her cigarette on the table, and grabbed it back up quickly, putting it out with a pinch of her fingers. She pushed away from the table and stood up with an explosive urge to kick him out of his chair. He had arranged all of this. "Why was any of that necessary?"

Julien sighed and leaned against the sink. "What can I say? I love a good show. But Dylan and Isadora deserve a chance to get to know each other without your interference. Instead, you're here, where you can be of much greater use . . . to me."

For a moment Stella could not feel her legs, as though they'd turned to stone beneath her. Her breath rode hard in her lungs. She was looking into the eyes of a lunatic!

"I slept in your *house*. You could have done whatever you wanted to me that night. Why wait? Why orchestrate this?"

Julien turned the faucet on, but no water came out. "I loved this house," he said in a melancholy voice, as though he hadn't heard a word she said. "We came here a lot in the early days, had raucous sex. She decorated it—she was into that Frank Lloyd Wright kind of Americana, so masculine for such a feminine beauty."

He turned to look at her. Her breath was coming out in short gasps. There wasn't going to be anywhere to run, and if the empty look of the kitchen told her anything, there were no knives in those drawers. She'd have to keep him talking until she could figure out a solution. "Who? Brooke? So you screwed her, knocked her up, and then what? Did she fall in love with someone else? Did she refuse to give up her addiction for you?"

Julien's brows furrowed and he suddenly focused back in on her. "Brooke? Brooke was a child. I didn't touch her. I never touch any of my girls. She was like a . . ."

He turned quickly toward her, his body tensing. "Lina's jealous of you, Stella, that's why she told you those things. She's angry at me, and she wants to see it all fall apart. She'd be happy if I were in jail. She'd tell anyone anything to get me in trouble."

Stella almost laughed at his bald-faced lies. "You're full of shit. She told me that she *didn't* want things to fall apart, that she was happy where she is, where the company is. Why would she want to sabotage you?"

"Because. I *have* to move!" He stood up fast. "Ernestine is going to make life impossible for me if I stay. He's convinced we stole some ancient jewelry that night at the Spectacle and he's too powerful for me to do anything about it. I'm just a visionary with a dream, Stella. A dream you have to admit you are just as taken with."

The edge of the door frame suddenly pressed against Stella's spine. She hadn't realized she'd been backing away from him until then.

"Where are you going?" He stood up, his eyes narrowed to slits. "I'm trying to talk to you. I've been trying to talk to you for months but you won't listen."

"You're a narcissist, you know that? Nobody exists but you— we're all just puppets in your little mental theater!" She quickly wondered why she was antagonizing him.

His face creased, as though with injury. "No, I care about you. That's why I hired you. I don't think there's any other way I could have gotten close to you. Your mother certainly hasn't been any help." He looked close to tears, and his whole body seemed to droop, though his hands reached out, beseeching her.

Stella found her legs acting without the knowledge of her mind, and suddenly she'd backed into the next room, a living room by the sight of an empty, blackened fireplace, though there was no furniture, and raced for the back of the house, knowing there had to be a back door in a house this size.

She passed through another empty, denlike room, and turned a corner, the only sound her own blood pumping in her veins. She found her way easily to the back of the house, a tiled hallway, and the back door.

She skidded to a stop and tried the knob, but it was locked. Without much thought she reared back and kicked her foot right through the glass top half of the door, vaguely aware of jagged edges penetrating her skin, but she didn't stop to investigate. She unfastened the lock and raced out onto the back porch straight into what looked like just a patch of muddy grass at first glance but turned out to be a murky pond with gooey mud and thick, reedy plants that groped at her like some swamp creature trying to pull her into its depths.

She began to cry as she treaded water, and before long, Julien appeared in the doorway.

"Come on out, Stella. Don't be silly." She struggled a little, just to prove that she wasn't helpless and wasn't coming willingly.

"Stella, honey, why are you struggling so hard away from the truth?"

"What truth?" Her words were wrapped in sobs. "If you brought me here to rape and kill me, then just do it already! "I should have known this was too good to be true from the day you came stalking me in the woods at night." When she tried to wipe her nose, she left a trail of stinky mud across her face.

Julien sat down at the edge of the pond and took her muddy hand in his, pulling her out of the swamp. "Tell me something, do you ever wonder how your life might have turned out differently if your mother hadn't been so busy all the time? If you had two parents and a normal life?"

Stella laughed. Her emotions were so tangled inside her she wasn't even sure if she was afraid of him anymore. "Honestly, no. That life was all I knew. I hated her for being gone, but I loved the stage and the theater, too, from an early age."

"I know," he said. "And I wanted to share that with you."

"Well, you have. The job has been great. Why does it have to get all weird now?"

"Because I have to leave town, and I knew that you wouldn't come away with me easily. Or at all."

"What does it matter if I come with you? You say you're not in love with me but . . ."

"Stella, your mother never gave me the chance. She denied me from the moment she became pregnant, even though I knew whose bed she had been in primarily. And I didn't have any money or resources in those days. You didn't go get a paternity test in the mail like you do now."

Stella began to shiver involuntarily, the wet of the pond coupled with Julien's words feeling like some unique form of torture.

"You can't be my . . ."

"I've been following you, your career, your life, since you were born, Stella. But she wouldn't let me close, kept me just at arm's length, your mother. Diva bitch. You call me a narcissist? *She* wanted full control of you and your life . . ."

"Why? If you're telling me the truth, then why? What did you do to her that would make her want to keep you away?"

He shook his head sadly. "I wanted her to make time for us. Put me before ballet."

Stella heard herself laugh, a chortle of disbelief. "You spin a good story. I can almost believe it. But you told me that Lina was your daughter, too, and she denied it to my face."

Julien's pale cheeks went blazing hot. "She'd deny the sky is blue if she had to."

"So what, you just left a trail of women and children behind in your dubious career of failed businesses?"

"No," he said, his voice now sounding sharp and tight. "Only you and Lina."

"And Lina's mother?"

"I told you . . . she died."

"When? How? Or is that another big mystery?"

He shook his head. "In the same accident that killed your mother's dancing career. I'm not proud of my actions, Stella. I slept with Sarafina to get back at Margaret. Your mother was a cold, cold woman. Lina's the only one of the lot of you that I still have to show for those years."

Stella turned slowly and looked at him, at his feline eyes and angular face. She'd never seen anything familiar in him before, never felt a kinship or familiarity, not the way that she could see Izzy in Dylan with just a glance. But Lina, with her hair the same color as Izzy's—she'd always assumed that red hair came from Dylan, though she'd heard that redheads had to have the gene on both sides of her family. Her mother's hair had been dyed blonde all her life, and the old photos of Margaret were all in black and white. What if?

"No." Stella stood up. "If, and I say this very skeptically, *if* you're telling the truth, you're my father in biology only. I don't love you. This whole time, in fact, I've been sure you wanted to sleep with me. It's too convenient. And anyway, what does it matter? You couldn't have written me a nice letter or something? You had to kidnap me at gunpoint?"

"I needed it to seem like something had happened to you, Stella. I didn't want anyone in law enforcement to think you were involved in any of the nasty stuff that's following me. And I knew you wouldn't come on your own. So yes, I needed to do this. And if it allows your daughter and her father a chance to get to know one another as we never got to, all the better."

Stella shook her head, brushed now drying mud off her cheek. "Involved in what nasty stuff exactly?"

"Come inside," he said, as though she hadn't asked the question. "Let's get you clean and dry."

*   *   *

The only two furnished rooms in the house, it turned out, were a bathroom and a bedroom upstairs, and these were slapdash, just a few shampoos and a ratty towel in one, a couple of cheap blankets in the other, all signs that told Stella he was squatting here at best. Stella willingly submitted to the bath only with the door locked shut. The lacerations on her legs from kicking it through the window were not going to need medical care, but they stung in the warm bath water.

When she emerged and put on the clean clothes Julien had left for her, she found him on the floor of the bedroom, candles lit for light, and a map of the United States spread out before him.

"It's a beautiful country we live in," he said. "And most of us never see more than a sliver of it. You'd love Wyoming, I'll bet. Beautiful country. Or we could go east—Chicago is an amazing city."

"Julien, I'm not going anywhere with you. You're going to take me back home, because it's the right thing to do."

Julien looked up at her from the floor with an expression that set her blood to ice. It was a somber drooping of the eyes and cheeks. "We can't go back, Stella."

"What did you *do*? Why won't you just tell me the facts?"

"Because facts lie. They don't reveal the gray areas between things."

"Who was Brooke? What really happened to her?"

Julien slapped the map closed. "She was one of my Frivolity girls, like a daughter, Stella, and a drug addict, and a lovely, lovely girl otherwise, one whose parents did not deserve her. And she died, but I didn't kill her."

"Okay. So I already know I'm barking up the wrong tree, but why didn't you go to the police?"

"Because . . . the Frivolity family doesn't involve police. It's not what we do."

"Spoken like a guilty man."

Julien hung his head. It swayed like a piece of heavy fruit on a branch. "Please tell me your mother didn't get so deeply under your skin, Stella. I'm counting on you to be more like me—warm, open, brave—than the cold women who spawned us."

36

FOR A LONG TIME, Izzy felt like she couldn't move, even after the hands let go of her and she heard footsteps retreating into the distance. Her body kept standing there, despite the voice in her head that screamed "Do something! Run!" She could only look in the direction of Dylan, who had fallen behind his car somewhere after the man in the ski mask hit him. She was afraid to move. Her mom was gone—she'd been taken away, and her father might be dead on the other side of his car, and she would be an orphan, except for her grandmother, who might or might not ever leave the hospital.

She realized that her violin case was still on the ground nearby, at her feet, and she was able to get her body to move forward and pick it up. The case was a little scuffed, but it didn't look like the kind of damage that could have injured the instrument. Feeling a little bolder, she inhaled and crept quietly around the car.

There was blood, but not a lot of it, mostly in a streak from Dylan's scalp down his cheek. He was laid out on the ground almost as though he was just reclining, surrounded by shattered glass. As Izzy came nearer she realized he was moaning. She hurried over and set her violin down next to him.

"Are you okay?" she asked him.

His eyes sprang open, and then he reached up and grabbed her with more force than she expected, pulling her forward onto his chest in a kind of awkward hug, then released her.

"Where's Stella?"

She shook her head, and felt tears start to form. "They—those men—took her."

Dylan tried to sit up but then he groaned and put his hand on his head. "Ow. Can you help me?"

She moved behind him and pushed against his back until he was sitting, brushing off the glass that clung to his sweater. She helped prop him against the car.

"Can you run inside and call the police, Sweetie, call 9-1-1?"

"Are you going to be okay?"

He squinted at her. Blood had run into his eye and was making him blink furiously. "We'll find her, okay?"

She nodded and turned and ran into the lobby of the hotel shouting, "Call 9-1-1, call 9-1-1."

Sometime later, she didn't really know how long, she let a paramedic examine her as Dylan sat undergoing a similar process.

"The police are going to ask you a lot of questions, Isadora."

She nodded, and squeezed her violin case between her knees.

"Like about Stella, and . . . who I am . . . I mean, why I'm suddenly in your life." He winced as the paramedic swabbed his scalp with something wet on a cotton pad.

"You're my dad," she said, and it felt good, right to say it. She didn't even care if he squinted funny at her when she said it. "That's all anybody needs to know."

The paramedic stood back from Dylan with the air of having finished something incompletely. "Sir, we can't rule out concussion even though your pupils look normal and you're sitting up talking. We highly recommend that you go down to the hospital and have them check you out."

Dylan waved a hand at the man and smiled. "Will do." The paramedic frowned as though he wasn't convinced, but walked away.

Izzy looked at her hands, which were red and chapped since she hadn't been putting on regular lotion. She noticed that Dylan's hands looked the same, and she wanted to ask him if he forgot his lotion, too.

"So . . . are you mad at her for not . . . telling you before?"

He gave a curt smile. "No. I just only wish I'd known a long time ago."

Izzy looked at him with his kind eyes and his face that was so familiar and nodded with a great gushing sense of relief flowing through her that this truth was out in the air.

"Right now we're just gonna worry about getting her safely back, all right?"

Izzy bit at the cuticle of her thumbnail because otherwise she was going to cry and she really didn't want to make a bad impression in front of him, the man who was her father, and the only adult she could count on for the immediate future.

When they got back to his car, Dylan brushed glass off the back seat, sighing the whole time. "I'm sorry it'll be a chilly ride home. You can wear my jacket."

Izzy accepted the black corduroy coat that looked like the kind sailors wore. It was only a ten-minute drive to her house, but it felt longer, as questions rose up in her throat with a yucky swirling, sort of like when she had to throw up.

When they pulled up to the house, Izzy felt as though she couldn't swallow. "Are you going to come inside?"

"Of course," he said. "I'm not leaving ye here alone."

"Of course," she repeated, gripping her violin case even more tightly.

Dylan opened her car door for her and waited patiently while she fitted her key into the lock of her front door. It felt weird to be coming home to an empty house, dark and quiet.

Izzy found herself slightly embarrassed at the dark, cluttered box they called home, as she imagined it looked to Dylan. She quickly switched on the hall light but that only made it worse, revealing clutter and mess.

She looked around, forlorn. "It's not usually so messy. Mom's been busy lately, and Gigi can't really do much for herself."

Dylan's hand was suddenly on her shoulder, and the next thing she knew she was crying into his chest as he patted her.

"I guess it's just us, lass," he said in a voice that sounded as unsure as she felt.

"I'm sorry," she said. "I didn't mean to . . ."

"Didn't mean to what?"

"To mess things up sending you that message on Facebook . . . I just wanted you and my mom to meet again. I just wanted . . ."

Dylan's eyes looked like clouds about to rain. He frowned, but not as though he was mad, just heavy with some kind of feeling. She knew her feelings only by how they came out of her violin.

"Oh, lass," he said. "I'd have done it, too. Only in my day there was no Internet; in fact we hardly ever had a working phone. I'd have had to set up a stakeout. Hired a thug from the pub to get a handle on things."

Izzy smiled; she could tell he was trying to cheer her up.

"She picked a really inconvenient time to go disappearing on us, huh?"

Izzy nodded again. "Are you going away too?"

Dylan pinched his lips together. "Well, I do have work to do, and a business to run."

Izzy tried to stop the tears but they came too fast.

He reached out and took her chin in his hand. "No, what I meant to say is, I guess ye're just going to have to come with me until yer mum turns up. And she will." He blinked very quickly, as though he had something in his eye. She hoped he wasn't fighting back tears. She wanted to believe him, but she couldn't catch her breath. The house felt too small and tight around her. She'd hated her mother lately for being so selfish—but now she'd give anything, even if it meant never playing the violin again, to have her come walking in that door just now in all her stage makeup.

37

STELLA WOKE UP TO FIND herself levitating off the ground, while footsteps crunched over gravel. It took her a groggy moment to realize she was in someone's arms, carried like a sick child, still dressed in the sweatpants and flannel shirt Julien had given her the night before. Or was it the same night? She couldn't see the sky through the canopy of trees. Her limbs felt rubbery and heavy, and she was dimly aware of panic inside her, locked as though behind a thick wall.

"Whaaa—" she managed to gurgle out between thick slab lips.

"I'm sorry, Stella." Julien's voice. "It probably sounds like a back-handed compliment, but I hadn't guessed you'd be so stubborn."

Where are you taking me? Ran through her head but wouldn't make it past the dull gate of her mouth.

"You want a little bit of truth? Even if there was no Brooke, no ghostly thief at Ernestine's mansion, eventually this is where we'd be. On the road again. Good ol' Jack Kerouac knew what he was talking about. I'm a believer in the temporary nature of things. That's why my Spectacles are what they are—one-of-a-kind shows, never to be repeated. Never do the same thing twice. What's the point? The universe doesn't. Even identical twins and cloned animals are unique."

Modern-day circus, Stella thought but couldn't say. *But you're the freak show.*

Stella felt herself lowered to the ground, though he kept her leaning against him because it was clear that her legs would not hold her satisfactorily. After months of having reconnected with the strength and power of her body, it was more than disconcerting to have no control over it.

He opened a door and slid her into the back seat of some sort of minivan. It was not the same one she'd been herded into on the way up here.

He'd laid a series of pillows beneath and around her so that he could buckle her in and leave her half-reclining. And then she heard a metallic-sounding snick and felt something cold close over her wrist.

His eyes had a milky softness—she'd have called it tenderness if she didn't know now what he truly was. "I know how it must seem, lovely. Handcuffs, I'm sorry. But I know you won't come with me willingly. I think you'll see that my lifestyle is quite exciting once you get used to it."

"Izzzzzzz . . ." Her daughter's name attempted to slither out from her lips.

"She'll be fine. She has an upstanding father, and her grandmother . . . She's safe. Nothing to worry about. I think of everything."

Stella's lungs felt as though someone were standing on them, like when Izzy was a toddler and would insist that her mommy *wie down* so she could lie on her belly to feel it rise up and down. She felt tears run down her cheeks, freed from the prison of her body, but she couldn't muster the energy to wipe them away.

"Your muscles will be useless for quite some time. You'll be fine. Try to rest, my sweet. I'll wake you when we make our first stop."

The insistent drug in her system, combined with the lull of the car on the road, dragged her back into sleep, try as she did to stay awake and become aware of where they were going.

*   *   *

She woke with a jolt to the sound of a door being slammed. She was pleased to realize she could move her body again, but it was with the noodlelike sense of limpness that comes with a very high fever, and a pounding headache accompanied it. She was mortified to feel a damp lump between her legs, clearly having peed into the diaper he'd placed on her.

He rolled down her window. "Hungry? Thirsty?"

She shook her head and strained at the handcuff, which was attached to the inside handle of the car door. She'd have to tear the door off its hinges to get free. Now that the drug was wearing off she felt a bleak film noir kind of despair: all the world seemed drained of color, of hope. This man, whoever he was, father or not, was a sociopath. He didn't care about her, or what happened to her.

"Where are we?" she asked.

He smiled. "A few hours away. One of these middle-of-nowhere towns that you can't remember because there's no soul here. Just passing through, don't worry. We're on our way somewhere a little more interesting."

"And then what?" she asked. Her lips still felt heavy, as though she'd had a dental shot of Novocain.

"And then we will work for our bread, love. Until we find the perfect place."

"Perfect place for what?" she asked wearily.

"To make art that people will never forget!"

He returned to the car with bags of chips and little chocolate doughnuts, bottles of water, and chewing gum. She refused to eat anything.

She slept on and off, feeling returning to her body in the form of muscle aches and her strength returned little by little.

By the time they stopped again, it was night, and it seemed they'd been driving for hours. She had basic control of herself but felt weak.

"I need to get this fucking diaper off."

"Of course. This is where we'll call it a night."

He had pulled down a dirt road. In his hand he referred to a crumpled piece of paper that looked like some sort of spreadsheet. There were no street lights. He parked in front of a faded gray house with weeds so tall they threatened to hide the house entirely. A bank "For Sale" sign hung from a tilting picket.

He got out and with a flashlight, looked in all of the windows, and disappeared around the house. He returned with a victorious smile, then carefully helped her out of the car and uncuffed her. She thought about running, but having eaten nothing and with the remnants of the drug still in her system, she didn't think this was her optimal chance to make a break for it.

She leaned against him and let him help her around back, where he had smashed in a window, crawled in, and opened the back door.

There were no neighbors to hear the sound, no heroic rescue about to ensue, so she wearily followed him in, trying hard to keep in mind a vision of Izzy as safe and secure, to send her a silent thought: *I will be back. I love you.*

* * *

After she'd used the bathroom, wiped herself down with cold but clean water that still ran in the house, and finally consented to eat the chocolate donuts, he laid out two sleeping bags in the empty living room and made her swallow a pill. "I can inject you if you'd rather do it that way," he said, so she took the pill.

As she lay there waiting for the drug to do its work in the ratty sleeping bag he'd rolled out for her, she sighed loudly, wondering what Izzy and Dylan were doing right now, if the police were looking for her, if her mother had any idea what had happened, or was waiting, alone, at the hospital for someone to claim her.

"I can hear you thinking," he said to her. "I know you must find me barbaric."

"That's an understatement." She vowed to stop being even remotely nice to him. "I was actually thinking that I can't imagine my mother ever being in love with someone like you."

She hoped that he'd get angry; she was itching for something like a fight. Instead he laughed. "Well, *she* certainly was her number one priority, but even divas fall in love."

"How can you be both a sociopath and a romantic?"

He was quiet then, and suddenly fear slapped down a chair at her table again. He'd kidnapped her and drugged her, and who knew what weapons he might have on him to see that she didn't flee.

"All I'm asking is that you give me a chance, Stella."

"A chance at what?" She rolled away from him inside her sleeping bag.

"At being your father."

She couldn't help it; she laughed hard until she was snorting and crying all at once. "Father of the Year," she said. "Total PTA material."

*   *   *

Whatever drug he'd given her made waking a sudden and brutal act. Sunlight made her eyes water, or maybe it was the headache, like her head was being smashed between two wrecking balls. The rich scent of coffee gave her a tiny impetus to rise. She dragged herself upright, then had to bend nearly in half to walk so she didn't vomit. She found Julien, smiling and humming, in the kitchen. He'd run out for food. Some kind of breakfast burritos and coffee sat on the counter, and hanging over the door between the kitchen and the living room was a slinky purple dress.

"You'll be dancing tonight," he said. "We've got to get working on the number now because we only have about eight hours until performance time. I've got makeup and wig."

"Glad to see you thought ahead," Stella said, suddenly ravenous. She grabbed her burrito and ate it in three bites, then washed it down with a lukewarm but still satisfying cup of coffee.

"Always," he said.

38

THE DOCTOR WAS A WOMAN. She wore blue scrubs and white shoes, and to Izzy her eyes looked red and tired. Dylan leaned back in his seat with his eyes closed.

"Are you Margaret Russo's family?"

Dylan snapped his head forward. "Yes."

Izzy chewed nervously at her thumb. Her mom would tell her to stop it if she were there.

"We're so glad you came. We've been calling Miss Russo's phone over and over, but she wasn't answering. Margaret's awake, but she needs a lot of rest. You can see her briefly, but then we need you to come back tomorrow for visiting hours.

Dylan nodded, stood, and reached for Izzy's hand. They followed the doctor to the recovery room.

Izzy was shocked at the sight of her grandmother—small and crumpled in her bed, propped up to half-sitting, her mouth open like that of a dead person, the skin of her neck thin and fragile-looking. She'd never thought of Gigi as really old before. When Gigi saw Dylan her eyes widened and she sat forward.

"Hi, Margaret." He took her hand in his.

"Well . . . never thought . . . see you again," she said. She was breathing heavily, as if she'd been doing physical exercise, and one side of her mouth drooped a tiny bit downward, as though it had just gotten tired.

He smiled but his eyes looked sad to Izzy. "I know."

Margaret looked from him to Izzy and back again. "Where's Stella?"

Izzy opened her mouth to tell Gigi the sad tale but Dylan interrupted. "On a job with the troupe. They're traveling for a few days."

Margaret raised an eyebrow. "She just left? With me . . . like this?"

Dylan frowned. "I guess it was sort of last-minute. And I said I would help out."

Margaret stared at him, her chest heaving. Izzy put her hand out and grasped her grandmother's other hand. "I hope you feel better soon, Gigi."

Gigi smiled, and the lines at her eyes feathered out. "I will . . . darling. Can I talk with . . . Dylan, alone?"

Izzy squeezed her grandmother's hand. She understood Dylan was not telling her grandmother the truth because she might not be able to stand it. She had a terrifying hollow feeling, like she was standing on a shore watching her mom and Gigi drift away out into the ocean without her. "Actually the doctor told us we have to go," Izzy said, a sob creeping up beneath her words. "We can't stay."

Dylan shot Izzy a look, but nodded. "I'll come back tomorrow, Margaret." He tried to pull his hand free of Margaret's but she held on tight. "She's . . . precious. You understand?" Margaret looked briefly at Izzy. "Be responsible."

Dylan's face moved through a series of expressions Izzy didn't understand but settled on a tight smile. "Absolutely. Ye can trust me, I promise ye that."

Margaret exhaled, closed her eyes, and leaned back in her bed. "Okay. See you both tomorrow."

Izzy kissed her Gigi good-bye and took Dylan's outstretched hand, where he led her back out into the hall. "I don't know how long before the police locate your grandmum here and want to talk to her, but I'm worried about her."

"I know," Izzy said. "Me too."

"Ye hungry, lass?" he asked.

"I don't know. My tummy is empty but I feel sort of . . . sick," she said.

He nodded. "I know what you mean. That's nerves, but we should try."

39

STELLA ENTERED the womblike nightclub ragged with resentment. She would perform the stupid routine as Julien requested, but she would not infuse it with any joy. It would be a robotic act, a body moving through a series of steps, paint-by-numbers for a dancer.

To her surprise, the club, which was painted in gold-flecked dark purple and red, hosted a well-coiffed-looking set of people in fancy dress. Women with expensive jewelry and hair pulled up in chignons. Men wearing ties and shiny shoes. There were more glasses of wine on tables than there were beers or coffee. Modern-sounding jazz played in the background and attractive young waiters and waitresses roamed the floor.

She was to go on after a jazz musician. Julien kept her close to him the whole time. Julien himself would be part of the show — seated in a chair the entire time as she did a mashup of Flamenco and tango around him. Her costume was not traditional for either dance form, however, and she hoped that there was no expectation.

She sipped a glass of champagne Julien had ordered for her and tried to fight the feeling of sleepiness that jazz always inspired in her.

She felt her chin graze her shoulder and her head snap up. Julien jammed a finger into her side. "You're almost on. Come with me."

She followed him up toward the stage, which was lit by one single but powerful can light, and through a curtained-off area.

A tall, broad-shouldered man in a velvet vest over a blue silk shirt stood with his back to them. His legs plunged from fancy black trousers. Stella assessed him to be nearly seven feet tall. Julien made a hissing sort of sound, and the man turned. His face was handsome, the color of milk chocolate, with dark penetrating eyes, and full lips.

"This is . . . Lola," he said, and when Stella snapped him a look, Julien met her gaze with one that suggested she stay quiet.

"Lola," said the man in a rich, deep voice. "A pleasure. I'm Stan." He put out his hand, and when Stella reached hers to him he took her entire arm and pulled her close to him. "I can't wait to see you dance."

Stella smiled. And then the audience was clapping and the jazz musician was hurrying off stage.

"Come, Lola." Stan escorted her out onto the stage where he sat in the big black chair where she'd expected Julien to sit.

She was about to protest, to ask questions, when she realized that she wouldn't be dancing for Julien at all, that Stan was her prop, and he was looking at her with a raised eyebrow that managed to convey both anticipation and menace all at once.

And then she heard the first strains of the music begin, and her body began to move, her arms lifting in the fierce, proud stance of Flamenco, her heels twisting and clicking. She walked around Stan, rested her hands on his shoulders, then pulled them away as he caressed her fingers. Flamenco was all about the tease. And despite her best intention to do it as monotonously as possible, her body delighted in the movement, in the ardent eyes of the audience upon her, of the feeling that only a stage and its spotlight could give her.

Stan's raised eyebrows and curved smile told her he was enjoying it too, and she finished the routine with the flourish that Julien had taught her only hours before, a series of twirls that deposited her right into Stan's lap. She was alarmed to realize, as she executed the final of these moves and the curtains closed to applause, that she was sitting upon an immense erection.

Stan began to kiss her neck before she could think of what to do. "I'm sorry," she said quickly, but his mouth was suddenly on her mouth, and he was kissing her so forcefully she couldn't quite pull away.

When he released her from the kiss, he lifted her up and onto his shoulder. "What do you think you're doing?"

"Where do you want to do the job?" Stan said. "I've got a nice little couch in my office, or we could just do it in the car."

His hands groped her ass. "I'm not going to have sex with you," she said.

Stan laughed as he carried her off stage. "Whatever you say, baby."

"Julien!" she shrieked.

But Julien was nowhere to be seen. She began to kick and pound Stan's back as he carried her through a side door and up some stairs.

"You're a fierce little thing," Stan said. "I'll settle for a blow job."

He'd reached the top of the stairs and put her down with a thud in a dingy faux-wood-paneled office.

It all made sense suddenly. Julien was exploiting her for money. Faced with the size of the man before her and his insistence, added to the fact that he probably didn't realize she was an unwilling participant, she knew she'd have to play this somewhat cool if she hoped to get out of here with her life, much less her dignity.

"Sorry," she said. "I just find this so . . . uninspiring."

"Are you insulting me?" His mouth was caught between a grin and a sneer.

Stella folded her arms across her chest. "No, in fact, I was going to say, you're a handsome man, and I'm guessing you get ladies in here all the time who would throw themselves at you willingly. So . . . this," she waved her hands at herself. "I'm just saying, there are lots of ways to get paid. You couldn't think of something more original?"

He was staring at her with an assessing grin, as though trying to figure out whether or not she was being serious. "So, you're not a professional, I take it."

"You knew that," she dared.

He shrugged. "I don't know anything but what the big J told me. And since he's the one in debt to me, I took the payment he offered."

Stella sneered. "Payment. Sex is fleeting; pleasure even more so. Don't you want something you can use, like money or things?"

Stan smiled now, a big, easy smile. "Now that's where you're wrong. Pleasure is something you can hold onto long after you have it, replay it in your mind. It's a living thing. It keeps in a way that money and stuff don't."

Stella sighed, realizing she couldn't talk her way out of this. "Whatever. I want you to get undressed first."

He looked at her with a raised eyebrow. "You want *me* to get undressed."

She cocked her head. "Honey, I may not be professional, but if it's pleasure you're after, I'm good at what I do." She put a hand against his chest and pushed him slightly so he stumbled a step backwards. "But it comes with a certain order, a protocol."

"Okay, baby." He began to undress in front of her, unsheathing his long, muscular body from his elegant clothes. When he was fully naked—and Stella was not entirely unmoved by the sight of his perfect body, feeling a tingle of sexual power—she commanded him, "Lie down on that couch."

When he did so, she hiked up her skirt and kneeled over him, alarmed at the part of her that considered doing exactly what he wanted. The rational part of her calculated every step she would have to make to get out unharmed and without regret. She only hoped that Julien was waiting somewhere close by, and then realized how desperate she must be to be hoping for such a thing.

"Now close your eyes."

He closed his eyes with a sigh of expectation, and she put her hand on his cock and gave it a few slow tugs, just to let him know she was serious. Then she slowly lifted herself off, while keeping hold of him, and made a silent apology in her mind before slamming her knee into his testicles.

She'd only ever heard the sort of groan Stan made from men running into each other at full speed on the football field. Guilty as she felt, she took the chance to bolt out of his office and down the stairs.

Julien was standing by the bar chatting with the pretty brunette bartender and sipping a cocktail. When he caught sight of her, wild-eyed, and her dress tucked halfway up into her tights, he bolted for her, and together they raced out of the café.

Stella simply ran, high heels making her ankles twinge. She wasn't even trying to escape from him, just to get far away from the feeling of being property, and of having had to injure a man for no good reason.

When Julien finally caught her, he grasped her painfully by the arm and dragged her back to their car, throwing her in. He jumped in and began to drive.

"What the fuck was that, Julien? This is how you win me over as a father, by pimping me out?"

"I figured after the way you gave yourself to that man at the gallery, you were fairly liberal when it comes to sex."

"Liberal? I don't fuck strangers for money, and even if I did I sure as hell would want to know in advance."

"Well, we have to keep on driving now, Stella, because Stan is going to be criminally angry now."

"What the hell was that? You owe that man money and you pay him with *me*?"

Julien sighed heavily. "He's a handsome man, respectful. I honestly don't see what the problem was. It wasn't some back-alley trick."

Stella laughed and found it turning into a kind of sob. "That's the problem—you don't have human emotions. God . . . I should have slept with him, and then begged him to save me from *you*."

Julien frowned and pouted like a little boy, his bottom lip jutting out. "Don't say that. You're hurting my feelings."

"No, I'm convinced by now that's impossible. It's only your pride or your megalomania that can feel any injury."

Julien slammed his lips together. Stella remembered to be afraid of him.

"So, where to now? Will I be turning more tricks for you, or would you like me to sell crack on a street corner? Or wait, I know, I could pose as a crippled person and we could panhandle on the street."

"Look, I'm sorry, that won't happen again. It was coincidence that we came through here and I owed Stan. Just thought I could settle a debt, but now I'm in deeper shit than before. Ah well . . . just makes the moving on all that much more necessary."

Stella sank into her seat, her fingers gripping the edge of her dress with the urge to tear it in two.

*   *   *

When Stella opened her eyes again she saw that they were approaching Santa Monica.

"Oh God," she groaned. "I can only imagine what you have in store for us here."

"I love L.A.," Julien said. "If it weren't so damn expensive I'd even consider living here permanently."

"Yes, a town famous for its empty hearts and insincerity—fits you perfectly."

"For someone who was raised to love the theater you're such a cynic," Julien said. He pulled off the freeway and into a McDonald's drive-through, where he ordered them both breakfast. The sun was just breaking above the dark clouds, casting a grimy light on the world around them.

"You know, I think the FBI is looking for you." She'd remembered the man who'd approached her and Izzy in the park. Up until this moment she'd forgotten about him, assuming he was part of the outfit that had kidnapped her.

"I think that's unlikely," Julien said, but his voice quavered.

"The man had a photograph of you. If he wasn't FBI, then he's something worse. Mob after you, Julien?"

A stony silence settled over the car. Julien had set down his breakfast muffin. "And what did you tell the man?" he asked at last.

"That I didn't know you," she said. "Before I took off running."

"That's good," he said. "Better not to say too much to strangers."

"Damn, Julien, are you ever going to just tell me the whole story? You want me to trust you, to give you a chance, then you have to tell me the truth."

Julien sighed. "The truth," he said simply. "Everyone always thinks they want to hear it, but it can't be un-heard or un-known."

"I want to know," she said. "You call this a life of impermanence; I think you're just running from something."

Julien took a bite of his food and then turned around to face her. "You're a wise girl, Stella. And I would like to tell you everything you want to know. But it's safer for you that you don't know everything. The more you know, the more danger it puts you in."

Despite herself, Stella felt that he was being sincere. "So tell me what you can, then. Are you in trouble with the law, or with other . . . parties?"

Julien sighed. "Both, I guess."

"That's a start. Why do you guess?"

"Because, Stella, I've learned that even the most egregious of problems can be shaken off like water from a duck's back. It's just a matter of being creative."

Stella felt like whatever moment of true vulnerability he'd revealed had been tucked away. "If you aren't going to tell me the truth, don't bother talking to me."

"Well here's a truth I can give you," he said, stuffing the last of a breakfast muffin into his mouth.

"Oh?"

"You're not going to like it."

"Well then, nothing will have changed about my feelings regarding this impromptu trip we're taking . . . so shoot."

Julien cleared his throat. "I don't think you were ever a true ballet dancer. You didn't love it; you did it because it was all you knew, because you were all but shoved into it by your mother."

Stella worked up a protest in her mind about how much crap that was—her mother had never suggested she become a dancer; she had simply followed the only path that made sense to her, the one that soothed the wild madness in her limbs that otherwise leant itself to breaking things and tripping over cracks in cement. "Oh, now you're an armchair psychologist too?"

"Let me finish," Julien said. "You got that position at the San Francisco Ballet because of your mother's reputation, and because everyone is prone to nostalgia."

"That was a highly competitive position, Julien. I'll be the first to admit that I was not the best dancer in the country, but I competed hard for it, and they don't just hand those out, not even for nepotism."

"Oh I'm not talking nepotism," Julien said. "In lieu of your mother's career, the one that accident ruined, the director of the ballet wanted to recreate her in you because the audiences missed her. You were good, even great, I'm sure. But had you been anyone else, I highly doubt they would have taken you."

Stella couldn't finish her breakfast muffin. His arrogance and audacity made the bit she'd already swallowed rise up again.

"So is it your plan to break down my self-esteem and will by humiliating me, telling me how terrible I am? Go on then, get on with it."

Julien sighed and turned around to look at her. "It's almost like you are willfully mishearing everything I'm saying because you're mad at me. Which, come to think of it, is rather charming in that it's what daughters *should* do to their fathers."

"You're not my father. Margaret told me the truth—what kind of a man you were. You didn't raise me, you didn't invest a stitch in my life, so you can stop with that line of bullshit."

"Oh I invested in you, Stella, and hopefully soon I'll be able to show you just how much. And I know that your mother sold you a line about you being the spawn of the greatest dancer in the world. Occam's razor, Stella: what do you think is true: your mother managed an affair with that Russian pretty boy, or that she didn't want to share you with anyone, not even your own blood?"

A chill ran through Stella. She hadn't, exactly, believed, not for sure, the story about her paternity, but she'd liked the way it sounded, felt, to see herself as born of someone great. Julien's words left a sick hollow in her chest.

"Meanwhile, what I'm trying to tell you, who are now balking at the truth you asked for just like I said you would, is that ballet was never your calling. It isn't you, and no matter how perfectly you learned the techniques, no matter how efficiently you performed them, you are no ballerina. And that, my dear, is a beautiful thing, because ballet is the Ice Queen of dance. And you are a fire goddess. You are Kali, Hera, Hecate. You see? Your talent is a dance of heat, and before you get on some jag about sex, I'm not talking about that. You burn when you dance, and you can't burn in ballet."

She wanted to refute him, to tell him off for his self-important rant about what was good for her, as if he knew anything about her, but the words wouldn't come. Inside her, like a tiny ember buried beneath dead coals, she felt the certainty that he was right, and it killed her. She chose not to answer him, but it didn't matter; he carried on as though they were having a two-way conversation.

"So . . . I think the best thing that ever happened to you was giving up that company role before it tried to freeze the life out of you. And you got Isadora out of the equation, and look at *her* talent! My God, these genes . . ."

Stella's heart felt as though it had been clamped inside a tiny metal box at the sound of her daughter's name. "Don't you *dare* try to take any genetic credit for Izzy. Whichever part of it isn't hers alone comes from her father's line, I'm sure, so you can forget your grandiose notions."

Julien chuckled. "How's the truth feel so far?"

"Fuck you," Stella curled her knees up to her chest, feeling sick and angry and confused. "What talent do you have anyway? Nothing that I've seen so far other than being a pathological liar."

"Oh my dear . . . my talent is that I harness and direct the talent of others so that it can be seen and allowed to shine."

"Oh yes, look at me shining back here in this probably stolen minivan in the middle of Los Angeles. Wow."

"I try not to lament the career you could have if I'd been there from the start. But things are about to change, Stella. Nothing will be the same."

40

DANCING HAD GIVEN Dylan an actor's ability to slide behind the truth. It was the only way he was keeping himself from splattering into a whirlwind of panic that presented itself every time he looked at the girl. She chewed on her lower lip so viciously he expected to see blood, and her violin case was tucked firmly between her legs in the hospital waiting room, as though it contained the last vestige of her safety, familiarity. He wished he had an object to hold onto to provide him some sense of stability himself. The events of the past two days unspooled in his mind as they waited for the doctor to give them a sense of her grandmum's prognosis.

He wasn't sure which thing disturbed him the most at that moment: the sight of the once-famous ballerina in a weak and gray state; the girl who looked the spit of his sister Maggie at the same age and all the implications therein, including the lies that Stella had likely told; or the fact that with her mum's whereabouts unknown, he might end up being her sole caretaker. There was also concern over how the hell he would run his company and get Izzy to and from school . . . but these were all overshadowed by a deeper, more visceral fear for Stella's safety. That just when he'd gotten a chance with her again, she might be wrenched out of his life.

Izzy was now tapping her fingers on her violin case.

"Ye want to play it," he said, no question in his voice.

She looked up at him as though startled, and he realized she had been hearing music in her head, had possibly even tuned out the sterile and overstimulating scene of the hospital to slip away.

"I always want to play it," she said simply.

He couldn't help but smile. It added up to the case for her being a Wheeler. His grandmum and mum had played the strings, too, and though neither had pursued a performing career, his grandmum had been playing the violin right up to the hour of her death. "It's music will ease my passage," she had said, and though her hands were weak, she had somehow managed to make a mournful dirge sound almost comforting.

"Well I think we should go find a place to do it then," he said.

"This is a hospital," she said, "I don't think they let you make that much noise."

"Are you kidding? Think how many people would prefer the sound of your music to the nasty beeping and static of all these devices," he said. "Come on."

She sighed, chewed her lip again, but then nodded and stood up. He walked her down corridors until they came upon an empty sort of lounge between a closed pharmacy and the cafeteria.

"No one's here. And if ye'd like privacy, I'll stand just outside the door."

Izzy nodded. She extracted the violin from its case. It was a beautiful, expensive instrument, gleaming and sturdy. It fitted nicely under her chin. She held the bow up to it and then raised her eyebrows at him.

"Right, out in the hall," he said.

He knew she'd been practicing for some time, but he was not prepared for the mature, full-bodied sound that burst from the room behind him, a thing so alive it seemed to press up against the edges of him, as though it were a body, and shoulder past him, wander out into the hall. It wasn't a piece of music he recognized, so he suspected a modern composer.

Within minutes, people were poking their heads out of doors, and drifting down the corridor from the cafeteria as though pulled by invisible ropes, craning their heads toward the source of the music. The hairs on his arms and neck stood up at the sheer power of the notes, which moved as though intentionally into the ear of the listener.

Minutes in, a small crowd had formed around the doorway where Dylan stood, feeling like a guard at the throne of some powerful queen who commanded her subjects with her instrument. In contrast to the feeling he'd had earlier, the terror of realizing that this possibly orphaned child might be his daughter, a reality he had no schema for, suddenly he wanted to shout to the crowd: "That's my girl!"

A large bald man with a billy club and a Taser on his belt elbowed through the crowd suddenly with a look of fierce determination. He peered over Dylan's shoulder with a smile that quickly worked its way back into a frown of authority.

"Sorry sir, but that little girl's creating a disturbance, crowding up the hallway here and blocking passage. I got to ask you to put an end to that."

The crowd of people made disappointed sounds. Izzy, however, didn't seem to notice a thing. Her eyes were closed, and her chin tilted toward the ceiling, cradling her violin and working its bow like someone in a trance.

Dylan sighed and nodded. "I know. But can she just finish the song?"

"No sir, what if there's an emergency and someone needs to get a stretcher or a wheelchair through here. We got babies being delivered up one floor and lots of new mothers coming through here . . . can't do it."

What about new fathers? Dylan thought, but nodded, and turned to Izzy. "Isadora, sweet girl . . . we have to stop."

Izzy strummed her bow over the strings for one last shimmering note, then dropped her instrument without opening her eyes. The crowd broke out in applause and Izzy's eyes sprung open in surprise. A tiny smile broke the surface of her freckled face and then retreated into the bright red flush of her cheeks.

The guard dispersed the crowd except for one middle-aged nurse in scrubs. "Honey, what was that music you played? I want to get that for my dad, he'd love it. You are a talent!"

Izzy smiled again, this time it had the mark of pride he'd seen too many times in a Wheeler face. "I wrote it myself," she said. "I don't have a recording."

"Well my goodness, you're a prodigy," the woman said. "You just keep on playing that music, sweetie."

Izzy nodded politely and said goodbye to the nurse.

"Sorry I got ye in trouble," Dylan said to her.

Izzy shrugged. "It was worth it." The look on her face, a euphoric satisfaction, was something like he'd seen in the faces of dancers after an intense workout, or a marathon runner after crossing the finish line.

"Guess we better go back and see how your grandmum is before we call it a night."

All the rapture left Izzy's face then, and he felt sorry for having reminded her of reality.

They returned to her grandmother's room to find a team of nurses and doctors crowding in with a crash cart.

"Oh no, what's wrong?" Izzy all but screamed.

The nurse nearest the door put a hand out to prevent them from coming closer. "You need to take your daughter away," she said to Dylan. "Now."

Dylan grabbed hold of Izzy and steered her down the hall, her heart beating like an injured creature beneath his arm.

41

ALL OF JULIEN'S RANTING mania dulled to a low buzz when they came into town, a reaction that put Stella on the alert. She had almost begun to enjoy the lull of the road, meditative in its constancy; this emergence into urban life, with stoplights and traffic and buildings, made a sudden claustrophobia clutch her lungs, squeeze her ribs. Worse, Julien's silence suggested he was thinking hard about something. About the next thing. And if the nightclub scene and her near-prostitution were indicative of anything, Julien could be capable of anything.

Though the last round of drugs had worn off, her limbs still retained a rubbery density, as though she weighed more than usual. She had the panicked sense that she should have been paying attention to street signs and exits, but she had let her mind wander, relieved of the burden of thinking too hard. And now they were nearing a destination; she could feel it as a buzz of negative anticipation, the way she'd once felt as a child when the doctor's office came into view

"We'll stay in a motel," Julien said in a strangely flat monotone. "And you'll take on a new role for me." He sat at a stop sign a beat too long, and she caught those strange multicolored eyes of his in the rearview mirror. Though it was absurd, she had a powerful feeling of déjà vu, of a time long before. "This time, Stella, everything depends upon you learning this . . . spectacle. No questions asked."

She wondered why he hesitated at the word spectacle. "What motivation do I have?"

Julien whipped around and there was nothing but cold steel in those eyes, a look so chilling it made her doubt he'd ever looked at her warmly before. "Everything and everyone you love, Stella."

She felt the threat like something cold and sharp was pressed to her throat. A threat of harm to her daughter, her mother, maybe Dylan? Hairs rose upon her arms, her instinct for danger alerted. "Well then," she said, aiming to keep her voice steady, "you better make yourself a damn good teacher."

He had pulled up to shabby motel with faded pink paint and palm trees, classic Los Angeles Americana.

"I won't be the teacher," he said. And, as if she'd been waiting for them, cued to his words, even, a motel room door opened, and out stepped . . . Isis. Or was it? She was bleached-blonde and tanned within an inch of her life—clearly the orangey spray-on variety. She wore red-and-white pedal pushers with red espadrilles and a tight white button-up top that revealed more cleavage than it covered. She was Marilyn Monroe's rougher, tougher cousin.

"I don't understand. I thought Isis left you. I thought she was running away from you!"

Julien parked the car. "Family sticks together. Blood is thicker than water." Perhaps it was the blonde hair, but suddenly Stella could see it—a family resemblance. His younger sister, no doubt. No wonder she had put up with Julien. Stella almost felt like laughing.

Julien helped Stella out of the car; her legs half-buckled beneath her. He looked every bit the gentleman helping her out, taking her arm in his, when it was this weakness alone that kept Stella from kicking him in the jewels or gouging a new scratch to match Aja's in his cheek.

"Isis," Stella breathed, the moment the woman closed the motel room behind them.

"When you speak of me aloud, you call me Betty." There was no trace of irony or apology in her voice.

Julien quickly closed all the shutters and scanned the room with a paranoid frenzy.

"You're fine," Isis said drily, lighting up a cigarette. "Nobody has been looking for you."

"You don't know that." He lifted the phone to his ear, listened as though one could hear a bug.

"What are you doing here?" Stella asked, flopping back on the bed with the urge to fall asleep so she could wake up from this nightmare.

"I'm here to make sure you don't bolt while Julien does whatever it is Julien does." Her tone was heavy, weary.

Stella groaned. "He won't even include you in the plans, huh? You must feel so special. Wish you'd gotten away before he roped you back in."

Julien exhaled heavily, strode across the room and took her arm in his fingers so tightly she felt frozen in shock and pain. "Don't you talk to your aunt that way."

Isis took a languid step toward them and stroked Julien's hand, which released its grasp of Stella's arm, though her arm throbbed painfully even after. "Now, now, Stella will be a good little girl. Relax."

"But can't you just tell me what, why?"

Julien had dropped to his knees and was inspecting a corner of the carpet for further surveillance. His behavior bordered on lunacy. He didn't look up as he spoke. "If you can just stop being so damn stubborn, after tomorrow our luck will change. Turn our fortunes on their heads. By which I mean, we'll never want for anything again."

"Yes, if." Isis's tone was dry, as though even she had stopped believing in Julien. As if perhaps, she, too, was here by force.

Suddenly all Stella could think of was Izzy, her plaintive eyes, the grief in her face every time Stella'd failed to come through for her. "We want very different things, Julien," she said, almost spat. "All I want is my family."

He spread his arms out wide. "As do I. And I have it here, the key players."

Stella couldn't be sure if it was her own projection or reality, but it seemed that Isis's face drooped a tiny bit, something weighty and full of grief that was erased almost as quickly as it appeared. And she remembered the way Isis had seemed to be running away back in Luma.

"What happened to Lina, then? Your real daughter? I think maybe I know now why she didn't want to admit you were her father," Stella said.

Julien's face flushed red and he sneered. "She is an ungrateful little bitch. You're not going to be the same way, are you Stella? I would be very unhappy if that were so."

"You're a shyster, a snake-oil salesman. Nothing you promise is real."

Julien's face hardened into a frightening mask that sent a chill of not only dread, but something like familiarity, through Stella.

"You do as you are told, Stella, and it won't matter what's real. I'm going out." With that he stormed out of the motel room. Stella assessed how easy it would be to overpower Isis, to escape.

Isis took bottles out of a little travel bag. "We're going to bleach your hair again, and dye it red. Just in case anyone is looking for you."

Stella looked at the door, ran her hand through her hair, which had started to lose its violet, had faded to something like the shade old ladies used to tint their hair, a bad lavender.

"And, if you have any problems with that—" Isis put a little red clutch purse on her knees and opened it casually, as though reaching for a lipstick but withdrew a tiny silver handgun—she was like something out of an old comic strip, a gangster moll.

"I see," Stella said, dread making her leaden. "I have to say, I didn't think you capable of this. You seemed to have integrity."

"You see what you want to see, Stella."

"Yeah, well the last time I saw you, you looked like a woman scared for her life, on the run. What happened? Julien catch wind of your escape?"

Isis sighed heavily and the gun-holding hand wavered. "This is not where I planned to be right now, but it's where I am, so I'll make the best of it."

"Oh, if this is the best of it, I don't think I want to know anything more. If I believe what I'm presented, then a man who had a couple of one-night stands with my once-famous mother is claiming to be my father and benefactor. And he's shown me this kindness by kidnapping me and leaving my child with a man who is little more than a stranger to her."

"Your mother was not the star she'd have you believe." Disgust muddied Isis's tone. "And what Julien ever saw in her . . . well, he has always been easily led by his smaller head." She wagged a finger like a wilting erection.

"You didn't know my mother," Stella said, a quaking suddenly running up her legs; perhaps more withdrawal from Julien's sedatives.

"*Au contraire, ma petite.* Knew her better than you ever did. Shared a dressing room for a while, a stage, a couple of lovers . . ."

"No. I don't believe you."

"Oh, *cherie*, you are so naive. I was no star like her, but I was a great dancer too, once."

Stella gagged, her empty stomach, already a near constant acid churn from anxiety and drugs, disgorged of this awful truth. She made it only as far as the bathroom floor before weak yellow, watery vomit splashed on the dingy white linoleum.

Isis followed behind. "Denial does nobody any good. I told Lina this, I've even told Julien himself many times. Accept the truth and then everyone can get on with their lives. Your mother felt she was too good for any mere man. And the one man she wanted, the only one she deemed worthy, if anything ever happened between them, I assure you he saw her as nothing more than a one-time fuck, honey. But she wouldn't let it go. I don't suppose she ever told you about the restraining order he put on her? Hmmm? You know who I mean, don't you? Your mother made him afraid for his life. Can you imagine such a thing? What kind of obsession must it take to cause a man that wealthy and famous to fear for his life?"

Stella vomited again. "You bitch."

Isis was quickly at the bathroom door. "Talking about the past is not especially motivating, I can see. Let's try a new tack—let me show you the pretty outfits Julien bought for you. He's not all cold. He wants you to be happy, Stella. I'll put on a little music, I know how music makes you feel alive, we'll dye your hair back to red—it'll be just like old times, sweetheart."

Stella felt like a husk of herself, hollow and shaky. She lifted her head. She must look like some kind of junkie, like the poor late Brooke. "I can believe you danced with my mother. But I don't believe the rest of it."

Isis pouted her lips and looked up, as though remembering something funny. "I believed Margie, you know, that she really did have a fling with Baryshnikov. Our company went to do a workshop with him in New York—well, *they* did. I got fired because your mother lobbied for it—and the prima donna always got what she wanted. *If* he fucked her, I'd be surprised that he came inside her. A man like that wears a condom, don't you think? Julien, however, it was on again, off again. On again." She flicked the bathroom light on so that a blinding, buzzing florescence filled the room and gave Stella an instant headache; she covered her eyes and groaned. "Off again." Isis flicked the switch off. "Your mother was a tease. A cold fish. She burned hot just long enough to get her hit of adoration and then she stole the world right out from under him. Your mother is a terrible person."

Without thinking, Stella lunged at Isis's legs. Caught off guard, Isis fell easily, surprisingly light for the density she took up in the world, hitting her head and hip on the wall and floor with a wail. Her little purse flew back out into the main bedroom area of the motel, and the tiny silver gun skittered out across the floor, landing not far from the front door. Blood welled from the top of her swelling lip, and her eyes flew open with something between horror and indignation as she pressed her hand there, her fingers coming away smeared. The blood pooled out of her mouth in swift, snakelike trails, and she spat out a piece of a tooth, which was Stella's cue to scramble toward the other room. She made it past her, but just; Isis was surprisingly strong, and Stella was weakened by all the drugs and lack of proper sleep or food. Isis clamped down on her ankles. Stella thrashed, kicked, suddenly fixed on the little glint of silver at the motel door. There was her key to freedom, and all she had do to was put a foot in this woman's face.

She glanced behind her; Isis was a terrifying blood-smeared vision, her blonde coif wild with released tendrils, white blouse unbuttoned, revealing a flowery bra now stained with blood, and exhibiting a gnashing grimace of rage as she grunted to hold Stella in place. Stella army-crawled forward, the cheap rug rubbing burns into her arms, her breasts squashed painfully into the floor. She felt nauseated and hot, as though she had a fever, but her vision would not waver from the tiny gun just inches from her grasp.

How had it all gone so bad so quickly? It was something about the gloating in Isis's voice as she called Margaret a slut that had done it. Whoever Julien was, no matter whether his putrid DNA ran in her veins, whether her mother had slept with him, then for some brief window in time, Margaret had believed he loved her. That was the kind of woman her mother was—a romantic to a fault. Not a stalker or starfucker.

Stella gave a great heave forward, the carpet tearing open the dry skin at her elbows, and with a mighty kick her fingers clasped the pistol. It was so small it didn't seem possible that it contained enough brute force to kill. She had the feeling that if she shot it, a little bird or a rose would burst out with a whistle.

"Please!" Isis cried, begging in her eyes, as Stella wheeled around and pointed the gun at her. It was an old-fashioned weapon; there was nothing more to do than pull the trigger. But she didn't have a chance to contemplate what she'd do next before the door flew open. Isis's eyes widened as a hand reached down and plucked the gun from Stella's own weak fingers.

And before she could make another surprised peep, the person aimed in one quick motion at Isis's head and fired. A bright spot of red opened up in Isis's forehead—and for just a moment she looked incredibly surprised, the way one might if a lover had brought an enormous bouquet of flowers, and then she dropped face first on the floor.

Expecting Julien, though numb and terrified at why he would do such a thing, Stella could barely make sense of the familiar female face looming over her, even as she reached down and grasped Stella by the scalp.

"She stole my fucking gun."

Lina.

42

LINA LOOKED THINNER and red-eyed, hair in a messy pony-tail, though it had barely been two weeks since she'd disappeared.

Lina released Stella's hair and leaned back against the door. "He always trusted Isis to a fault, even when she was ready to run off and take him for everything he had left—which isn't fucking much."

"I don't get it, are you rescuing me?"

Lina barked a laugh. "You wish. And really, what is it you want to be rescued from, Stella? Do you even know?"

A sob heaved out of her chest. "I just want to go home to my daughter."

"Yeah, that'd be nice. If all mothers and daughters could be reunited. Too bad mine died."

Stella refused to look toward Isis's body; she didn't know if she could handle seeing the still and bloodied corpse. How grotesquely frail the human body was—that a lifetime of memories and experience could be collapsed in a single second.

"What did Isis do to you? Why would you . . . kill her?"

Lina grimaced at Stella as though she'd asked the dumbest question possible. "She collaborated, Stella. She helped him perpetuate the fraud that was my life!" She raised her voice and began pacing the room on her muscular dancer's legs.

"I'm sorry," Stella offered, feebly.

"Oh you're sorry. I'm sure you are. You had a mother. I had a father. Neither one was any good at it. And you know, you get used to it. I knew he wasn't my father, I knew Isis wasn't my mother—I knew in my bones that they had something to do with her death, but what choice did I have? They took care of me. They raised me." Lina's eyes kept widening as though someone were pushing a button in her back.

"And I'd made my peace, I had a decent life—even though we had to move from city to city to city every few years because Julien's big dreams would come crashing to the ground, usually in the form of the cops or some guy who wanted to take a toe or worse away with him. Then we moved. Brooke was the only one he would ever confess to. He would tell her things when she was high. And she would tell Aja . . . and Aja would tell me little snippets, thinking I was on her side. House of Cunts—that's what we should have been called. He spent all of my life looking for *you*. His 'true' daughter. His star. I hated you before I even knew you, Stella."

Stella shook her head, not wanting this to be true, any of it. She'd spent her energy in the scuffle with Isis. "If you're going to kill me, just do it."

Lina moved with Julien's fierce, leonine grace toward Stella. She took Stella's chin in her cold, thin fingers. "I'm not going to kill you, idiot. I need you to find out what Julien is up to. He's hot on some trail and the only two things that motivate him are money and adoration."

Stella shook her head. "You killed Isis," she said, almost drily; laughter rose like a bubble to her lips but died down. "He's not going to be happy about that."

Lina, however, did laugh, heartily, too. "Yeah. But I can play her on the phone really well."

"What about . . . her?"

Lina glanced at Isis as though she were a mannequin, with a mad, manic glint in her eye. "Yes, well . . . how handy are you with bleach?"

43

MOST OF THE BLOOD puddled in the bathroom where Isis had been knocked down in their initial fight, and it came off easily with Windex and paper towels. Stella told herself it was costume blood, just grenadine and chocolate syrup. But when she turned to find Lina squinting over the limp form of Isis on the carpet she nearly tilted onto the floor in shock herself. Lina was staring at Isis, inspecting her. She touched her forehead, then ran her finger down the bruised bridge of her nose, the cheekbone.

Isis had fallen backwards onto the little throw carpet, which had collected most of the blood. *Oh, God, the blood.* Stella had to pant through her mouth just to stay upright. Lina looked up at her, red tendrils of hair pressed in sweat to her face. Her eyes were heavily dilated, her face flushed. She looked like a wild beast about to tear open the throat of its prey, capable of anything.

Somehow, by continually telling herself this was just a play, not real, Stella helped Lina roll up Isis's body in the blankets. They hefted her now immensely heavy form but Stella was too weak; she dropped Isis's legs, which hit the ground with a thud.

"Get it together, Princess," Lina sniped.

Stella tried again. She held the woman's legs and tried to pretend the victim had just passed out drunk—they were merely carrying her to the back seat of a car to let her sleep it off. Tears snuck down her cheeks. The car was parked right out front of the motel, and

Lina popped the trunk with an automatic key in her pocket. It had become night in the madness of her world. Another year or era could have passed. Once they swung the woman's body into the trunk, Lina grasped Stella by the elbow and hurried her back inside.

They spent another half an hour bleaching out drops of blood, but Stella had that sickening feeling that they'd missed some; of course they had. That even after wiping down the surfaces, her fingerprints persisted. That now she was an accomplice to covering up a crime. She pictured herself handcuffed and tossed into a cell with Lina, who might choke her in her sleep. She knew these were shock thoughts, clouding the greater horror that sat like a blood blister beneath a bruised nail; and somewhere down the road the horror would seep out and contaminate her.

Soon enough Isis's phone rang, and Lina answered it, launching into an astonishing mimicry of Isis as she garnered whatever information the speaker had to reveal.

Then they crowded into the car and Lina drove with an offensive mania that rivaled Julien's, weaving in and out of cars and closing the gap too fast, only to slam on brakes. Stella clutched the grip over her seat, eyes clenched shut, as if she could will herself home and out of this hell.

And then suddenly they were at a house. No, not a house, some kind of side alley of small warehouses, like storage units, and all her fear came roaring back in. This was where Lina would kill her.

Lina inhaled a bracing breath, and Stella wondered what she could do. In any other situation she'd try to humanize herself to her captor, but all reminders that Stella had a life worth getting back to were likely to further enrage Lina.

Lina snapped a sharp look at her. "You don't say a word about Isis, you got me? As far as you know, she bailed, lost her nerve, took off."

Stella nodded.

"I'm getting out, and you are going to walk ahead of me and we will meet Julien for the next step."

Stella's body was cold with adrenaline sweat that had cooled into clamminess on her skin.

She waited as Lina got out, then did as she was told and walked over cigarette butts and broken glass toward the entrance of the small building. Inside it turned out to be a storage shed full of broken machines—lawn mowers and mopeds covered in rust, missing wheels. Stella quickly glanced around for a weapon, something she could use to defend herself, when the sound of voices beneath their feet became a head appearing from beneath the ground. And then Julien was suddenly standing there as though he'd risen from the very earth itself, a human mole, then he slid out and snapped shut the door in the floor.

Julien held what looked like passports in his hands. He gazed between the two women with shock on his face for only a second, and then he composed it, tucked away surprise along with the blue booklets in his pocket with nonchalance.

"Isis bailed," Lina said simply. "She's been biding her time for so long, Julien, it's amazing she didn't rat you out a long time ago for one scam or another."

Julien put on a showy smile that Stella knew was fake, but in its own way it made her feel safer—he would work his charm and save her from Lina's madness.

"Sweetheart. You had us so worried running off like that. I thought you left me."

"I see you have the bank books," Lina said, her arms limp at her sides. The tone of a person who has been betrayed.

Julien suddenly looked at Stella. "Your hair was supposed to be red. That's the photo I have. We'll need to fix that." He shook his head, then muttered, "Goddammit, Isis."

"Julien, you didn't answer my fucking question," Lina shouted.

Julien's head snapped up and his face went hard again, like it had been in the hotel room until it softened in a singsong way, as one might talk to a snarling dog. "Honey, you disappeared. And let's face it, you're the one always saying you're not my daughter. You would never let Isis and me be parents to you!"

Lina barked a laugh that broke into a tiny sob. "You and Isis, parents! Ha. What an idiot I am. Why don't you ask Stella just where Isis went?"

Julien narrowed his eyes and looked warily at Stella. She couldn't hide the horror, she supposed, her eyes as wide and probably revealing of the awful truth as the day she'd stood at the basement leading down to Brooke's body.

Julien clapped a hand over his mouth and fell into a lean against the wall. "Your own blood."

"Don't start with that bullshit." Lina's mouth was pulled into a nasty sneer, but in its contortions Stella wondered if she saw clearly what she'd missed before—true likeness between them in the narrow noses, the sleek triangular chins. "We both know you're little more than a kidnapper. Probably a pedophile too. Did I repress a bunch of early memories, hah, hah . . . eh, *Max*?"

Julien's face had gone ashy white. When he spoke again, his tone was soft, his words pressed back against his throat like arrows to be unleashed. "I gave you everything. You have never wanted for anything. We fed you, clothed you, taught you. We trained you to dance, to sing . . ."

"Oh fuck off with your story of giving, Julien. We always moved, sometimes four times a year—do you know what that does to a kid? I never had any friends." She swung a look at Stella again. "She was the closest thing I had to a friend but you had to fuck that up, too. Why couldn't we just have stayed in town? It was nice."

"We never made you stay. You could have left at any time. Oh, Isis." He buried his face in his hands.

"Don't pretend you have feelings for her. Sure, she played mommy to you, since your own mother would have preferred you'd never been born. You're just sad because she's been the one picking up your slack all these years and now she can't. But she couldn't pick up Brooke's slack, huh? Left a little too much rope to hang herself on . . ."

"Stop it!" Julien lunged forward toward empty space, as though to do something, but then reeled back as he spotted Lina holding out her dainty little gun.

"Do you know how I got Brooke to do it?" Lina's voice was now a low, feral whisper that made Stella want to shout, to sing over her, to stop her if not for that gun. "I told her that you always complained about what a shitty dancer she was. That she would never be any good. That you kept her around to make the other girls feel better about themselves. That she would be replaced, and soon." Lina laughed.

Julien slumped to his knees, and for the first time since he'd abducted her, Stella wanted to run to him. His cheeks sagged like he was having a stroke. "No. Please," he whispered.

Lina's voice dropped to a menacing rasp. "I got her a last baggie of meth and I watched her do it, and then I told her it would be simple, painless. She got up on the stool herself, Jules. Only thing I had to do for her was kick out the stool."

Julien lunged. It was a bold and stupid move, even Stella knew that. The gun went off; Stella closed her eyes and felt her own scream as a vibration more than a sound. But when she opened them Julien was not dead, though blood trickled from a hole in his left shoulder. He'd pinned Lina to the floor, her gun flung just past her head on the floor.

"Stella, get the gun." He said it softly. Lina thrashed beneath him, but he exhibited a powerful strength in holding her down.

For a moment, Stella contemplated simply running out the door, but here were two people alive with a gun on the floor. She was weak. The world slowed. Stella felt as though she'd entered that stage of a dream where your legs simply won't run despite the monster on your heels. Lina grunted and made a frustrated shout.

"If you give him that gun, I'll tell the police you were my accomplice with Isis. I'll tell them it was your idea. Your fingerprints are all over her!"

Julien put a hand on Lina's mouth. "Give me the gun, Stella."

She moved toward it. Her hand closed around it. It felt cold to the touch and surprisingly heavy for such a tiny instrument. At last, she was in control. She lifted it with a shaking hand and pointed it at them. "I just want to go home."

Lina bit Julien's hand hard, the crunch audible. Julien howled and pulled the hand off her mouth but stayed pinned atop her. Lina began to rant, "You killed my mother, you fucker. Why did you kill her? Why not Stella's mother? She's the one that scorned you. Why mine? What did my mother ever do to you?"

Stella walked backwards toward the door.

Julien looked down at Lina, who had stopped thrashing and was now simply sobbing. He stroked her face with a finger. "I didn't kill your mother." When he looked back up at Stella, his expression unnerved her. She held the gun, yet his eyes were loaded with something equally dangerous.

"Margie killed your mom, Lina. *Her* mother." He pointed at Stella, whose body began to shake as though she'd stepped out into sudden snow. "Jealous, petty, self-centered, always getting what she wanted. That's who your mother really is, Stella. Until she finally couldn't have one thing. One person. That narcissist of a famous dancer never wanted her. She couldn't live with that. Couldn't bear it. And I'd already moved on. Sara and I had a baby. She gave me willingly all that your mother withheld from me."

Stella felt the tears in her eyes, hot down her face, but she didn't brush them away. They weren't tears of sorrow, but indignation, disbelief.

"We all want to believe the best about those people we love." He'd dropped into his hypnotic tone. Even Lina had gone still beneath him. The gun shook in his hands from the effort of holding it up.

"She lost her ability to walk, to dance, in that accident." Rage thickened Stella's words. "You can't tell me she did that on purpose!"

Julien smiled and then moved his hand to Lina's neck, stroked it like you might a sick child.

"It's not so strange, is it, Stella? If you can't get what you want, you simply take it out of the picture." His fingers wrapped around Lina's throat and just as quickly he squeezed. Lina bucked underneath him and moaned.

"Don't do that, Julien. Let her go!" The words rushed out in a scrape of horror.

"Put down the gun, Stella, or I won't stop."

"That's no way to rebuild the bond with your daughter, Julien. She'll hate you after this."

Lina was breathing raggedly; he had her throat squeezed to a pinhole. Tears leaked out the sides of her eyes.

"She already hates me. She made that perfectly clear when she killed my *sister!*" He shouted the last. Now he pressed his nose against Lina's. "Your own blood, Lina."

"Julien, Julien, it's okay. Just take your hand off her neck," Stella crooned.

The curve of Julien's hand around Lina's throat, under other circumstances, could almost have been tender, as well as the way they lay, nose to nose, their heads pressed together.

"If you're going to shoot me, Stella, I hope you are a really, really good shot. Or, you can have two for one. Maybe that's your goal."

Stella felt the hopelessness of the situation. If she tried to shoot, she'd kill for sure. If she didn't shoot, he'd kill Lina or at least seriously injure her.

She'd have to focus here and find another way out. Win Lina back over to her side.

With a sigh that squeezed every last molecule of air from her lungs, she dropped her arm and set the gun on the floor at her feet.

"No, bring it to me."

"How do I know you won't use it?"

He squeezed Lina's throat again so hard her eyes bulged out of her head and a twisted scream stuck in her throat.

"You don't have the luxury of worrying about that. I need you."

Stella picked it up, held it with a couple of fingers like it was a dead thing, hiccupping so as not to cry, and walked it over to Julien. He snatched it out of her hand and sat up. Lina gasped for breath, heaving and crying. Stella wanted to pull the woman into her lap, stroke her head.

Julien smiled at Stella. "Good girl." Then with a swift motion he brought the gun down on Lina's temple and knocked her clean out.

"Why'd you do that?" Stella cried. "You could kill her with a blow like that."

"Because we'll never get out of here if she's awake!" He picked her up as though she were a child, winced, and tossed her over his shoulder, steadying her there as he lifted the gun up toward Stella.

Stella now saw that his arm was losing a lot more blood than she'd first realized, but she couldn't get close enough to see where the bullet had lodged, or if it had at all.

"Fish her keys out of her pocket."

She did as asked, wishing there was a can of pepper spray or a knife in Lina's pockets.

"Go outside."

Stella hesitated.

"Move! Walk."

She did as told. The evening air felt bracingly cold, though it couldn't have been less than sixty degrees. She was vaguely aware of a world beyond this; people sitting down to dinner, making love, watching TV shows, all unaware of this hell unfolding. Her mind thought: *Izzy*, a pulse, a heartbeat for one second, and it was as though every ache her body had sustained, every bruise and agony were all present at the same time, for a split second, a full-body stab of pain.

In the alley were two cars. The one Lina had driven, and Julien's. "Get the bag out of my car," he instructed. Stella did as asked, and found inside the dark blue Honda the same duffel bag she'd seen Isis carrying away from the bank that day back in Luma. Had Isis not been running away from Julien, but toward him? Why had she sounded as though she was warning her? Had she known? Did she, for a second, hope she could rescue Stella from this whole fate? The bag was heavy, and she suspected it contained more than just cash. She hefted it onto her shoulder.

Julien nudged her back toward Lina's car. "Open the trunk and toss it in," Julien said.

Stella froze, hand poised on the keys. "No," she whispered.

Julien's eyes narrowed into that feline shape. "Open the god-damn trunk, Stella."

"Please . . ." She shook her head.

Julien's hand with the gun rose to her face with a jerky energy, as though mind and limb were not working together. His arm bled steadily, dripping like a leaky faucet that left dark splotches on the ground.

Tears burned in her eyes as she pointed the keys at the trunk. Her fingers were sweating so badly she could barely press the button. It popped with a click, like a seal breaking. Julien's face rippled, muscles twitching at random, his lips curling up. Stella didn't wait to be ordered; she pushed the trunk up and looked away.

Julien made a horrible squeal and moaned *Whyyyyyyy?*

Lina groaned on his shoulder, coming to consciousness. And with a quick move, careless of her physical safety, he tossed Lina down next to the wrapped and still body of Isis and slammed the trunk shut.

Stella slapped her hands helplessly on the trunk. "You can't do that! She'll die in there."

When Julien turned to her his face was so grotesquely twisted, tears seeping out his eyes, mouth a red gash of a grimace, that she took a step back away from him.

"Get in the car, Stella." His voice was hoarse, as though he'd been shouting or coughing.

Now terrified he might toss her into the trunk, too, she moved swiftly toward the passenger side of the car.

"Driver's side. You drive, I'll navigate."

She heard the first thump of Lina, awaking to the horror of her prison. She could almost feel the tight dark space as if it enclosed her too. Her breath wanted to hitch in her chest, but she had no doubt now: she couldn't trust Julien to be in his rational mind. Calmly, as though she hadn't heard a thing, Stella turned on the radio.

And it became clear to her what she was going to have to do if she had any chance of making it home alive.

Become the good daughter.

44

AS INSTRUCTED, Stella pulled up to another motel, this one seedier than the last, with fake palms and perfumed air freshener to cover up scents she didn't want to think about; it brought up her gag reflex. An ebony-skinned teenage girl in a skin-tight dress and stilettos sat smoking in the lobby. The clerk sized Stella up with a snap of his eyes, while she clutched Julien's arm. For all he knew, like all the other regulars likely to frequent such a joint, they were here to fuck.

Julien had tossed on a sweatshirt to cover up his bleeding arm. Stella didn't mention Lina, tried not to think about her sweating and gasping for breath away from the noxious odors of Isis's silent decay in the trunk. He'd parked the car a block down the road, in a pay-to-park lot. They wouldn't be here long, he said. She would do whatever had to be done swiftly, and maybe, somehow, she could save Lina from Isis's fate.

Once inside the room Julien stripped off sweater and shirt and tossed something at Stella. She caught it. A bottle of hair dye.

"Are you sure I should go red? It's so noticeable, Julien. If you're aiming for stealth . . ."

"It's less suspicious if you seem unafraid of scrutiny," Julien muttered. "And it's how you look in the photo I've got in your new ID."

Good daughter, good daughter, she reminded herself. "Good point." She laughed, trying to sound lighthearted, like she'd realized what fun running away with an armed criminal could be. Tried not to think of Lina in the trunk of the car. The bathroom light was dim, yellow and buzzing. It barely brought anything that qualified as light to the space, which Stella realized was the purpose, to hide the grime. If "grime" even described the extent of the dark clumps of mold that clustered in the corners, brown water stains snaking down the walls and ceilings as though the room were bruised like an abused lover. She took one look at the pale green slick on the shower floor and knew that she'd not be taking off her shoes to rinse the dye out. She choked down a cloying feeling of despair. This was the kind of place a person came, if not to have sad, empty sex, then to take one's own life. A leftover anguish hung here, a thin film of prior people's pain, and she wished she could wash it from her person.

Time condensed into nothing. Next thing she knew she was toweling off red hair. The bleached, starched white towel of the motel was stained a garish pinky-red, the color of movie blood.

Julien sat on the edge of the bed, gun resting in one hand, his fingers looking massive in comparison to its almost dainty silver weight. He stared up at the television, which was off. He hadn't moved since Stella began her hair transformation. In the arm of the sweatshirt he'd tossed on over his wound, there was now a sizeable red stain that continued spreading.

"Julien, you're bleeding." She whispered, in the hopes that she wouldn't startle him. He looked up at her sharply anyway. "Let me look at it."

He sat, wary, eyeing her.

"You can hold the gun on my head with your other hand if you're worried. I'm not going to hurt you."

He tilted his head up slightly, then sighed deeply.

Stella went to turn on the sink. The handle came loose in her hand but it turned on. She left it running and soaked the washcloth which she then brought to him.

"I don't care how you do it, but please let me look at that arm."

Julien stared up her, his multicolored eyes moist, as though she were a beautiful nurse and he a war-torn soldier. There was longing and hope in his now open eyes, guileless, as though he had no idea what he'd done.

Transferring the gun from hand to hand, he slowly worked off his sweatshirt, then unbuttoned his shirt and pulled it off. Stella tried to look at him objectively—as just a person in suffering. She tried not to notice that he had the same high-protruding collar bones as she did, the same bony ridges at the tops of her shoulders—surely these were just things that people had, not convincing markers of genetic inheritance. The wound was oozing not only blood but a lot of pale pink fluid. The bullet had opened a significant gouge into his shoulder. The edges of the wound were puckered and raw, the wet, open flesh like the center of a raspberry Danish, still leaking. She pressed the cloth there and he gasped. She could feel the heat of the wound beneath the cloth.

"When I was little," she began in a gentle voice, "I didn't imagine I had a father because my mother was larger than life. She was always in costumes, too, you know—big skirts that fanned out around her, and all that dramatic stage makeup. I felt like I'd been spawned by her in some magical moment."

Julien looked at her now, his face empty of all poses and roles, and in this light both eyes looked momentarily the same color, a grayish blue. For a moment she felt as though this is how a father might actually look at a daughter he loved.

"I wanted you," he said. "I wanted to be a father to you."

"I know. I believe you. Margaret wasn't a prima ballerina for no reason; she came by that attitude naturally. Izzy, your granddaughter, is the third in line of women raised without fathers. It's like a family legacy. I'm sorry, Julien. I'm sorry that she kept us apart. I didn't know."

It was working. Tears sprang to the corners of his eyes. He was vulnerable, he was open.

"My mother was the same, Stella." His voice had a wavering shake to it like Izzy's after a bad dream. She had a genuine urge to hug him. "She was also well known, beloved at her craft, adored. She took lovers at her leisure and she cast them off just as quickly. Isis and I . . ." His voice rent like fabric on a nail. "We didn't know our fathers—or whether we have the same father. We knew her cruelty. We knew that we were burdens. That we would never amount to anything. But my daughters . . ."

He pulled back a bit to look at her and for a second she could almost imagine him there in the audience when she was a child, a swelled chest, and beaming eyes as he rushed the stage to toss her roses.

Now, however, his eyes were so hollow and far away, Stella feared what he might do if he realized how vulnerable he had become. This was a dangerous place where any image might remind him this intimacy wasn't real. She could just as easily picture the pressure of his fingers around her own throat.

"We really should get some kind of antibiotic cream on that arm. Maybe get you to the hospital. We shouldn't wait; it could become infected."

He shook his head violently. "No hospital. We're so close, almost there, Stella."

Though panic kicked suddenly against her ribs, she took a deep, slow breath, softened her voice. "Where, Julien?" She brushed a lock of hair out of his face. "Where are we going?"

He smiled and grasped her fingers with his good one. "Home, sweetheart."

With great effort, the muscles of her jaws painful as she prepared to sound out the next word, she said, "Okay." She worked the word "Dad" around in her mouth but no matter how hard she tried, she couldn't spit it out.

45

IF EVERY HOUR WERE NOT more surreal than the last already, Stella thought, the looming white Hollywood sign clinched it as they came over the hump of the freeway. She'd been clenching her jaw so hard, as they inched along in the omnipresent traffic, alarmed by the fact that there were no sounds from the trunk, it now hurt to open it. She knew they'd been near Hollywood, in the general vicinity, but now arriving here in the land of performers seemed a sign that there was nothing more to do here than to play a role until she could soften Julien sufficiently to get his phone away from him or escape to the police. She'd been a fool not to run when she had hold of the gun. Either way, Lina's life was likely measured in hours.

They pulled up to a lovely brown craftsman-style home in a tailored, tree-lined neighborhood. The freeway was forgotten. She could almost believe this really was her home in the movie version of her life, the one in which her mother had not denied Julien his paternity and become this monster, the life in which her mother had kept her legs.

Julien glanced up at the house darkly for a moment, his brow rolling toward the bridge of his nose in either physical or emotional pain—Stella couldn't tell which. But then he opened his car door and plastered on that about-to-sell-you-something smile she had once believed in.

She glanced down the street in both directions. Gardener-sculpted bushes adorned a neighbor's lawn, but otherwise the street was empty. Julien's smile had dropped when she looked back at him; he tapped the gun on the top of the car casually, as though it was nothing more than an umbrella. His action said *Don't even think about it*. Stella sighed and walked to the sidewalk ahead of him.

"Go on in. Mom will be thrilled to meet you."

Mom? She'd thought this whole thing a ploy up till now—him having staked out another empty home to squat in while he figured out their next plans. And then—she knew it was idiotic, but she felt the pang of movie terror anyway—pictured a skeletal body tucked in a chair, worshipped long after death. Her legs shook a little. She realized she couldn't remember the last meal she'd eaten.

"Does she cook? I'm starving." Ever the good daughter, she reminded herself.

"All her meals are delivered; there's always a full larder. Mom always takes care of hers, even when she can't do it herself." Julien was suddenly standing right behind her, and she moved faster up the walkway, red flagstone, neatly manicured grass, sturdy bushes with no flowers—the kind of foliage that is easily maintained but expresses no personal taste.

The knob twisted beneath Stella's hand. It was cool to the touch, perhaps rarely turned. The hallway smelled like lavender and mothballs—fake flowers faded from red to pink in glass vases on a pert shelf beside an empty coat rack and umbrella stand. A pair of beige fluffy slippers and a sturdy pair of brown walking shoes rested, toes pressed up against the wall, like the feet of sleepwalkers.

She paused, panic leaching acid bile up her throat. She choked it down and turned around to Julien with a smile she hoped looked more real than it felt. "It's cozy."

He nodded and waved her on. They entered a living room with velvet-clad furniture in jewel tones: sapphire, ruby, and gold brocade. Posters hung on every wall, so that she could barely make out the grayish wallpaper in a cabbage-rose design between them. The posters, she saw, as her eyes focused in the dim light, featured old movies as well as signed glossies of famous actors and actresses from the thirties and forties. And over the fireplace mantel, a row of family photographs. She wanted badly to go closer, inspect them for answers.

"Mom, it's me. Don't be alarmed. I've brought someone very special!" Julien bellowed toward the ceiling like a teenager too lazy to get up and find his parent. They heard a thumping sound from above.

Julien grasped Stella's arm, led her around the corner and up a set of carpet-covered stairs. There were more crowded walls—the entire home an altar to the craft of acting, or maybe just fame, with its faces of flawless pores and expensive trappings. But Julien gave her no time to stop. Suddenly they were at a bedroom, shuttered and dark, its door ajar. A petite hand pressed the door open with painful slowness, and anxiety set off flashbulbs in Stella's nerves. A delicate, shriveled woman stood there precariously balanced within a walker. Julien flipped on the hallway light.

"Mom, I'm home. I've brought someone."

The tiny woman edged toward them with jerky motions, lip pressed in fierce determination as though it hurt her to move but she was going to do it anyway, goddammit. She came all the way to the edge of the room, just to the doorframe, and raised her hand to Julien's face. Now Stella could see the badly dyed red hair, not unlike Stella's own favorite color—patches of it were still white, or pinkish, as though she'd done it herself, which seemed impossible given her stiffness and frailty. Stella wanted to clap a hand to her mouth with the shock of it. She was the shriveled, wizened, spitting image of Isis. She saw the truth, then, of Isis's relationship to Julien. A sister indeed. At the very least, this woman's daughter.

Now "Mom" turned her eyes to Stella and narrowed them in an assessing manner before opening wide, their piercing blueness mirroring Julien's one blue eye. She looked to Julien with questions hanging in them.

"This is my Stella." His words came in a proud sounding breath. "The real deal."

Confusion twisted through her. At moments she almost believed he did love and care for her. And then she thought of Lina and knew that whatever he felt for any of them was probably no more than the fondness one had for an old stuffed animal or a well-loved car. They were objects in his bizarrely staged production.

"That's right." Stella made jazz hands around her face. "Prodigal daughter, returned at last!"

Julien glanced at her sharply. She realized her hunger pangs had turned to low-blood-sugar–borne hysteria.

"I see." The woman's voice was hoarse, as though she rarely used it. She didn't smile.

"I have a great idea. How about I put together lunch for all of us? I'm starved, and when I don't eat I get hypoglycemic, which makes me moody and unpredictable." Stella laughed a little louder than she intended.

The woman's eyes brightened before Julien could protest. He did, however, manage to grasp Stella's arm before she bounded back down the steps in search of a kitchen . . . or an escape, she figured.

"I'll show you where everything is."

"Sure, of course. Dad."

Julien's eyes clouded over. She worried he thought she was making fun of him.

His arm holding hers, his gun hand in his other pocket, they retreated down the steps to the kitchen, its counters and floor so clean it looked as though no one ever used it.

Stella opened the fridge and found it full of pre-packaged salads and cold cuts. The freezer held frozen dinners. She rifled around, pulled out salads and small bottles of orange juice, setting them on the counter, humming. With a little fuel in her body she would be strong enough to do what she needed to do next.

"Stella, I can just order a pizza."

"Why? There's plenty of food here. I can't wait. I get crazy when I'm hungry."

"Stella."

She pried tops off, opened cupboards looking for plates, found them, and pulled them onto the counter.

"Stella." His voice was pleading.

She turned around at last, stuffing deli ham into her mouth. "What?"

The gun dangled from his hand, which was coated in dark liquid. The entire sleeve of his shirt was soaked with blood. The pose was garish, almost like something out of a bad horror flick. She rolled up another slice of ham and ate it in two bites. Hunger made her head cloudy, the world feel indistinct around her, but at the back of her lizard brain was a pulse of terror like a strobe light that flashed every few minutes.

His voice limped out. "I want you to know I have been sincere to you. I really do want to be a father to you. I want to find a way past . . . all that's happened."

She sighed. "I'm here, I'm trying. Don't you believe me?"

Blood trickled down his fingers and onto the clean white floor in perfectly round little splotches. His blood. Did it run in her veins too?

"I want to, but . . . the things I've done." His voice walked the border of tears.

She shook her head, reached a hand into the air between them as though to pat him. "Hey, it's okay. We're going to get past it. You know . . . you don't have to keep a gun on me. I'm not going anywhere."

He shook the gun slightly, causing more blood to splash the linoleum. "I just, it's just . . . insurance."

"For what? For how long? How long are you going to mistrust me? If you want to build a relationship with me, it won't be over the barrel of that."

Julien swayed on his feet and his head lolled toward his chest. "I'm feeling a little woozy. I'm going to sit down."

Stella nodded. He was losing blood a little at a time, but steadily for the past few hours—her work might be very simple after all. Wait for him to weaken, maybe pass out, then she could escape, take Lina to safety. *God, let her be alive.*

"I'll set the table." She took two plates of salad out to the dining room, adjacent to the living-room shrine to the movies, paused and took a deep breath to keep the plates from clacking together in her shaking hand. Julien wandered after her, moving with the lethargic energy of a just-awakened teenager. This was almost too easy. She could break a lamp over his head, or maybe just steal the gun from him after he set it down to eat.

Julien slumped into a chair, panting slightly. "We . . . have to be . . . at the bank in a few hours."

"Of course we do," she said softly, placating him.

She turned and looked back at the living room and its walls of images. Again her eyes were drawn to the mantel and this time, she went right to it, to the row of photos all sitting there so innocently, just like those of any other family.

The few bites of food helped her blood sugar and cleared her mind some. Enough to know these photos were not a hallucination:

herself as a child, maybe four years old, holding an arabesque on a stage next to photos of a young Lina with glasses and a book, frowning up at the photographer, hers and Stella's likenesses undeniable. This was mindfuck enough if not for more photos of *other* girls, maybe five other girls all about the age of seven or eight. And in their youthful poses Stella could see a clear similarity between them all—it was in the eyes, the tilt and shape of them, and the similar bridge of nose: sleek, aquiline. Chills snaked across her. And suddenly the door she'd shut on the horrors opened up again. What did it mean? Who were these girls? *Sisters*, a voice slithered through her mind. *Sisters.*

She looked back at Julien slowly, as though she'd noticed nothing, but even in his fatigued state, head propped up by a fist, he was now alert, head held high, eyes sharp on her. His hand tightened around the gun.

"So I guess I come from a big family." She wasn't sure what she expected—his anger, his false pride.

"I tried, Stella." His voice had a scraped, raw tone. Defeat. "Tried to bring just one of you home, but there was always something keeping me . . . away . . . Couldn't give Mom what she wanted . . ." Julien's eyes suddenly rolled back in his head. For a second his head all but levitated inches off the table. "Oh so many," he said on an exhale and then slumped, unconscious, onto the table.

Stella wasn't sure what this bubbling sensation inside her was—elation, relief, terror? She rushed over and lifted the gun, now sticky with blood, out of his hand, then jammed her hands into his pants pockets, found the cell phone, and dialed 9-1-1. Halfway between a sharp stab of joy at the realization that she was free, and a punch of nausea at what she'd find when she opened the trunk of the car, she turned to see a jerking flash of red. She dropped the phone into Julien's lap.

Mom stood at the lip between kitchen and dining room with a shotgun in her hand, trained with surprisingly steady aim at Stella's head. Dangling from the finger that held the butt of the gun was a pair of silver handcuffs. She'd abandoned her walker.

"Drop that little excuse of a pistol," Mom said. The woman's voice was rather silky, not as crusty as she looked. And it nudged a faint feeling of familiarity awake inside Stella.

Surprise erupted out of Stella as laughter. She called Mom's bluff and aimed her gun at Julien's slumped head. Mom smiled, then burst into her own guffaw. "Do it. Useless and thankless excuse for a son. Don't think I won't kill him myself."

Shit, this woman played a serious game. Stella kept her aim, hopeful that at any moment the emergency crew would bust down the door. Mom shuffled her way toward her, tiny sprigs of her thin hair sprouting up above her forehead, lips pressed flat in concentration. She never dropped aim. Such cognitive dissonance: the frail body, the determined will. Stella was so caught up in the strangeness of the situation, she didn't realize the old woman's intention until Mom pressed the barrel of the gun to Stella's forehead. Stella felt her bladder weaken, and the minuscule amount of food she'd consumed churned and frothed inside her. *Get a grip, Stella. This woman is certifiable. She'd kill her own son.*

"What did you do to him, to mess him up?" Stella asked.

Mom deftly slid the handcuffs off her finger onto the floor. The gun shook too, and pressed its edges harder into Stella' forehead, which was now slick with sweat. "Radiator. To your left and just behind. Handcuff yourself. Move slowly. Back up."

Stella obeyed, grasped the handcuffs and closed one end around her wrist, loosely. Mom's gnarled hand snaked out and clasped the metal circle, pressed harder, cinching it painfully. She slid herself to the left and back until she was crouched beside the metal radiator, cold to the touch. Mom had pulled the gun off of her head, but still looked at her straight down the barrel of Stella's nose.

"Click it on, Missy." Mom ordered.

"My *name* is Stella."

"Well la-dee-dah."

Mom's eyebrows were drawn on in dark blue pencil, crookedly. Stella had the urge to lick her finger and wipe one of them clean.

"You're one of the lucky ones, aren'tcha? Didn't rot your pretty face with the methamphetamines or ruin your pretty figure with a bunch of ungrateful little shits, huh?"

"You mean the rest of my . . . sisters? Julien's girls."

"*Julien.*" Mom said his name like *herpes* or *Hitler*. "Never thought what I gave him was good enough. His real goddamn name is Max, always was, always will be. Big aspirations, no follow-through."

"Where are the other girls?"

Mom's thin blue brows pressed together, making a child's scribbled W. "How the hell should I know? Not a one ever stays."

"Stays? You mean he's brought . . . brings . . . them here?"

Mom pulled out the chair next to Julien at the table and slumped into it. She wore house slippers, open at the top, where thick toes with yellowed nails poked out.

"Can't fix a guilty heart with false generosity." She propped the shotgun in her lap.

"What do you mean? Why am I here, uh . . . Mom?"

"Name's Faye. Harlowe—not my maiden name but it carried me far, so I'm keeping it. I'm not your mama, and don't even think about calling me Granny." She sat taller in her seat, as though proud, and that earlier tingle of familiarity solidified in Stella.

"Faye Harlowe? The actress who starred in *When the Rooster Crows* and *Oh Mother*?"

Faye wiggled one of her blue brows. "The same. And thirty other movies. And to answer to your stupid question, he brought you here because he needs something I have."

"That doesn't seem like a good reason," Stella said. "He's made a huge production out of all of this—you don't know the least of it."

"I have ideas." She looked at Julien—or Max's—slumped head with something almost like tenderness for a moment. "He's my son after all."

"He courted me into his dance company. It was pretty great for a while. I was a ballerina when I was young, then I got pregnant . . ."

Faye frowned, her penciled eyebrows briefly meeting in a V that reminded Stella of Disney villains. "I don't want your damn résumé, girl."

Stella felt oddly stung by Mom's demeanor. "Why are you holding a shotgun on me? What have I done to you?"

Mom's lips curled into a grimace. "I don't know what your mother did to him way back when—but that one, that one woman undid him more than any other. Drove him insane. I wanted to see what made you so damn special. Didn't realize he'd try and get killed in the meantime. Or Eileen." Her voice dipped down near something like a real feeling.

"Eileen?"

"What name was she going by? *Isis.*" She sneered. "Back in my day we had names that made sense, dignified names."

"Why did he bring me here?"

Now Mom's face made an alarming slump, skin pulling down in an almost horrifying mask of feelings. "Oh brother. Still trying his luck." Mom slapped her knee and shook her head. "It's about the money."

"What? I have no money."

"*I've* got money, you dummy. Made a pretty penny in the movies, and more so, my own daddy had a bit, too, which he left me. It's a good-sized nest egg. And I told him I'd only leave it to him if he brought me an heir." She laughed hard and rattling again. "Got that idea out of one of my own movies! A female heir. Damn if he didn't try. It made Eileen hate him—she had to stick close to him all these years so that when I finally kicked the bucket, she could get her cut of the estate."

"I still don't understand. He's got Lina, why didn't she count as an heir?"

Faye frowned and shook her head. "I wanted an heir that looked like me, like my lost babies." Now Mom reached out and stroked Stella's cheek softly.

She wanted to pull away, but resisted for fear of losing her head to that shotgun. Faye's fingers smelled like menthol.

For the first time since she'd dialed and dropped the cell phone, Stella heard the obvious ring of sirens out in the world beyond the house, loud enough she prayed they were really coming for her. Mom snapped upright again. "What did you do, girl? Did you call emergency?"

Stella shook her head but couldn't bring herself to lie in words.

The shotgun resumed its point between her eyes. "Moment of truth, girl. I don't know what Max has told you about me. And now you've gone and called the police." Desperation made big ovals of her small eyes, and Stella could picture her, suddenly, all horrified beauty on the big screen as she found her lover dead in *When the Rooster Crows.*

"Nothing! He's told me nothing. I didn't even know you existed until we walked into this house. I mean, I knew your movies, but I didn't know you were his . . . oh, God . . ."

Faye smiled with one corner of her mouth, revealing yellowed teeth. "Of course that's what you're going to say. You don't know a thing about me? My babies?"

Stella shook her head furiously, heat and cold moving in alternating streaks through her nerves. "And I don't want to know."

"Well here's the thing." Mom reached into her robe pocket and pulled out a handkerchief. Then she bent forward with a groan, and picked up the gun which Stella had dropped on the floor. She turned it over and over. "Eileen took this from me. It was a prop in one of my movies, did you know? Only shot blanks, we thought. Near killed my co-star!" Her laugh was full of phlegm.

Stella took a deep breath. If these were indeed her relatives, she wished she could strip these crazy genes right out of her cells. Insanity upon insanity.

Mom cocked back the hammer of the pistol and placed it gently, almost lovingly up against Julien's ear. He stirred slightly, mumbled something.

"No, please!" Stella tried to lunge forward. She'd spent her life letting powerful women dictate her future and here she was again, helpless, having done nothing but be a coward.

"Oh, do you love him now? Dear old Dad? He's been so good to you, after all, such a *big* part of your life."

"It's not his fault! My mother . . . she kept him from me." What had her life come to that here she was defending Julien? Did she have that condition, where she'd bonded with her kidnapper? *But the signs have stacked up. He's probably my father.*

The sirens were blaring just outside the door. This should have brought relief but instead it brought terror. It gave Mom power.

"Stella, fates are sealed much earlier in our lives than we know. Don't you realize that? He took my babies from me. Smothered them in their sleep, each one, ever time, when he was a boy. We knew he had problems. They didn't have words for it like now— sociopath, whatnot. He was just a 'bad seed.' I never caught him doing it, thought they all had the crib death. Cops thought I did it. Police investigation and everything—can you imagine, losing your babies and then the police grill you for hours and hours about what an evil person you must be if only you'd confess? *The agony.* But there was no evidence I did wrong. I only figured it out years later, when he started sending home those pictures—all the pretty danc-ing girls—like he was trying to make up for what he did to his own brothers and sisters."

Stella felt as though she'd just dropped down a long empty shaft, was on her way to crashing painfully at the bottom. *What he did to his own brothers and sisters.*

There were three loud, hard knocks on the front door.

Mom didn't even look as though she'd heard. "Six babies, smoth-ered in their sleep, none but him made it past a year old. Lucky for Eileen she came before him."

A male voice shouted, muffled through the door, "Paramedics, anyone home?"

Julien's multicolored eyes snapped opened—the pale, milky blue-gray one gazed up at Stella, searching for her—and in its sad depths she felt as though she could see the young boy who never had a chance, born into insanity. For one long moment she felt a pull of grief—for the boy he'd been and the father she never had.

Mom smoothed the hair back off Julien's face almost tenderly and put the gun into his ear like a thermometer. "You thought you could get the family money, after what you did, you little monster?" she whispered.

"Noooo," whimpered Stella, then "I'm sorry," though she wasn't sure who she was apologizing to, or for what.

The door bursting open seemed to happen at the same time as the gun going off, but that couldn't be because she knew it was the sound of the shot that forced the paramedics to break in the door.

They moved like a swarm—though logically she knew they were maybe only three or four paramedics, maybe one cop. All she could feel were the ridges of the cold radiator pressed against the knobs of her spine; the rest of her body was a numb heavy thing her mind was attached to. She spoke to the air, unable to focus on a single face. "The trunk of the car out front—please, there's a woman in there, might still be alive . . ."

Someone nodded. Another said, "Holy shit."

46

SINCE THEY'D LEFT the hospital Izzy refused to put down her violin. Its sleek body felt at home in her hands, and though she wasn't playing it, she twanged a note here and there, like they were having a conversation.

Her dad sat behind his laptop and phone, making calls to important people, arranging things so that he could stay longer.

How long?

How long before her mother came back again?

What if she never did?

She tried to imagine a life that was as odd as this—Dylan, who, though really nice, maybe nicer even than she'd expected, clearly had no idea how to take care of a kid. He hadn't asked her if she was hungry, or tried to get her to do her homework. No Gigi. No Mom? She'd be making her own food and walking to school with nobody watching over her. Or worse—what if she had to move in with him? San Francisco seemed far away, and full of tall buildings and low clouds, a place you got lost in and never felt warm. She shivered slightly and clutched the violin to her body like the teddy bears that no longer provided comfort.

Dylan clicked off his phone and tossed it onto the table with a sigh. "Y'okay, lass?"

She shrugged.

"I know."

"You don't know." The words came out meaner than she meant.

Dylan ran a hand through his hair and looked at her peripherally. "I guess I probably don't. I'd like to try."

She shrugged again, because she didn't trust herself to say anything nice.

"I have t'admit, when I imagined having kids I'd always thought I'd have a good few years before I had a teenager to deal with."

"I'm not a teenager."

Dylan raised a soft red eyebrow. "Yer a girl, though. Girls mature faster than boys, if ye haven't noticed."

Izzy smiled despite herself.

"Maybe ye could make me a cheat sheet. Favorite color, food, boy band, etc. Give me a head start?"

"I hate boy bands," she said, but a smile spread across her face. He was trying. It was kind of embarrassing really, like when the boys did stupid tricks at school on their skateboards in front of the girls to show off.

Her mom's phone suddenly vibrated on the table. The number was blocked but she picked it up, her hands suddenly sweaty.

"Answer it, lass." Dylan's eyes were wide and alert.

She pressed *talk* with a feeling in her stomach like she'd eaten too many bowls of ice cream.

"Hello, I'm looking for family members of Stella Russo." The voice was strong, male, serious. For a moment, Izzy couldn't swallow. "Hello?" The man said again.

"Yeah, um, yes, this is the family of Stella Russo." She tried to make her voice sound adult.

"Young lady, is there an adult I can speak to?"

Her guts went into churn, like that time she'd had the stomach flu and threw up at school out of the blue, a day she'd never live down.

"You can speak to me. I'm her daughter."

There was a beat of silence. Dylan's eyes snapped to hers. He looked frowny and scared, the way adults got when they were trying to pretend they weren't nervous but couldn't help themselves.

"Uh, okay. Well, Stella Russo is your mother, then?"

"Yes."

"Your mother is here at Memorial Hospital. She's in stable condition. We wanted to let you know that she's been found."

Izzy couldn't help herself. She jumped up, fist pumped the air, and Dylan made a half smile, as though unsure. "Is she . . . okay?"

"She's okay, sweetie," said the officer. "Now is there an adult present that I can speak to?"

"Oh, yeah, my dad," she said quickly, before an aftershock of embarrassment swept over her." She handed the phone to Dylan, who took down some information and then hung up.

"She's alive!" She only realized her eyes were filled with tears when Dylan leaned in and wiped one of her eyes. "She's at the same hospital as Gigi."

"That's the best news, my girl." They hugged tightly.

Izzy pulled back for a second. She liked that he called her 'my girl' but she felt like she'd taken a bite of something too big that she couldn't swallow. "So I guess you'll be going home now?"

Dylan raised that eyebrow—it was like his signature move. "Right now, we're going to the hospital to see yer mum."

Izzy tried not to think past the hospital, past her mom. Right now, this was enough.

47

DYLAN WAS SHAKY with anxiety at seeing Stella, at the entire question mark of the future that now loomed before them all. Stella sat up in a hospital bed, her face wrinkled in annoyance, as though this was all just a big hassle to her. Her hair was back to red, but it looked unevenly dyed, and stark against her extremely pale skin. Puddles of dark skin ringed her eyes, which were themselves bloodshot, and bruises marked her collarbone and wrists, and the edge of one eye.

Izzy rushed to her mother and they hugged tightly. Stella closed her eyes and pressed her chin into her daughter's head. *Their* daughter. He looked at them and thought: *They are mine if I want them,* though it was quickly followed by the realization that though he felt love for both of them—odd how the love for Izzy snapped on the moment he knew she was his—family still had to be earned. This might be the first of many such moments of togetherness, or the beginning of a series of exchanges around their daughter. His daughter.

Stella opened her eyes. "I'm not contagious or anything. Throat's a little raw from shouting, not a cold or anything." There was a note of humor in her voice and it softened the tight breath he held. He moved toward her and placed a hand on her shoulder. Her skin was cold.

"Sweetheart, let me put a blanket on ye. Yer like ice, love."

Her eyes crinkled sweetly, as though she liked these terms of endearment. She nodded and he pulled the thin, coarse hospital blanket up over her.

"I'm dehydrated and anemic—nothing life-threatening."

"I'm glad it's nothing worse than that." Their eyes exchanged a conversation they could not have yet.

"Izzy, sweets, do you want to go get yourself a treat from the café? A donut or something?" Stella petted her hair.

Izzy frowned, as though she knew it was a ruse to get rid of her, but at last stood up. "Okay. Can I get you something, too?"

"How about a nice cup of coffee. Black. And maybe a cookie."

Izzy gave a wan smile and skipped out of the room to get her treat.

Stella sighed heavily. "I'm just so damn glad to see both of you." Her scratchy voice broke into tears.

Dylan sat on the edge of the bed and put his arm around her, pulled her head into his shoulder. "That girl, Stella, she's writhing with talent, ye know. I heard her play a piece on the violin she wrote herself. She's an echo of me grandmum, of Ireland. It's nothing short of awesome."

Stella exhaled a half laugh, half sob into his chest. "I may come from corrupt genes, but yours, thank God, are made of beauty and art."

"Shall I suppose you'll tell me more about that later?"

She nodded, her face mashed into his shirt, which was damp now with her tears. "I like to think there will be a later for us."

He pulled her tighter to him. "I like to think so too."

48

MARGARET WAS SO STILL in her bed it reminded Stella of the years when the Bigger Than Life Ballerina took sleeping pills to knock herself out the night before a big performance, her face a smooth landscape that Stella would trace with her fingers to see if she was real and not made of marble or plastic.

She slumped down beside her mother, took her still nicely warm hand in her own. "I'm here, Mom. I'm here."

Margaret didn't respond, but her breathing deepened, and Stella took that as enough, for now.

She didn't realize she'd fallen asleep until the pressure of her mother's hand squeezing hers dragged her out of a strange dream of dancing on the roof of a moving car. She bolted upright. Margaret's eyes were open, and she was blinking blankly.

"Mom!"

"Sara . . . fina," her mother said.

"No, it's me, Stella."

"Oh Sara, I'm so sorry for what I did to you." Her mother's voice was small, faraway.

"Mom, listen to me, it's Stella, it's okay. You didn't do anything."

Her mother's eyes continued to look just past her, as though at someone standing behind Stella. "Oh but Sara, I did. I was so jealous over Max, when he went to you. Even though I turned him away. I hated you. I was so selfish. Our accident was no accident." Margaret clapped a hand to her mouth, stifling a sob. "I killed you."

Stella leapt up, wedged herself onto the free edge of the bed, and took her mother in her arms as best she could, leaning her mother's frail head against her own bruised body.

Margaret dissolved into wracking sobs that turned to a rattling cough. When her sobbing subsided she turned her head up. "Stella?"

"It's me, Mom. You're okay."

Margaret sighed. "There's . . . a box . . . in my closet. Find it. You need to."

"Okay, Mom. When you get home, you can show me."

Margaret shook her head slightly against Stella's bosom, then slipped back into her near comatose sleep.

*   *   *

She didn't know she would be driving to Headquarters until she suddenly turned left into its steep driveway. She'd gone round and round in her head about whether she could stand to see any of the girls again—set foot in that house. But Aja, of all people, had called a dozen times since she'd been gone. Gone. That's how it felt. Though the entire ordeal added up to about a week of her life, she felt as though she'd been on some nightmarish six-month vision quest. Frivolity Inc. and its spectacles seemed a lifetime before. And Dylan's presence felt as though the wires of her life had been unhooked and rehooked in a new configuration in that time, reset.

She found the front yard full of furniture and boxes. The screen door was completely off its hinges and lying flat on the porch. No sounds of Daft Punk (Chloe's choice) or Mozart (Yvette's) or even Aja's moody Belle and Sebastian music radiated out from the house. It felt like an abandoned institution. But when she turned the knob, the door opened beneath her hand.

The house was nearly bare, most of its innards already dumped on the front lawn. She wandered down the long hallway and caught a dark glimpse of motion in the kitchen that had her stop and catch her breath. Ghosts, shadows. What lived in this house? But it was only Aja sitting in a lone chair—the table already outside. Her dark hair was pulled up into a massive twist at the top of her head, her face free of makeup. The room was stripped of all kitchen appliances, even the ceramic chickens and salt and pepper shakers. She looked up at Stella with her usual impassive face, but before Stella could think of how to even begin a dialogue, Aja launched up from the chair at Stella—who braced herself to be choked or punched. But Aja *hugged* her.

Stella rocked on her feet, shocked. For a beat her arms hung limply, loose, at her sides before she hugged her back. The girl felt thin and bony beneath her hands. She realized Aja was crying. "Hey, hey, it's okay."

Aja shook her head into Stella's shoulder.

"Here, here, sit down, let's talk." Stella pulled the other chair closer to the first and seated Aja in it.

"Are they all dead?"

Faces windmilled through her mind. "Julien . . ." Suddenly the tears were in the back of her own throat. "Max, actually. Max is his real name. What his mother called him, anyway."

Aja wiped her tears. "You met Mom? Holy shit."

"How do *you* know Mom? There's a lot of backstory I don't know, huh?"

Aja nodded, chewed a finger that was already bitten down to a nearly bloody quick. "Yeah, there is. First tell me about Isis? Lina?"

Stella sighed. Coming home, seeing Izzy and Dylan, had made her feel okay for a few hours. But now she felt the sickness of what she'd survived underneath her skin, like a sac of poison. "Julien and Isis did not survive."

Aja bit her lip and slammed her eyes shut. "And Lina?"

Stella, despite herself, smiled. "She is in a hospital in Los Angeles. Recovering." She wouldn't soon forget the look in Lina's eyes once they'd gotten her on the stretcher and pumped an IV full of fluids into her arm: eyes wide and horrified as though Stella had sprouted horns and exhaled smoke.

Aja exhaled deeply. "Fuck. You don't know how crazy we've all been going. We're being kicked out, you know? Julien was behind on the rent here like six months. Only way the landlord let us stay was because he used Brooke to score pot. Not that I ever liked it here. Fucking drafty piece of shit."

"Where did you live before this, Aja? What life do you have to go back to?"

Aja clutched herself. She wore her signature outfit of white tank top and black leggings, even though it was cool outside. "I wish I could say I could go make a life for myself in L.A. again. But I'm guessing they'll take Mom's house, right? Because fuck knows Julien was up to his balls in debt."

Stella reached out and put a hand on Aja's knee. The animosity between them was for a moment gone, and she wanted to keep it that way. "How do you know Mom? Surely now that there's nothing left, you can tell me what I don't know, help me figure it out? Do you know about the pictures of the girls on her mantelpiece? Sisters, I'd say. My picture was there."

Aja sighed, reached back and let down her bun, her hair spilling down around her shoulders and past her hips, a fairytale-worthy length. "Not your sisters, Stella. Think most of them were picked because they reminded him of you."

"What do you mean?"

"Julien and Mom—that dastardly old bitch—took me in when I was a twelve-year-old runaway after my Olympic dream fell through—I know Lina told you about that. Thought I could make it as a model or an actress in Hollywood. My mom had OD'ed. My dad was a pimp or a junkie she never wanted me to know. Was going to be raised by the same grandparents that fucked up my mom in the first place and I was not having that. Back in those days Julien worked as a talent scout—or pretended to be one, anyway. One of his many grand schemes. Lina and me never did really like each other. She was moody and spent a lot of time by herself writing stories. But both of us could dance and sing. I just went where they went. He moved a lot. Always had a new 'production' or 'studio.' I wasn't always good to them—back talked and had a brief spell of drugs myself."

"How old are you, Aja? I honestly can't even tell."

Her smile was sweet, coy almost, and Stella couldn't remember when she'd ever seen it before. "Twenty-eight. But I look good for my age, right?"

Stella smiled. "I'd never have guessed we were almost the same age. So, what, you and Lina grew up in the shadow of some mystery daughter Julien was always chasing. Little Miss Perfect Stella, am I right?"

Aja scowled, but it was almost as though she was working at keeping it on her face for show. "Honestly, for years Lina and me didn't even think you were real. I mean, he had a picture of himself with a pretty ballerina and a little dark-haired girl on his lap that he said was you, but Julien was always bringing home girls . . ." Aja stopped and looked up sharply. "You know he never touched us, right? He wasn't a perv."

"But what about Brooke? I mean, okay, technically she was a woman, but the rumor had it she was pregnant by him. Did he just wait until they came of age?"

Aja's entire face crimped inward at the mention of Brooke. The air in the kitchen seemed to go dead. Stella almost smacked herself in stupidity. They were feet away from the stairs that led to the basement where she'd found Brooke hanging. A chill shook her body.

Aja looked at the ground. "I brought Brooke in. She was my friend. Okay, so we met at a party and shared a crack pipe, but we both got off it for a good long time. She was—oh, Stella, you should have seen her dance. I never saw such a fucking angel, you know? Perfect. She was perfect. She was an angel until the heroin and meth made her lose her mind. She came to live with us when we were fourteen, on and off. Drove Julien batshit with her BS, but I think he kind of likes the crazy ones especially. I mean he comes from crazy. Go with what you know, right? Anyway—it's funny; I always rebelled against being treated like his kid, but Brooke, man, she wanted a family so bad, she took to it. She became more like his daughter than even Lina."

Stella nodded. For the first time she was struck with a gut feeling she had never caught onto before. Aja had loved Brooke—and not just as a friend. "So, naturally, Brooke hated me too. This idea of me he was chasing, right? Like here were all these perfectly good, loving 'daughters' under his nose and he wasn't happy."

Aja nodded. "You're pretty fucking smart."

Stella raised an eyebrow. "Brooke's pregnancy?"

"She'd gotten sober for a long time, and Frivolity—or the version of us we had down in L.A. called "Spectacular Inc." was working out pretty well—and she felt she wanted to be a mother. You probably figured out Julien's got a lot of parent-child issues. He wanted to reward her for her good behavior. He donated sperm. Paid for the insemination."

"That's a pretty whacked form of reward." Stella couldn't help herself.

Aja frowned. "Haven't you been paying attention, Stella? Everything Julien does, touches, loves—*loved*—it's all whacked."

Stella bowed her head. In her own way, she saw that Aja had loved Julien, too.

"So...things were going okay, Brooke was pregnant, and then what?"

Aja spread her fingers into wings and laid them on her knees. "And then you came along."

Thickness lined Stella's throat. "So you're saying I'm responsible for her death?"

Aja held Stella's eyes for a long, hard moment, then licked her lips. "I held you responsible for her using again, her disappearance and her death, Stella. I did. She was everything to me. More than a sister. Do you understand? We might have made . . . a life together." Aja shook her head. "But since everything went to shit, Lina gone, then Isis, Julien and you took off and there were reports that you'd be kidnapped, I realized we all make our own shit paths. She was a drug addict. And she was afraid of change. You're not to blame. But yeah, Julien's attentions turned to you."

Stella sighed, rubbed her sweaty palms on her pants leg. "I guess Julien was hoping to use me to get Mom, Faye, to leave her estate to him, or that's what she told me."

Aja shook her head with a scowl. "You really don't know the full story on Mom, do you? She was one of those what do you call it, Munchausen moms? Her babies were always mysteriously sick, and then they'd all die. Isis told me she did it herself but blamed Julien—even convinced him that he'd done it." Aja inhaled and tilted her head back in exultation of the smoke's entry.

"You're saying Mom . . . smothered her own babies and blamed it on Julien?"

Aja nodded. "Fucked up, right? Then, she'd go out again and get knocked up with some grip or small time PA on her sets. Once, Isis told a story that when Mom found out she was pregnant again, she made Julien punch her in the stomach. He was about twelve, I think. Isis said he sobbed and sobbed, but Mom just kept after him, calling him a wuss, saying he had no balls and would never be a real man. . . . I guess he finally did it."

Stella's stomach seemed to hit her knees, disgust twisting her all up. "That poor kid," she said. "No wonder he was so fucked up."

Aja jabbed her finger right into the air as if through a phantom smoke ring. "I guess she used to rant about how men were good for nothing but giving their sperm, that dear old Julien would never amount to anything. She just dangled that bullshit about the money over his head because she knew it would keep him coming back. I don't believe she had much left, the way she lived—spent more money on clothes and hair than her own home. She sort of had her own son whipped, you know. Julien was going to prove her wrong. He was going to be the one man who did not turn out to be worthless. But, unfortunately, the only talent he had himself was spotting it in others."

Aja fished around in the black jacket slung over her chair and produced a pack of cigarettes, holding one out to Stella, who shook her head. Aja had already smoked one down to ash and moved on to the next.

As Stella watched the match ignite into flame at Aja's mouth an idea came over her. "Aja, do you think the other girls would stick around if there was a reason to?"

Aja shrugged. "I can't think of a reason, if I'm real honest."

"What about a real dance studio? Where we teach classes, maybe a range—kids to adults. We could still do events, too."

Aja inhaled deeply, let the smoke dance out of her lips in slow spirals. "You're saying like, you'd be in charge of it, run it?"

Stella shrugged. "Or you."

Aja made a scoffing laugh. "Right."

Stella stood up. "I don't buy the fucked-up little girl routine, Ayj. You're capable. I've seen it. All you need is someone willing to share a little power for a change, instead of always trying to run the show."

For the first time in memory, Aja smiled—a real smile, all teeth and gums—revealing a tiny little dimple in one cheek that made her look about twelve years old. "You're a fucking surprise, Stella. Not what I thought you were."

"Well, that makes two of us. Now, put me to work. There's gotta be boxes to pack, right? She opened cupboards, pulled down the mismatched plates they'd eaten on many times.

Aja stood up. "Right. Hey, Stella. So, is he, or was he, do you think he, really your father?"

Stella looked over her shoulder. "It doesn't matter. I grew up without a dad, and he's dead now. Whatever he is, or was, he was just a man I crossed paths with for a while."

"But if he is, then the rest of them—Lina, Isis, Mom: they're your family, too. And if there is any money . . ."

"It should go to Lina and you. And I'll see that it does, if I can."

Stella now realized that family meant a lot to Aja. But family wasn't only blood. "This makes me think of a quote I read once by this spiritual teacher, Ram Dass. 'In the end, all we're really doing is walking each other home.'"

Aja bit her lip, looked away. "That's some deep spiritual shit."

Stella laughed. She grasped a crimson-colored mug that turned black when you put hot liquid in it. It had been Lina's favorite. "Yeah, it really is."

"Walking each other home. I like that." Aja started to hum.

49

THE HOUSE FELT EMPTY to Stella without her mother in it, emptier still with the knowledge that Margaret might not be coming home anytime soon.

She had learned to respect her mother's space as though she were a sullen teen, not a grown woman. She cleaned only that which she could reach and see, and otherwise, closets and cupboards were kept closed.

She was surprised to find her mother's closet more organized than she'd expected, given that Margaret had to take every item down with a special stick attached to a hook. At the very back of the closet were a series of cardboard boxes, including photographs and newspaper articles of her days in the spotlight, old costumes, everything bearing the scent of mothballs. It took Stella the better part of an hour to comb through it all and find, at last, the box her mother had mentioned: file folders with labels such as "Letters" and "Court Documents."

She extracted an envelope of letters penned in a masculine scrawl. These, she noted, were dated all within the last couple of years, from the same Los Angeles address. The envelope was heavy, though, and as she leafed through what appeared to be love letters from Max she turned the envelope upside down and dumped the heavy contents into her lap. What she saw choked her breath for a moment. A heavy gold necklace, set with big green stones—they looked like emeralds to Stella. These were rough cut, though, and the gold had an ancient, flaky quality. The necklace that had been stolen from the Ernestine mansion, she realized with a frisson of shock and disgust. All this time, and Julien—aka Max—had sent it to her own house, her own mother sitting on a piece of jewelry worth millions of dollars, possibly the catalyst for all the chaos that had followed. Now that she understood her mother a little better than before, she had probably thought it was just the sort of thing a man had to produce to earn her respect. She'd probably thought it ugly, unwieldy. If the detective had taken Aja's threats seriously when he'd come to investigate, insisted on searching Stella's house, Stella might be in jail now. As it was she'd have to decide if it was even worth turning it in to the cops, or letting it molder in the back of her mother's closet, a lost and ancient artifact.

The files revealed more items of interest, but most intriguing was a legal document in a light-blue stapled folder. Not, as she'd anticipated, an order against Max—but a letter from a lawyer claiming to represent Mikhail Baryshnikov. "My client states that Margaret Russo is a delusional woman who has convinced herself she engaged in a sexual act with my client, which my client categorically refutes. My client states that he never even met her, much less touched her. He is certain that he is not the father of her child and will submit to DNA testing if necessary to prove it."

Stella's heart raced. A DNA test . . . what *might* a test have shown? She flipped through the remaining documents quickly, unsure what such a report would even look like. But after a further half an hour of careful sifting and stacking, she could find no evidence that it had ever existed. What she did discover were articles detailing her mother's accident, an artsy piece in the *San Francisco Magazine* on the fall of a great star. Tragedy writ in fading ink.

And at the bottom, a photograph: Margaret in prima ballerina finery—feather headpiece, frilly tutu and pointe slippers, cuddled up against a young, handsome Julien—*Max,* she reminded herself. In his arms, a tiny Stella who resembled Izzy in the expression—maybe two years old, grinning, the top of her head tucked beneath his chin.

There it all lay, in Stella's lap: the truth in its broken bits and pieces. And it was more than Stella had ever had before.

Epilogue

STELLA GLARED ONE last time at the elderly matron who sat between her and Dylan, the crone's eyes already at half-mast, hidden between a heavy gray wig that had slipped well over her forehead.

"You're sure you won't consider moving just one seat over so my friend and I can sit next to each other?" Stella tried again.

The woman's head wobbled on her shoulders. "Oh dear, this is the perfect seat for me—I've a direct line to the stage." Potent liquor oozed from her mouth, and Stella recoiled.

"Our ten-year-old daughter is the featured violinist in this concert," Dylan said softly.

Stella felt her breath catch just a little. After all they'd been through, this was the first time he'd said those words with such authority and pride. No matter what—if they would be driving an hour each way to see each other, or if time would turn their relationship into something more solid, or even if the best they had was this easy kind of friendship, Stella was grateful for that pride in his voice.

"Your daughter? Didn't you just call him your friend?" The woman said, nose wrinkled in obvious disapproval. "Your generation baffles me."

Stella smiled despite the urge to topple the bad wig off the woman's head. And then the woman closed her eyes again and her head nodded backwards. Sloppy snores barreled out of her open mouth. Dylan raised an eyebrow and shrugged at her.

And then the auditorium lights dimmed, and the spotlight hit the stage. Heavy blue curtains whisked apart slowly, and Stella felt the same heart-in-throat anticipation as if she were up there.

The musicians were all decked in black—all of them twice as old as their star. Stella pictured her backstage, chewing her thumb bloody, nervously running one hand along the velvet of her dress. She wished she could rush the stage and give Izzy some sort of support, but Izzy had begged her not to do any such thing. She twisted the program in her hands until it was a tight tube of paper, damp with her sweat.

As a tall young woman strode across the stage, she heard Dylan's sharp intake of air as the conductor announced, "Isadora Wheeler Russo, our ten year-old star of this evening's program, will first be performing a composition she has written herself."

The audience went wild. People were whistling. And even from the distance Stella saw two roses bloom hot on her daughter's cheeks. The noise did nothing to rouse the elderly woman between them, Stella noted with some resentment.

At the conductor's firm gesture the packed auditorium settled into a sudden hush, and then he tickled the air with his baton and the air was suddenly transformed into music that settled in and around Stella's body, chills rising up her arms and neck.

The old woman roused suddenly and put a hand to her heart, then turned to Stella with tears already leaking down her heavily powdered cheeks. "Oh my goodness," she said in a choked voice, "I could die satisfied right now, it's so beautiful."

Stella thought of Margaret, or rather felt her then, as she was when Stella had been young, before the accident, queen of the ballet, light and graceful in white satin, commanding the same stage where her granddaughter now entranced a crowded hall.

Acknowledgments

Every book is an act of collaboration in one way or another. This book wouldn't exist at all if I hadn't stumbled into a hip-hop class taught by my dearest friend, Suzi Sellers, who truly moves like no one else, and can pull off all the shades of hair in this book. I want to express thanks to other friends and writers who gave me necessary feedback: Amy McElroy, my anchor and confidante, without whom my characters would all be flat, unfeeling stereotypes; Julia Park Tracey for constant support; Emilya Naymark for some of the most incisive plot and character analysis possible; Kari Jensen Milich for true insight into the intense world of professional ballerinas; Kari Ramirez for thoughtful early com-ments; Marge Rubenstein Bloom, for loving it enough to encourage me to revise; to the rest of my Scarlet Letter Creative Support Team: Eros-Alegra Clarke, Nanea Hoffman, Becca Lawton, Christina Mercer, Stephanie Naman, Tomi Wiley James; to Jessica Barksdale Inclan for a quick read and kind words; to Ellen Meister, for always trying to set me on the right course to publishing; to my marvelous team at Booktrope; and last, but never least, to Erik and Ben, who make my writing life possible with support and unending love.

Made in United States
Orlando, FL
29 May 2022